MURDER MOST MALICIOUS

Books by Alyssa Maxwell

Gilded Newport Mysteries
MURDER AT THE BREAKERS
MURDER AT MARBLE HOUSE
MURDER AT BEECHWOOD

Lady and Lady's Maid Mysteries
MURDER MOST MALICIOUS

Published by Kensington Publishing Corporation

MURDER MOST MALICIOUS

ALYSSA MAXWELL

KENSINGTON BOOKS
http://www.kensingtonbooks.com

KENSINGTON BOOKS are published by

Kensington Publishing Corp.
119 West 40th Street
New York, NY 10018

Library of Congress Catalogue Number: 2015951102

ISBN-13: 978-1-61773-830-2
ISBN-10: 1-61773-830-1
First Kensington Hardcover Edition: January 2016

eISBN-13: 978-1-61773-831-9
eISBN-10: 1-61773-831-X
First Kensington Electronic Edition: January 2016

10 9 8 7 6 5 4 3 2 1

Printed in the United States of America

For my mother, who was so proud of my accomplishments.
Miss you and love you, Mom.

CHAPTER 1

25 December, 1918

"Henry, don't you dare ignore me!" The shout burst from behind the drawing-room doors, a command nearly drowned out by staccato notes pounded on the grand piano. "Henry, I'm speaking to you!"

Stravinsky's discordant *Firebird* broke off with a resounding crescendo. Voices replaced them, one male, one female, both distinctly taut and decidedly angry. Phoebe Renshaw came to an uneasy halt. She had thought the rest of her family and the guests had all gone up to bed. Across the Grand Hall, light spilled from the dining room as the butler and footmen continued clearing away the remnants of Christmas dinner.

With an indrawn breath she moved closer to the thickly paneled, double pocket doors.

"I'm very sorry, Henry, but it isn't going to happen," came calmer, muffled words from inside, spoken by the feminine voice—a voice that sounded anything *but* sorry. Dismissive, disdainful, yes, but certainly not contrite. Phoebe sighed and rolled her eyes. As much as she had expected this, she shook her head that Julia had chosen Christmas night to break this news to her latest suitor. And this particular Christmas, too—the first peacetime holiday in nearly five years.

A paragon of tact and goodwill, that sister of hers.

"We are practically engaged, Julia. Why do you think your grandparents asked my family to spend Christmas here at Foxwood? Everyone is expecting us to wed. Our estates practically border each other." Incredulity lent an almost shrill quality to Henry's voice. "How could our union be any more perfect?"

"It isn't perfect to me," came the cool reply.

"No? How on earth do you think you'll avoid a scandal if you break it off now?"

Phoebe could almost see her sister's cavalier shrug. "A broken not-quite-engagement is hardly fodder for scandal. I'm sorry—how many times must I say it? This is my decision and you've no choice but to accept it."

Would they exit the drawing room now? Phoebe stepped backward intending to flee, perhaps dart behind the Christmas tree that dominated the center of the hall. Henry's voice, raised and freshly charged with ire, held her in place. "Do I? Do I *really*? You listen here, Julia Renshaw. Surely you don't believe you're the only one who knows a secret about someone."

Phoebe glanced over her shoulder and sure enough, the two footmen, Douglas and Vernon, met her gaze through the dining-room doorway before hurrying on with their chores. Inside the drawing room, a burst of snide laughter from Henry raised the hair at her nape.

"What secret?" her sister asked after a moment's hesitation.

"*Your* secret," Henry Leighton, Marquess of Allerton, said with a mean hiss that carried through the door.

"What . . . do you believe you know?"

"Must I outline the sordid details of your little adventure last summer?"

"How on earth did you discover . . . ?" Julia's voice faded.

It registered in Phoebe's mind that her sister hadn't bothered to deny whatever it was.

"Let's just say I kept an eye on you while I was on furlough," Henry said, "and you aren't as clever as you think you are, not by half."

"That was most ungentlemanly of you, Henry."

"You had your chance to spend more time with me then, Julia, and you chose not to. I therefore chose to discover where you *were* spending your time."

"Oh! How unworthy, even of you, Henry. Still, it would be your word against mine, and whom do you think Grampapa will believe? Now, if you'll excuse me, I'm going to bed."

"You are not walking away from this, Julia!" Henry's voice next plunged to a murmur Phoebe could no longer make out, but like a mongrel's growl it showered her arms with goose bumps.

The sound of shuffling feet was followed by a sharp "Oh!" from Julia. Phoebe's hands shot instinctively toward the recessed finger pulls on the doors, but she froze at the marquess's next words. "This is how it is going to be, my dear. You and I are going to announce our engagement to our families tomorrow morning, and shortly thereafter to the world. There will be parties and planning and yes, there *will* be a wedding. You will marry *me,* or you'll marry no one. Ever. I'll see to that."

"You don't even know whether or not anything untoward happened last summer," Julia said with all the condescension of which Phoebe knew she was capable, yet with a brittle quality that threatened her tenuous composure. "You're bluffing, Henry."

"Am I? Are you willing to risk it? What would *Grampapa* think of his darling girl if he only knew the truth?"

Phoebe's breath caught in her throat at the thud of something hitting the rug inside. She gripped the bronze finger pulls just as Julia cried out.

"Let go of me!"

Phoebe thrust both doors wide, perfectly framing the scene inside. Julia, in her pale rose Poiret gown with its silver-beaded trim, stood with her back bowed in an obvious attempt to pull free of Henry's hold. A spiraling lock of blond hair had slipped from its pins on one side to stream past her shoulder. At her feet, a vase lay on its side, thankfully unbroken, the flowers and water it held now blending with the Persian weave. Four empty indentations in the rug testified to the side table having been rudely knocked askew. Meanwhile, Henry's dark hair stood on end, no doubt from raking his fingers through it. His brown eyes smoldering and his cheeks ruddy with drink, he had his hands on her—*on her!* His fingers were wrapped so tightly around Julia's upper arms they were sure to leave bruises.

For a moment no one moved. Phoebe stared. They stared back. Henry's bowtie hung loose on either side of his neck, his tailcoat and waistcoat unbuttoned with all the familiarity of a husband in his own home, his garnet shirt studs gleaming like drops of blood upon snow. Anger twisted his features. Then recognition dawned—of Phoebe, of the impropriety of the scene she had walked in on—and a measure of the ire smoothed from his features. He released Julia as though she were made of hot coals, turned away, and put several feet between them.

Phoebe steeled herself with a breath and forced a smile. "Oh, hullo there, you two. Sorry to barge in like this. I thought everyone had gone to bed. Don't mind me, I only came for a book, one I couldn't find in the library. Julia, do you remember where Grampapa stashed that American novel he didn't want Grams to know he was reading? You know, the one about the boy floating up that large river to help his African friend."

"I don't know. . . ." Julia looked from Phoebe to Henry and back again. She brushed the errant lock behind her ear before hugging her arms around her middle. "I'll help you look. G-good night, Henry."

"Were you just going up?" Without letting her smile slip, Phoebe glared at Henry and put emphasis on *going up.*

A muscle bounced in the hard line of his jaw. His eyes narrowed, but he bobbed his head. "Good night, ladies. Julia, we'll talk more in the morning."

He strode past Phoebe without a glance. Several long seconds later, his footfalls thudded on the carpeted stairs. Phoebe let go a breath of relief. She turned to slide the pocket doors closed, and as she did so two black-clad figures lingering in the dining-room doorway scurried out of sight.

There would be gossip below stairs come morning. Phoebe would worry about that later. She went to her sister and clasped her hands. "Are you all right?"

Julia whisked free and backed up a stride. "Of course I'm all right."

"You didn't look all right when I came in. You still don't. What was that about?"

Julia twitched her eyebrows and turned slightly away, showing Phoebe her shoulder. Yes, the light pink weal visible against her pale upper arm confirmed tomorrow's bruises. "What was *what* about?"

"Don't play coy with me. What was Henry talking about? What secret—"

"Were you listening at the door?"

"I could hear you from the middle of the hall, and I think the servants in the dining room heard you as well. Lucky for you Grams and Grampapa retired half an hour ago. Or perhaps it isn't lucky. Perhaps this is something they should know about."

"They don't need to know anything."

"Why are you always so stubborn?"

"I'm done in, Phoebe. I'm going to bed." Her perfectly sloping nose in the air, she started to move past Phoebe, but Phoebe reached out and caught her wrist. Julia stopped, still facing the paneled walnut doors, her gaze boring into them. "Release me at once."

"Not until you tell me what you and Henry were arguing about. I mean, besides your breaking off your would-be engagement. That comes as no great surprise. But the rest . . . Are you in some sort of trouble?"

Julia snapped her head around to pin Phoebe with eyes so deeply blue as to appear black. "It's none of your business and I'll thank you to mind your own. Now let me go. I'm going to bed, and if you know what's good for you, you'll do the same."

Stunned, her throat stinging from the rebuke, Phoebe let her hand fall away. She watched Julia go, the beaded train of her gown whooshing over the floor like water over rocks.

"I care about you," Phoebe said in a barely audible whisper, something neither Julia, nor the footmen, nor anyone else in the house could possibly hear. She wished she could say it louder, say it directly to her prideful sister's beautiful face. And then what—be met with a repeat of the disdain Julia had just shown her? No. Phoebe had her pride, too.

Eva Huntford made her way past the main kitchen and into the servants' dining hall with a gown slung over each arm. Lady Amelia had spilled a spoonful of trifle down the front of her green velvet at dinner last night, while Lady Julia's mauve and silver beaded gown sported an odd rent near the left shoulder strap. It almost physically pained her to see such damage to the clothing she took such loving care of, and she briefly wondered what holiday activities could possibly result in such a tear. She dismissed the thought. Today was Boxing Day, but she had work to do before enjoying her own brief holiday later that afternoon.

"Mrs. Ellison, have you any bicarbonate of soda on hand? Lady Amelia spilled trifle—oh!" A man sat at the far end of the rectangular oak table, reading a newspaper. A cup of coffee sat steaming at his elbow. She draped the gowns over the back of a chair. "Good morning, Mr. Hensley. You're up early."

"Evie, won't you call me Nick? How long have we known each other, after all?"

It was true, she and Nicolas Hensley had known each other as children, but they were adults now, she lady's maid to the Earl of Wroxly's three granddaughters, and he valet to their houseguest, the Marquess of Allerton. Propriety was, after all, of the utmost importance in a manor such as Foxwood Hall. Familiarity between herself and a manservant would hardly be considered proper. "A long time, yes," she replied with a lift of her eyebrow, "but it's also been a long time since we've seen each other."

He smiled faintly. "I saw you yesterday. And the day before that."

"You know what I mean. We've been surrounded by the others, or have passed each other in the corridors as we've gone about our tasks." She turned to go. "In fact, I should—"

"Evie, do stay. I've craved a moment alone with you. Don't look like that. I only wish to . . . to express my deepest condolences about Danny. My very deepest, Evie. A sad business, that."

Her throat squeezed and the backs of her eyes stung. Danny, her brother . . . She swallowed. "Yes, thank you. A good many men did not come home from the war. They are heroes, all."

"Indeed."

Hang it all, this would never do, not on Boxing Day. In a couple of hours she would be free to trudge home through last night's dusting of snow to spend the afternoon with her parents, and they must not glimpse her sadness. She gave a little sniff, a slight toss of her head. There, better now. She smiled at Mr. Hensley. "Tell me, what are you doing down here at this time of the morning? Won't his lordship be abed for hours yet?"

"My employer is already up and out, actually."

"On such a cold morning?" Shivering, she glanced up at the high windows, frosted over and sprinkled with last night's flurries.

Mrs. Ellison turned the corner into the room, her plump hand extended. Eva's requested soda fizzed away in the measuring cup she held. She handed Eva a clean rag as well. "Who's up and out on this frigid morning?"

Eva moved a place setting aside and spread the velvet gown's bodice open on the table. She dipped the rag in the soda. "Lord Allerton, apparently." She looked quizzically over at Mr. Hensley.

He set down his newspaper. "At any rate, his lordship isn't in his room. I inquired with the staff setting up in the morning room and no one's yet seen him today."

"One supposes he's gone out for a walk despite the weather, then." Eva dabbed the dampened cloth lightly at the stain on Lady Amelia's bodice, careful of the embroidery and the tiny seed pearl buttons.

"Or perhaps a ride in that lovely motorcar of his?" Mrs. Ellison sighed longingly.

"No, I called down to the carriage house and his Silver Ghost is still there." Mr. Hensley frowned in thought, a gesture that did not diminish his distinguished good looks. He was several years older than Eva and had briefly courted her sister before entering into service as an under footman here at Foxwood. The years had been more than kind to him, she couldn't help admitting. The slightest touch of silver at his temples might be premature for a man of thirty, but on Nick Hensley the effect was both elegant and charming.

Perhaps more so than a valet needed, she added with a silent chuckle.

"Wouldn't I relish a ride in that heavenly motorcar!" Mrs. Ellison took on a dreamy expression, but only for an instant. "Ah well, back to work."

"I'm sure he'll turn up." Eva dabbed one last time at Amelia's frock and gave a satisfied nod. Voices sounded in the corridor.

"That was some show last night."

"You can say that again. They were like a couple of—"

"Good morning, Vernon, Douglas." Eva injected an implied reprimand into the tone of her greeting. She didn't know whom the head footman and under footman were discussing, but the gossipy nature of their observations didn't escape her. The pair had the good grace to blush guiltily as they clamped their lips. Mr. Giles had strict rules about gossip-mongering, and had he overheard them they'd have suffered a hearty tongue-lashing, as would everyone else within hearing range.

Other staff members arrived for breakfast, having completed their morning chores of laying fires, sweeping floors, and setting up the breakfast buffet. Connie, the new housemaid, came barreling into the doorway and skidded to a halt with a visible effort to catch her breath. She regarded Eva with large, worried eyes. "Did Mrs. Sanders notice my late start this morning?"

"Were you late? Well, no matter," Eva assured her. She hoped she was correct, and that Connie wouldn't be facing a scolding later from the housekeeper. "It's Boxing Day and I suppose we're allowed a bit of leeway. Is everyone ready for their holiday later?"

Boxing Day, the day after Christmas, was a rare treat for the manor staff. Some visited their families if they lived locally, while others attended the cinema or shopped or simply spent private time in their rooms reading. Eva planned to spend the afternoon at her parents' farm outside the village, but first she needed to set her ladyships' gowns to rights. After a final inspection of the now nearly invisible stain, she moved Amelia's velvet off the table to make way as more staff gathered round.

She was on her way to deliver the gown to Mable, the laundress, before settling in with needle and thread to mend the beaded strap on Lady Julia's frock. Suddenly Lady Amelia bounded down the back staircase and launched herself from the bottom step. She landed with an unladylike thwack mere inches away from Eva.

"Good heavens, my lady!" Eva sidestepped in time to avoid being knocked off her feet and spilling her burdens to the floor. She hugged the gowns to her. "Is there a fire?"

"I'm terribly sorry, Eva. I didn't mean to give you a fright." Lady Amelia's long curls danced loose down her back, and in her haste to dress herself she'd left the sleeves on her crepe de chine shirtwaist undone. "I was looking for you."

"You know I would have been upstairs to help you and your sisters dress in what"—she glanced at the wall clock—"ten minutes?"

Amelia Renshaw's sweet face banished any annoyance Eva might have felt. At fifteen, she was a budding beauty. Not Lady Julia's glamorous, moving-picture star beauty, but a quieter, deeper sort one often finds in country villages like Little Barlow. Her hair was darker than either Julia's or Phoebe's but still golden, a color reflected in her eyes, which sometimes shone hazel and other times brown, but always with bright gold rims. If Phoebe took after their dear but somewhat plain mother and Julia took after their dashing father, Amelia had inherited a pleasing combination of both that would surely endure throughout her lifetime.

"If you're worried about your frock, my lady, look." Eva held out the gowns, using one hand to unfold the bodice of Amelia's green velvet. "I've almost got the stain out and Mable will vanquish what's left."

"I don't care about that," Amelia said with a dismissive wave. "You keep the gown. I wanted a private moment to wish you happy Christmas."

"Lady Amelia, wherever would I wear such a garment? And as for Christmas, you wished me happy yesterday." Slinging both gowns over her shoulder, she reached to button the cuffs that traveled halfway up Amelia's forearms. "Had you forgotten?"

"Yes, but yesterday was a work day for you and this afternoon you'll be free to enjoy as you like." She switched arms so Eva could button the other sleeve. "I may wish you happy from one carefree person to another. That's quite different, don't you think?"

Puzzled, Eva frowned at her young charge, but only for an instant. "I think it's a lovely gesture and I thank you very much, my lady."

"There's more. I wanted you to know there's a special surprise in your box from Phoebe and me. There's something from Julia, too, something she purchased, very lovely and thoughtful, but Phoebe and I made our gift ourselves. But you're not to open your box until you're at home with your parents." Amelia bounced on the balls of her feet with excitement. "We made one for your mother as well."

"How terribly sweet of you. But you're very mysterious,

aren't you?" Eva reached out and affectionately tucked a few stray hairs behind Amelia's ear. In some ways she was blossoming into a gracious young lady, while in others she was still very much a little girl. Sadly, one with too few memories of her mother. Poor child, one parent lost to childbirth—along with the babe—and the other to war. Eva hoped she helped fill the gaps, on occasion at least, even if only in the smallest ways. "Whatever it is, Mum and I are sure to love and treasure it always. Happy Christmas to you, my lady."

To her mingled chagrin and delight, Lady Amelia reached her arms around her and squeezed.

"With this deplorable weather keeping us inside, we'll have to use our imaginations to keep ourselves occupied this afternoon."

Maude Renshaw, Countess of Wroxly—Grams as Phoebe and her siblings called her—stood as tall as she had as a young woman, if the photographs were any indication. If anything she seemed even taller now, although Phoebe knew that to be an illusion created by the uninterrupted black she habitually wore, from the high-necked collars of her dresses to the narrow sweep of her skirts. With smooth hair the color of newly polished silver worn in a padded upsweep culminating in a topknot at her crown, Grams was a study in dignified elegance that caught the eye and held it whenever she entered a room.

Strengthening the illusion of Grams's Amazonian height, Phoebe's youngest sibling, Viscount Foxwood—Fox— walked at Grams's side, holding her hand in the crook of his elbow. Fox had yet to enjoy a major growth spurt, much to his chagrin as this set him a good head shorter than many of his classmates at Eaton. Together Fox and Grams led the small procession of family and guests into the Petite

Salon, tucked into the turret of what had been the original portion of the house.

This room was one of Phoebe's favorites. Crisp wainscoting offset by calming green walls and an airy cove ceiling made a welcome contrast to the dark oaks and mahoganies in other parts of the house. Best of all, the room was a partial oval, with a rotunda of windows overlooking the south corner of the gardens.

An enthusiastic blaze danced behind the fireplace screen, and Mr. Giles and the footmen, Vernon and Douglas, stood at attention, waiting to serve. The table had been laid with leftovers from last night's dinner—roast goose and venison and medallions of beef, with Mrs. Ellison's apple-chestnut stuffing, among other delicacies, and for dessert, the left-over Yorkshire pudding and cranberry trifle. Supplemented by a platter of sandwiches, the leftovers provided easy fare designed to allow the kitchen staff, along with the rest of the servants, to finish up early and set out on their after-noon holiday. The day promised adventures for every-one—for the servants as they pursued their personal interests, and, Phoebe thought wryly, for the family and guests as they endeavored to look after themselves for these next several hours.

"Where is my son? It's not like Henry to be late to a meal." Lucille, Marchioness of Allerton, regarded her son's vacant seat at the table. Whereas Grams's stoic self-discipline had sculpted her figure into lines of angular ele-gance, a longstanding habit of overindulgence had softened the marchioness's figure, rounded her hips and shoulders and upper arms, and produced rather more chins than a body re-quired.

"Come to think of it, he wasn't down for breakfast ei-ther." Grams spoke lightly, but shot a suspicious look at Julia. Julia didn't appear to notice, but Phoebe winced, wondering if somehow Grams had gotten wind of the debacle in the drawing room last night.

"He and Lord Owen must have gone out." Grampapa turned his broad face toward Mr. Giles for confirmation.

"I believe Lord Owen is still in his room, my lord. If Lord Allerton has gone out, he left no message that I know of."

Lady Allerton's frown deepened. "Hmm . . . That, too, is most unlike Henry. Did he take his motor car?"

"No, my lady. His Silver Ghost is still in the carriage house."

"Hmm . . . How very odd, indeed."

"Really, Mama, why all the fuss?" Lord Theodore Leighton—Theo—reached for a roll and his butter knife with a bored expression. "Henry's a grown man."

He fell silent without any further reassurance and buttered his bread with meticulous strokes as if creating a work of art. This proved no simple task, not for Theo, and Phoebe quelled the urge to reach over and offer assistance. The knife quivered in his grasp, bringing attention to the scarred flesh of his fingers and the backs of both hands. The rippled skin ended at his sleeves and reappeared in angry blotches above his collar to pull the left side of his face into a perpetual sneer. Phoebe wondered that he hadn't grown whiskers to hide the scars. Like Henry, this second son of the Leighton family was handsome, or had been, before the war had left its mark on him.

Mustard gas, in the trenches of the Battle of Somme. Phoebe remembered the day a distraught Lady Allerton had telephoned to deliver the awful news. Theo's injuries had taken him out of action for nearly six months—he'd very nearly died—but when everyone had expected him to return home, he returned to the trenches instead. He made it abundantly clear at every opportunity he wanted no one's pity, no one's help. He'd butter his own roll, thank you, if it took all morning.

Phoebe tried never to feel sorry for him, even tried to like him, but he made it a ticklish task, especially in moments like this. This might be Henry they were talking about, but he and Theo were, after all, brothers, and Theo exhibited not the slightest concern.

While the elder generation discussed where Henry might be, Phoebe glanced across the table at Julia. Had her argument with Henry driven him away? She noted that Julia's arms were well-covered in deep blue chiffon, with a velvet shawl draped over that, to hide any evidence of last night.

What Julia needed, what they *all* needed, in Phoebe's opinion, was a life free from the old pressures to marry and marry well. The war had changed life for so many others, but those changes seemed worlds removed from Foxwood Hall. It was as if the Renshaw family, and other families like theirs, had become mired in an earlier time dictated by an endless procession of luncheons, dinner parties, and potential beaux. She sighed.

A mistake.

"What's wrong, Phoebe?" Beside her, Amelia looked both pretty and smart in a new shirtwaist with blouson sleeves.

She should know better than to show even the slightest sign of distress in front of Amelia, for where Julia cared little about the goings-on around her, Amelia was apt to care rather too much. She regarded her younger sister's concerned expression.

"Wrong? Nothing, Amelia."

"Then why are you moaning?"

"I am not moaning. I sighed. There is a difference." She didn't dare discuss what happened last night with her innocent sister, but it was too late to pretend nothing was wrong, for Amelia was far too perceptive to be fooled. Phoebe cupped her mouth to prevent Fox overhearing. Fox always seemed to be listening in on other people's conversations,

storing away bits of information to be used at his convenience. "The truth is, I'm horribly bored. I miss . . ." She
paused. How to phrase this without sounding unfeeling
and self-absorbed? "I miss the activity of the war. Not the
war itself, mind you. I'm happy and relieved it's finally
over. But we made a true difference to a good many people. And now . . . I fear life has lost its color."

Her sister nodded, her large eyes keen with understanding, just as they had always been from Amelia's earliest
age. Even as a baby she had seemed to possess an uncanny
wisdom when it came to reading the moods of others. Sometimes Phoebe yearned for those plump, little-girl arms hugging her tight as they once so often had. Julia could use
one of those hugs now, though it had been years since she
had admitted to vulnerability of any sort or accepted that
kind of closeness—not from Amelia and certainly not from
Phoebe.

Amelia nodded sagely. "You're afraid all we'll have to
look forward to from now on are parties and such, like in
the old days?"

"You have read my mind exactly." Yes, let gentle Amelia
believe that was all that was wrong. "The old ways seem so
purposeless now. I've been thinking—"

"You should be thinking of finding a husband before
the dust gathers on that shelf you're sitting on," Fox whispered out of the side of his mouth, his gaze still fixed
across the table at the elders as if he hadn't been listening
in on Phoebe and Amelia.

"I'm *nineteen*, Fox. That hardly qualifies me for any shelf
and besides, what difference should it make?" Phoebe shook
her head at him. "It's a new world and women will no
longer be relegated exclusively to the home. We have choices
now." Or should, she silently amended.

"That's right," Amelia put in eagerly. "Many choices."

Fox finally deigned to turn his face to Phoebe, his lips

tilting in a mean little smile. "You think so? As you said, the war is over. The men have come home. Time for you ladies to return to the roles for which God designed you."

She nearly choked on her own breath. Only a throat clearing and a glare from Grams prevented her from retorting—and perhaps wringing her brother's neck.

"I propose that directly following luncheon, Julia play the piano for us." Grams pinned her light brown eyes on Julia, turning her *proposal* into an adamant command that brooked no demurring.

"And following Julia, I wouldn't mind regaling everyone with a song or two." This came from Lady Cecily Leighton, Henry's maiden great-aunt. Phoebe glanced up at her, alarmed by the suggestion. Lady Cecily had already proved herself thoroughly tone deaf, and on one occasion Phoebe had had to endure an entire hour of jumbled and stumbling notes. If that weren't enough, the woman's outfit today reflected sure signs of a growing disorientation, with her striped frock overlaid by a knee-length tunic of floral chiffon. A wide silk headband sporting a bright Christmas plaid held most of her wiry white curls off her shoulders and neck, giving her the appearance of a garish, holiday gypsy. The poor woman's maid must have been mortified this morning.

"Of course, Cecily, dear." Grampapa spoke softly and gently, as he had when Phoebe was small. His perfectly trimmed mustache twitched as he smiled. "We shall look forward to it."

Phoebe managed to suppress a groan, but Fox could not. Grams shot another glance across the table while Grampapa's eyebrows gathered in warning.

"After Julia serenades us"—fourteen-year-old Fox pulled a face—"and Lady Cecily, too, may we find something exciting to do? Grampapa, couldn't we take the rifles out for some skeet shooting?"

"Fox." Grams arced a crescent-thin eyebrow. "I believe indoor activities are more appropriate for days such as this."

"Oh, Grams. . . ."

"Fox." Grampapa's stern tone forestalled any impending complaint.

The boy made a grinding sound in his throat, and Phoebe whispered to him, "When are you going to grow up?"

"When are you going to stop being so boring?"

"Terribly sorry to be late for luncheon, everyone. I had some letters to write. Do forgive me." Clad in country tweeds, Lord Owen Seabright bowed ruefully and took the vacant seat beside Julia. His gaze met Phoebe's, and she raised her water goblet to her lips to hide the inevitable and appalling heat that always crept into her cheeks whenever the man so much as glanced her way.

Lord Owen Seabright was an earl's younger son who had taken a small, maternal inheritance and turned it into a respectable fortune. His woolen mills had supplied English soldiers with uniforms and blankets during the war. He himself had served as well, a major commanding a battalion, and for his valor he'd been awarded a Victoria Cross. Unlike Theo Leighton, Lord Owen had returned home mercifully whole but for having taken a bullet to the shoulder.

If only Papa had been so fortunate. . . .

She dismissed the thought before melancholy had a chance to set in. Of course, that left her once more contemplating Owen Seabright, a wealthy, fit man in the prime of his life and as yet unattached. After years of war, such men were a rarity. He'd been invited to spend Christmas because his grandfather and Phoebe's had been great friends, because he'd had a falling out with his own family who disapproved of his business ventures, and because Fox had insisted he come, with Grams's blessing.

If an engagement between Julia and Henry didn't come about, Owen Seabright was to be next in line to seek Julia's hand. Phoebe wondered if Owen, or Julia for that matter, had been privy to that information. She herself only knew because Fox had told her, his way of informing her he'd soon have Julia married off and Phoebe's turn would be next.

Or so he believed. What Phoebe believed was that Fox needed to be taken down a peg or two.

"Henry isn't with you?" Lady Allerton asked.

Lord Owen looked surprised. "With me? No, I haven't seen him today."

"No one has, apparently." With a perplexed look, Lady Allerton helped herself to another of last night's medallions of beef bordelaise. "I do hope Henry hasn't gotten lost somewhere."

"He can hardly lose his way." Grampapa's great chest rose and fell, giving Phoebe the impression of a bear just waking up from a long winter's rest. "He knows our roads and trails as well as any of us. Spent enough time at Foxwood as a boy, didn't he?"

"Yes, but, Archibald," Grams said sharply, "things look different in the snow. He easily could have taken a wrong fork and ended up heaven only knows where. Or he might have slipped and twisted his ankle."

"Good heavens," Lady Allerton exclaimed. "Is that supposed to reassure me?"

"Should we form a search party?" Amelia appeared genuinely worried. Phoebe sent her a reassuring smile and shook her head.

"Grams, don't be silly." Fox flourished his fork, earning him a sharp throat clearing and another stern look from Grampapa. The youngest Renshaw put his fork down with a terse, "Sorry, sir," and shoved a lock of sandy hair off his forehead. "But even if he *was* lost, he'd either end up in the village, the school, or the river. He's not about to jump in the river in this weather, is he?" The boy shrugged. "He'll be back."

He sent Julia a meaningful look. She ignored him, turning her head to gaze out the bay window at the wide expanse of snow-frosted lawn rolling away to a skeletal copse of birch trees and the pine forest beyond that. Farther in the distance, the rolling Cotswolds Hills embraced the horizon, with patches of white interspersed with bare ground where the wind had whipped the snow away.

Phoebe brought her gaze closer, and noticed a trail of footprints leading through the garden and back again. Henry? But if he'd gone out that way, he had apparently returned to the house.

Grams narrowed a shrewd gaze on Julia. "I do hope there is no particular reason for Henry to have made a sudden departure."

This, too, Julia ignored.

"As Lawrence Winslow did last summer," Grams muttered under her breath. Although everyone must have heard the comment—Phoebe certainly had—all went on eating as if they hadn't. Grams seethed in Julia's direction another moment, then returned her attention to her meal.

Apparently, not everyone was willing to pretend Grams hadn't spoken. "Julia, you and Henry get on splendidly, don't you?" Fox snapped his fingers when she didn't reply. "Julia?"

She turned back around. "What?"

Phoebe was gripped by a sudden urge to pinch her. Though last night had obviously left her bewildered, this sort of indifference was nothing new. It began three years ago, the day the news about Papa reached them from France, and rather than fading over time her disinterest had become more pronounced throughout the war years. By turns her sister's apathy angered or saddened Phoebe, depending on the circumstances, but always left her frustrated.

"Stop it," Amelia hissed in her brother's ear, another comment heard and ignored around the table. "Leave it alone."

Phoebe observed her little sister. *Had* Amelia found out about last night's argument, or had she merely grown accustomed to Julia's fickleness when it came to men?

"My, my, yes, he'll be back." Lady Cecily spoke to no one in particular. She used her knife to scrape food around her plate with an irritating screech. "He must return soon, for isn't there an announcement Henry and Julia wish to make today?"

Lady Allerton leaned in close and, with an efficiency that appeared to be born of habit, slipped the knife from between her aunt's fingers. "You asked that this morning, Aunt Cecily. And no, there is no announcement just yet. Why don't you eat something now?"

"No engagement yet?" Lady Cecily looked crestfallen. "Why is that? Julia dear, didn't Henry ask you a very pertinent question last night?"

Julia finally looked away from the window as if startled from sleep. She blinked. "I'm sorry. Did you say something?"

"We were all very tired last night, what with all the Christmas revelry." Grams's attempt to sound cheerful fell flat. In the old days the house would have been filled with guests, but first the war and then the influenza outbreak that sped through England in the fall heavily curtailed this year's festivities. The Leightons might be second cousins, but they would not have been invited to spend the holiday at Foxwood Hall if Grams hadn't held out hope that Father Christmas would deliver a husband for Julia. The war had left so few men from whom to choose. "Henry and

Julia shall have plenty of time to talk now things have calmed down. Won't you, Julia?"

"Yes, Grams. Of course."

Phoebe doubted her sister knew what she had just agreed to. Fox sniggered.

"If you don't stop being so snide," she whispered to him behind her hand, "I'll suggest Grampapa send you up to the schoolroom where you belong."

Fox cupped a hand over his mouth and stuck out his tongue before whispering, "Then you should stop impersonating a beet every time Lord Owen enters a room."

"I do no such thing." Good gracious, if Fox had noticed, was she so obvious? She sucked air between her teeth. But no, Lord Owen was paying her no mind now, instead helping himself to thick slices of cold roast venison and responding to some question Grams had just asked him. She relaxed against her chair. Lord Owen was a passing fancy, nothing more. He was . . . too tall for her. Too muscular—good heavens, his shoulders and chest filled out his Norfolk jacket in the most alarming ways. Approaching his late twenties, he was too old as well. And much too . . .

Handsome, with his strong features, steely eyes, and inky black hair that made such a striking contrast next to Julia's blond.

Yes, just a silly, passing fancy. . . .

"Well, now, my girls." Grampapa grinned broadly and lightly clapped his hands. "I believe it's time to hand out the Christmas boxes, is it not? The staff will want to be on their way."

"Yes, you're quite right, Grampapa." With a sense of relief at this excuse to escape the table, Phoebe dabbed at her lips and placed her napkin beside her plate. "Girls, shall we?"

Amelia was on her feet in an instant. "I've so been looking forward to this. It's my favorite part of Christmas."

Julia stood with a good deal less enthusiasm. "Not mine, but come. Let's get it over with."

Eva could finally feel her fingers and toes again after trekking across the village to her parents' farm. Mum had put the kettle on before she arrived, and she was just now enjoying her second cup of strong tea and biting into another heavenly, still-warm apricot scone.

Holly and evergreen boughs draped the mantel above a cheerful fire, and beside the hearth a small stack of gifts waited to be opened. Eva eyed the beribboned box from the Renshaws. She wondered what little treasure Phoebe and Amelia had tucked inside.

Mum huffed her way into the room with yet another pot of tea, which she set on a trivet on the sofa table. "Can't have enough on a day like today," she said, as if there had been a need to explain. "As soon as your father comes in from checking the animals we'll open the presents."

"I think they're lovely right where they are," Eva said. "It's just good to be home."

"It's a shame your sister couldn't be here this year."

"Alice would if she could have, Mum, but Suffolk is far, especially in this weather."

"Yes, I suppose. . . ." With another huff Mum sat down beside her, weighting the down cushion so that the springs beneath creaked and Eva felt herself slide a little toward the center of the old sofa.

A name hovered in the air between them, loud and clear though neither of them spoke it. Danny, the youngest of the family. Eva's chest tightened, and Mum pretended to sweep back a strand of hair, when in actuality she brushed at a tear.

Danny had gone to France in the third year of the war, just after his eighteenth birthday. Not quite a year later, last winter, the telegram came.

"Ah, yes, well." Mum patted Eva's hand and pulled in a fortifying breath. "It's good to have you home for an entire day, or almost so. I'd have thought we'd see more of you, working so close by."

"Tending to three young ladies keeps me busy, Mum."

"Yes, and bless them for it, I suppose. It's a good position you've got, so we shan't be complaining, shall we?"

"Indeed not. Especially not today. But . . . I hear you huffing a bit, Mum. Are your lungs still achy?"

"No, no. Better now."

The door of the cottage opened on a burst of wind and a booted foot crossed the threshold. A swirl of snowflakes followed. Eva sprang up to catch the door and prevent it swinging back on her father, who stamped snow off his boots onto the braided rug and unwrapped the knitted muffler from around his neck.

"Everyone all right out there, Vincent?" Mum asked. She leaned forward to pour tea into her father's mug.

"Right as rain." He shrugged off his coat and ran a hand over a graying beard that reached his chest. "Or as snow, I should say."

"Come sit and have a cuppa, dear. Eva wants to open her gifts."

"Oh, Mum."

They spent the next minutes opening and admiring. Eva was pleased to see the delighted blush in her mother's cheeks when she unwrapped the shawl Eva had purchased in Bristol when she'd accompanied Lady Julia there in October. There was also a pie crimper and a wax sealer with her mother's initial, B for Betty. For her father Eva had found a tooled leather bookmark and had knitted him a new muffler to replace his old ragged one.

From them Eva received a velvet-covered notebook for keeping track of her duties and appointments, a linen blouse Mum had made and embroidered herself, and a hat with little silk flowers for which they must have sacrificed far too much of their meager income. But how could she scold them for their extravagance when their eyes shone so brightly as she opened the box?

Mum gripped the arm of the sofa and pulled to her feet with another of those huffs that so concerned Eva. "I'll just check on the roast. Should be ready soon. Oh, Eva, you've forgotten your box from the Renshaws."

So she had. "There's something inside for you, too, Mum."

"You have a look-see, dear. I mustn't burn the roast."

"All right, I'll peek inside and then I'll come and help you put dinner on, Mum."

She picked up the box and returned to the sofa. Her father grinned. "So what do you suppose is in there this year?"

"We'll just have to see, won't we?" She tugged at the ribbons, pulled off the cover, and set it aside. The topmost gift was wrapped in gold foil tissue paper. The card on top read: *To Eva, with fondness and appreciation, from Phoebe and Amelia.* She carefully unrolled the little package and out tumbled a set of airy linen handkerchiefs edged in doily lace, each adorned with its own color of petit point roses: a pink, a yellow, a violet, and a blue. Eva didn't think there were such things as blue or violet roses, but her heart swelled and her eyes misted as she pictured the two girls bent over their efforts, quickly whisking away their gifts-in-the-making whenever Eva entered their rooms.

"Look, Dad. See what the girls have for me. Aren't they perfection? And here's a fifth, with a tag that says it's for Mum."

He craned his neck to see. "Look a mite too fine for the use they're meant for."

Eva chuckled and glanced again into her box. "And here's a card. . . ." She took out a simple piece of white paper, folded in half. She unfolded it. "It reads, '*For the Huntfords, for their pains.*' Odd, there's no signature."

"Isn't that jolly of the Renshaws to remember your mum and me."

"I'll bet it's a bit of cash, like last year. Let's see. . . ." Eva bent over the box to peer inside. The breath left her in a single whoosh.

"Well? What's next in that box of surprises?" Dad leaned expectantly forward in his chair. "Evie? Evie, why do you look like that? Surely they haven't gone and given us one of the family heirlooms, have they? Evie?"

"I . . . Oh, Dad. . . . Oh, *God*."

"Evie, we do not blaspheme in this house," her mother called from the kitchen. She appeared in the doorway, drying her hands on a dish rag. "Eva, what on earth is wrong? You're as white as a sheet of ice."

"It's . . . it's a ring," she managed, gasping. Her hands trembled where they clutched the edges of the box. Her heart thumped as though to escape her chest. "A s-signet ring."

"That's lovely, dear. So why do you look as if you've just seen a ghost?" Her mother started toward her. Her father's rumbling laugh somehow penetrated the ringing in Eva's ears.

She held up both hands to stop her mother in her tracks. "Mum, stay where you are. Don't come any closer."

"Why, Eva Mary Huntford, what *has* gotten into you? What sort of signet ring could make my daughter so impertinent?" The sullenness in her mother's voice mingled with that incessant ringing. A wave of dizziness swooped up to envelop Eva.

The room wavered in her vision. "One that's still attached to the finger."

CHAPTER 2

Vernon delivered his message in a whisper near Phoebe's ear. She sprang to her feet, drawing the attention of the other ladies in the second-floor Rosalind sitting room, so named for her great-great-grandmother, who had furnished the room to reflect the pinks and reds of the rose garden in summer. "Excuse me, everyone. I'll . . . er . . . be back."

"Phoebe," Grams called after her.

"Where on earth is she going in such a hurry?" Lady Allerton said as well, but Phoebe didn't stop to explain.

She couldn't, not without alarming ladies Allerton and Cecily. Grams was aware of the macabre developments that brought the servants home hours before they were expected. Several of them were directly affected and word had quickly spread among the rest. Grampapa had explained to Grams, and she in turn had brought Phoebe into her confidence. This had been too much to bear alone, even for stoic Grams. Grampapa, meanwhile, was telephoning all over the village and nearby inns for any sign of Henry.

She repressed a shudder and traveled the corridor a brisk clip. With Vernon following close in her wake, she made her way to the back of the house and down the service staircase. Eva, her eyes wide and her face blanched of color, stood shivering at the bottom.

"Milady, I'm so terribly sorry Vernon disturbed you. I asked him not to, but—"

"He was acting at my request, Eva. I wished to be notified immediately if you returned to the house."

Vincent Huntford, the bearded, burly man beside Eva, placed a calloused hand on his daughter's shoulder. "Perhaps we should have gone straight to the Chief Inspector's office rather than burden poor Lady Phoebe with this."

Phoebe shook her head. "No, Inspector Perkins is already here. So I am to understand you also found . . ."

Eva's eyes opened wider still. "Do you mean there were others?"

"Several. Phelps and Dora, and two of the shopkeepers in the village to whom Grampapa sent gifts." A sudden queasiness tempted Phoebe to find the nearest seat. Instead, she drew herself up straighter. "Tell me what you found. Was it in your Christmas box, too?"

"A finger," Eva whispered through quivering lips. "A severed finger with a signet ring."

"I see." Not for the first time since this began, a chill swept through Phoebe. "The inspector will need you to help identify the . . . the . . . victim."

"I know exactly who it is." Eva's next words confirmed Phoebe's own suspicions. "Lord Allerton."

Eva preceded her father and Lady Phoebe into the jarred goods pantry, where she had deposited that dreadful Christmas box. She loathed involving Phoebe in the sordid details, wished she could prevent the girl from peeking inside. After all, she *had* just divulged the contents of the box, so what was the point of looking, really? But Lady Phoebe had that determined set to her chin and there would be no deterring her.

Her father drew the box to the edge of the counter and lifted the lid, whereupon Lady Phoebe rose up on her toes and glanced in. A second later, she turned away and reached for Eva's hands.

Her face was pale. "I'm so sorry."

"You've no reason to be sorry, my lady."

"To have your holiday ruined by this . . ." Lady Phoebe let out a breath. "I think you and Mr. Huntford had better come upstairs. The inspector will want to speak to you both."

A few minutes later, Lady Phoebe knocked on the morning-room door. Ranged along the corridor were others staff members—Josh the young hall boy, Dora the scullery maid, and Lord Wroxly's valet, Mr. Phelps. Phoebe had mentioned two of the villagers as well, but Eva saw no sign of them. Perhaps the inspector had already interviewed them in their homes.

Apparently, Inspector Perkins and his assistant had set up for questions in this relatively small room set back from the main part of the house, and where there would likely be fewer distractions. He glanced up as Lady Phoebe led Eva and her father across the threshold. Her father held the box, his face slightly averted as if the contents gave off a vile odor. Which perhaps they did. Eva didn't believe she'd drawn a full breath since first opening it.

"My lady's maid discovered a gruesome surprise in her box as well," Lady Phoebe said with an authority that belied her nineteen years. "I thought you might wish to see her."

Had Eva been wrong to leave the new handkerchiefs at home with Mum? Were they evidence, too? She didn't care. She wouldn't hand over the gifts her girls had labored over especially for her.

Her girls. She often thought of them that way despite being only seven years older than Phoebe.

Douglas, the young under footman, sat at the table across

from Inspector Perkins, his right hand tugging at the left cuff of his livery coat. The inspector's assistant, a young man and a stranger to Eva—rare in a village like Little Barlow—sat to his employer's right, a pencil poised above an open notebook. He wore the blue woolen tunic of a constable; his high-domed helmet sat on the table beside him.

Inspector Perkins spoke quietly to Douglas.

"All right, lad, that'll do for now. I'll send for you if I have further questions." He looked up at Eva. "Have a seat, Miss Huntford. Ah, Mr. Huntford, nice to see you. Well . . ." He let out a bark of a laugh. "Not *nice*. Surely not, with such business afoot." He gestured to the chair Douglas had vacated and the one beside it.

"Do you wish me to stay?" Lady Phoebe whispered to Eva.

"No, it's all right, my lady. How is Lady Amelia? When I think of her setting your lovely gifts on top of that horrible thing, it's almost worse than the thing itself. What if she'd seen it?"

Lady Phoebe placed a manicured hand over Eva's. "She didn't. The boxes were up on a shelf and she slipped our present inside right before Julia and I tied the lids closed with ribbon. None of us ever thought to glance inside."

With that Phoebe stepped out and closed the door behind her, leaving Eva and her father to face the inspector's questions. Five minutes later she began to feel as though she were running round and round the hedge maze with the exit nowhere in sight. The inspector asked myriad questions several times each, as if he couldn't remember her answers from one moment to the next despite his assistant jotting everything down. Had she seen any strangers in the house recently, either above or below stairs? Did she talk to anyone on her way to her parents' farm? Had she left the box unattended anywhere for any length of time as she crossed the village? Had she argued with anyone recently?

Did he think the daily squabbles above and below stairs could result in this kind of act? If so, there wasn't a safe manor house in all of England.

She studied the chief inspector's eyes with their webbing of red lines and surrounding pockets of flesh. A pocked nose shot through with tiny purple veins completed the picture. It wasn't hard to guess how he had spent Christmas Day—with his feet up in front of a hearth fire and a bottle of whiskey close at hand. It was no great secret that Isaac Perkins liked his spirits, but in a parish that hadn't seen a major crime in over a hundred years, no one saw much reason to complain.

Until now.

"Inspector Perkins, I don't understand why you don't examine the ring itself. If you do, you'll see that it belongs to Lord Allerton." She gulped and continued lower. "As does the finger, one can only assume."

"Lord Allerton?" Inspector Perkins exchanged a look with his assistant. The assistant, a man about Eva's age with a curly mop of dark red hair and bright blue eyes that marked him most likely of Irish or Scottish descent, merely kept writing in his notebook. The inspector looked back at Eva. "Are you certain? I was to understand he's not been in the house all morning."

"Yes, and there could be a very significant reason for that. Look at the ring." Eva tried to smooth the frustration from her voice. She gestured at the still-closed box sitting in front of her father. "The A on the signet is as clear as day. Who else could it belong to? It would also explain why no one has seen Lord Allerton. Because he's . . ."

Her throat ran dry. Her father reached over and rubbed her shoulder gently. Inspector Perkins stretched an arm over the table, a wordless request for the box. Her father complied and pushed the thing across the surface.

"Ah, yes. Sorry to say, this has become an all-too-familiar sight today," the chief inspector declared upon peering in.

"What was found in the other boxes?" Eva wanted to know.

Inspector Perkins pulled a handkerchief out of his coat pocket and mopped it across his brow. "More of the same, I'm afraid. Except without identifying circumstances. An appendage lying beside a gold watch. Another with a tie pin. Yet another with a set of sapphire shirt studs. And so on. A half dozen in all. Makes no sense."

"Have you shown the other items to his man?" Dad's voice rang with impatience. "He could identify them as Lord Allerton's or not."

"We had no reason to, not until now." Inspector Perkins's assistant stopped scribbling and leaned forward with an elbow on the table. "But now that we have an identity," he said in the slightest of brogues, "the question for the time being is not so much the who or how of the crime, but the *where*. As in, where is the rest of Lord Allerton?"

Eva groaned in queasiness.

Phoebe stared out the Petite Salon's bay window at the sweep of lawn bordered by white-crested shrubbery and icy flowerbeds. At the sound of a spoon tinkling against the fine porcelain of a teacup, she turned to Julia, who was sitting at the table.

"You're awfully calm about this," Phoebe noted. "Especially seeing as it was your beau who met his demise this morning. Or last night."

Julia offered one of her trademark shrugs and sipped her tea. "As far as I am concerned, Henry was neither my fiancé nor my beau. He was little more than an acquaintance."

"Good heavens, Julia, that's terribly unfeeling of you.

We've known the Leightons all our lives. You might at least feel a smidgeon of sympathy for his mother."

Julia stared impassively back. "It's not as if I wished him ill. I'm simply not devastated that he has left us."

"Left us? Henry hasn't gone off on holiday. He is most assuredly *dead,* Julia."

"Is he?" She wrinkled her pretty nose, which, unlike Phoebe's, had never known a single freckle. "Thus far we have no real proof of that. Inspector Perkins said there isn't a speck of blood in Henry's room, nor anywhere else they've looked."

"His blood is *somewhere,* Julia. His fingers were severed from his hands!" Phoebe paused to regain her composure.

Though the others had assembled in the drawing room to await their turn to speak with Inspector Perkins, there was no telling when one of them might come looking for either Julia or herself. Julia had sneaked away earlier to avoid questions about the night before, especially the constant ones posed by Henry's aunt Cecily, who hadn't quite grasped the gravity of the situation and still believed an engagement to be imminent.

"Julia," Phoebe began again more calmly, "it is a foregone conclusion that Henry did not survive such a vicious attack on his person. And that everyone in this house could be viewed as a suspect."

"That's ridiculous."

"Which? That Henry is very likely dead, or that any of us might be considered culpable?"

"The latter, of course." Another shrug followed.

Phoebe wanted to shake sense into her. No, not sense. Feeling. Empathy. *Life.* During these past years Julia had seemed less than alive, disconnected from the rest of the world and everyone in it.

Papa's death had done that to her, just as it had turned

Fox from an unruly but good-natured child into a grasping, self-centered adolescent. And Amelia . . . poor Amelia worried about everyone all the time, constantly seeking ways to ensure the happiness of the entire family. Well-meaning though she might be, there was often something quite desperate and grasping in Amelia's vision of how life should be.

If only Papa hadn't gone to war. If only he hadn't died in the trenches.

And if only Henry Leighton had been a decent man, one with whom Julia could have fallen in love. But none of that had happened, and Phoebe knew they must face what did happen head-on, or they would never be free of it.

She sat at the table across from her sister. "When the inspector questions you, it would be best if you come clean about last night. About your argument with Henry."

Julia paled. Her eyes narrowed within their dark rim of lashes. "That is no one's business. Not yours, and certainly not Inspector Perkins's."

"Don't you understand? I'm not the only one who overheard you last night. The servants clearing the dining room witnessed a good deal. Wouldn't it be better for you to explain yourself rather than allow them to speculate on your behalf?"

"I feel no need to explain myself, Phoebe. And how dare you imply that I might have had something to do with Henry's death." Her expression smoldering, she stood and thrust her napkin to the table.

"I implied no such thing. And I thought you weren't convinced Henry was even deceased." She raised her eyebrows, a silent dare for Julia to backtrack once again.

"I've had more than enough of this." Julia headed for the door.

"Of course I don't believe you had anything to do with what happened to Henry," Phoebe called after her. "That's exactly why you should speak honestly with the inspector. Julia, wait. . . ."

She came to her feet, but too late. Julia was gone. With a deep sigh Phoebe returned to the bay windows. Whose footprints were those, leading through the garden, around the fountain, over the footbridge, and to the edge of the woods? Another set of prints also marred the fresh snow, but only near the house. The inspector's assistant had been out for a look and had no doubt determined that whoever had ventured out that way had returned to the house. But Phoebe wondered about that. Had anyone bothered to trace the footsteps and determine whether they entered the woods? And if so, where they had gone from there?

"I need my Wellies and a warm coat," she said to herself, and turned to discover a figure in the doorway.

"My lady?" Eva still looked pale and shaken, though she offered Phoebe a patient smile. "I just thought I'd check to see if you needed anything."

"Has the inspector finished with you and your father?"

Her hands folded primly at her waist, Eva stepped into the room. "With me, yes. He's still questioning my father. I didn't like being asked to leave. It felt wrong, leaving Dad there alone."

"Why do you think Inspector Perkins dismissed you?"

"It seems the note I found in our box raises some questions about . . . well . . . about whether my parents had any dealings with Lord Allerton. Which they never have, of course. Why would they?"

"What did the note say?"

" 'For the Huntfords, for their pains.' " Eva's shoulders quivered. "As if a severed finger were reward for . . . for I cannot imagine what, my lady."

"That *is* ghastly." Phoebe folded her arms and considered. "Of course, the ring must be very valuable. One supposes it was meant as payment for something. Any idea what?"

"None at all." Eva opened her hands, then clutched them together again. "My father occasionally supplies meat to various butchers and manor houses, and of course his dairy cows provide milk to the village. But I don't know that Lord Allerton did business of any sort with my father since before the war." After a pause, she added, "It's all rather befuddling."

"Indeed it is." Phoebe came to a quick decision. "Eva, would you mind accompanying me outside? Just in the garden."

"If you like, my lady, of course. We must dress warmly. It's quite cold and your grandmother would never forgive me if I allowed you to catch a chill." She studied Phoebe with an assessing gaze that suddenly had Phoebe wanting to squirm like a child. "May I ask the purpose of this trek into a frozen garden, my lady?"

"I'll answer that with another question. Do you trust Inspector Perkins to conduct a thorough investigation?"

"My answer is no . . . and *no,* my lady."

Phoebe blinked. "Why a double no?"

"Phoebe Renshaw, I entreat you to leave police business to the police."

"I only suggested a walk through the garden." She struggled to keep her expression clear of all controversy. "And if we should happen to notice any significant details about those footprints out there, so much the better."

Phoebe held her breath as Eva continued to study her. Had she been wrong to involve her maid? She should have simply slipped out alone with no one the wiser. If Eva refused, she would watch Phoebe like the hawk she sometimes became. And here Phoebe had believed she had outgrown the need for a governess. Sometimes Eva could be sterner than even Miss Dawson of years ago.

Finally, Eva spoke. "Absolutely not, my lady. I won't help you become involved in a criminal investigation. It's far too dangerous. You would do best to return to the drawing room with the others and let Inspector Perkins and his assistant perform their duties."

Some ten minutes later, Eva let out a sigh. "Honestly, my lady, I don't know how I let you talk me into coming outside." Swirls of steam accompanied each word and she shivered inside her wool coat. The cold knifed at her lungs and penetrated thick stockings, a flannel petticoat, and calf-high boots. She could not return to the house quickly enough.

She glanced over at Phoebe, who had assumed one of her "Who me?" expressions. "Here, put your collar up. My goodness, it's grown colder even than this morning. We'll both be frozen through in a matter of minutes and it'll be spring before they manage to thaw us out."

She raised the fur collar of Phoebe's coat more snugly around her neck and tightened her muffler for good measure, but that did little to soothe her guilt about agreeing to this excursion. They had exited the house through the library, and Eva supposed if anyone happened to glance out of the drawing-room windows, they would merely think Phoebe needed a bit of fresh air. Lord Wroxly in particular favored nothing so much as a brisk wind in his face, so he would find nothing out of place in his grand-daughter seeking the same, especially on so distressing a day as this.

"Do stop fussing, Eva." Phoebe raised a gloved hand to tug at her muffler. "This wretched thing makes me sneeze. Besides, I'm not in the least bit cold."

"I am, so humor me." But she made no more adjustments to her mistress's clothing.

Phoebe studied the ground and frowned. "I thought Henry would have exited the house through the drawing room or the library, but apparently not. Where *do* the tracks originate?"

True, Eva noted, theirs were the only footprints to be seen in last night's fresh snow, at least until they reached the central walkway. With her gaze Eva followed the tracks to their source at the farther end of the house.

"It looks as though he came out through the service courtyard." She pointed to the wing that jutted out perpendicular from the main edifice. High stone walls separated the service courtyard from the formal gardens. Around the corner of the wing, a wooden gate led out to the kitchen garden tucked behind a towering evergreen hedge. Beyond that stood the sprawling greenhouses and then the orchards.

"Why would Lord Allerton come outside through the servants' entrance?"

"If it was Lord Allerton who made this trail, perhaps he raided the larder for something to eat first," Eva suggested.

"Come on, then, let's start where he started." Phoebe took off at an undignified trot, and as Eva followed at a brisk walk she glanced up at the drawing-room windows to see if Lady Wroxly observed them with one of her disapproving frowns. She saw only the backs of heads ranged along the settee beneath the central window and a few moving shadows beyond. She hurried after Phoebe, who had disappeared from sight. Eva found her just inside the service gate.

"This must be how Henry went out," she murmured absently. Her gloved finger swept the double trail of footprints between the gate and the door that led inside the servants' corridor. "He returned this way, too. See the prints? The same ones—note the size of the shoes being the same—go both in and out." She moved farther into the courtyard, still pointing at the ground. A jumble of prints went to yet another, wider pair of gates where deliveries were brought in each morning from the village. "Here are some smaller ones, probably those of Mrs. Ellison and her assistants, and I would wager these larger ones here are from Vernon and Douglas carrying in the heavier parcels."

"Perhaps one of them decided to walk through the gardens early this morning."

Phoebe scrunched up her face as she studied the prints. "No, Vernon and Douglas are taller than Lord Allerton and their feet are larger." She paced back to the garden gate. "There is only one set in and out here, and they don't appear to lead to the kitchen garden or the hothouses."

Even through her woolen gloves, Eva's fingers stung from the cold. "All very astute deductions, my lady. Perhaps you'd like to offer your assistance to Inspector Perkins."

She suppressed a smile at Phoebe's little frown of perplexity. "You're teasing me."

"I suppose I am, but you *have* made some astute observations. Shall we follow the trail and see where they lead?" *And return to the warmth inside all the more quickly,* she thought.

"Yes, but we should stay well away from the prints. We don't want to obscure them with our own."

Before Eva could comment on that strategy, a voice interrupted.

"That is something the inspector and I would vastly appreciate, ladies."

Both Eva and Phoebe whirled at the sound of the brogue to find Inspector Perkin's assistant letting himself out through the kitchen door. Over his uniform he wore a deep blue trench coat, double breasted with polished brass buttons and belted at the waist. He strolled over to them and tipped his helmet, his hair fiery against the background of snow and overcast sky.

"Is Inspector Perkins finished asking questions, then?" Phoebe asked.

The young man shook his head. "No, he's still questioning the staff, but he didn't think he needed me for the time being. I thought I'd come out and take another look at these very same footprints that seem to hold you in such fascination, my lady."

Though he spoke to Lady Phoebe, he cast several quizzical glances at Eva. Something in the acuity of his gaze put her on her guard, as if she might be a suspect. Silly of her, she knew, yet the gentle brogue and the sharp blue eyes seemed to work in conjunction, suggesting a strategy of setting people at ease while missing nothing.

A beneficial talent for a policeman, to be sure, but why use it on her? Had some development arisen inside—something to do with her father?

The notion unsettled her nearly as much as the man's piercing scrutiny. "Has the inspector discovered anything—any clues as to who might have wanted to harm Lord Allerton?"

"I am afraid I'm not at liberty to discuss that."

Phoebe frowned, and Eva said, "Come now. This is a small village where there are few, if any, secrets. If someone amongst us performed this despicable deed, we shall all know soon enough."

"I don't doubt that," he said as he clasped his leather-clad hands behind him, "but you'll not hear about it from me, I'm afraid. Not at present, at any rate."

Phoebe's frown hadn't diminished, and now she said, "You are new to the village, Constable. . . ."

"I am. And it's Brannock. Constable Miles Brannock, my lady, at your service." He swept a little bow aimed primarily at Phoebe. Eva pursed her lips. She easily imagined him to be a charmer with ladies, for though his gesture might have been one of deference to a daughter of the house, his smile held too much familiarity for Eva's comfort. He reminded her of Nicholas Hensley, teasing her this morning by insisting she call him Nick. This, however, was quite a different matter and set off a trill of warning. Did the constable have the cheek to flirt with Phoebe while trying to gauge Eva's reaction? Or was he *daring* her to react?

She'd show him a reaction, all right. She would nip his insolence in the bud immediately, and in no uncertain terms. "If you'll excuse us, Constable Brannock." She raised her chin dismissively, as she had had to do on occasion with the butcher's rather presumptuous delivery man. "Lady Phoebe and I were just about to return to the house."

"No, we weren't," Phoebe blurted, much to Eva's frustration. "We were about to follow these tracks to wherever they lead. You see, constable, they suggest the person went out and later returned to the house, but if they belong to Lord Allerton, where is he? And where were his . . . Oh dear. I shouldn't like to say it aloud, but after what was found in the Christmas boxes, you comprehend my meaning."

All impertinence faded from the policeman's manner. "I did notice that about the prints, my lady, which is why I'm here for another look. Perhaps, as your maid suggests, you should return to the house."

Eva couldn't have agreed more and placed a hand on Phoebe's sleeve to coax her back inside. "Come, my lady."

The determined young woman stood her ground. "No, I intend to have a look. You can't stop me from walking on my own grandfather's property, can you?" This she asked with a grin and a lift of an eyebrow. At the constable's nod of acquiescence, she gestured toward the gate. "Shall we, then?"

They filed into the garden proper. Eva made sure to position herself between Constable Brannock and Phoebe, and they kept well to one side of the footprints and allowed Constable Brannock to perform his task. Through the garden, past the dormant fountain whose bubbling waters had been replaced by icicles, over the footbridge that spanned a half-frozen stream, and onto the lawn they went. Other than a bit of scattered snow that suggested the shuffling of feet, Eva detected no hesitation in their quarry's stride. He—for the shoes identified the wearer as undoubtedly male—seemed to have walked with a clear purpose all the way to the edge of the forest. But from there . . .

Constable Brannock studied the spot where the footprints ended in what appeared to be a bit of pacing back and forth before turning about and retreating to the house. Eva stole the opportunity to study the officer again. She hadn't considered it previously, but given his age and healthy physical appearance, it was odd he walked without a limp, bore no visible scars, and . . . to put it bluntly . . . that he lived at all. Not that she would wish ill upon him, but with so many young men swept away by the war, she couldn't help wonder how Miles Brannock had spent the previous years. Had he shirked his duty to his country, hidden away in a rural police department in order to escape the horrors other men his age faced?

True, the British government hadn't extended military compulsion to Ireland, but Eva would swear, given the man's Anglicized accent, that he had spent the war years and possibly more right here in England. Perhaps his heart and loyalty had neglected to follow where his feet had brought him.

"Are there no trails from here into the woods?" he asked.

"Not from here, no," Phoebe said. "The riding trails begin about a half a mile off to our right." She glanced in the general direction of the stables, whose pitched slate roofs poked up above the surrounding oak and pine. "No one uses the trails much these days, though."

"And why is that, my lady?"

Sadness shadowed her features. "Most of the horses are gone. Grampapa sent them to help the war effort, along with the hounds." She shrugged. "They would have been conscripted into service eventually."

"I see." To Eva's relief, Constable Brannock didn't comment further, offered neither commiseration nor approval for what had been a sacrifice of a most painful nature. Phoebe had been inconsolable the day the horses were led away, including her own gray hunter, Stormy. An eleven-year-old Amelia had cried, too, though her pony, Blossom, had been spared, too small to be of any use to the army. Eva had cried, secretly, for the dogs, taken to be trained to deliver messages and supplies between the trenches.

Once again Eva couldn't help but wonder if Miles Brannock had made any sacrifices for the war effort.

After a lengthy pause, he asked, "Are there any other trails or paths?"

The question seemed to shake Phoebe out of her melancholy and brought her back to the present. "The gamekeeper's paths. They begin some several hundred yards beyond the stables, at the gamekeeper's cottage."

"I'd like to speak to the man."

"I'm afraid you cannot," Phoebe replied flatly. "He's gone."

"Gone where, my lady?"

"To a grave in France, sir. He died during the war."

"I see. I'm sorry." Sorry, perhaps, but he seemed to dismiss the matter quickly. He craned his neck to see past the birch copse into the forest. The dense canopy had prevented the snow from accumulating at the bases of the trunks, and patches of bare earth and dead undergrowth formed murky shadows between shallow pools of white. Constable Brannock pushed heavy boughs aside, releasing a shower of snow, and stepped between the trees.

"Do you see anything, sir?" Phoebe called after him. "More footprints?"

"That I don't, my lady," he replied after a moment. He pushed farther in, setting off more powdery cascades as he himself disappeared into the embrace of the forest. "But I wonder . . ."

Presently, he returned, brushing the snow from his shoulders. "The bare ground is too frozen for anyone to have left prints, but the patches of snow are smooth and undisturbed, but for occasional animal tracks. You say there is nothing beyond this point unless one heads either toward the stables or the gamekeeper's paths?"

"Nothing but empty forest for several hundred acres, until one emerges at the home and tenant farms," Phoebe said. "The trees are thick here and Grampapa, like his father before him, was opposed to clearing them. He maintains there are too few old forests left in England."

"Very wise of him." The constable contemplated the ground another moment before flicking his gaze back to Phoebe. "It does appear as if Lord Allerton—or someone— walked to the edge of the woods, perhaps stopped and looked about, and then retraced his steps. A brief morning stroll. However, the inspector will no doubt organize a search party to inspect the riding trails and gamekeeper's paths."

"And the stables and the gamekeeper's cottage?" Lady Phoebe suddenly became animated. "There's a storage room attached to the cottage. Lord Allerton could be there."

"We'll check of course, my lady." Constable Brannock spoke with rather less enthusiasm than Phoebe had. "It does seem doubtful, though, considering these footprints indicate whoever came out here went no farther than this point before returning to the house."

"I just thought of something." Phoebe turned to Eva.

"Has Lord Allerton's valet checked his employer's boots for dampness?"

Eva had wondered about that herself. Poor Nick Hensley would bear the brunt of the investigation, at least until the authorities had gathered the facts and devised a theory. "I'm quite sure he will, if he hasn't already."

Constable Brannock concurred and then let out a long, frost-tinged breath. "Inspector Perkins and I had hoped to avoid this—hoped another scenario might present itself. But I'm afraid the house will need to be searched from top to bottom. Every square inch."

Those last words sent Eva's stomach plummeting as she considered their precise meaning in relation to the contents of the six Christmas boxes. She looked to Phoebe and realized she, too, understood the implication. Her cold-pinched cheeks paled, and at that moment she appeared very much a young girl, no more worldly than Amelia.

"You believe Lord Allerton is somewhere in the house right now?" Phoebe said. A soft hissing filled the momentary silence. It had begun snowing again, tiny flakes that drifted through the air like fluffs of down. "Somewhere without his fingers? Somewhere . . . dead . . . and perhaps no longer whole at all?"

Eva stroked her arm. "It doesn't do to speculate, my lady. We don't even know for sure that these are Lord Allerton's footprints. Please, let's go back and leave this to Constable Brannock and Inspector Perkins, shall we?"

If she expected further argument, it didn't come. Phoebe merely nodded weakly and let Eva lead her away. They had passed the fountain when Phoebe suddenly dug in her heels and turned. She peered over her shoulder at the constable, and Eva expected her to call out to him.

Instead, she spoke barely above a whisper. "Oh, Eva . . . if you knew something . . . something that might incriminate someone you cared about . . . or at least cast doubt over their recent actions . . . would you tell the authorities?"

Eva didn't reply right away. It was a question that deserved thought and an honest answer.

Whom did Phoebe mean? Surely not Fox or Amelia—they were children. Her grandfather? Eva hesitated over that one, but no, Lord Wroxly never allowed anyone or anything to perturb him to any great extent. What argument could he have had with Lord Allerton, the man he expected his eldest granddaughter to marry?

Lady Julia?

Again, she paused. Julia and Lord Allerton. . . . She searched Phoebe's face for clues, but found none.

All right, then, the question. Her father had been interviewed—alone—and that had left Eva . . . well . . . worried. Not that her father could be guilty, but that the inspector might assume guilt where none existed. If she had known of some argument between Lord Allerton and her father, would she have confessed it to Inspector Perkins?

She knew her father. She believed in the kind of man he was, believed in his good character, his honesty, his gentle nature. She knew—*knew*—that even if some resentment *had* existed between Vincent Huntford and Lord Allerton, the man who had raised her would never lift his hand to another person in anger. So then . . .

She smiled gently at Lady Phoebe. "My answer is no, my lady. In all honesty, no. If I believed wholeheartedly in that person, if I trusted beyond a doubt that the person I cared about could never commit such an act of violence, then I would hold my tongue."

Phoebe thought it over a moment. "Thank you, Eva. I thought that would be your answer."

They started once more toward the house, and Eva couldn't help noticing that Phoebe continued to look less than reassured.

CHAPTER 3

❧❧❧

After shedding her coat and boots in favor of velvet house shoes and a lamb's wool shawl, Phoebe met Henry's valet outside the morning room.

"Yes, my lady, these are Lord Allerton's boots."

"Are they damp?"

"They are, my lady. The soles have dried, but the leather of the vamps still shows traces of moisture. And here"—he turned them so Phoebe could view them from the side— "here are traces of the salt Mrs. Sanders sprinkled about the service courtyard."

"This is very odd, Mr. Hensley. It means Lord Allerton did indeed walk out through the servants' entrance some-time between midnight and dawn. He obviously returned to his room, removed his boots, and promptly disappeared." She tightened her shawl, tapping her foot as she considered. Surely then the police would not find him at either the sta-bles or the gamekeeper's cottage.

"Not *all* of him disappeared, my lady."

Her gaze snapped to the man's face, to nicely formed features drawn tight with distress, tinged with sorrow. And then she remembered. When Henry had gone off to serve as a colonel in the Royal Fusiliers, his valet had gone with him. From what she understood, Henry had given orders mostly from behind the lines. Mr. Hensley walked with the slightest of limps, one he usually kept well hidden but which she had noticed just now as he'd traversed the corridor toward her. A sniper's bullet had got him, perhaps, and likely in times of distress and great fatigue, the wound made itself known. Whatever had occurred in France, Henry and Mr. Hensley had served together, creating, no doubt, a bond that far exceeded that of nobleman and servant.

"I am so sorry, Mr. Hensley. This is obviously deeply disturbing for you. The inspector should have asked one of the footmen to retrieve the boots."

"No, my lady. Lord Allerton's effects are my responsibility. It is just that I can't help feeling somewhat responsible for . . . that is . . . if he is indeed . . ."

"Oh, no, Mr. Hensley! You mustn't blame yourself. Lord Allerton released you from your duties last night. Of course you assumed he put himself to bed and all was well."

"I did, my lady." He stared down at the black half boots in his hand and breathed in sharply. "Well, I should bring these in to Inspector Perkins."

"Is he still questioning the staff?"

"I believe so, my lady."

"All right. But, Mr. Hensley, if there is anything I or my family can do for you, please let us know." It did not escape Phoebe's understanding that if Henry was really and truly dead, Mr. Hensley would now be without a position, unless Theo were to hire him on. That seemed the most likely course, yet one never knew with Theo.

"Thank you, my lady." His face suffused with color. "That is most generous of you."

With that he tapped on the morning-room door and, at a reply from within, went inside. Phoebe, having received the answer to her latest question, made her way back to the drawing room.

The others were all there. Grams and Grampapa sat with Lady Allerton and her aunt Cecily over a game of bridge. Lady Allerton was leaning over Aunt Cecily's hand and pointing to the card she should play next. The old woman merely smiled and nodded passively.

Neither woman had been told yet. They knew only that Henry was apparently missing, and the inspector had come to help search for him. Grampapa, who had weathered the news splendidly earlier, thought it best to wait until Inspector Perkins discovered something concrete. Phoebe doubted the inspector's ability to do that, but she had little choice but to respect Grampapa's decision.

The younger set—Julia, Amelia, and Theo Leighton—were gathered on the settee and easy chairs beneath the central floor-to-ceiling windows, speaking quietly. That is, Amelia seemed to be doing most of the talking. Julia fidgeted with a tassel on the pillow beside her, while Theo stared down at his hands, flexing and unflexing his fingers as he so often did. Did they ache beneath their scars? Or . . .

Was Theo contemplating his brother's fate, those ghastly surprises in the Christmas boxes? He glanced up and Phoebe looked quickly away.

Fox and Lord Owen sat in two armchairs facing each other across the chessboard. Fox hunched forward, elbows on his knees and chin in his palms as he studied the pieces. Thank goodness someone remembered to keep Fox occupied—and blessedly quiet. Lord Owen lounged back in his chair with a patient half smile as he waited for Fox's next move.

Neither of them had noticed her yet, and Phoebe allowed her gaze to linger. Even sitting, Lord Owen towered over Fox, and her brother might have fit twice within the breadth of Owen's shoulders. And the depth of subtle color in his hair, dark upon darker even in the brightness of the electric lamps . . .

Phoebe sighed. Obsessing over the man's hair color, indeed. A ridiculous indulgence, this fascination of hers. But to be sure one that would slip by unnoticed. A man such as Owen Seabright would see her as little more than a child, one of scant experience and even less wisdom, whereas he had commanded men, led attacks, and survived battles so that such as she might continue in her safe, comfortable existence. They all owed Lord Owen, and Theo and even Henry, for such cozy, familial scenes as this, complete with vigorous fires in the room's two hearths and a snowy backdrop glittering through the expansive windows.

Only the glaring absence of one significant guest belied the tranquility of the afternoon.

That tranquility shattered further still with the pounding of approaching footsteps. A frantic cry of "Lord Wroxly! Lord Wroxly! My cleaver has gone missing!" destroyed any further illusion of this being an ordinary winter's day.

The elders around the card table looked up from their game. Grampapa sprang with a youthful surge to his feet. "What the devil?"

The drawing-room doors burst open and Mrs. Ellison, Foxwood Hall's cook since before Phoebe was born, appeared on the threshold, her face as blanched as her apron. "My cleaver. It's gone, milord. Gone!"

Mrs. Sanders, the housekeeper, came running up and stopped directly behind her. "I'm so sorry, Lord Wroxly. I couldn't stop her."

Phoebe's breath caught. A cleaver missing from the kitchen, and those awful Christmas boxes . . .

The rest of the gathering came to their feet as well. The men—Grampapa, Lord Owen, Theo, even Fox—rushed forward while the women held back, trading alarmed glances. All except for Aunt Cecily, who remained seated and continued to contemplate her cards. "It is most irregular for kitchen staff to appear above stairs, don't you think so, dear?" she asked her niece.

Lady Allerton shushed her.

Grampapa went to the cook, took her pudgy hand in his, and coaxed her to sit in the nearest chair. He dragged another close and sat facing her. The way he gave her the whole of his attention told Phoebe he took her most seriously. "What is this all about, and please explain from the beginning as calmly as you can."

The woman's ample bosom rose as she filled her lungs. "Well, milord, since our holiday was cut short I set Douglas to sharpening the knives I used to prepare Christmas dinner yesterday. I'd had to carve up the joints of venison and beef, as you know, sir, and I used my largest cleaver and . . . and now it's nowhere to be found! I distinctly remember Dora washing it and returning it to me last night, so it had to have disappeared sometime after midnight. . . ." Her hands went to her mouth, and she whispered behind her fingers, "Milord, do you suppose someone used my cleaver on . . . on . . ."

"Shhh!" Grampapa leaned closer to the woman and spoke in her ear. Her eyes went wide as her gaze darted to Lady Allerton. She whispered something to Grampapa in turn, and he shook his head.

"What is going on?" Amelia murmured to Phoebe.

Phoebe replied with a shake of her head, but inwardly she cringed. First the footprints and now this. More and more it appeared that Henry Leighton had been attacked . . . dismembered . . . *killed* . . . in this very house, and might still be here now, somewhere . . .

Good heavens—*moldering!*

She shut her eyes, but that did nothing to banish the gory images from her mind. She had never particularly liked Henry, and after last night she downright abhorred him for the way he had treated Julia—but this! This she would not wish on anyone.

Oh, Henry. . . .

She stole a glance at her elder sister. Julia looked on impassively for all appearances, until Phoebe studied her more closely and detected the anxiety sparking in her dark blue eyes. Theo Leighton stood beside her—when had he retreated from the other men?—and moved his scarred hand to touch the back of her arm, just a slight graze before he let his hand drop to his side again.

Phoebe watched them another moment. Odd, that physical contact. She had never observed much of a rapport between them. If Henry *had* met his end, Theo stood next in line to inherit the title, the estate—everything. Phoebe might be staring at the new Marquess of Allerton. Julia would be aware of that fact as well.

Could Julia's rejection of Henry have something to do with Theo? Or was Phoebe reading too much into what had been, after all, a fleeting touch in the face of yet another shock.

Grampapa pushed out of his chair and bellowed to no one in particular, "Where is the inspector? I must speak to him immediately." To Mrs. Ellison, he said more gently, "I need you to return below with Mrs. Sanders and see that the staff is assembled in the servants' hall. No one is to leave. Tell Giles these are my orders."

"Yes, milord." It was Mrs. Sanders who spoke, her tone brisk with authority.

Like the old-school gentleman he was, Grampapa offered a hand to help Mrs. Ellison up from her seat. He walked her to the door, offering a pat of reassurance on her shoulder just before she disappeared into the corridor, her footsteps muffled on the runner but her sniffles still audible. Mrs. Sanders swept out after her.

"All of you are to remain here, please." Grampapa's

order was soft-spoken but firm. His gaze honed in on Phoebe. "And that most especially includes you, my dear. No more tracing footprints for you."

"What did he mean by that?" Julia demanded when Grampapa left in search of Inspector Perkins.

Phoebe shrugged. "No idea. I merely went out for some air earlier." But she longed to run and find Eva and discuss this latest development.

Across the room, Lady Allerton huffed loudly. "All this fuss over a missing kitchen utensil? Is no one the least bit concerned about Henry?"

CHAPTER 4

"You know they'll be rummaging through our things," Douglas, the under footman, murmured with no effort to hide his resentment. His Cornish accent became more pronounced the angrier he became. His finger traced nervously back and forth over the wood grain of the oak tabletop. "Probably emptying our drawers onto the floor this very moment and toeing through our personal things."

"I doubt very much they're using their toes," Eva told him in an effort to alleviate the tension in the servants' hall. It did no good, didn't raise so much as a half smile among the servants sitting around the long table.

"Doesn't matter how they search. There's nothing we can do about it," Connie said with a furtive glance at the others before sinking down into herself, her shoulders stiff and angular beneath her black dress and starched pinafore. A plain girl about the same age as Lady Phoebe, Connie had come to Foxwood Hall only two months ago. Eva thought she had sensed a loneliness about her, or perhaps a painful shyness, and had tried to draw her out with friendly conversation only to discover the girl seemed to prefer being left alone. By all accounts she performed her duties with competence and no complaints, despite being a few minutes late earlier this morning. Though not disliked by anyone, she had yet to form close ties with any of the other staff members.

"No one is in a position to protest," Mrs. Sanders reminded them in clipped tones. "The inspectors have a job to do and we'll stand aside and allow them to do it. And anyway, Mr. Phelps and Miss Shea are with them to ensure the search is conducted in an orderly manner."

Mrs. Sanders referred to Lord Wroxly's valet and Lady Wroxly's personal maid, respectively. Eva doubted Mrs. Sanders's claim, an opinion Dora, the young scullery maid, apparently agreed with, for she said, "Miss Shea and Mr. Phelps think lower servants don't deserve any privacy at all."

"The inspector believes it's one of us, doesn't he?" This observation came from Douglas. He absently toyed with the braided trim on the cuff of his livery coat. "No one ever thinks to suspect the fine folk upstairs. No, it's always the servants—"

"You'll mind your tongue, Douglas. You, too, Dora." Mrs. Sanders snapped to her feet in a blur of black bombazine, high-necked and floor-sweeping in the old style. While most every other woman in England had raised her hems above her ankle bones, Mrs. Sanders still insisted on covering all but the tips of her shoes. "You'll mind, or you'll both find yourselves trudging down the high road with your suitcase in hand."

Douglas muttered something under his breath.

"What was that?" the butler demanded.

"Nothing, Mr. Giles, sir."

Eva could easily guess what he'd said. With her dark gray eyes and wiry, peppered hair, Mrs. Sanders had earned the nickname of Old Ironheart from some of the staff. Eva found that unfair. The running of a house like Foxwood took discipline and order, and Mrs. Sanders certainly commanded both. But true, at times like these she often showed a decided lack of sympathy. If there were sides to be taken, Mrs. Sanders's opinion unwaveringly favored the family above stairs.

Douglas apparently couldn't help himself. He jerked his chin at Vernon. "You're awful quiet about this. Don't you have anything to say?"

"I, er . . ." Vernon glanced first at Mrs. Sanders, then Mr. Giles, and remained silent. Newly made head footman, George Vernon straddled a fence between the upper and lower servants, desiring the acceptance of the former without alienating the latter. It wasn't an easy position to be in, as Eva knew from experience.

Douglas flashed him a look of disgust. Murmurs of discontent broke out around the table.

"That will be quite enough. If I hear one more complaint out of any of you—" Mrs. Sanders didn't finish. She didn't need to for everyone to understand her meaning.

"Everyone calm down, please." Mr. Giles stood up at the head of the table, prompting Eva and the others to jump to their feet in one swift motion. It had been ingrained in them: When the butler stands, everyone stands. He held up his hands and made patting motions at the air. "Sit back down, all of you. I only wish to make a point. And that is that no one here has any reason to fear, as long as none of you has broken any rules . . . or worse."

By *worse* the butler referred to Lord Allerton. The faces around Eva registered every emotion from apprehension to suspicion, frustration, and out and out fear. By that last sentiment, Connie seemed most affected, sitting stiffly and staring down at her lap as if afraid if she looked up some terrible fate might befall her. Had she something to hide? What about Douglas? Or Vernon, who seemed to be avoiding meeting everyone's gaze.

Any of them might harbor a secret they dreaded revealing, a happenstance that could send them out into the street this very day. Never mind what happened to Lord Allerton. *Any* broken rule, from a liquor flask or forbidden reading material hidden under a pillow to some evidence that a member of the staff had sneaked out after curfew . . . offenses other people never gave a second thought could threaten a servant's livelihood.

She began to worry, not for herself, but for her fellow domestics. She'd grown fond of them all in these last few years. She didn't wish to see any of them cast out without a reference.

Sitting next to Eva, Mrs. Ellison kept clasping and unclasping her plump hands. Eva reached over and stilled them. "Don't worry, Mrs. Ellison. Your cleaver might turn up innocently enough."

"I do hope so. How I loathe to think a blade from my kitchen could have been used in so fiendish a way. It's almost blasphemous! Lord knows, if it was used to . . . to . . . Well, I should never be able to chop chickens with it again, shall I? The very thought . . ." She shivered.

"If that is indeed the case, you'll have a new cleaver, to be sure, Mrs. Ellison," Mrs. Sanders said.

"What's taking them so long?" Dora spoke with a groan, yet not one of distress or worry, Eva deduced, but, judging by the light in her eyes and the vivid color in her cheeks, anticipation. The girl found something exciting in all of this, the kind of vicarious adventure one gleaned from reading sordid details in mystery novels.

Mrs. Ellison must have noticed this, too, for presently she compressed her lips and then said, "Dora, I think you might return to the scullery and start polishing the copper pots used for last night's dinner. If the inspector needs to speak with you, I'll let you know."

"But Lord Wroxly said—"

Mrs. Sanders cleared her throat. "It is irregular for you

to be in the dining hall at all, Dora. I'm quite certain Lord Wroxly would have no objection to you restoring the shine on the sauce pots."

She had a point. As the lowliest servant in the household, Dora took her meals in the kitchen with the hall boy rather than here in the servants' hall. With another groan the girl scraped back her chair and pushed to her feet. Like a child being sent to her room, she dragged herself away.

Rather odd behavior for a girl who had found a severed finger in her Christmas box only a few hours ago, in her case accompanied by a gold watch chain. In her mind, Eva lined up each recipient of Lord Allerton's appendages: herself, Dora, Mr. Phelps, Josh the hall boy, and Rupert Garth and Myron Henderson from the village. Many others had received boxes today, of course, but only these six contained the ghastly surprises.

Each had little in common with the others. True, the first four all worked here at the Hall, but while Josh and Dora worked exclusively below stairs, Eva, as a lady's maid, and Mr. Phelps, as Lord Wroxly's valet, enjoyed a much higher status among the servants. The two men from the village each owned a business, the tailor shop and haberdashery, respectively.

There must be some connecting factor among them, but what?

"I don't see what you're all worried about." Nick Hensley leaned back in his chair with a somber expression. "If anyone should be suspect, it's me. I'm the one who deals with—dealt with—" He shook his head, the corners of his mouth pulling taut. He began again. "I am Lord Allerton's valet. If they wish to blame one of the servants, they'll likely blame me, won't they?"

For the briefest moment a horrible thought chilled Eva's heart. As Lord Allerton's valet, Nick certainly had access to the marquess's person. Could he have had some reason to want his employer out of the way?

Nodding heads around the table shocked her out of her own thoughts and prompted Eva to speak up. "No, Nick, you mustn't think that. And neither must any of you. We must stick together. Support each other. Nick is no more guilty than any of you."

He met her gaze with a gleam, and she realized she had called him Nick, not once but twice—not Mr. Hensley as she had insisted on doing only that morning.

The significance of that gleam made her feel as if they were the only two people in the room. It warmed her even as it left her disconcerted and fumbling for an appropriate response. It made her glad she had used his first name, even as she longed for the comfortable formality of his surname again.

And then, remembering they were *not* the only inhabitants of the room, she blinked and looked away, but too late. The others had seen and would speculate. Let them, Eva decided, even as she resolved not to give them further cause to gossip. A strained silence settled over the room, all the more nerve-racking for the clunking and clattering coming from Dora in the scullery.

Finally, Douglas broke the silence. "It's not like we've given the toffs any reason to suspect us. They should look to themselves."

Mr. Giles reared his head. "Whatever do you mean by that?"

"I mean . . ." Douglas swallowed, his Adam's apple bobbing sharply. "Things weren't exactly all roses last night between Lord Allerton and a certain member of the Renshaw family."

Mr. Giles slapped his hands on the tabletop. "I will not

suffer this staff to spread gossip or speak ill of our employers. Nor will I countenance footmen eavesdropping on private matters when they should be concentrating on their work. Whatever you overheard last night, Douglas, you are to put out of your mind this instant. Is that clear?"

Douglas gave a petulant nod. At the same time, a wash of scarlet stained Vernon's neck, and he dropped his gaze.

Mr. Giles was not satisfied. "Is that clear?" he repeated with the full boom of his baritone.

Connie flinched, and even Mrs. Ellison pressed a hand to her breastbone. Douglas raised his chin. "Yes, sir. Quite clear, Mr. Giles, sir."

Footsteps sounded in the stairwell. Everyone around the table, Eva included, tensed, sat up straighter, and craned their necks to see who was coming. A moment later, Constable Brannock entered the hall. He scanned the room, his gaze falling on each of them in turn. Eva's pulse quickened when his regard lingered on her longer than the rest.

He pointed. "Mr. Vernon."

Another crimson wave swept over Vernon's fair complexion. "M-me, sir?"

Brannock nodded and pointed again. "And you, Mr. Hensley. You both need to come with me."

Eva gasped, and it was all she could do to keep from jumping up in protest. The others stared with saucer-like eyes as Nick quietly came to his feet, but before he stepped away from the table, Mr. Giles stood. "Not to interfere in police business, but Vernon is under my direct supervision, as is Mr. Hensley while he is here in this house. Will you please explain the nature of this summons?"

"Inspector Perkins has further questions for these two men," Brannock said, looking almost bored and giving away nothing in his manner.

"Was something found during the search?" Mr. Giles moved to stand behind Vernon's chair, his hand coming to rest on the young man's broad shoulder. "Was the murder weapon discovered?"

"Did you find my cleaver?" Mrs. Ellison squeaked.

"Good heavens, did you find Lord Allerton?" Mrs. Sanders laced her fingers together as if in prayer.

"I cannot discuss anything at present. All I can say is the rest of you are to remain here. We might have more questions for some of you." He regarded first Nick and then Vernon with an expression approaching pity, or so Eva thought. She liked this man less and less with each passing moment. "Gentlemen, please follow me."

Vernon stood up shakily from the table and looked so much like a lost child Eva wished to offer him a reassuring hug. She remained where she was, hearing other footsteps and then two sets of murmurs from the corridor. Constable Brannock led Nick and Vernon out as Harlan Phelps and Fiona Shea entered the hall.

Around the table, a barrage of questions drowned out even Dora's clashing of pots and pans.

Mr. Giles held up his hands. "Silence, all of you. That's better. Now, Mr. Phelps, what can you tell us?"

The man, tall and thin with a full head of silver hair neatly slicked back from his brow, shook his head. "Officially, we can tell you nothing." He cupped his palm behind his ear and raised his head to listen to the retreating footsteps on the stairs. "But unofficially . . ."

"Did they find Mrs. Ellison's cleaver?" Douglas demanded.

Miss Shea and Mr. Phelps exchanged a glance and a nod, and Mr. Phelps said, "Indeed they did."

"Where?" Several voices spoke at once.

Her dark hair parted in the middle and pulled back into a severe bun, Miss Shea puffed up with self-importance, as the lady's maids of countesses were apt to do. "I don't know if we should say. Inspector Perkins might disapprove."

"Hang Inspector Perkins." Douglas drummed a fist on the table. "Tell us what you know."

"Douglas, a modicum of patience, if you will," Mr. Giles counseled. "I'm sure the inspector has his reasons for being reticent on the matter. However, we all have our reasons for wanting to know the truth. Vernon is a valuable member of this staff, and a decent bloke all around. I don't believe there is a one of us here who has ever had a gripe against George Vernon." He aimed a significant glare at Douglas, who could not always make the same claim. "And as for Nicholas Hensley, why, the senior staff such as Mrs. Sanders, Mrs. Ellison, and myself remember when he worked here, before Lord Allerton took him on as his valet. Mr. Hensley is family, and so is Vernon. So please, Mr. Phelps, Miss Shea, if you know something of consequence, do not leave the rest of us in the dark."

"The imagination is always more detrimental than the truth," Mrs. Sanders added.

Mr. Giles turned to her as if she had just imparted the greatest wisdom. "Indeed."

"All right." Mr. Phelps dragged a chair from against the wall over to the table. "Make room for us." Loud scraping filled the room as the others scooted aside. Mr. Phelps held the chair as Miss Shea primly sat, then brought another one over. Once situated, he leaned over the table in a conspiratorial hunch. "The cleaver *was* found."

Gasps were followed by exclamations of "I knew it" and demands as to where the item had surfaced. With all the drama of stage actors, the valet and lady's maid once again traded knowing looks and nods. In fact, Eva believed they might have missed their calling. Her patience was wearing thin when Mr. Phelps gestured to Miss Shea, and said, "I'll allow you to do the honors."

The woman moistened her thin lips, dragging out the

moment until Eva wanted to scream. Then she said, "Beneath a floorboard in the room shared by Vernon and Mr. Hensley."

Another barrage of gasps followed. Eva remained silent, her mind reeling. What did this mean? That one of them had attacked—perhaps killed—Lord Allerton? *Vernon or Nick?*

She rejected the notion. It simply wasn't possible. Someone else must have planted that cleaver in their room. When or how, she didn't know, although the servants' bedrooms were never locked, so anyone in this house might have found the opportunity to sneak in.

"Why was Mr. Hensley sharing with Vernon anyway," Douglas asked, and several others nodded their concurrence with the question.

"Well, certainly *I* shouldn't have been expected to share my room with him," Mr. Phelps replied, "even if Hensley does technically outrank me as the valet of a marquess. I am, after all, valet to the master of this house. As such I have always enjoyed a room to myself. I saw no reason to change that now, even temporarily."

Mr. Phelps's arrogance and the smugness of his tone penetrated the veneer of gentility Eva had cultivated over the years, and she wished nothing so much as to throw something—for instance, the kerosene lantern in the middle of the table—against the wall for the simple satisfaction of watching it shatter. "How can you go on so?" she demanded. "Have you no compassion at all?"

Even as she confronted the valet, she knew her anger wasn't truly directed at him, but at the situation, the awful revelation that her childhood friend—they *had* been friends of a sort—might be implicated in a horrific crime.

"I am merely explaining the situation to Douglas, who did ask, Miss Huntford."

Eva clamped her lips around the point she longed to

make, that if Mr. Phelps had observed proper etiquette by allowing the marquess's valet to room with him, Nick might not be undergoing questioning at this moment. Might not be a . . . She could barely bring herself to think the word: *suspect.*

An argument wouldn't have done anyone any good. But she did have a question. "Mr. Phelps, you are among those of us who received the Christmas boxes in question. Can you think of any reason why you or any of us should have been singled out?"

His upper lip curled in disgust at the reference, and for this she could not blame him. "Indeed I cannot, Miss Huntford. I believe perhaps it was random. That whoever performed the dreadful deed disposed of . . . of the . . ." His lip curled again, baring his teeth. "The *you know what* . . . in the first boxes available."

"But were they the first available?" she persisted. "Does anyone know what order they were placed in?"

"Why, I believe they were switched around multiple times," Mrs. Sanders said, "as members of the family placed their gifts inside. There's hardly any way of knowing which boxes sat where on the shelves at any particular time."

"There must be some way to figure out why some and not others." Eva let her chin sink into her palm.

"There is," Mr. Phelps said flatly. "By allowing the inspector and his assistant to do their job and staying out of their way. And by not pestering the rest of us with silly questions."

Her mouth dropped open on a huff. Of all the rude, condescending . . . She counted to ten to regain her calm, and immediately noticed Connie trembling and breathing so rapidly Eva feared she would hyperventilate.

"Connie, are you all right?" she whispered across the table.

Connie stared back like a startled doe before abruptly

pushing to her feet. The talking around the table ceased and all eyes turned to her.

"Is something wrong?" Mrs. Sanders asked with a perplexed frown.

"N-no, ma'am. I . . . I need to use the water closet."

"Go on, then."

Connie hurried off. Eva watched her go, wondering. Then she, too, vacated her chair. "She didn't look well. I'm going to go see if she's all right."

"I think that's a good idea." Mrs. Sanders's mouth flattened a moment; then she added, "She's a nervous sort, that one. I don't wonder this has upset her."

Eva knocked on the door of the water closet. When no answer came, she knocked again. "Connie? It's Eva. Are you all right, dear?" More silence. "Are you ill?"

Not a sound came from within. Had the girl passed out? Both puzzled and mildly alarmed, Eva tried the latch. It moved easily beneath her thumb and the door opened into the tiny and quite vacant room.

"That's odd." Listening, she heard the murmur of voices from the servants' hall, and the continued banging and clanking from Dora in the scullery, but no sound of Connie's voice. Down the narrow corridor, dusty shafts of light poked through the window in the courtyard door. She hesitated, doubting the day had gotten any warmer. Still, she didn't stop to don one of the cloaks hanging on pegs near the door. The sooner she found Connie, the better.

It didn't take long. Connie stood beside the coal chute, although *standing* was something of an exaggeration since the girl had her arms wrapped around her middle as she leaned, half-bent at the waist, against the stones of the house.

Eva wrapped her arms around herself, too, in an effort to stave off her shivering. "Connie, what on earth are you doing out here? Dear, what is it?"

Connie lurched upright, seeming ready to bolt away. Merely a response to being caught unawares, Eva reasoned, but she stepped into her path anyway, ready to catch her if necessary.

"It's nothing, Miss Huntford. I . . . I just . . . needed some air."

Eva eyed her suspiciously. "Well, now you've had it. Let's go back inside, shall we?"

Connie made no move to go.

"Surely you don't intend holding up the wall all afternoon."

"I . . . no, miss. I . . ."

"Connie, come now. Something is terribly wrong and . . ." She thought back to the moment Connie had transformed from merely nervous, to use Mrs. Sanders's word, to out and out panicked. For surely it had been panic that made the girl lie about needing to use the water closet and instead brave the chilling temperatures.

Vernon. And Nick. Yes, it had been the announcement that the missing cleaver had been found in their shared bedroom that drove Connie into the cold.

"You're worried about Vernon and Mr. Hensley, yes?"

"I . . . well . . ." She fidgeted with her apron, her cap, a strand of hair that hung loose. "Who isn't? Aren't you worried?"

Yes, she was, but at this point she hadn't enough information to warrant panicking. Did Connie know something Eva didn't?

Of the two men, George Vernon was the one Connie knew best. In fact, the girl barely knew Nick at all, so surely the prospect of his being charged with a crime wouldn't have such a drastic effect on her. One might even term her reaction . . . passionate.

Ah, a budding romance, Eva guessed. But there was something more here. She glimpsed it in the wariness of

Connie's expression, rather like that of a fox who knows the hounds' snapping teeth will soon be in its flesh.

"Connie," Eva said as gently as if the maid were a five-year-old child, "perhaps I can help you. Do you know something about all this, something you should tell me?"

Connie's eyes filled with tears. She raised a hand to wipe them away, and what Eva spied peeking out from the edge of the girl's sleeve prompted her to seize her wrist.

"Dear heavens, Connie, where did you get that bruise?"

Phoebe listened silently while Eva filled her in on what had occurred below stairs. They stood at the end of the hallway that linked the morning room and solarium to one of the back staircases, where Phoebe had asked Eva to meet her to compare notes from above and below stairs.

"And the bruises on her wrist, my lady. Connie tried telling me she got them cleaning out Lady Wroxly's hearth, but I'd swear those marks were left by fingers. A vise grip, my lady."

Phoebe felt her eyes widen. Another set of bruises? Could it be a coincidence that both Julia and the chambermaid sported such marks at the same time? It seemed highly doubtful. "Did she mention Lord Allerton at all?"

"No, my lady. Nor did she mention Vernon. But it was the news of the cleaver being found in Vernon's room that sent her running scared."

"From what I understand, Mr. Hensley has been staying in that room as well."

"Yes, but Connie barely knows *him*." Eva blushed faintly, just enough for Phoebe to perceive it.

"True. Do you believe Vernon could have bruised Connie's wrist like that?"

Eva shook her head. "I don't, my lady. I don't believe he has an aggressive bone in his body. I would practically stake my life on it."

"Practically?"

"We can never fully know someone, can we? Never know what they're capable of until we've seen them in a dire situation."

"No, I suppose you're right. I fear . . ."

"Yes, my lady?"

"Eva, do I have your word this will be kept in the utmost secrecy?"

Her maid drew back with a hand to her breastbone, as if greatly offended. "Of course, my lady!"

"I'm sorry. I should not have asked that." Phoebe seized Eva's hand and drew her into the recess of a nearby window. "Connie is not the only woman to have been recently seized in so ungentlemanly a manner."

Eva gasped and reached for Phoebe's hands. Her shawl fell away, and Eva's gaze dropped to her forearms, exposed by her three-quarter sleeves. "My lady! You mean to say someone dared lay his hands upon you—"

"No, not me. I cannot say who, for that would be betraying a confidence. And please do not try to guess. But I will tell you the name of the brute in question."

At that moment the door to the morning room burst open and Miles Brannock strode into the corridor. He looked right and then left, and upon spotting Phoebe and Eva, started toward them.

"My lady," he said with a nod before turning his attention to Eva. "Miss Huntford, we'll need to speak with the housemaid again. If you wouldn't mind relaying the message downstairs."

"Connie? Why? What's happened?" It was Phoebe who spoke, knowing the constable could not ignore her questions as easily as he might Eva's.

"I'm afraid I cannot discuss—"

"The details. Yes, we know," Eva said.

"But you've already questioned Connie," Phoebe persisted.

"New questions have arisen, my lady."

Phoebe was about to inquire—adamantly—as to the nature of those questions, when another figure stepped from the morning room. Eva's color rose again, as it had done moments ago, and for the same reason, apparently.

"Nick—er—Mr. Hensley."

Phoebe caught Eva's slip. She had called the valet by his Christian name. But then, he once worked here as a footman. Except that had been before Eva was hired as a lady's maid. . . .

Constable Brannock nodded again. "Miss Huntford, you'll have Connie sent up?"

"Yes, yes," Eva agreed absently. She waited until the constable went back into the morning room before she said, "Ni—er—Mr. Hensley, what happened in there? Can you tell us anything?"

He raked a hand through his hair. "It's not looking good for Vernon, I'm afraid."

"What do you mean?" Eva asked.

Phoebe felt the weight of the valet's gaze on her, as well as his palpable hesitation. She said, "Mr. Hensley, I may be a daughter of this house, but I assure you I am no wilting flower. You may speak freely in front of me without fear of causing me any undo distress."

Eva frowned and looked about to protest, then evidently gave in to the idea that Phoebe was no longer a child. "Go ahead, Mr. Hensley. Please tell us what you've learned. And how Connie is involved, for I've already figured out for myself that she is."

"Quickly," Phoebe added, "before Constable Brannock comes looking for Connie again."

Mr. Hensley's reluctance was clear to see. He blinked in

the frozen light coming through the window and sighed. "It wasn't said outright as the footman will admit nothing, but it appears Connie and Vernon have been carrying on a"—he glanced at Phoebe again—"a courtship."

"I thought as much," Eva said. "They'll both be in trouble now. It's against the rules."

"Is it?" Phoebe hadn't known that. "Why? How are the servants supposed to get on with their lives?"

"It's Mrs. Sanders's rule, my lady, though a common one on estates," Eva explained. "In her view, the younger servants should stay focused on their duties and not much else. If they wish to court or be courted, they are to seek companionship elsewhere, on their own time."

"That hardly presents much opportunity."

"As Mrs. Sanders would say, that is not her concern." Eva turned back to Mr. Hensley. "Now, then, about Vernon and Connie? How did this information come out?"

The valet sighed again. "I'm afraid the truth came out as a result of something I said. And—if you'll forgive me, my lady—I'm damnably sorry about it, too."

CHAPTER 5

"If Miss Robson wishes you to stay, you may do so, Miss Huntford, but do be quiet. And by quiet, I mean silent."

Isaac Perkins didn't appear at all pleased that Eva had followed Connie into the morning room, but Connie had latched on to the downstairs banister with both hands and refused to let go until Eva promised to stay with her during the questioning. The poor thing was beyond terrified. Anyone in her position would be. Connie hailed from faraway Manchester, from a family of seven siblings. Her mother lost her employment in a munitions factory when the war ended and now labored as a laundress, and her father had returned from the front with a severe case of shell shock and was unable to hold steady employment. On any particular day, they were mere shillings away from the workhouse. If Connie was sacked, she would have nowhere to go.

Inspector Perkins reviewed a sheet of notes in front of him and cleared his throat. "Now, then, Miss Robson . . ."

At the sight of Connie's freely falling tears he trailed off and rolled his eyes at Miles Brannock, who was once more installed at the table with pencil and tablet. Despite the inspector's edict that she remain silent, Eva leaned closer to

Connie, and murmured, "It's all right, dear. No one is accusing you of anything. If you'll simply answer Inspector Perkins's questions, this will all soon be over."

"Yes, perhaps," the man said, most unhelpfully.

Despite her reassurance, Eva's own optimism faded as quickly as a winter's twilight, especially after Nick's earlier admission. When asked by the inspector—with no small amount of sarcasm, apparently—if he could attest to Vernon's whereabouts all night long, Nick had felt honor bound to tell the truth, which was that he had awakened some time before dawn to discover Vernon's bed empty. Nick's agony over the disclosure had been palpable, even after Eva assured him the truth would always come out, and lies only ever turned a bad situation worse.

"Here." Eva handed Connie her own handkerchief—an older one, not one of the gifts from Phoebe and Amelia. "It's clean."

Inspector Perkins waited patiently while Connie dabbed at her tears and made a visible effort to collect herself. Finally, only the occasional sniffle slipped out.

"Miss Robson," he began again, "how long have you been a member of the staff here?"

"About two months, sir."

"And where did you work previously?"

A tide of crimson engulfed her face. Odd, but before Eva could consider the reason, the inspector shot another question at the maid. "Does that question distress you, Miss Robson?"

So he had noticed, too.

"N-no, sir. It's just that I suppose I'm a wee bit homesick still. My old situation was closer to home, you see."

"Was it? Then why did you leave?"

"I . . . well . . . the cook's daughter . . . she needed employment, sir. The cook's worked there a long time, and her son died in the war, so you see . . ."

"Yes, yes, fine." He leaned toward Constable Brannock. "Make a note of that."

Brannock's scratching pencil filled the silence while Inspector Perkins sat contemplating Connie over the table. A tear escaped Connie's eye and rolled down her cheek. She let it, apparently having forgotten Eva's handkerchief, twisted cruller-like between her hands. Eva realized Connie hadn't answered the inspector's question of where she had worked previously, nor did Inspector Perkins remember to inquire again.

"What is the nature of your association with George Vernon?" he asked instead.

"What?"

"I believe you heard the question, Miss Robson."

"I . . . he . . . that is . . ." She shrugged one shoulder, but far from nonchalant, the shaky gesture only emphasized her state of agitation. Her foot tapped nervously against the floor. "We work together, sir."

"That much is glaringly apparent, young lady. I am speaking of your personal association. Mr. Vernon claims you can vouch for his whereabouts early this morning, before sunup, and before the other servants had risen from their beds. Is that true?"

"Y-yes, sir."

"And why would that be?"

Connie turned to Eva. "Must I answer that?"

"Yes, dear, I'm afraid you must."

Eva feared for her handkerchief as Connie tugged with both hands, raising a staccato of tiny, ripping threads. "I'm up early each day, sir, earlier than the rest of the household, except for the hall boy. It's my job to clean the hearths and lay the morning fires, turn the hot-water heaters on, collect the previous night's laundry, and set out fresh linens for the servants, family, and guests."

The inspector drummed his fingertips on the table. "What has this got to do with George Vernon?"

"Sometimes, sir, he rises early to . . . er . . . help me."

Brannock stopped writing, his gaze meeting Eva's and becoming quizzical. She didn't give him the satisfaction of a response. Instead, she tensed, well aware of what would soon be revealed. Pity for Connie made her heart thump.

The inspector frowned deeply. "Why the blazes would the head footman deign to help the housemaid with her duties?"

Miles Brannock's mouth turned up at the corners. He had guessed the answer, no doubt.

Connie continued tearing threads from Eva's handkerchief. "W-what did *he* tell you, sir?"

With an exasperated exhalation Inspector Perkins reached into his inner coat pocket and produced a hip flask cloaked in leather. He unscrewed the top and took a generous sip, and wiped his mouth with the back of his hand. "*He* told me precious little, young lady, which is why you are here now. All he was willing to say is that you saw him in the predawn hours and can attest to his whereabouts. Now"—his free hand struck the tabletop, making Connie flinch—"do explain, Miss Robson, or would you prefer to continue this questioning at my office in the village? The one conveniently adjoining a jail cell."

"Inspector Perkins, please . . ."

Eva's caution was drowned out by Connie's protest. "Oh, no, sir! I . . . I'll answer. George often helps me with my morning chores because . . . well, you see, sir . . ."

"No, I do not see, Miss Robson, and I have reached the limits of my patience."

"We're sweethearts, sir." She whispered so low the man leaned across the table with his hand cupped to his ear.

"What was that?"

Constable Brannock's keen blue eyes twinkled. Obviously the younger man suffered from no such hearing impairments as Inspector Perkins. Once more, Eva held her features impassive, refusing to join in his apparent mirth over what was, for Connie, a dreadful ordeal.

"We're sweethearts," the maid repeated, this time in nearly a shout. "There!" She collapsed against her chair. "There," she said more quietly, "now Mrs. Sanders can sack me. And probably George, too."

Eva reached over to stroke the maid's forearm. Hers was obviously a reserved and nervous constitution, and Eva doubted the poor girl could take much more of this line of questioning. "May Connie go now, Inspector Perkins?"

His flask stashed away in his coat pocket, the inspector tented his fingers beneath his chin. "Indeed not. Events begin to make more sense to me. Tell me, young lady, are you acquainted with the Marquess of Allerton?"

She seemed rather taken aback by the question. "Well . . . yes, sir. He was—is—a guest in this house. I deliver his linens each morning, lay his fire, tidy his rooms. . . ."

"And beyond that, did you have occasion to speak with the marquess?"

Her spine went rigid. "I . . . I'm not sure what you mean, sir."

Eva did. She understood quite well where the inspector was leading with these questions. She herself had already begun to guess the truth. Now it only needed confirmation.

"I mean, if I may be so blunt, Miss Robson, did the Marquess of Allerton ever engage your services for courtesies *other* than linens, hearth fires, and tidiness?"

Connie gasped. Eva pushed back in her chair and jumped to her feet. "Inspector Perkins, your methods of questioning are unwarranted and most unkind. If Connie was a victim—"

"Victim, ha! I'll thank you to sit back down and hold your tongue, Miss Huntford, or leave this room."

"Well!" Eva remained on her feet another several moments, glaring back at the man as he attempted to stare her down into compliance. Even Miles Brannock no longer looked amused, but had dropped his pencil to the table, slid to the edge of his chair, and appeared about to intervene. Connie made a noise—part strangled sob, part sigh that rang with unmistakable capitulation. Eva resumed her seat. Mr. Brannock retrieved his pencil, his attention riveted on Connie as they all waited.

"Well?"

"It's true, sir. Lord Allerton did make . . ." Her voice plummeted yet again. "Advances."

Eva's breath froze. Even having been certain Connie *hadn't* got those bruises cleaning a hearth, she still felt a shock at hearing the truth spoken aloud. Eva's mind reeled when she considered what the girl had been forced to endure—the fear, the sense of violation, the humiliation. Her gaze dropped to Connie's lap, where the girl twisted her fingers together with Eva's handkerchief, the backs of her wrists facing upward and those telltale smudges peeking out from her cuffs.

"Aha. I thought as much." The inspector made no attempt to hide his obvious sense of triumph. Or his disdain. He turned to Constable Brannock. "Did I not tell you? It's always over a girl—always!"

"W-what do you mean, sir?"

The elder man's eyes narrowed within their florid, bloated pockets of flesh. His pocked nose flared. "I mean, girl, that George Vernon murdered Lord Allerton because of you."

"No, sir! No!" Connie flattened her palms on the tabletop, her whole body tensing as if she were about to spring over the table and attack Inspector Perkins.

Eva reached for her, wrapping an arm around her shoulders while with her other hand she seized Connie's arm. But it was the inspector she addressed. "Inspector Perkins, isn't that a rather far-fetched assumption? What evidence do you have?" But the evidence lay only inches from her own fingertips—those bruises. Connie had admitted to Lord Allerton's advances. . . .

Inspector Perkins ignored her and continued his rant. "Oh, yes, my girl. It's all too clear that George Vernon discovered what Lord Allerton had done. Either you told him, or he caught Lord Allerton in the act. Which was it?"

"He saw," Connie rasped without inflection.

The admission rendered Eva immobile.

"And he went for the cleaver." Inspector Perkins's hand slapped the table.

"No! The cleaver had nothing to do with Lord Allerton. I swear! It was—" She broke off, shoving a fist against her mouth.

"It was what, Miss Robson? Why did George Vernon hide that cleaver in his room?"

Her tears streamed and she spoke around choking sobs. "Because it broke. He was putting away some trays and knocked it off the counter—"

Eva gasped. Good heavens, had Vernon taken the cleaver after all? "Connie, what are you saying?"

Connie shoved both hands into her hair, knocking her maid's cap askew. "Didn't you see the handle was cracked? George accidentally dropped it and it hit the floor just so, and the handle cracked." She raised her clasped hands, with Eva's handkerchief sandwiched between them, in supplication. "He was going to take it into the village to have a new handle put on this very afternoon, and Mrs. Ellison would be none the wiser. He's already telephoned the cutler to make sure he'd be open for business today."

Inspector Perkins sat back in his chair, a satisfied look

swelling his cheeks and making him appear more bloated than before. "A confession, of sorts. That cleaver didn't make its own way beneath the floorboard in George Vernon's room. He put it there himself."

"Only so he could take it to be fixed. . . ."

"So you say, Miss Robson. And even if that's all true, and the cutler expected him today, if you ask me, the handle broke during the heinous crime perpetrated against Lord Allerton."

"No, I swear, it fell off the worktable. I saw it happen."

"Yes, and what girl wouldn't lie to save her sweetheart?"

Eva felt ill. She sat unmoving, not daring to breathe and willing Connie to offer up a more tolerable explanation. None came. The fight had flowed out of the girl, leaving her limp, shaking. She slumped forward onto the table, head on her arms.

Her muffled voice, strangled by tears, broke the silence. "George didn't hurt Lord Allerton. He would never do such a beastly thing."

"Can you prove that, Miss Robson? And mind you speak the truth or you'll be charged with obstructing justice and aiding a murderer."

Her head came up a scant few inches and she peered through swollen eyes across the table. Even from beside her Eva felt, if not saw, the full force of the loathing contained in her gaze. Then Connie dropped her head to her arms again. "Oh, George, forgive me."

"I believe it is your move, sir."

At Lord Owen's patient prodding that Fox make a decision regarding his remaining chess pieces, Phoebe felt as if she might crawl right out of her skin. Just a little while ago Eva had quickly filled her in about Connie's interview with Inspector Perkins. Phoebe had immediately drawn Grampapa out of the others' hearing and implored him not to allow Mrs. Sanders to sack Connie, at least not until all the facts were known. He had hesitated over his answer, mumbling, "I don't typically involve myself in the daily running of domestic matters."

"Grampapa, you're master of Foxwood Hall, and Eva tells me Connie would be quite destitute without employment. It is no exaggeration to say it's a matter of life and death. And we have no proof either she or Vernon did anything wrong." She had resorted to slipping her hand into his broad one, like grasping a friendly bear's paw, and rising on tiptoe to look directly into his kindly eyes. "Please. For me, Grampapa. At least until we know the truth."

His capitulation had taken all of another second or two, the time it took to draw a breath. He smiled and patted her hand. "Anything for you, my dear."

Inspector Perkins had then entered the drawing room and asked to speak with Grampapa privately. They were still gone now, and with each tick of the mantel clock, she thought she'd go mad.

"Phoebe, come let's make etchings on the window-panes."

The idea brought her no pleasure, but she conjured a smile for her younger sister and followed her to the window. Amelia used her thumbnail to trace patterns in the frosted glass and with a sigh Eva did the same, but without *Phoebe* much enthusiasm. From the corner card table came the clink of coins as Grams raised the stakes for the round of cribbage the elder ladies were about to play. A glance over her shoulder revealed Theo making a slow circuit of the room, pretending interest in the various paintings along the wall. Julia stood at the piano, absently picking out notes with a forefinger.

Was she remembering how Henry had pounded on the piano last night as they'd argued?

"Look, Phoebe, see how I've swooped the A in Amelia differently than I usually do? I'm going to embroider this onto my uniform blouse before I return to school."

She dutifully admired her sister's tracing. "Yes, that'll be lovely."

"You know something, don't you?" Amelia said much lower, her entire demeanor changing. Gone was the naïve schoolgirl intent on frost drawings, while before Phoebe stood a much more mature, intuitive young woman she hadn't known existed. "I suspect you know what happened to Henry." She peeked over her shoulder. "And ladies Allerton and Cecily have yet to be told. Isn't that true?"

It took Phoebe several seconds to overcome her stupefaction. Then she followed her sister's gaze to the corner of the room, where Lady Allerton was just then tossing down a card with the smug expression of someone expecting to win.

"It is, but we mustn't breathe a word until Grampapa decides the time is right." Phoebe still doubted the wisdom of keeping Lady Allerton in the dark when harm had almost certainly befallen Henry. Now his mother must learn of it all at once, rather than in bits as Phoebe had. She feared the effect the shock might have on the woman.

After a pause, Amelia whispered, "The cleaver. Dear Lord, Phoebe, Mrs. Ellison's cleaver!"

"Shhh!" Phoebe lifted her hand to the window and dragged her fingernail through the icy condensation. "We'll discuss it later. Alone. Though in all honesty you'll be better off not knowing."

"I am not a child."

"Yes, you are." But even as Phoebe made the claim, her heart squeezed around the truth. Although Amelia had always been perceptive, her relationship with Phoebe had been one of older and younger sister, with Amelia looking up to Phoebe, hanging on her every word and believing all she said. This new Amelia felt . . . Phoebe groped a moment to identify it, then seized upon the only fitting word. Amelia seemed her equal now, with opinions and judgments of her own, no longer reliant on an elder sister's guidance.

She should have expected it, should have seen it sooner, and should be proud of her sister. But all she felt just then was sad.

Presently, the drawing room's double doors slid open upon Grampapa and Inspector Perkins. If Phoebe had believed she alone had been counting the minutes, she was mistaken. The cards were slapped to the table, the chess pieces abandoned, and Julia closed the piano with a thunk that left the strings rumbling.

They gathered around the two men, voices jumbled as several questions were blurted simultaneously. Grampapa held up his hands for silence. Anticipation veritably pulsed among them—Phoebe felt it in the pounding of the blood at her temples. Before anyone could speak, however, Lady Allerton pushed her way past the others and stood before the inspector.

"Have you found my son?"

"I'm afraid not, my lady."

"Then why are you here? You should be out searching for *him,* not vanished meat cleavers. I must inform you, sir, that I have quite lost my patience."

"My lady . . ." Looking mystified, Inspector Perkins trailed off. He appealed to Grampapa. "My lord, have you not explained . . . ?"

Grampapa cleared his throat. "I thought it best to wait until we knew more."

Lady Allerton whirled toward him. "Archibald, have you been keeping something from me?"

Grampapa looked distinctly uncomfortable. "Lucille, perhaps you and I should speak privately, in my study."

Phoebe felt a protest rise up inside her, but she held her tongue. Lady Allerton, however, showed no such constraint. "You shall speak to me here and now, Archibald. I insist! I demand it! I have been quiet long enough. I *will* know what has happened to Henry."

Silence descended, so thick Phoebe thought she might drown in it. Grampapa exchanged a questioning look with Grams, who closed her eyes and nodded. Phoebe marveled at how calm Grams had remained in light of the situation, how in control. If Phoebe hadn't already known something awful happened today, she would not have gained an inkling from Grams's stoic mannerisms.

It was Lord Owen who broke the silence, coming forward like the commander he had been and speaking softly, yet quite firmly, to Lady Allerton. "You are entitled to answers, ma'am. I suggest we all sit down, along with brandies for the gentlemen and sherries for the ladies."

"Amelia, go to your room, please." Grams raised a delicately veined hand to point Amelia's way into the hall, but Amelia held her ground.

"Grams, really. I have already deduced that something dreadful has happened to—ouch!"

Phoebe poked her elbow—hard—into her sister's upper arm. But at the same time, she took up her sister's cause. "Grams, forgive me for speaking out of turn, but I believe we should stay together and hear what Inspector Perkins has to tell us. There's no telling what Amelia might imagine on her own."

"And I'm certainly not going anywhere." Fox drew himself up and widened his stance.

"Very well, but don't say I didn't warn you." Grams held her hands out, drawing Lady Allerton and Lady Cecily to her. Together they went to the settee beneath the central window. The snowy garden behind them made an icy backdrop for the chilling news about to be shared.

"Owen, would you be so kind as to pour those brandies and sherries? I fear we are going to need them. Julia, you may help pass them around, please."

"This had better be important," Miss Shea griped yet again. She and Eva walked briskly side by side through the butler's pantry and across the dining room, or as briskly as Miss Shea could manage while carrying a basin half-filled with ice water. Eva couldn't remember the last time she had been in this part of the house. Upstairs, yes, and along the corridor to the morning room, but there was little reason for a lady's maid to ever be in the manor's formal rooms. Only minutes ago, Phoebe had called down on the inter-house telephone requesting both she and Miss Shea come as quickly as possible.

"It's certainly must be important, or Lady Phoebe wouldn't have instructed me to bring smelling salts." Eva held up the glass vial and looked up at the taller woman. She paused to catch her breath, the quick climb up the steep back stairs having left her slightly winded. "Nor you, ice water and a rag. I do hope Lady Wroxly hasn't taken ill. Or one of the girls."

Miss Shea snorted. "Are we nurses? I'm sure it's nothing. And it isn't as if Lady Wroxly won't expect her gown ironed and her jewelry polished by dinnertime, same as always. Except now I'll barely have time to complete the tasks I was hired to perform. And you—when do you suppose you'll find time now to freshen three frocks and dress three young ladies' hair?"

"In light of today's goings-on, I sincerely doubt there will be a formal dinner tonight," Eva replied.

"And anyway," the woman murmured as if Eva hadn't spoken, "this was supposed to be our holiday. Some holiday, I say."

"Quite frankly, I think you're being unkind." Eva sped

up to walk ahead of the woman rather than endure more of her complaints.

In the drawing room, she found the family and guests hovering around the long settee, their faces etched with concern. She hastily sought out her girls—Phoebe, Julia, Amelia—and saw that each appeared sound enough. Her relief grew at the sight of Lady Wroxly standing straight and tall by the settee, looking her usual, hearty self.

"Thank goodness you're here," the countess said with enthusiasm, as if lady's maids could magically remedy any situation. After today, Eva only wished that were true.

It was Lady Allerton who lay stretched across the cushions, her head supported by a satin pillow. Her eyes were closed and the fingertips of one limp hand skimmed the carpet. She must have been told about her son . . . about the Christmas boxes. Eva hurried across the room, opening the vial as she went. Lady Wroxly moved aside, giving Eva room to kneel beside Lady Allerton's prone form. She waved the smelling salts under the marchioness's rather wide nose.

Lady Allerton snorted and coughed, and after a moment lifted a hand to swat the vial away. "She's coming to," Eva said. "Miss Shea, the cold compress if you would."

The senior lady's maid did as Eva bade, but let Eva know she didn't appreciate being given orders with a severe look that promised a repercussion or two once they returned below stairs.

Lady Allerton groaned. "What happened?" She slurred her words, as if she was tipsy. "Where is *my* maid?"

"You fainted." Lady Wroxly leaned over to say, "And as your maid was upstairs, I thought it quicker to send for ours below stairs, where the ice is kept. Are you feeling better?"

The woman drew her hand up to finger the compress, then thrust an arm across her eyes. "I must have imagined . . . oh, the most appalling thing. About . . . about Henry. But surely it couldn't be."

"What couldn't be, dear?" Lady Cecily sounded as if she was enjoying a pleasant afternoon's entertainment. Poised beside the closer of the two hearths, she reached up to press her thumb against the point of a sabre mounted on the wall.

Eva wondered if they had discussed Lord Allerton's fate out of his great-aunt's hearing. But then again, Phoebe and Amelia often giggled together over the odd things Lady Cecily said and did. Eva frowned as she took in her clashing attire—a flowered tunic over a striped afternoon dress. Oh, dear. Clearly Lady Cecily no longer exercised full control over her faculties, but perhaps in this case her infirmity was a blessing in disguise.

Lord Theodore went to his aunt and gently drew the woman's arm down to her side. "Come away, Aunt Cecily. You'll hurt yourself playing with that."

At a movement from the sofa Eva turned her attention back to the marchioness. She nearly touched the woman's shoulder but stopped an inch or two shy. "Ma'am, perhaps you should not attempt sitting up just yet."

She pushed Eva's well-meaning hand away. "No one need fuss over me. I'll be fine." She sat upright, but immediately swayed and let out a moan. Lady Wroxly scooted next to her on the settee.

"Our Miss Huntford is right. You've had a terrible shock, Lucille."

"Oh, Maude, what the inspector said. There can be no truth in it."

"Perhaps not. We shan't give up hope."

At that last, Eva was careful not to meet the marchioness's eye, for her own hopes for Lord Allerton had dwindled to none. She rose and moved away as Lady Julia approached with a long-stemmed cordial glass. Lady Wroxly took it from her and pressed it into both of Lady Allerton's hands. "Drink, dear. It'll fortify you."

"I cannot bear to think of them searching the house for him, Maude."

"Now, now, we must have courage." Lady Wroxly's pale hand closed around Lady Allerton's plumper ones, and she helped the woman raise the glass to her lips. "Drink."

When the marchioness bowed her head to obey, Lady Wroxly caught Eva's gaze. She merely nodded, then repeated the gesture for Miss Shea. They set the vial and basin down and quietly left the room.

Miss Shea grumbled the entire way as they retraced their steps, but Eva paid her no attention. Downstairs, she met with a sight that stopped her cold.

Vernon, with his head down and his hands cuffed behind him, was being led down the service corridor by a grim-faced Constable Brannock. Sobs echoed from inside the servants' hall. Eva didn't have to peek in to know those whimpers came from Connie.

"Constable, please wait. I'd like to speak with Vernon."

"What can you possibly have to say to a murderer?" Miss Shea brushed by her and disappeared into the valet's service room.

"My assistant needs to bring the accused to the village, Miss Huntford." The inspector's raspy voice filled the stairwell behind her. He descended each riser with heavy footfalls and huffing breaths. "Is there something I can help you with?"

"I merely wish to have a word with Vernon. Just for a moment."

"That's highly irregular. . . ."

"What can it hurt?"

Several faces filled the dining-hall doorway, and Mrs. Ellison and Dora poked their heads out from the kitchen.

Murmurs reached Eva's ears, comments ranging from disbelief to sympathy to, "Didn't I tell you so?"

That last came from Miss Shea herself, who had joined Nick Hensley in peering out from the service room. For the briefest moment Eva wondered what tasks had brought Nick to that room, where he typically would have brushed his employer's suits and polished his shoes. Then she remembered. With the marquess gone, his younger brother, Theodore, would take over the title, with all the privileges—and servants—that went along with it.

She waited until Inspector Perkins reached the bottom of the stairs. "I promise I won't keep Constable Brannock waiting but a moment."

"Sorry, it's against regulation."

He didn't sound at all sorry. If she was going to get any kind of favor out of this man, she would have to make him believe it would be to his advantage. She steeled herself and thought quickly. "Inspector Perkins, Vernon trusts me. Perhaps I can . . . learn something important, something he wouldn't readily tell you."

The inspector regarded her, a pensive frown growing deeper with each laboring breath he drew. Then he nodded. "Hmm . . . you might at that. See if you can't get him to confess, Miss Huntford. Make things easier on him, and on all of us. I should like to have this matter cleaned up by the New Year. A foul business, this."

Eva bit back a cry of exasperation. It was as if the man were speaking of mucking out the stables. Dredging up her patience, she said, "May I speak with him alone . . . in Mr. Giles's office?"

"Are there windows in that room?"

"Windows?" Did he think she might help Vernon escape? "The only windows are high up at ground level and too narrow for a man to fit through. Hardly convenient for making a getaway. Besides, you've got him handcuffed."

"So we do. All right. A few minutes. And"—he leaned in closer, bringing the rancid odors of spirits and cigars to sting her nose—"do utilize all your feminine wiles to persuade him to confess. And to tell us what he did with the rest of the marquess."

Eva fisted her hands and all but bit her tongue to keep from retorting. She thanked him, but before she moved away, he said, "Thank you, by the way, for your assistance with Miss Robson."

"My assistance? I only provided her with a bit of moral support."

He grinned and wagged a forefinger in the air. "So you did. Were it not for that, I fear we'd not have gotten a peep out of her. As it is, she rather neatly stitched up this case for me."

"But, Inspector Perkins, nothing she said provided any proof of anything."

"Didn't it? She provided us with the motive." He leaned closer still. Eva recoiled, but he seemed not to notice. "And she told us the footman himself hid the cleaver in his room. I may not be through with our Miss Robson, so see she doesn't go running off. It's highly likely she conspired with Mr. Vernon to rid herself of Lord Allerton's unwanted attentions."

Anger engulfed Eva. "I do not believe that."

"Never mind. I'll speak with Mrs. Sanders about keeping close watch on the girl."

"Inspector Perkins, don't. Please. Mrs. Sanders doesn't know yet of the connection between Connie and Vernon. The moment she hears of it she'll send Connie packing."

"Is that my problem?"

Eva fisted her hands to stop her fingers trembling with rage. "It's positively arctic outside. With nowhere to go, she'll freeze to death. Do you want that on your conscience?"

"Relax, Miss Huntford. Lord Wroxly has no intentions

of allowing the girl to be sacked. Yet. Besides, I need her here while I gather enough evidence against her to put her away. She won't freeze to death in a jail cell, now will she?" With that he let go a nasty laugh and stalked away.

"That heartless man," she murmured under her breath. "Justice will never be done with him in charge."

Outside Mr. Giles's office, Constable Brannock called after his employer. "Do you wish me go inside with them, sir?"

Eva held her breath. She wished to speak with Vernon alone.

The inspector gave a flick of his hand. "Just stand guard at the door. Did you remember to load your weapon this morning?"

Eva didn't wait for the answer. Grasping Vernon by the upper arm, she walked him into the office and closed the door.

"Are you all right?"

He stared back as if she had taken leave of her senses.

"I mean . . . I don't know what I mean. I'm sorry, that was a stupid question. What I mean is . . ." Again, she didn't know how to continue, except to ask a blunt question. "Vernon . . . George . . . did you have anything to do with Lord Allerton's disappearance?"

"Are you a policeman now, Miss Huntford?"

"No, but I simply don't believe you're guilty. You aren't, are you?"

"What difference would it make either way?"

"It makes a world of difference! An innocent man must be exonerated."

"And how do you propose to do that? I've already declared my innocence and told them what I know. I cooperated, and see where it got me."

"Please sit." She again grasped his upper arm and helped him keep his balance as he lowered himself onto the wooden-backed settee against the wall. She sat beside him. "It's true I don't believe you're guilty. But I do think you tried to withhold certain information from the inspector, and that is why you're in this position."

He glowered at her from beneath his brows.

"You were trying to protect Connie."

The scowl persisted, and he hesitated so long she didn't think he would answer at all, but then he said, "None of this is her fault."

"No, I agree. What can you tell me about the hours before Lord Allerton was discovered missing? We know you rose early to help Connie."

"They think I murdered him to protect her." He spoke with his head down, but now it swung upward, and louder he said, "And maybe I would have. Don't think I didn't consider it. Give the bugger exactly what he deserved—"

The door burst open and the inspector stopped short on the threshold, his chest heaving and his rotund belly bouncing. "Was that a confession?"

"No, Inspector Perkins, that was not. Please give us another moment." It was all she could do to stop herself from chiding him for eavesdropping.

"Very well." He stepped out and the constable reached in to close the door.

She lowered her voice. "Now, then, while you were helping Connie with her chores, did you see the marquess at all?"

"No."

"And what did you do once Connie's chores were complete?"

He blew out a breath. "I hurried upstairs with the broken cleaver so I could take it to town later. I swear, Miss Huntford, that's the only reason the cleaver was under that floorboard."

"Oh, Vernon, I wish you'd told the constable about that in the first place. You should have spoken up as soon as

Mrs. Ellison discovered the cleaver missing. Why did you keep silent then?"

"I never thought anyone would find it under the floor-board. It's Boxing Day, and no one should have been working all afternoon. I'd already called down to the cutler in the village and he said he could change the handle this very day. Then I'd have sneaked it back into the kitchen this evening. That would have been the end of it. I didn't think Mrs. Ellison would notice it missing today of all days."

Tears filled his eyes. Eva pretended not to notice and hurried on. "All right, then. After you hid the cleaver, what did you do next?"

"I already told the inspector, Miss Huntford. I ate break-fast—you saw me in the dining hall—and afterward I went upstairs to bring in the hot water for Lord Theodore's morning shave."

"You were serving as his valet, weren't you? Doesn't he have his own?"

"No, Lord Theodore doesn't keep a valet. The head foot-man at the Leightons' estate serves him just as I've been doing here. Word has it he can't afford a valet, and his brother wouldn't increase his allowance for one."

A marquess who denies his brother the luxury of a valet? Interesting. Eva stored that information away for later. "Did he speak to you at all while you shaved him?"

"Barely a word. He had a rough look about him, like he hadn't slept much. Maybe like he'd been drinking, although there was no smell of spirits hanging about him. He'd sent me away that night, said he wouldn't be needing my ser-vices. And in the morning—I told the inspector this—he hadn't changed out of his clothes from the night before."

Eva fell silent as she digested this information. Both Lord Allerton and his brother sent their valets away last night. If Lord Theodore hadn't changed for bed, could it be because he never *went* to bed? Then where was he all night? With whom? Beneath her sturdy broadcloth sleeves, gooseflesh swept her arms.

"What did Inspector Perkins say when you told him this?"

"He said, and I quote, 'If a toff wishes to sleep in his clothes, what's it to me?'"

She felt a spark of outrage on Vernon's behalf. "Did he not stop to consider—" She broke off, realizing that kind of rhetorical question wouldn't solve a thing.

"He thinks I deserve to hang. Guilty or not."

"Why would you say that? I'm sure he doesn't feel that way. He's merely trying to do his job . . ." She trailed off, wondering why she felt the need to defend an inspector who would arrest a man on such poor evidence.

Vernon shook his head. "It's on account of my not having served in the war. He called me a shirker. Said I have no business demanding justice after being too cowardly to defend my country."

Eva gasped. "He did not! Oh, Vernon, how awful. Didn't you tell him about your medical exemption? Your heart, wasn't it?"

"Irregular heartbeat, the doctors said." He made a disgusted face. "I told him. He called it a convenient excuse. Said if my brother was fit enough to serve, I certainly should have been."

"Oh, Vernon," she repeated, not knowing what else to say. She understood Vernon's grief, for like him she, too, had lost a brother. But she could not share in Vernon's guilt at having seen his brother off to war when he himself could not go, only to discover that brother would never return.

So many men . . . so many *boys*.

A rap on the door came; then it opened. Constable Brannock poked his head in. "I'm afraid time is up. The inspector gave me the order to escort Mr. Vernon to the village."

For one furious moment Eva wanted to seize Constable Brannock by the shoulders, shake him, and demand to know how *he* came through the war so utterly unscathed. But her anger receded as quickly as it had risen. For all she knew, Mr. Brannock, like Vernon, had some hidden physical defect that had kept him from the fighting, or some other hardship that had rendered him ineligible. Or perhaps he had fought after all. Some men—precious few—had somehow managed to escape injury.

How ironic that Lord Allerton had been one of those lucky few.

Sighing, she came to her feet and helped Vernon to his, a task made difficult by his wrists pinioned behind him. "This isn't the end of the matter," she told him, not caring if Constable Brannock heard or not. In fact, she hoped he did. She hoped he saw that others had faith in George Vernon and were not prepared to give him up to the gallows. The fact that she had little to base that faith on other than having observed the young man's good character these past several years did not for a moment cause her to falter in her opinion.

Vernon hesitated before setting his feet in motion. "Please don't do anything that will get Connie sacked."

Eva touched his sleeve. "You care about her very much."

He dropped his gaze to the floor and left with the constable.

CHAPTER 6

Through her dressing-table mirror, Phoebe watched Eva pin up her hair and affix the mother-of-pearl combs. Eva had already helped her into her dinner dress, a simply-draped chemise of sapphire silk with an overlay of satin netting that swirled about her ankles. Dinner would not be a sumptuous affair tonight, and Lady Allerton might not even descend from her room. Under the circumstances, and were Henry her son, Phoebe didn't think she'd have much appetite either.

"Lady Allerton was splendidly brave about the whole thing, once she got over her faint," Phoebe said.

"Yes, her ladyship is holding up most admirably, considering."

"I wonder how poor Vernon is faring. Grampapa has arranged for meals to be brought to him. He can't bring himself to believe Vernon is guilty either. I hope that helps make his confinement rather easier to bear."

"I'm sure it will, my lady, both the meals and Lord Wroxly's faith in him. Douglas brought his supper down about an hour ago. He should be back by now and ready to serve in the dining room, so I'll ask how Vernon appeared to him."

"Be sure to tell me what he says." She reached into the jewelry cask Eva placed on the dressing table before her. "Something simple." Her fingers lingered over a string of jet and vulcanite beads. "No, these would suggest mourning, and we aren't yet certain of Lord Allerton's fate. Mother's scent bottle necklace, I think." She selected a simple gold chain holding a tiny flask decorated with an art nouveau pattern of marcasite and amethyst stones.

"A good choice, my lady." Eva slipped the necklace around Phoebe's neck and fixed the clasp.

Through the mirror, her mother's necklace glinted pinpoints of light. Phoebe sighed at her reflection. "It seems silly to be dressing for dinner at all. Even before Lord Allerton disappeared, I'd been thinking how stuck in the old ways we are here. The war changed so much. I've heard that in London girls go about alone, or accompanied by their beaux. They go to music clubs and the cinema and shopping all on their own, or with friends, without a chaperone in sight. And no one thinks anything of it."

Eva let go a quiet laugh as she stepped back to inspect her handiwork on Phoebe's hair. "I suspect there are many people thinking a great many things about what some young women are doing nowadays. And I equally suspect precious few of those young ladies hail from families such as yours, my lady."

"Pish. Sometimes I wish Grampapa were a barrister or a physician, or even a baker."

Eva laughed again. "I'm afraid we all have our crosses to bear, my lady."

Phoebe joined in her laughter. Eva was quite correct. It served no purpose to lament one's lot in life, especially for someone as fortunate as she. Despite what she often perceived as restrictions or silly traditions, she knew hers was a privileged existence and she had no right complaining. Not when so many families across England struggled to scrape together the pieces of their lives, torn apart and scattered by the war.

And not when young men such as George Vernon made convenient suspects for crimes without a shred of evidence, merely because he lacked a fortune and pedigree.

She went to sit on the bed, leaning against one of the posts supporting the brocade and velvet canopy. "Come and sit, Eva. We need a plan to help Vernon."

Eva hesitated before perching stiffly at the edge of the mattress. Phoebe hid a smile. No matter how familiar or friendly they often became, it was always Eva rather than she who maintained the invisible barrier between them. Another silly tradition, wherein one person could be seen as having been born superior to someone else. True enough that some people were stronger, faster, more clever, or more beautiful. That was nature at work. But to be better than others simply because one bears a title—what utter nonsense. Phoebe hoped such notions dissipated along with the lingering ashes of the war.

She absently fingered the chain looped around her neck. "I've been thinking about what Vernon told you concerning Lord Theodore. It's odd, his having sent Vernon away when he retired, and then sleeping in his clothes. I'd like to know more about Lord Theodore's whereabouts last night. I was up rather late myself, but I never saw him."

"It could be nothing," Eva pointed out with a shrug.

"Or it could be something. I wonder . . . Lord Allerton kept tight reins on the family's money and often treated his younger brother like a poor relation. . . ."

"That reminds me of something else Vernon said. It was the reason Vernon was serving as Lord Theodore's valet. He said Lord Theodore had no valet of his own because

Lord Allerton wouldn't give him sufficient allowance for one."

Phoebe nodded slowly. "Yes, so you see, Lord Theodore had reason to resent his brother. And since returning from the war, Theo's become so aloof . . . so indifferent to everyone around him."

Rather like Julia, she thought.

"Do you believe Theodore Leighton is capable of murder, my lady?"

"That, Eva, is precisely the question. Did Lord Theodore often want to wrap his hands around his brother's throat? I wouldn't doubt it." Phoebe herself had contemplated doing just that in the drawing room last night. She believed Henry inspired the sentiment in a good number of people. "But the question remains, is he capable of such an act?"

"I don't know that I wish *you* to be the person to answer that question, my lady." Eva's hand came up, hovered in the air a moment, then descended tenderly on Phoebe's cheek. "In fact, I'm quite sure I do *not* want you answering that question."

Phoebe leaned into the warmth of Eva's palm, remembering the feel of another comforting hand, that of her mother, gone these eleven years. If she inhaled deeply enough, Eva's light soap almost transformed into the lavender oil her mother had favored.

She lifted her face. Eva was not her mother for all she often slipped naturally into a maternal role. Only seven years older than Phoebe, she had dark hair where her mother's had been Phoebe's own auburn-tinged blond, and green eyes where her mother's had been blue with gold rims. With her softly pleasing features, glowing cheeks, and determined chin, Eva was pretty in that distinctly English way, whereas Mama. . . . Mama had looked much like Phoebe herself. Her features had been rather thin and plain, but with a kindliness and patience that made her nonetheless beautiful in Phoebe's eyes.

Eva was her maid, but also her friend, no matter the difference in their positions. A valued, beloved friend.

"I will be as careful as you would have me be, Eva, but if you and I do nothing to help Vernon, who will? Not Inspector Perkins. That much is obvious by the way he is all but patting himself on the back for having solved the case."

"I'd hardly call it solving the case when Lord Allerton is still missing."

"All the more reason to find the truth. Now, you'll ask questions downstairs?"

"I will." Eva folded her hands in her lap and thought a moment. "There was something about the way Vernon held himself, how he responded to me. I can't quite explain it, but I believe he *is* hiding something. If the inspector senses it, too, it won't help Vernon's case."

"Something to do with Connie, you think?"

"That could be, my lady, but I'm not sure. And then there is the cleaver, which Vernon admitted to hiding. This suggests there must have been another blade used on Lord Allerton. If it were found, it could exonerate Vernon."

Phoebe pondered this a moment, but found a break in Eva's logic. "Possibly. But Inspector Perkins still believes Vernon had a strong motive."

"Very true." Eva's shoulders seemed to sink as she exhaled a long breath. "What is needed is someone else with a motive, but who? There is no one else in this household I can imagine carrying out such a brutal act on another person. And it would have to be someone with a deeply rooted grudge against Lord Allerton."

"What about Mr. Hensley?"

"What? No, not him, my lady. I'm certain it's not him."

Phoebe studied the high color staining Eva's cheeks.

"Hmm. You didn't need to think about that at all, did you?" She smiled. "You know him rather well, I'd say."

"My lady . . ."

"Go on, admit it." She grinned at Eva's apparent embarrassment. "It's perfectly all right with me."

"I assure you, there is nothing between Mr. Hensley and myself. In fact, he once courted my sister, Alice. It was briefly, and years ago, before he went into service for the marquess."

"I remember when he worked here as gamekeeper's assistant, and then an under footman. But you weren't with us yet."

"No, Mr. Hensley is a bit older than I. But we digress, my lady."

"Yes, we do." Phoebe leaned against the bedpost again. "But tell me, is your faith in Mr. Hensley based merely on past association?"

Eva shook her head. "Not only that, no. Mr. Hensley served in the war at the marquess's side. You know the kinds of bonds forged between soldiers. If Mr. Hensley had harbored a grudge against Lord Allerton, he might easily have arranged an incident on the battlefield."

"Yes, quite right. But if neither Vernon nor Mr. Hensley, then who?"

"I can't see *any* of the staff having committed this act." Eva's smooth brow puckered to a frown. "Not Vernon, nor Douglas, nor even persnickety Miss Shea."

"Douglas can be rather grumpy when assigned a task he doesn't particularly relish. I've occasionally heard him muttering his resentment against Mr. Giles or Vernon when he thought no one could hear."

"Douglas is all bluster, my lady."

Phoebe nodded and blew out a breath. "But you and I are not necessarily searching for the guilty party. We are searching for overlooked clues that might exonerate Vernon and force the inspector to continue investigating. For all we know, an intruder might have committed the deed."

"I should like to think so," Eva conceded gravely. "Not that I wish to think of poor Lord Allerton being attacked by anyone, but to exonerate all who dwell beneath this roof, both above and below stairs, would be a blessing, wouldn't it, my lady?

Phoebe reached over and gave Eva's hand a squeeze of agreement.

Eva returned below stairs to the controlled chaos of a dozen or so men, all of whom she recognized from the village, searching through cupboards, storerooms, the cellar, and even the old bread oven built into the bake house walls, which hadn't been used in well over a decade. The search party and the staff performed a kind of frenetic dance as they circled and sidestepped one another. Josh, the hall boy, nearly collided with a village man while carrying kitchen trash out to the bins in the courtyard, and Mr. Giles, shorthanded now that Vernon was gone, dropped a full box of flatware when another man went scurrying by him without warning. Eva cringed at the resounding clatter of forks, spoons, and knives of all sizes showering the oak planks in the corridor.

Meanwhile, having returned from the village, Constable Brannock strode back and forth from group to group, issuing instructions, checking if anything—or anyone—had been found, and overseeing the proceedings.

Eva hurried into the boot room and deposited an armful of shoes and half boots onto the wooden table. They needed to be cleaned and polished before she went to bed tonight in order to be back in the dressing rooms of their respective owners and ready for use tomorrow. But her ladyships' shoes could wait another few minutes. She went back out to the corridor. Mr. Giles stood in the midst of the silverware, a perplexed frown on his face and no won-der. He was dressed in his formal frock coat and black tie, ready to serve dinner to the family. A sojourn on the floor, however brief, would leave his clothing wrinkled and the knees of his trousers dusty.

"Let me help you with that, Mr. Giles. So clumsy." She knelt and began reaching for scattered cutlery.

"Yes, it was exceedingly inept of me."

Eva paused to look up at Mr. Giles's lined face, still al-most handsome for a man of his years; she guessed him to be close in age to Lord Wroxly. "I didn't mean you, Mr. Giles. I meant the oaf who nearly knocked you off your feet."

That brought a smile. "Ah, indeed. One can only hope they'll soon be finished and out of our hair. So disruptive." He reached for the butter knife she had just retrieved and studied it in the glow of the electric lights. "Good heavens, is that a scratch?"

He might as well have asked if one of Lady Wroxly's priceless diamonds had been damaged, for the horror that filled his eyes.

"Let me see." Eva stood and took the knife from him, holding it up to the overhead light. She turned the knife to and fro, watching the reflections slide back and forth across the silver surface. "No, it must have been a bit of lint. Looks as smooth as the day it was made." She knelt down again and nestled the knife with the rest of the set in the velvet-lined box. She collected the remaining flatware and handed Mr. Giles the box.

"Thank you, Eva. These knees of mine . . ."

"You've been working hard, Mr. Giles. And now with-out Vernon—"

"We've had to make do with a shorthanded staff these four years of war, Eva. We can endure a little longer until more can be hired." He regarded the box in his hands, the flatware tossing glints of light over the planes of his face. "Now, to bring these into the silver room so Douglas can get to work polishing them."

A frisson of alarm went through Eva. "But, Mr. Giles, it's nearly dinnertime. The food needs to be brought upstairs." Her consternation grew. "Please tell me the table has been set, Mr. Giles."

"The table?"

"Dear heavens . . ."

"It's quite all right." Douglas came down the service stairs. "Mr. Giles and I set the table a half hour ago. All is ready for dinner, isn't it, Mr. Giles?" He placed a hand on the older man's shoulder, a gesture that would have been impertinent, not to mention presumptuous, under ordinary circumstances, but Mr. Giles showed no sign of taking offense.

"Yes . . . yes, that's correct." He glanced down at the box of flatware in his hands. "Then I'll just . . ."

Douglas reached for the box. "I'll just put this in the silver room so I can get to work on it first thing tomorrow. I think another washing before polishing is in order."

"Thank goodness for Douglas," Mr. Giles said. "We'd best bring dinner up before the family begins to wonder if all their servants have run off."

Douglas reappeared and the two men headed into the kitchen, leaving Eva with a gnawing sense of worry. What had seemed to be Mr. Giles's calm acceptance of a difficult situation had instead been confusion over the natural course of the day's schedule—a schedule so ingrained in everyone at Foxwood, both above and below stairs, that only a catastrophic event could cause a deviation. Even a man's possible demise would not stand in the way of dinner.

"Excuse me, Miss Huntford."

A village man squeezed by her and kept going, at the same time shouting the name of another member of the search team. Eva suddenly understood what constituted a catastrophic event in Mr. Giles's world. Disorder. There was far too much of it at present, and the poor man had lost his equilibrium.

Well, she would do something about it. After several minutes of poking her head into doorways, she found Constable Brannock in the main kitchen, standing at one of the wooden counters set to one side of the range with its multiple ovens and numerous burners. His back was to her. Mrs. Ellison and Dora were at the center worktable, transferring tonight's dishes from pots and pans to elaborate silver platters and fine porcelain tureens. They seemed to be ignoring the constable, but they nodded at Eva when she entered the room.

"Constable Brannock," she called out, injecting a bit of force into her greeting. "A word, if you please."

He shot her a glance over his shoulder but remained at the counter.

"Constable, I'm speaking to you."

"Yes, Miss Huntford, can I help you with something?" He didn't turn around and sounded more irked than eager to offer assistance.

That didn't deter her. "You most certainly can, sir, and you might begin by turning and addressing me, rather than the wall presently in front of you."

No effect, other than to elicit a harrumph from Mrs. Ellison. She raised her eyebrows at Eva as if to ask her what she intended to do next. Eva answered with action, crossing the room with angry strides.

"Constable Brannock, you cannot continue to disrupt the work of this staff. I would greatly appreciate your exercising some form of organization over your search, finish up down here in an orderly fashion, and leave us in peace. Please."

"It doesn't seem quite right, does it," he murmured absently.

"What doesn't?" Eva plunked her fists on her hips. "What in heaven's name are you talking about?"

Douglas came into the kitchen to pick up a large tray holding several platters. A subdued-looking Connie followed. She hefted a tureen and trailed him, presumably up the stairs to the butler's pantry that adjoined the dining room. Connie must not be seen above stairs and Douglas or Mr. Giles would have to carry the tureen into the dining room, but with Vernon gone everyone else must pitch in where they could.

Eva returned her attention to Constable Brannock and noticed that he held an item—a cleaver, much like the one found in Vernon's bedroom. As everyone knew, Mrs. Ellison favored the one Vernon had taken. The steel was of finer quality and the thicker handle fit her hand more comfortably.

"What are you doing with that?" she demanded.

He finally turned to look at her. "Put your hand on the counter."

She scowled and drew back.

"Please, Miss Huntford. I have a point to make and I promise no harm will come to you."

"All right." She placed her hand palm down on the counter.

"Spread your fingers."

She did as he said, flinching and gasping when he held the cleaver above her hand.

"It's all right, Miss Huntford." He spoke quietly, so that only she could hear. A peek over her shoulder revealed Mrs. Ellison and Dora craning their necks to hear, but the frustrated tilts of their mouths suggested their efforts were in vain. "Do you see that if I were to sever your fingers from your hand using this cleaver, I could only go straight across them all at once."

Eva did see that would indeed be the case. The cleaver was too long and unwieldy for anything but one fell swoop, but Mr. Brannock's point eluded her. "I don't understand the significance. Besides, I don't believe the cleaver found in Vernon's room was the weapon used on Lord Allerton."

"And I'm beginning to believe you." He lowered the cleaver until its edge rested lightly on the backs of her fingers. "See how if I were to strike, due to the shape of your hand, each finger would be severed at a different distance from the knuckle. It's because the cleaver's edge is perfectly straight, but the placement of your knuckles isn't."

She fought back a rising tide of excitement as she studied the curve of her hand. Judging by the straight edge of the cleaver and the angle of her fingers, were she wearing a signet ring as Lord Allerton had been, the ring would actually be below the sever line. It would not have come off with the finger. She snapped her gaze to Mr. Brannock's and spoke breathlessly. "Are you saying you don't believe the cleaver found in Vernon's bedroom could have been used on Lord Allerton?"

"I'm saying it's highly unlikely."

"Then you've got to tell Inspector Perkins. He must release Vernon at once."

"I intend to tell him, but I can't guarantee he'll accept my deduction."

"Why ever not?" she said in her full voice, then remembered their audience, which grew as several of the village men came lumbering into the kitchen.

"Constable Brannock, sir?" one of them called. "We've been all through the premises and found nary an onion nor an egg out of place."

"Good. Gather up the others and wait for me near the staircase." He turned back to Eva. "Inspector Perkins is feeling extraordinarily gratified with having apprehended his suspect so quickly. He's not likely to give him up without a fuss."

"But you just proved it would have been impossible—"

"Not impossible, Miss Huntford. Merely more difficult. That won't be enough to satisfy my superior."

Eva was silent a long moment, her gaze connecting with his, seeking out what she believed to be the truth. She believed she found it in those deeply blue irises and dared to voice her thoughts aloud. "You are under no illusions when it comes to our inspector, are you, Constable Brannock?"

He glanced down at his feet with that grin that was becoming all too familiar: amused, confident, and decidedly cheeky. Then he raised his chin, took her arm, and led her out of the kitchen. She felt Dora's and Mrs. Ellison's curious gazes heavy on her back. She and Mr. Brannock traveled down the corridor to the dining hall, empty at this time of day.

"Inspector Perkins is my employer, Miss Huntford," he said quietly, "and I make it my stringent policy never to speak ill of the person who fills my purse. That having been said, there is something we can do."

"We?" Something about speaking that word to this man made her uncomfortable and sent heat to her face. She was glad she had not switched on the overhead lights. "Are you asking for my help?"

"If you discover any other sharp implements that have gone missing, let me know immediately. The only way to replace the cleaver in the inspector's mind is to present him with a more probable weapon. Until we can do that, I'm afraid the man will not be budged from his conclusions."

"If I discover anything, I will certainly come straight to you."

"Will you now?" His brazen smile flashed at her again, and she stiffened.

"For Vernon's sake, of course I will. And since you've enlisted my assistance, there is something else I can do. I am on familiar terms with everyone who received . . ." She drew a fortifying breath. "Who received a ghastly surprise in their Christmas box. I thought it might be a good idea to question them, to see why only certain individuals were chosen and not others."

He gave a dismissive shake of his head. "The inspector will have thought of that."

"I've seen how the inspector questions people. It's no wonder he's arrested the wrong man."

"Now, Miss Huntford, all we have done here is admit the possibility that events might not have occurred as we originally thought. If there is further questioning to be done, I shall do it. Not you, Miss Huntford. Is that clear?"

"You cannot forbid me to speak with my fellow employees, can you, Constable Brannock? It would certainly interfere with the smooth running of this household were we all to go about with gags over our mouths."

She immediately regretted her flippant words. This was a grave matter. The constable, for all his impertinence, was a trained professional and she should not be making jokes. Before she could apologize, his grin reappeared—an assessing, amused curve of his lips.

"You're quite the challenge, Miss Huntford, to be sure." He laughed softly and headed out of the room, repeating as he went, "To be sure."

"Oh!" Eva gaped and then scowled, not quite certain if she had just been complimented or insulted.

CHAPTER 7

Phoebe forced her way out of the dream, thrashing like a drowning victim desperate for air. She *knew* she was dreaming, knew she must awaken or the sorrow would be too great to bear. Just as the swimmer seeks the light above the surface, she sought the daylight behind her eyelids.

She awoke with a start, gasped, and took in the reassuring sights of the canopy above her head, the flowered wallpaper, the silk and velvet furnishings. All comforting and yet . . .

Sometimes, so empty.

She had been dreaming of Papa. They had walked together in the gardens and circled the pond. The morning rays streamed golden through the trees, gilding the water and warming the grass. The air had been sweetly fragrant. Papa held her hand and spoke quietly, his deep voice settling in her heart as he explained, as he had while he lived, the responsibilities of her station, of being born a noblewoman.

That had been right before he'd gone to war. Phoebe had been fifteen. Papa said she was almost a woman and he depended on her to help watch over her sisters and brother, the servants, and the villagers.

Her. Not Julia, though she was older. Phoebe and Papa had always enjoyed a special bond. And then he, who had led men through the Boer War with hardly a scratch, died less than a month later.

Phoebe put her hands to her ears as if she could actually hear the bombs falling. She shut her eyes as if to block out the horrible sight of the explosion that shattered the dugout, ejecting ragged shards of weapons and equipment and men into the air.

Papa.

She let her hands fall to the mattress. Just a dream. And yet the words Papa had spoken were real enough. They lived inside her, always. What would he think of her now, with poor Vernon sitting in the village jail? Would he think she'd failed in her responsibilities? That she could have done more?

"I *will* do more, Papa," she whispered.

A soft knock came at the door, and it opened upon Eva. "Good morning, my lady."

Phoebe didn't waste time in pleasantries. Her dream wouldn't allow it. "What did you learn yesterday?"

They hadn't been able to talk last night because Amelia had been feeling poorly. Eva had swiftly helped both Phoebe and Julia change into their nightclothes and then went to tend their youngest sister.

"All in good time, my lady." Eva leaned to press a hand to Phoebe's forehead. "Are you feeling well? You're look-ing rather peaky."

Phoebe didn't meet her gaze. "I'm fine. Have you looked in on Amelia yet this morning?"

"Yes, and she's much better. I brought breakfast to her room, though, and advised her to take her time coming down." Eva went into the dressing room and returned with the high-waisted gabardine skirt and simple cream shirt-waist she had laid out the night before. Phoebe nodded her approval and swung her legs over the edge of the bed to sit up. "If you ask me, it was all the upset of yesterday that did it."

"I'm sure you're right. Any word on how Lady Allerton is?"

"Shea helped Lady Allerton's own maid tend to her."

"It took two of them?"

Eva nodded as she selected an embroidered silk scarf, deep blue like the skirt, from Phoebe's dressing table. "The shock seems to be taking its toll today. She may not come downstairs."

"I wouldn't blame her a bit." Despite what Phoebe might think of Henry Leighton, no matter what he might have done to Julia, he didn't deserve to meet a violent end, and no mother deserves to suffer with that knowledge.

"I'll draw you a bath now, my lady, and then I'll tell you everything."

An hour later, Phoebe left her room armed with last night's revelations from Eva and a new sense of purpose. Whereas yesterday she simply couldn't believe George Vernon could have harmed a fly, today saw her faith in him bolstered by Constable Brannock's very scientific conclusion about the cleaver.

Not that matters had gotten any easier. Missing sharp items . . . in a house of this size? She couldn't begin to calculate how many ornamental swords, daggers, and bayonets hung on Foxwood's walls or inhabited the numerous glass-fronted cabinets. The Renshaw men had been collectors from far back. At least she felt certain if any more knives had gone missing below stairs, Mrs. Ellison, Mrs. Sanders, and Mr. Giles would know. Not an implement existed in the kitchens or pantries that had not been meticulously entered into the household catalogs.

Subdued male voices coming from the guest wing reached her ears as she entered the upper gallery, and she craned her neck to see. The door to Henry's room, which Inspector Perkins had ordered locked yesterday, stood open. Curiosity sent her down the corridor, and she peeked round the doorjamb to discover Constable Brannock sitting at the desk with his tablet and pencil, and Inspector Perkins standing in the middle of the room. He appeared to be scanning his surroundings, his arms clasped behind him.

"I think we're done here," the inspector murmured. "I see nothing that could possibly negate the conclusion we reached yesterday."

"Perhaps, sir," Constable Brannock ventured in an equally low voice, "we should search more thoroughly into Lord Allerton's personal effects. There may be a clue we've overlooked."

"Bah. Nonsense. The case is straightforward. Besides, one doesn't simply rummage through the personal possessions of a marquess, alive or dead. The family would be outraged. No, sir, the footman did it, and for quite substantial reasons."

Phoebe wanted to barge in and give the inspector a good shake. Instead, she eased away from the door and retraced her steps to the gallery. She heard the commotion in the Great Hall even before she reached the half landing of the staircase. Mr. Giles, Douglas, Mrs. Sanders, and even Mr. Phelps, Grampapa's valet, were all working diligently around the Christmas tree, removing the trimmings and placing them carefully in the straw-lined crates used to store them in the attic. The side of the tree facing the stairs greeted Phoebe with a sad droop of its now-bare branches. The star had been removed, and as Phoebe reached the bottom landing, Mrs. Sanders cradled the crystal and gilt tree topper in her arms and sighed.

"What a shame," she said. Then she noticed Phoebe. "Good morning, my lady. We apologize for this. Your grandfather's orders. He thought it seemed—"

"Inappropriate, under the circumstances," Phoebe finished for her. She peered through the dining-room doorway. The holly branches had been cleared from the sideboards, the gold garlands from the window valances. She expected Christmas would have disappeared from every room throughout the house by luncheon.

The morning room felt akin to a gentlemen's club when she entered, being inhabited by only Grampapa, Fox, Theo Leighton, and Lord Owen. Phoebe knew Amelia and Lady Allerton were breakfasting in their rooms, and Grams often took advantage of a married lady's prerogative to be served in bed as well. But Julia's and Lady Cecily's absences struck her as odd. Especially Julia's.

"Good morning, everyone," she said, and immediately wished she could recall the words, or at least her tone. She hadn't meant to sound cheerful, as if this were an ordinary morning. But perhaps the others hadn't noticed. They stood as they greeted her, then resumed their seats.

"Someone is awfully chipper," Fox said with a sardonic twist of his mouth. Ah, she might have known nothing would slip past him. "Hasn't anyone told you what happened here yesterday?"

"Fox, manners," Grampapa rumbled at him.

Phoebe went to the sideboard and spooned eggs, kippers, and tomatoes onto her plate. "Fox is quite right. I apologize."

"No need. It's heartening to hear a cheerful voice."

Phoebe's eyebrows went up in surprise, not so much at the statement but the fact that it had come from Theo Leighton. Theo, who was usually so reserved, one might even say surly. Was he in a more sociable mood today? Though she wondered why, she decided his overture would suit her purposes nicely. She decided to reward him with a smile, but his gaze slipped away too quickly. He missed the gesture and went on eating.

She took a quick moment to study him. He appeared freshly shaven, his informal Norfolk jacket brushed and pressed, his shirt collar starched and snowy white. Who had attended him? Not Vernon, surely. Perhaps Mr. Hensley, Henry's valet, had helped him dress. But it wasn't only his clothes making the difference. No shadows peeked out from beneath his eyes to proclaim a lack of sleep. The subdued lighting of the morning room even helped smooth the appearance of the scars on his neck and the side of his chin. He was almost handsome, and one might have thought him an agreeable fellow.

But did his refreshed appearance signify a better night's sleep due to the fact that a suspect had been arrested for a crime he, Theo, had committed?

That might be jumping to conclusions, but according to what Vernon told Eva yesterday, Theo seemed not to have occupied his bed the night Henry went missing. Circumstantial evidence perhaps, but no more so than that which had shed suspicion on Vernon.

She returned to the table and the uneasy silence that had fallen. They must have been discussing Henry and broke off abruptly when she entered the room, believing her too delicate to join in the conversation. She would dissuade them of that notion and see where it led.

"Has the search yielded anything so far?" she asked bluntly.

The gentlemen traded glances, confirming her suspicion. It was Theo who surprised her—again—by responding.

"If you are referring to additional pieces of my brother, no."

Phoebe's mouth fell open—she certainly hadn't expected quite that level of candor. A rush of angry red suffused Lord Owen's face. "Theo!"

Fox grinned with delight, and his gaze darted back and forth between Phoebe, Theo, and Lord Owen. Theo calmly met Lord Owen's gaze. "Phoebe asked, and I replied. Truthfully, I might add. Henry has not been found, nor has there been any more of him popping up in odd places."

Grampapa looked decidedly uncomfortable. Though he might be master of Foxwood Hall, little in his experience had taught him how to take a guest to task for behavior he obviously found ungentlemanly.

"Theo is right," Fox said brightly. "I've been looking and I haven't found any of Henry either."

"Fox, leave the table this instant." Grampapa shot an extended finger toward the doorway. He might not know how to reprimand a guest, but he exhibited no such qualms when it came to his grandson. Phoebe silently applauded him.

"But I haven't finished my breakfast."

"Now, Foxwood. To your room. I do not wish to see you downstairs again until luncheon."

"I'm banished 'til *then*?"

"Longer if you don't get up and go this instant. And during your banishment you might reflect on the sort of conduct befitting a future Peer of the Realm. Is that clear?"

"Yes, sir." Shoving a last forkful of fried potatoes into his mouth, Fox dragged himself out of his chair.

Theo waited about five seconds before he, too, rose, made his excuses, and followed Fox from the room.

Lord Owen leaned across the table toward Phoebe. "That was uncalled for. Are you all right?"

The dratted blush crept up her cheeks, fired, as always, by the man's attention. She compressed her lips, realized an opportunity had just been served to her on a silver platter, and shook her head. "No, frankly." At Grampapa's concerned look, she added hastily, "It's just a bit early for talk of that nature. My own fault for raising the subject. I'm sure Theo didn't mean to offend me. He's suffered a terrible shock, after all. But I do seem to have lost my appetite. Please excuse me."

"Of course, my girl." Grampapa seemed eager for her to go. As much as she would like to stay and hear what he and Lord Owen discussed next, she had something else in mind. Both men stood as she did. Grampapa patted her hand. "Have Eva bring a tray to your room. Honestly, all of you ladies should rest today. Don't think about anything. Read a book. Let us men worry about things."

"Yes, thank you, Grampapa. I believe that's exactly what I'll do."

She left the morning room sedately, but nearly broke into a run partway down the corridor. She had no intention of locking herself away in her room. Now, which way had Theo Leighton gone?

Eva followed Josh into the servants' hall, where he set down the coal bin he was carrying and began to transfer small shovelfuls into the hearth. "Josh, may I have a moment, please?"

Apparently satisfied he'd properly fed the fire, the hall boy turned to face her. "Aye, Miss Huntford?" A bit of coal dust smudged his cheek, tempting Eva to reach out and brush it away. She forewent doing so, knowing the fourteen-year-old would not appreciate being fussed over.

Instead, she leaned a hip against the table and tried to choose her words carefully. "Josh, yours was one of the Christmas boxes that held an unhappy surprise, no?"

"You know it was, miss. We were thrilled at first. Finding a gold watch like that. Mum and Da could have fed the little 'uns for the next year or two on that. But the other . . ." The boy's mouth pulled down at the corners.

"Believe me, I do understand. But can you think of any reason why you and your family were singled out?"

"Don't know that the family was singled out, miss. It was in *my* Christmas box." He shrugged a thin shoulder beneath his woolen work shirt. "Yours, too, ain't that right, miss?"

"That's right. And I can't for the life of me understand why. I was wondering—had you had any dealings with the marquess?"

His chin went down and his gaze became hooded. "Inspector Perkins already asked me that, miss. And I'll tell you what I told him. I ain't never spoken to the marquess—not to any marquess. I never even spoke to Lord Wroxly upstairs. Why would I? I know my place, Miss Huntford, and it ain't among the toffs."

"I wasn't suggesting otherwise, Josh. But perhaps your father had some business with Lord Allerton?"

Josh's father had specialized in fine saddles and tack before the war, a good business, but with so many horses having perished for the cause, he had been forced to close his shop. He still plied his trade from home when occasion called for it, but mostly he performed odd jobs around the village. He had jumped at the opportunity for his son to take over the hall-boy position at Foxwood when the former boy, Arnold, enlisted two years ago. Unlike the gamekeeper, Arnold had returned from the war, but had gone to London to seek, as he put it, "modern" employment in a factory.

"Dunno, miss," Josh said in answer to her question. "I s'pose I could ask."

"Yes, would you? That would be a great help."

The wary look returned. "We won't be getting into any trouble, will we, miss?"

"Oh, no, Josh. Of course not. Don't worry about that."

But as she watched him retrieve his coal bin and go on his way, guilt niggled. She could make no such promise. In attempting to exonerate Vernon, she very well might incriminate someone else. There was no telling whom that might be.

To find Dora, her next quarry, she had only to follow the clanking of the breakfast pots and pans. The girl stood in the scullery at the long trough sink, elbow-deep in steaming water. Eva went to her side, shoved up her sleeves, grabbed an extra dish rag, and submerged the next pot that needed washing. She sprinkled in Dora's mixture of salt, flour, and vinegar and started scouring.

Dora went utterly still but for the repeated blinking of her eyes. "Are you having some sort of an apoplexy, Miss Huntford?"

"Of course not. Why would you suggest such a thing?"

Dora blinked again. "A lady's maid helping in the scullery?"

Eva scrubbed at something stubborn and crusty on the side of the pot. "Yes, I'm sorry you don't often receive help, Dora."

"Connie pitches in when she can. She's a good sort, that one." Her eyes narrowed. "Not that *you're* not a good sort yourself, Miss Huntford, but . . . surely you must want . . . something."

"Dora!" She might have gone on with her shock and indignation, but the undeniable truth settled over her. She *did* want something, or she would be busy ironing the blouses that had just come from the washhouse. "Yes, you're correct," she admitted. She kept scrubbing, rinsed the pot, and next hefted a cast-iron fry pan. "Tell me, Dora, do you believe Vernon is guilty?"

"Well . . ." She let both hands dangle in the water, the wash rag floating like a bit of seaweed. "I'm not sure. I think, well, he *might* have done it."

Eva went still. She hadn't expected this. "Do you? I thought everyone here believed in his innocence."

"I like Vernon well enough, but . . ."

"Please go on."

Dora blew a strand of dull brown hair away from her face. "I wouldn't blame him if he did go after the marquess, after what the marquess did to Connie."

Eva's patience had worn about as ragged as the cloth in her hand, but she spoke her next words calmly enough. This might not be the information she came for, but her buzzing senses told her she might be about to learn something important. "What do you know about Connie and the marquess, Dora? If it involves Vernon, you shouldn't keep it to yourself."

"Well . . ." She flicked excess water off her hands and went to the doorway, looking into the short corridor that separated the scullery from the main kitchen. She returned to Eva's side. "You know my room is down here, and Christmas night I couldn't sleep, so I got up to go find something to nibble on. Just a scrap of cheese or something," she added hastily. "Nothing that would be missed."

"It's all right, Dora. I don't think Mrs. Ellison would begrudge you a bit of cheese."

The girl nodded. "I heard voices from the stairwell, angry ones. They frightened me a little, so I crept along the corridor a ways so I could hear what they were saying. It was Connie and the marquess, and she was begging him to let her go. He was laughing—not loud, mind you, just a mean little laugh, and I heard scuffling on the steps, and Connie saying no over and over again. And the marquess said, 'Too bad, my dear, you owe me this.'"

Eva braced her hands on the edge of the sink. "What time was this? Do you have any idea?"

"Sometime after midnight. I don't know exactly."

"And then what happened?"

"I heard footsteps coming down, and a voice—Vernon's—asking what was going on. That's when I peeked round the corner. I saw Vernon and the marquess staring

each other down like two bulls in a pen, and Connie cowering against the stairwell wall. She was crying, Miss
Huntford, and her dress—it was all crooked-like. Finally,
the marquess pushed past Vernon and stormed upstairs,
and Vernon reached to help Connie. He hugged her and
she cried on his shoulder, and she said . . ."

Here Dora compressed her lips and plunged her hands
back into the water, searching for the rag that had submerged beneath the suds.

"Please, Dora. This might be vitally important. I promise,
whatever you tell me, I shall reveal to no one that you and I
spoke." Her conscience gave another whisper of warning.
She seemed to be making questionable promises this morning, so she vowed silently that she would not use any information unless she could verify it herself—however she may.
She said again, "Please."

Dora blew out a breath. "Connie said she would kill
Lord Allerton if he ever touched her again."

Phoebe lightened her tread on the stair runner. No sound
came from above her. She could only assume both Fox and
Theo had reached their destinations. Where had Theo gone?
She hoped not to his room. That would make it impossible
to strike up a conversation. But the billiard room or even
Grampapa's smoking room—no longer used for smoking
ever since his physician forbade him—would suit her purposes. Before the war, both rooms would have been off
limits to Phoebe and her sisters unless Grampapa invited
them in, but the preceding years had loosened the old
rules. As long as the door stood open and she and Theo
didn't occupy the same settee, no one could raise an eyebrow, or at least not much of one.

Yet murmurs led her, not to either male domain, but to
the Rosalind sitting room that overlooked the dormant
rose garden and the bare willows scraping against the ice-

covered pond. She again muffled her steps, this time along the hall runner, and stopped a door away from the one from which the voices emanated. How familiar it seemed— Phoebe eavesdropping outside a door. But while the feminine voice once again identified Julia, the other held Theo's deeper, gruffer tones. And unlike Christmas night, Phoebe heard no anger. What she did hear kept her rooted to the spot, albeit tempted to move closer.

"Do you suppose anyone else knows?" Julia said, her voice low and rushed.

"I don't think so, at least not yet. But as for the evidence—"

"It must be destroyed, Theo."

"What are you doing?"

Phoebe bit back a cry. She spun about to find Fox lurking several feet away, his eyes glinting with speculation. Wouldn't she like to hang a bell from that boy's collar, or better still, put him on a leash.

She seized him by the wrist and dragged him away, down the corridor. "You're supposed to be in your room," she whispered. "What would Grampapa say if he discovered you disobeyed him?"

"Tell him and I'll tell Julia you were eavesdropping on her and Theo."

She was tempted to twist his arm behind his back. If not for her devious little brother, she might have learned about this evidence Julia and Theo must destroy. Evidence of what? Murder? Something rather less diabolical? Could they have been referring to the secret Henry held over Julia on Christmas night, the one that robbed Julia of her usual cool aplomb?

Had that secret spurred Julia to rash action? Or had Theo finally had enough of Henry's arrogance and tight-fistedness?

It wasn't the first time Phoebe's thoughts turned in either

direction. But even with Fox's untimely interruption, she had learned something new: Julia and Theo were somehow in league together. Yes, that touch she'd witnessed yesterday in the drawing room had not been haphazard. Now all Phoebe had to do was discover whatever common interest had joined two people who in the past rarely took the time to acknowledge each other's presence, much less strike up conversations.

She and Fox turned a corner and stopped outside his bedroom. Phoebe released him and attempted to stare him down, but he only stared back in silent, arrogant challenge.

There was nothing for it but to strike a bargain. "You keep mum and so shall I," she said. "Besides, I wasn't eavesdropping. I was on my way into the sitting room when I heard their voices. I hadn't wished to intrude, and was about to turn around and go to my room when you decided to frighten ten years off my life."

His cunning smile suggested he didn't believe her story for a minute. "If you say so."

"I do, and if I were you, Fox, I'd be in my room minding my own business rather than roaming the house looking for trouble."

"Is that a warning, dear sister?"

She reached past him and opened the bedroom door. "Merely a bit of advice you would be wise to heed."

She didn't wait to see if he took her counsel. She hurried back to her own room and rang for Eva, who came up straightaway, almost as if she had been waiting for the summons. She seemed out of breath, flushed, her eyes lit with urgency.

She and Phoebe spoke the same words at the same time. "I have something shocking to tell you."

They fell silent, regarding each other, and then Eva said, "You first, my lady."

Phoebe took her hand and brought her to the little settee facing the fireplace. Eva hesitated as Phoebe sat. Phoebe gestured at the place beside her. "Please, Eva. We cannot speak earnestly with me sitting and you standing. If we are to work together on Vernon's behalf, we must act as partners."

"Oh, dear," Eva muttered, even as she sat beside Phoebe and primly smoothed her skirt.

"Thank you. Now, then. I overheard something only moments ago. Julia and Lord Theodore were speaking together in the Rosalind sitting room, and—"

"You were eavesdropping, my lady?"

"Don't scold me. But yes. They spoke all in a rush about whether 'anyone else knew' and 'evidence that must be destroyed.' "

"My goodness! What were they talking about?"

"I cannot say, but Christmas night I quite accidentally overheard Julia and Lord Allerton arguing in the drawing room after everyone else had gone up to bed. She had just turned down his proposal of marriage, and in retaliation Lord Allerton threatened her with some secret he knew about her, something which left her obviously flustered."

Eva was silent a moment, then let out a breathy, "Oh." She placed her hand over Phoebe's. "That was why you asked me if I would tell the inspector if I knew something that might incriminate someone I cared about. You were struggling over whether or not to tell Inspector Perkins about Julia and Lord Allerton's argument."

"Did I do the right thing in not telling?" Phoebe searched Eva's features, which always exhibited such patient kindness. Would she see disapproval there now?

To her relief, Eva's forehead remained smooth. "I believe you did, at least for the time being. Inspector Perkins has botched this investigation so far, and I doubt this information would change anything for Vernon."

"I agree, but what about Constable Brannock? He seems an astute fellow."

"Perhaps . . ." Eva nipped at her bottom lip. "I don't fully trust him, my lady. I can't put my finger on it, but I sense he is hiding something of his own."

"Such as what?"

"To begin with, he seems frightfully whole and unimpaired, at a time when so many men have returned home maimed or scarred or emotionally wounded by the war . . . or simply never came home. I keep wondering why that should be."

"You think he was a scrimshanker?"

Eva drew back. "My lady, wherever did you learn a term like that?"

She shrugged. "I expect I heard Grampapa say it a time or two. He has little regard for healthy men who avoided their duty during the war. Why? Is it a bad word?"

"No, I don't suppose so. It's just not one I would expect to hear from you."

Phoebe waved a hand in the air. "Never mind that. You seemed agitated when you got here. Have you also learned something significant?"

"I might have. I've begun questioning the others who received . . ."

At Eva's hesitation, Phoebe hastened to reassure her. "You needn't fear being blunt with me. Not after the breakfast conversation I enjoyed a little while ago. What you mean to say is, 'the others who received bits of Lord Allerton.'"

Eva swallowed and nodded. "Yes, I've begun questioning them in an attempt to understand what each had in common. Why them—or us, I should say, since I was among them—and not others. One possibility that came to mind was business dealings. What else *could* link a workman or artisan with a marquess?"

"Good thinking. We should question the other recipients as well. The ones in town." When Eva agreed, Phoebe prompted her to continue with what she had learned below stairs.

"The hall boy's father deals in tooled saddles and tack—items certainly in demand among the aristocracy. Or at least they were before the war. I also spoke with Dora, the scullery maid, but we were sidetracked by another matter. My lady, on Christmas night, in the early morning hours, Dora overheard the altercation between Lord Allerton and Connie. Vernon intervened, and once Lord Allerton had gone back upstairs, Dora heard Connie say she would kill Lord Allerton if he ever touched her again."

"My goodness! This is far more significant than the matter concerning Julia." She scrunched up her nose. "At least I think it is. I—oh, hang it." She hopped to her feet and began pacing. "Vernon, Lord Allerton, Lord Theodore, Connie . . . and Julia." Sudden insight brought her to a halt in front of Eva. "This would have been soon after his argument with Julia. As if, having not gotten satisfaction from Julia, he went looking for satisfaction of another sort from Connie. How beastly! What a bully! And a coward. A man like that certainly makes it a thorny task to be sorry he's gone."

CHAPTER 8

Eva didn't enjoy riding in motorcars. Never had. They were jarring and drafty and moved at alarming speeds. But today she barely noticed as Phoebe steered her two-seater Vauxhall around the last curve to her parents' farm at a speed that normally would have had her cowering into her coat collar. She had other things on her mind, namely, her father's likely reply to the question she intended to ask him. Or confront him with, if the truth be told.

Apprehension overshadowed even her relief at climbing out of the Vauxhall, only to increase when the front door opened on her mother's quizzical surprise. "Why, Evie, we didn't expect you today." Mum's surprise quickly turned to alarm. "And Lady Phoebe, too. How . . . er . . . lovely." With only a shawl tossed over her dress, she hurried across the threshold, but a quick word from Phoebe stopped her short on the stoop.

"Mrs. Huntford, don't you dare come out in this bitter cold. We're coming in presently." And with that she and Eva hurried into the house and went directly to the fireplace to warm themselves. After trading pleasantries with Eva's parents, Phoebe followed a jittery Mum into the kitchen, leaving Eva alone with her father.

"Dad, there's a reason I'm here today."

"Any reason's a good one if it means we get to see our girl. And that Lady Phoebe—quite the young woman she's becoming." He waved a finger at her. "I see your influence on her, Evie, and she's the better for it."

"Thank you, Dad. But I need to ask you a question. It's about what happened, and you might not—"

"Ask, Evie, and stop beating about the bush."

"All right, then. Had the Marquess of Allerton owed you money?"

Sitting in his favorite easy chair, Dad crossed his feet, then uncrossed them, and tugged at his beard. "Why would a marquess owe money to the likes of me?"

"You know very well why." She sat at the end of the lumpy settee closest to his chair. "There must be some link between all of us who received those ghastly surprises in our boxes. I can think of no other rational possibility."

"You mean to say, someone might have been paying off the marquess's debts?" Skepticism oozed from both his tone and his expression. "Devil of a payment, that."

"Yes, but when you think about it, why does someone commit murder? Jealousy, revenge, and money top the list, don't they?"

"Perhaps . . . But the box was for you, Evie, not me. Did the marquess owe *you* money?"

His attempt to turn the question around left her uneasy. From where she sat in the front parlor, she could peer into the kitchen, where Mum was nervously pouring a cup of tea for Phoebe. Eva could understand how having a Renshaw in her kitchen might throw off her mother's equilibrium, but was there more to it? Had Mum overheard Eva's question? In an attempt to set her at ease, Phoebe, bless her heart, chattered nonstop about her grandfather's plans for the spring planting at the home farm and asked Mum her opinion on different grades of seed.

Eva drew a breath and turned back to her father. "The marquess did not owe me money, Dad. But someone knew I would be coming here on Boxing Day, just as he or she knew where the others would be going as well. So I'll ask you again. Did the marquess owe you money? He was furloughed for several weeks last summer. Perhaps you helped provision his estate during that time?"

Her father's forehead puckered. He tugged again at his beard.

"I've guessed it, Dad, haven't I?"

"All right, Evie, yes. He purchased several sides of beef while on furlough. What of it? Plenty of noblemen fell into arrears during the war. The toffs are pressured to keep up appearances no matter what. He'd have paid me sooner or later. He promised."

"Why was that so hard to admit? Did you tell the inspector?"

"It's none of his business."

"Then you lied by omission! Don't you realize how that looks?"

"Shh!" Her father darted a look into the kitchen and gestured for Evie to lower her voice. He whispered his next words. "I do not need your mum scolding me for extending credit during the war years. The man was a soldier, Evie, a commanding officer, risking life and limb for those of us left behind. I couldn't very well tell him no when he placed his order, now could I?" Rising, he went to the fireplace and took his pipe from the mantel. He didn't reach for his tobacco pouch, but instead tapped the bowl against his palm as he regarded Eva. "Why are you so interested anyway? What are you and her ladyship up to?"

"We are up to finding justice for George Vernon."

Dad shook his head slowly, now tapping the pipe's mouthpiece against his lips. "What if he's guilty, Evie?"

"You know him. Do you believe he could have committed a crime like that?"

A heavy pause ensued before he answered. "Do you believe I could have?"

"No, Dad, of course I don't," Eva said without hesitation.

She and Phoebe left soon after, retracing their way along the same road. With a grind Phoebe shifted gears, and the Vauxhall jerked twice as it slowed. A moment later they passed through the old medieval walls of Little Barlow. Cobbles lined the curving main road, which, when combined with the frigid air inside the motorcar, made Eva's teeth clatter until she feared they'd crack. To either side stood a few cottages and side streets, then rows of attached shops, followed by more cottages, the village church, the livery, and the Houndstooth Inn, all fashioned from the Cotswolds' distinctive, honey-colored stone. Thanks to the generosity of Lord Wroxly, the roads and structures had all once been kept in almost pristine condition. But the war years had created a shortage of men available to do maintenance of that sort, and an air of neglect had settled over the village along with a layer of grit only partially hidden now by the snow.

Phoebe brought the Vauxhall to a stop outside the haberdashery. The tailor shop, which doubled as a seamstress shop for ladies, was two doors down on the other side of the post office. Cloaked villagers, their chins tucked into their mufflers, hurried along the sidewalk, though many took the time to call out their greetings of "Morning, my lady," when they recognized the motorcar. A cart jostled its way around them, and a lorry rumbled by. Phoebe waved and called out her acknowledgments, addressing each passerby by name.

She set the break. "I think we should split up. You go into the haberdashery and I'll go down to the tailor."

"I don't think that would be a good idea, my lady."

Phoebe buttoned up her fur-trimmed coat and tightened her muffler around her neck. "There is no reason why we shouldn't. Entering a shop alone isn't anything new for me, and I have the legitimate reason of wishing to speak with Mrs. Garth. She was so helpful in facilitating our medical supply donations for the army, and I've a new idea I'd like to discuss with her. At the same time, I can also speak to her husband under the pretext of checking on some items Grampapa ordered for Fox. Meanwhile, you pretend to be shopping for buttons and ribbons and the like for my sisters and me. In fact, please do so and charge it to our account."

Eva didn't like it, but she couldn't come up with a reasonable explanation why. It simply felt like a dereliction of her duties to allow Phoebe to question a man alone. Of course, Mrs. Garth would be there, and even if *Mr.* Garth did have something to hide, he wouldn't dare be anything but polite to Lord Wroxly's granddaughter. "Very well, but we must be very discreet," she warned.

"It's not as though I intend blurting the question as to whether Lord Allerton owed the Garths' money." She tugged her velvet hat lower over her ears and reached for door handle. "Don't worry. I'll ease into the matter by showing my concern over his having received that gruesome gift." She opened her door and stepped out.

Eva did the same, sliding on a patch of ice and only just managing to catch her balance by gripping the Vauxhall's door handle. The sooner this was over and they could go home, the better. She watched Phoebe make her way down to the tailor's shop; then she stepped inside Myron Henderson's haberdashery. Myron Junior, that was. His father had died of the influenza that raced through England that autumn, only a month before his son returned to the village. Her own mother had somehow survived it, although she had still to fully recover from its ravages. Most hadn't been so lucky. She had not seen Myron Junior since his return, as his uncle had manned the shop after the elder Myron passed. Myon Junior had only recently taken over.

Coming in from the overcast day outside, she blinked at the kaleidoscope of colors and shapes that filled her gaze everywhere she looked. As always when she entered this shop, delight trilled inside her, as if she were a child in a room full of sweets. Perhaps, to a lady's maid who was always in need of a button, a bit of lace, or some lovely silk thread to hem a gown or fix a sash, a haberdashery was a sweet shop of sorts.

The shop was presently empty, Mr. Henderson the younger being nowhere in sight. She walked to the wall of shelves holding bolts of cloth like a library of colorful tomes and traced a gloved finger along a row of fabrics. The sea green satin would look lovely on Julia, and the black and cream striped would make a smart summer motoring outfit for Phoebe, and for Amelia . . .

"Why, Miss Huntford, forgive me. I didn't hear anyone come in." Myron Henderson ducked his head as he stepped out from behind the curtains separating the shop from the back room. Eva tried not to show her surprise. He looked . . . different from what she remembered.

"Mr. Henderson, how very good to see you again."

In the time it took him to approach the counter, her surprise melted into sympathy. A once vigorous young man, he now walked with the aid of a cane, and an odd squeak accompanied each uneven step. His short-cropped hair had receded, and though he was about her age, like many a soldier he had returned much older, at least in experience. Despite his kindly smile, his eyes were shadowed, no doubt obscuring the sights they had witnessed on the battlefield. Sights Eva's brother had witnessed as well, but hadn't survived.

She went closer, until only the counter separated them. "How are you?" She immediately questioned the wisdom of asking. Under the circumstances, was that prying? Did his condition—his limp—speak of struggles better left undiscussed? She had heard of his capture last winter. Had the Germans tortured him?

She wanted to bite her tongue.

"I'm much better, thank you," he said easily enough. "Looking forward to resuming a normal life again. And you? Your family?"

"Oh, we're all fine. . . ." How dear of him to ask, she thought.

"I heard about Danny. I'm so sorry."

"Yes, thank you. I'm very sorry about your father."

Silence fell, though oddly not an uncomfortable one. For several seconds they seemed joined in their reflections, their losses shared and jointly commiserated.

"Are you looking for anything in particular?" he asked at length. "If I don't have what you need, I can surely order it. Now that the war is over, England's young ladies may have their hearts' desires again." Having set aside his cane, he leaned his palms on the countertop and bent forward to speak on a more even level with her. So calm, so patient. She could hardly imagine this solicitous man charging on a battlefield, aiming bullets and bayonet into the bodies of other men.

A chill swept through her, and she shook the image away. "I need to replenish my supply of buttons and thread. Perhaps some ribbon. New shears, too, now I think of it. And I'm looking at some of your lovely fabrics."

"Perhaps something for Lord Wroxly or Lord Foxwood as well? Some rather dapper shirt studs have recently come in. Nothing too fussy. Very modern."

She smiled. "I'll leave that to Lord Wroxly's valet." She hesitated, then went to the bin holding glass containers filled with buttons, separated by color and size. She only now remembered she had come here for reasons other than replenishing her sewing basket. "How was your holiday, Mr. Henderson? Or need I ask? I believe you and I were both treated to a most unsavory shock on Boxing Day."

"Indeed. Who would ever suspect such a thing in our lovely village? And poor Lord Allerton. Good heavens."

Yes, good heavens. He had just given her the lead she needed. "Did you know him? Did he shop here?"

"I saw him upon occasion before the war, yes. Sometimes he came in himself, or he would send his valet, Mr. Hensley."

"Did Nick—er, Mr. Hensley—shop here for the marquess? I hadn't realized that." She assumed an expression of concern. "I do hope Lord Allerton's death hasn't left you short, then."

"Short?"

"Yes, you know. Unpaid bills." She held her breath as she awaited his reply.

"Ah. No, I don't believe so. At least, my father's records don't indicate any debts owed by Lord Allerton. Did you know I served under him in the Royal Fusiliers, Third Battalion."

"Then Lord Allerton was your commanding officer?"

"Not my immediate commander, but part of the chain of command, yes. And a fine officer he was, Miss Huntford."

"You thought well of him."

"Indeed, I had no reason to think otherwise. He won a D.S.O., you know." At her blank look, he added, "Distinguished Service Order award. They don't give those away for nothing."

"No, I don't suppose they do."

"A funny thing, war. Officers, foot soldiers—on the battlefield and in the trenches we were all brothers. It's hard to explain to those who weren't there. But there were moments when neither military rank nor social position made a difference. Life and death has a way of making equals out of men as nothing else can. Officer, soldier—the bombs and bullets treat us all the same in the end."

His voice took on a faraway quality and Eva sensed he was no longer talking to her, no longer even aware of her presence. A wild gleam entered his eyes as he stared past her, not at anything in the shop but somewhere beyond, somewhere invisible and inaccessible to her. Was he remembering the incident—bullet or bomb—that had incapacitated him? Or the day the Germans took him prisoner?

A breath shuddered in and out of him . . . and then he blinked. Brought her into focus. Smiled. "I'm sorry, Miss Huntford. You didn't come here to listen to me run on about the war. What may I show you?"

He picked up his cane again. The squeak she had heard resumed as he came around the counter, drawing her gaze to his right leg. He stopped, and she felt the weight of his stare upon her. Her face flamed, and she quickly looked up at him.

"I . . . Forgive me. . . ."

"No, Miss Huntford, it's quite all right. These prosthetics can be noisy and unwieldy, and walking with a cane is awkward, but without either I'd be confined to a wheelchair." With that, he tugged his trouser leg up several inches to reveal his shoe and black stocking and the wooden limb that extended toward his knee. He tapped his cane against his shin to produce a *clunk-clunk* sound. "It happened the day the Germans captured me. It was *how* they captured me, as I had not the capacity to run from them. But I was luckier than a lot of poor devils. They allowed me medical attention, or I'd have died of the gangrene. Mine came off below the knee. It's a much fouler business when the entire leg is lost."

"Oh!"

The gasp drew their attention to the street door, where a rosy-cheeked Phoebe stood gaping at Mr. Henderson and his prosthetic leg. He let his trouser fall back into place. "Good morning. Why, you must be Lady Phoebe. Do you remember me?" His greeting and his smile seemed to come naturally, as if nothing unusual had happened.

"Of course I do. G-good morning, Mr. Henderson. I didn't mean to . . . that is . . ."

"Your Miss Huntford was just about to make her selections. Have you come to give her your opinions?"

His straightforward, patient manner put both Eva and Phoebe at ease, and after another quarter hour they left with armfuls of parcels they dropped into the boot of the Vauxhall. As soon as they climbed in themselves, Phoebe turned to Eva.

"You were right. The marquess owed a goodly sum to the tailor. Mr. Garth said Lord Allerton came in several times last summer, as well as twice in the past month, each time running up rather extensive charges. Once Mr. Garth even asked Lord Allerton why he was 'honoring' his shop with so much business when surely there were more fashionably skilled tailors in London who were only too happy for the business now the war is over. Lord Allerton claimed he preferred doing business in the quiet of the countryside, that he didn't care for the bustle of London. Do you know what I think?"

"What is that, my lady?"

"I think Lord Allerton had been cut off by his London creditors, and was *forced* to do his shopping in the country. As I said, Eva, you were right about Lord Allerton owing people money."

But Eva shook her head. "I was only partly right. He didn't owe a cent to Mr. Henderson."

"Are you certain?"

"He told me as much."

Phoebe wrinkled her brow. "Could he have been concealing the truth?"

Eva had to smile at Phoebe's polite wording. "You mean *lying*, my lady? I didn't get a sense of that at all. Besides, Mr. Henderson could not have been responsible for what happened to Lord Allerton."

"How can you be so sure? Anyone might have broken into the house that night. Especially if a door or window had been missed when Giles locked up."

"His leg. He is reliant on his cane, and all balance and speed have been compromised. How could such a man overpower another who was both fit and young?"

Phoebe sat back and pressed her gloved hands against the steering wheel. "I do see your point. Then he would have no reason to lie about the marquess being in his debt."

"No," Eva agreed. "Which means there has to be some other factor linking all of us who received . . ."

"A bit of Lord Allerton on Boxing Day," Phoebe finished for her.

At the front door, Phoebe handed off the Vauxhall to Douglas, who drove with Eva round to the servants' entrance and then on to the carriage house. Though Phoebe would have liked to spend the next hour or so discussing what they had learned so far, Eva had other work to do. Not only must she tend to the wardrobes and needs of Phoebe and her sisters, but with the staff shorthanded she pitched in wherever Mrs. Sanders directed her. Keeping her otherwise occupied didn't excuse her from those duties. Rather, it meant Eva having to work later into the night to complete her chores, and Phoebe had no desire to add to those burdens.

Mr. Giles stood at the open front door to welcome her home. "Did you have an enjoyable excursion into town, my lady?"

"I did indeed, thank you, Mr. Giles. Mrs. Garth has agreed to help me start up a donation drive for the widows, orphans, and wounded veterans left destitute by the war. We'll begin first thing in the New Year."

"Splendid, my lady. A worthwhile cause. You must let me know how I may be of assistance."

As Phoebe stepped from the foyer into the Great Hall she couldn't help but notice the butler's harried appearance—his hair slightly out of place, his tie a fraction to the left of center. And, good heavens, what was that a smudge on his coat sleeve? Dust? Flour? This immediately elicited her concern. Mr. Giles was never anything but calm, organized, and perfectly groomed.

"Is anything wrong?" she asked him as he relieved her of her coat and held it cradled across his forearms. She piled her gloves, muffler, and hat on top of it, creating a little heap. "Are there new developments concerning Lord Allerton?"

She had dropped her voice to a whisper, wary that others could be within hearing distance. Lady Allerton had planned to keep to her room today, but one never knew whether she might change her mind and wander downstairs.

"Lord Allerton . . ." Mr. Giles assumed a blank expression, though only for an instant. "No, nothing new to report there, my lady. But all these guests . . . I have given orders for several more guest rooms to be prepared, but then I turn around and a new guest has arrived."

"New guests?" Surely Grampapa would have mentioned

at breakfast if they were expecting more company. "Who are they? And when did they arrive?"

"They began arriving yesterday, my lady. And more today. They seem to be everywhere. If you don't mind my saying so, before the war, guests did not assume they had the run of the place. A certain decorum was observed. But perhaps I have neglected to change with the times." He sighed.

Phoebe grew more and more confused—and alarmed—with each word he spoke. As far as she knew, there were no guests other than the Leightons, nor would there likely be any in the foreseeable future, considering present circumstances. She laid a hand on his sleeve, a familiarity she did not feel untoward for extending to this vigilantly loyal man she had known all her life.

"Mr. Giles, it sounds as if the constable's search party has upset your routine and made life exceedingly taxing for you, not to mention your being shorthanded now that Vernon isn't here. But please, do take some time to rest. A cup of tea, perhaps. You mustn't overexert yourself."

"Yes, thank you, my lady. I'll . . ." Trailing off, he wandered across the hall toward the cloakroom, only to stop again and turn back to her. "I do believe I'll have tea, my lady. Thank you."

Phoebe's throat tightened, and for a moment it seemed the world would never be right again. But surely Mr. Giles would be fine once all the commotion died down and life at Foxwood Hall returned to its usual tranquil, if tedious, pace. And she knew of only one way for that to occur.

Solve the mystery of what happened to Henry Leighton, Lord Allerton.

"Mr. Giles, one moment, please." She hurried across the hall to him. He reappeared in the cloakroom doorway, still holding her things. "I've decided to step outside again."

He helped her on with her coat. She took her hat, gloves, and muffler and set off through the house. Outside on the terrace, the biting wind that had followed her and Eva home from the village nipped at her ankles and plucked at her cheeks. Snowflakes churned through the air. She tucked her chin and descended to the garden path.

Back in town, she and Eva had ruled out one potential suspect—Myron Henderson of the haberdashery. But the tailor had been owed money by Henry . . . as had Eva's father. Phoebe didn't like to think about that. Eva adored her father, and to Phoebe he had always seemed an honest man, steady and hardworking, and devoted to his family. Could such a man commit murder?

Her thoughts returned to the residents of Foxwood Hall. It did seem more likely that someone from inside, rather than outside, had attacked Henry. She ticked off the possibilities on her gloved fingers: Vernon, Connie, Theo . . . Julia.

She liked those prospects no more than suspecting Eva's father.

But could Henry have been attacked by someone from neither the house nor the village?

The thought sped her down the garden path, around the fountain and over the footbridge, following alongside Henry's original tracks, which were becoming slightly blurred by the falling snow. The night he disappeared, he had not only engaged in an argument with Julia, he had attempted to press his advantage with Connie. Vernon had interceded, and Henry had apparently retreated back upstairs. Then at some time in the predawn hours, he had returned below stairs, exited the house through the servants' courtyard, walked through the gardens to the treeline, paced about, and simply turned around and went back again.

It all seemed too absurd. Why would Henry come out here? To look at the stars? To stand about in the bitter cold? That didn't sound like the Henry Leighton she knew.

She was certain they were missing something, a key element.

She halted at the edge of the woods, where the shadows between the birch trees deepened to a fathomless sea within the oaks and pines. Boughs, nudged by the wind, creaked like old bones.

If Henry *had* come out here, would he have continued through the trees? Or perhaps . . . her mind rushed ahead with a new notion. Perhaps he had come out to meet someone, a prearranged rendezvous.

She pushed her way through an icy tangle of underbrush where Constable Brannock had stepped through yesterday. As then, patches of snow—smooth but for scattered animal tracks—alternated with bare earth where the canopy grew too thick for the precipitation to penetrate. She tapped her toe on the ground, then gave a kick with her heel. The frozen earth sent reverberations up her leg.

Which meant if anyone had made their way through the woods to the garden, they would not have left footprints if they avoided the patches of snow. Had the inspector pursued that possibility?

She stood, thinking, staring into the frigid shadows. The stables lay to the south, and beyond it, the gamekeeper's cottage. She peered back through the treeline to the lawn and gardens. A sudden notion—a possibility—made her gasp, and she strode back into the clearing. Everyone had assumed Henry had exited the house, traversed the garden, and returned.

But what if Henry never left Foxwood Hall . . . and these footprints marked someone's trek *to* the house and then back to the woods? That would mean someone managed to gain entrance to the house when all the doors and windows should have been secured for the night.

Mr. Giles certainly hadn't been himself lately. True, he

had locked the doors and windows every night for some thirty years. But perhaps his present disorientation wasn't merely the result of recent events. Perhaps he had been growing forgetful all along, but they had failed to notice.

He might have left a door unlocked, and someone *could* have entered without using force. Money matters weren't the only area in which Henry might have made enemies. He had threatened and manhandled Julia, only to then corner Connie on the very same night. Perhaps some enraged father, brother, or husband had followed him here to Foxwood, awaiting his chance to teach Henry a lesson.

A permanent one.

Phoebe hoisted her thick skirt and flannel petticoat and hurried back to the house, uncaring whether Grams saw her in the undignified act or not. When she arrived she didn't bother removing her outerwear, but went straight to the library, where Grampapa typically spent the hour or so before luncheon. She found him alone, sitting in his favorite wing chair beside a cheery hearth fire.

He lowered his newspaper to his lap when he saw her. "Phoebe, you're flushed. And wearing your coat and boots through the house? What have you been up to?"

She answered his question with another. "Do you know where I might find Constable Brannock? He's still here, isn't he?"

Grampapa made a derisive face. "Here today and every day, or so it seems. I believe he was extending the search to the third floor and the old back stairs. Why do you— Phoebe?"

She had already about-faced and hurried away. By the time she reached the third floor she panted for breath and felt dampness spreading across her nape and between her shoulder blades. Only then did she remember to remove her outer layers, leaving all but her muffler draped over the railing on the landing.

A whitewashed corridor with wide-board flooring stretched to her right, and to the left, several yards down past what she knew to be a storage cupboard, stood a door that separated the manservants' bedrooms from the maids'. A completely separate staircase rose from the basement to the men's section, and the door between the two areas was always kept locked. Only Mrs. Sanders had the key. Not even Mr. Giles was permitted to unlock that door for any reason.

Today, however, it stood ajar. Voices, footsteps, and the thudding of wardrobes and cupboards being opened and closed echoed along the corridor. They wouldn't be going through dressers or lifting floorboards as they had previously. No, what they were looking for today, namely Henry himself, would not have fit in a drawer.

Or could he, if . . . No. She refused to follow that thought to its grisly conclusion. Still, it had been more than a day since Henry went missing. If he were here in the house, wouldn't his flesh soon begin to . . .

Rot? Is that how they would eventually find him, by smell? She shuddered and kept going.

Like a thief, she muffled her own footsteps as she passed through the forbidden door. Here she found herself in a corridor that exactly matched the one she had just left, down to the whitewashed walls and bare, oaken floors. Nothing distinguished one from the other but for Phoebe's sense of trespassing. She might have good reason to be here, but she was still breaking a host of strict rules.

A village man, one of Foxwood's farmers, stepped out from a bedroom and gave a little start upon seeing her. "Lady Phoebe."

"Good morning, Mr. Poole. Sorry to intrude. I'm looking for Constable Brannock. I have something important to discuss with him."

"He's down that way, my lady. All the way, then turn the

corner and keep going past the men's washroom. You'll find another door that leads into the old portion of the house."

She almost chuckled at the irony of this man knowing a part of her own home better than she did. But she assumed he referred to what Grampapa had termed the old back stairs. These had been part of the original structure, half manor and half fortress, erected as the Middle Ages gave way to the Renaissance.

She passed several other men along the way, and more than one tipped his hat and conveyed his wife's greetings. During the war years, rather than being used as a hospital for returning veterans, Foxwood Hall had become a Red Cross station headed by Grams and manned by Phoebe, her sisters, and many of the women from the village. They had collected clothing and blankets, and rolled bandages, made swabs, and fashioned splints and other first-aid necessities to be shipped to the Continent. At times the front hall had been stacked high with crates, and Phoebe had driven one of the delivery lorries to Gloucester and Bristol to drop off supplies at the train depots. Warmth filled her at the memory of them all coming together—wealthy and poor, noble and commoner—to help in the war effort.

It hadn't been long ago, yet the social barriers had fallen swiftly into place the moment peace had been declared last month. If Phoebe had her way, they would come together again, only this time to help the orphans, widows, and wounded soldiers the war had left behind. She hoped her plans would come to pass.

"Constable Brannock, a word if you please," she called out as she rounded a corner and caught a glimpse of the policeman in the doorway that had been described to her. Through it she could make out a rough stone wall. This stairwell, she knew, formed part of the turret that graced the south corner of the house, marking the delineation between the family's and servants' domains. The Petite Salon occupied the first floor of the turret, and the Rosalind sitting room the second floor. But in earlier times a staircase had filled the entire length, giving the servants access to each floor of the house. The upper half of the older steps still existed but were no longer used.

When Phoebe stepped through onto the landing, the odors of dampness, dust, and disuse enveloped her—but thankfully nothing worse than that. She sneezed into her muffler, still hanging around her shoulders.

"Lady Phoebe, can I do something for you?"

The constable's tone communicated a fervent wish that she reply in the negative, that perhaps she would simply ask if his men needed refreshment. She would disappoint him, then.

"I need to speak with you in private."

"I'm very busy right now. . . ."

Below them came more sounds of the ongoing search, echoing against the old stones like water rushing through a cave. Even if Phoebe whispered the sound would travel. There could be no privacy here.

"Please, come with me." Without pausing to see if he would follow, she turned about and retraced her steps. Even if she had not heard his tread behind her, she knew he wouldn't hesitate to comply with her wishes. Being an earl's granddaughter did have its benefits.

She brought him back into the maids' section of the attic. Here all was quiet, though a peek through the nearest doorway revealed an open wardrobe with its contents all shoved to one side. Were they truly expecting to find a marquess behind Sunday clothes and spare aprons? As if the staff didn't have enough to do without cleaning up after the constable's search party.

For now Phoebe dismissed her annoyance. "First, have you found anything? Any sign of Lord Allerton?"

"Beg pardon, my lady, but I could have answered that question where we were. No, we've found nothing yet."

"And did you check at the stables and the gamekeeper's cottage?"

"Nothing was found at either location, my lady."

"How does a man simply disappear without a trace? No signs of a struggle and, considering what was found of him, no bloodstains anywhere?"

"My lady . . ." He glanced down at his wristwatch, an aviator's watch, judging by the size of the face and numbers. She experienced a moment's curiosity about the piece, but realized she could claim his attention for only a limited time.

"Yes, sorry. I came because I have a new theory." He barely twitched an eyebrow, but Phoebe caught his skepticism nonetheless. "No, listen to me one moment. We've all assumed Henry—that is, Lord Allerton—left the house and walked out by the woods. We need to consider the possibility that someone else walked *in* from the woods."

"We inspected the doors and windows for signs of forced entry."

"But what if Mr. Giles neglected to lock the service entrance that night?"

"Is that possible? An experienced butler like Mr. Giles?"

Phoebe wished she could uphold the integrity of the man who had served her family so faithfully for decades. But given his recent behavior. . . . "As unlikely as it seems, I believe it is. He's been rather . . . disoriented lately, I'm afraid."

His eyes narrowed for a moment; then he angled his chin at her. "All right, then, let's say he did forget. But I'll also remind you, my lady, that the shoe prints matched Lord Allerton's, and the leather was still damp when we examined them."

"Many men wear similar-sized shoes, in similar styles.

And perhaps Lord Allerton's shoes were damp because he stood outside on the terrace to enjoy a cigar before retiring that evening. He liked his cigars."

"Seems unlikely given the weather lately. He could have used your grandfather's smoking room."

"Yes, but perhaps he thought the cold would do him good."

His eyes narrowed again. "Now why would that be, my lady? Why would a man seek out a cold wind before bed? Did something happen to upset him Christmas night?"

Phoebe's mouth snapped shut. Here it was again, that insidious morsel of information no one but she, Julia, and now Eva knew. And perhaps Theo, but she had yet to ascertain that for certain.

Should she tell the inspector what she had heard? Just come out with it—and possibly implicate her own sister? In all likelihood, Henry's and Julia's argument had nothing to do with what followed.

No, it was not her secret to tell, at least not yet. Not until she could find out more.

"Then perhaps Lord Allerton waited for whoever arrived outside in the service courtyard. There is such a jumble of prints close to the door that his might be among them. The point is, Constable Brannock, I came to you with a new possibility, based on the fact that someone easily could have walked through the woods without leaving clear footprints. But there could be other telltale signs, such as broken thickets, crushed undergrowth, or even pine needles swept aside by a man's stride. Has anyone examined the area beyond treeline?"

"You saw me walk into the woods, my lady."

"True, but you were looking for footprints. I suggest you refine your search to include smaller details."

His face turned stony and Phoebe realized she might have gone too far, telling the man how to do his job. This wouldn't help Vernon. She needed to find a way to convince Constable Brannock her theory warranted his attention . . . and she needed to exonerate Julia of all suspicion, at least in her own mind.

If she couldn't do that, should she tell the constable what she had overheard? Could she save a man's life by possibly sacrificing her sister?

CHAPTER 9

Eva set the pair of boots Phoebe had worn to town on a shelf in the boot room to be cleaned along with the rest of the shoes later tonight, after she helped the girls dress for dinner. Through the high-set window, she spied a pair of legs clad in dark trousers and button-up demi boots pacing back and forth in the service courtyard. Nick, she quickly deduced. She traversed the corridor, snatched a cloak from the row of pegs near the door, and tossed it around her shoulders. A biting wind circling the courtyard enveloped her as soon as she stepped out the door.

She spied Nick immediately. He wore only his suit, with no overcoat or even a scarf to ward off the cold. By the looks of things, he must have been out there a good long time; he had worn a path in the snow nearly down to the cobbles.

"Nick, whatever are you doing out here?"

He came to an abrupt halt and laughed. Not a happy laugh, but edged in bitterness. "What am I doing?" He laughed again. "Wondering where to go and what to do next."

The acrimony in his voice made her hold her ground,

shivering, rather than move closer to him. "I don't understand."

"My employer is gone, Eva. In essence, I am sacked without a reference."

"Nick, that's not true! Lord Theodore will need—"

"Lord Theodore has just informed me my services will no longer be required. As soon as Lord Allerton's remains are found and the constable ties up his case against Vernon, the Leightons will return home minus one valet."

"But . . . why? Why would Lord Theodore let you go? He'll be the Marquess of Allerton now. He'll need his own valet."

"He's planning to promote the footman who has been serving him in that capacity at home. He told me he has no desire to assume his brother's castoffs."

"What a dreadful thing to say."

He smirked and toed the ground. "It is, isn't it? But even more dreadful, Eva, is not knowing where I'll go now."

"Surely Lord Theodore—or Lady Allerton—will give you a reference of good character."

"Perhaps. But his lordship isn't exactly a man of many words, nor of good cheer." He said this last with cutting sarcasm. "And honestly, a woman's recommendation won't do much good for a valet."

"Perhaps there will be an opening here," she suggested, but he only shrugged.

"Lord Wroxly has Phelps."

"Well, Fox will be needing a valet soon."

"Lord Foxwood is an obnoxious fourteen-year-old who will soon be returning to Eaton. And I doubt any of his sisters will be needing a valet anytime soon."

"You mustn't despair. If nothing else, I'm sure Lord Wroxly will supply you with impeccable credentials. All Lady Phoebe need do is ask him, and you can be assured she'll do so eagerly. But do come back inside. It's freezing out here and becoming ill will do nothing to help your situation."

He flashed his first genuine smile. "You're right, Eva. I cannot argue with that."

He offered the crook of his elbow and she slipped her hand through, walking at his side to the door. "Oh, that Lord Theodore. If I weren't a lady's maid I'd give him a piece of my mind."

Nick stopped suddenly and gave Eva a gentle tug to bring her round to face him. "Eva, I haven't said this to anyone else, but it's been eating away at me ever since this all began."

Through the small window in the door, Eva could see Dora carrying a stack of dishes along the corridor. Nick saw her, too, and drew Eva off to the side, out of view of anyone else who might pass by inside.

"Mind you, I could be entirely wrong, but I've got a feeling in my bones, Evie."

A fierce light entered his gaze and Eva stepped back. "Nick, you're frightening me a little. What are you trying to say?"

"Just this. If anyone had reason to want Lord Allerton out of the way, it was his brother. They hated each other. I've seen it firsthand."

Yes, literally everyone had, at one time or another. Even Phoebe had mentioned their mutual disregard, and the fact that Lord Theodore hadn't seemed in the least bit concerned about his brother's welfare when he first turned up missing.

But for someone in Nick's position to accuse a toff, as her father liked to call them, was dangerous—exceedingly so. Before she realized what she was doing, she seized Nick by the front of his coat and tugged him farther away from the door.

"Do you realize what you're saying? Fratricide is one of

the worst of crimes. It would take a monster. Lord Theodore isn't the kindest of souls, but—"

"I know, I know." He dragged both hands through his hair. "Lord Theodore resented the control his brother kept over the money, and he made no secret of the fact that he believed the wrong brother had inherited the title and fortune."

"But Henry Leighton was the elder brother. Surely Theodore didn't contest that."

"No, but he made accusations, said Lord Allerton was squandering the fortune away and leaving nothing for anyone else. I'd even heard Lord Theodore threatening to have his brother's competency put to the test."

At those words, Eva went very still. "Are the Leightons facing bankruptcy?"

"I don't know . . . Lord Allerton always paid me monthly, which is generous. As you know, many employers pay but once or twice a year."

"Yes, but today in town, Lady Phoebe stopped in at the tailor—to inquire on some items for her brother—and in the course of conversing with Mr. Garth, she learned Lord Allerton did indeed owe him money for unpaid bills."

Nick's eyebrows went up, but then he shook his head. "All gentlemen run up bills. It's simply their way. They never carry much in the way of cash. Cash is vulgar, not to mention filthy, and as a result they purchase everything on credit. And with the war and all, and Lord Allerton only recently being home permanently . . . you understand, don't you?"

"I suppose. . . ." It wasn't as if she hadn't already known this to be true. And in questioning both Mr. Garth and Mr. Henderson today, she and Phoebe had all but ruled out unpaid bills as being the connecting factor among the recipients of the Christmas boxes.

"If you ask me, money isn't what killed Lord Allerton.

Jealousy did. Jealousy and resentment." Nick didn't finish the accusation, didn't name Lord Theodore again, but condemnation sparked in his eyes.

"If your suspicions are true, then it comes down to money all over again. If Lord Theodore resented his brother, it was because Lord Allerton controlled the fortune, thereby controlling the lives of the entire Leighton family. But, Nick"— she laid a hand on his coat sleeve—"You must be very careful what you say. If Lord Theodore were to be accused by your word and then proved innocent . . ."

"Yes." He blew out a cloud of frosty steam. "I'd never work in service again. Probably never find decent employment anywhere. So then you think I should let this go, forget all about it?"

She released his arm. "No, Vernon claimed Lord Theodore slept in his clothes Christmas night. Perhaps he didn't sleep much at all that night because he was busy elsewhere. What I think is that we should try to find out what the man was up to, and if we discover anything significant, we go straight to Inspector Perkins. Are you game?"

His calculating grin supplied the answer.

That evening, Lady Allerton descended from her room. Her appearance in the drawing room surprised everyone, there having been no prior warning that she intended to join them.

"Lucille, darling." Grams moved to her friend's side with a vigor that belied her sixty-seven years. "It's wonderful to see you."

"Is it, Maude? Then perhaps I should return to my room. It was not my wish to bring anything approaching relief or merriment to the household while my son is still missing. I merely wished to take a meal without forcing your servants to carry another tray up two flights of stairs."

Grams colored to the roots of her silvery hair. "Forgive me, Lucille. I didn't mean to give offense. It's just that we've all been so worried about you."

"Sherry?" Grampapa pressed a crystal cordial glass into Lady Leighton's hand, and Phoebe immediately perceived his ulterior motive of providing a quick distraction and a change of subject. "It will do you good."

"Finding Henry *alive* is the only thing that will do me good." But she accepted the glass nonetheless and took a dainty sip.

"Henry and Julia are going to be married, in the spring, I should think." Lady Cecily leaned over the Louis Quinze side table, arranging and rearranging a Rose Medallion vase filled with bright blue delphinium, pink clematis, and wide, blush peonies, all products of the hothouse. Though she had been present when matters were explained to Lady Allerton, the elderly woman appeared to have retained no notion of Henry's fate. "Spring weddings are always loveliest. Maude, dear, do you suppose that will leave enough time to plan?"

Grams sighed and didn't reply.

Fox and Lord Owen had resumed their ongoing chess game, while Amelia stared into the pages of a book. Theo sat ruminating in a wing chair, looking at nothing and no one in particular. The gathering before dinner had always been meant to start conversations that would carry on into the dining room, but with only one topic on everyone's minds, Phoebe saw the wisdom of the younger set in avoiding conversation altogether.

Unfortunately, she was never one to follow the wisdom of a crowd. She headed for Julia, once again at the piano. This time she sat on the cushioned bench, softly playing a rolling melody in the style from America called ragtime.

Phoebe slid next to her on the seat. Julia missed a note, then went right on playing as if Phoebe didn't exist.

But exist she most certainly did. "You've got to come clean about Henry."

Julia stumbled over the next note, recovered, and scowled down at the keys. "Again? When will you let it go?"

"When Henry is found. I know you and he had secrets, ones you both could use against the other. What did you know about Henry?"

"It's none of your affair. And if you know what's good for you—"

Phoebe whisked her hand over both of Julia's, silencing the song. Theo, as if prodded from sleep, jerked his head upright and stared from across the room. Lord Owen glanced over his shoulder, frowned slightly, and returned his attention to the game pieces.

"Don't you understand," Phoebe whispered between gritted teeth. "Whatever you know about him might have been known by others. By someone who followed him to Foxwood and . . . Julia, this is something the authorities need to know. It could be a vital clue as to what happened to Henry."

"Really, Phoebe, you're so terribly dramatic."

"Do you still deny that he's most likely dead? And does that not concern you in the slightest?"

"They arrested the culprit."

"Oh, Julia." Her sister's indifference pushed tears into Phoebe's eyes. If only Julia could care again—about anything. If only Phoebe could make her care. Simply reach inside and coax Julia's heart to beat again. Surely, deep down, her sister wasn't as empty as the lifeless mask she showed the world.

Phoebe had tried reaching her—tried and tried. She had come to the conclusion no one could help Julia until she herself wanted to live again. But Vernon, on the other hand, could possibly be helped, and Phoebe didn't intend resting until she had done her best for him. "You can't believe

Vernon is guilty. You cannot believe all avenues have been properly explored. He's one of ours, Julia. Like family. We cannot abandon family. We *do* not."

They locked gazes, and Phoebe saw a battle waging in Julia's dark blue eyes—eyes that nearly matched the sapphire on her finger, the one that had belonged to their mother. Had Phoebe gone too far in speaking of abandonment? Did Julia believe not one but both of their parents had abandoned them? Neither had had a choice, but sometimes even Phoebe felt angry and betrayed by their deaths.

Perhaps Julia read her mind, for she gazed down at her ring, closed her eyes, and drew a deep breath. "Henry owed a very large debt."

Phoebe held her breath and waited for more, but nothing further came. "How large? I already know he owed our own Mr. Garth in the village for unpaid tailoring bills."

"No, Phoebe. I'm not talking about the kinds of debt every gentleman runs up. I'm talking about a moral debt. Last summer while Henry was home, he fell in with a band of speculators, men of the worst sort, who were manipulating war bond values with false information about how the fighting was going."

Phoebe's hand flew to her mouth as she gasped. "How beastly and dishonorable. And downright treasonous. How did you find out?"

Julia gave a soft laugh. "It wasn't hard, really. I immediately took a distaste to Henry's new so-called friends. From there I began asking questions—direct ones to the right people." When Phoebe started to question that, Julia shushed her. "That's all you need to know."

Phoebe shot a glance across the room. "Does Theo know?"

"I couldn't say, really."

Phoebe didn't believe her on that count, but she let it go

as an observation pushed to the forefront. "This is why you turned him down."

"I'd have turned him down anyway, but this certainly helped. I could never marry a man I didn't respect."

Phoebe stole another peek at Theo, once more ignoring them and everyone else as he appeared to be contemplating his hand, turning it this way and that and studying the scars on both sides. Had he known about his brother's devious business dealings?

She turned back to Julia, who had resumed playing the same languid melody. "Will you please tell Inspector Perkins what you know?"

To her surprise and frustration, Julia shook her head. "No, it might lead to too many questions."

"Ah, the secret Henry knew about you."

Julia glowered at her.

"Whatever it is, it needn't be mentioned. Simply tell Inspector Perkins or his assistant what you learned last summer. Perhaps someone swindled in this scheme lost their fortune and came here seeking revenge. My goodness, Julia, this could turn the inspector's case on end."

"Very possibly," she said dismissively. "But I won't be involved. You may tell Inspector Perkins what you will. Perhaps the police will be able to trace Henry's actions and round up his cohorts." She gave a careless shrug of her shoulder, in typical *Julia* fashion. "Perhaps further insights will be revealed during the reading of his will."

A wave of fresh anger caused Phoebe to flip the fall board down into place. Julia barely managed to whisk her fingers clear in time. She surged to her feet and rounded on Phoebe. "What was that for?" she hissed. "You might have broken my fingers."

"The will cannot be read until Henry's body is found. However, Vernon can be shipped to Gloucester in the interim and stand trial for a crime he almost assuredly did not commit."

Julia's indignation slipped a fraction. "How can they try him without a body?"

"As they have tried other men without fortune or connections. Do you think there can be justice for a footman accused of murdering a marquess?"

Julia's nostrils flared, making her appear even haughtier than usual. "I'll . . . think about it. No promises, but I'll consider what you've said."

"Consider quickly. In the meantime, I *will* tell Constable Brannock what you told me. I can only hope he'll take me seriously."

Chapter 10

On Saturday, Phoebe woke to bleak skies and a fresh coating of snow softening the edges of the garden and lawns. . . .

And the footprints. From her bedroom window she could see they were all but gone, and her heart sank. Not so much because of the loss of the prints themselves, but a kind of symbolic declaration that hope for Vernon faded with each passing day.

With that disheartening thought she descended to the morning room, happy to find it empty but for Connie, her hands wrapped in two thick towels as she carried in the coffee urn.

"Good morning, my lady. I apologize for being above stairs, but—"

"Never mind, Connie. We appreciate your helping out."

The girl arranged the cups and saucers near the urn, then stood hovering at the sideboard, alternately peering at Phoebe and lowering her gaze to the floor.

"Is there something you'd like to say, Connie?"

She stepped closer. "There is, my lady. I . . . I believe you know about . . ." She hesitated, splotches of scarlet blooming on her neck. She shrank into herself and chewed her lip.

Phoebe went to her and spoke softly. "If you are speaking of you and Vernon, of your . . . regard . . . for one another, for now you needn't worry. I spoke to my grandfather. Mrs. Sanders will not turn you out."

"Oh, my lady . . . I swear he and I never stepped beyond what's proper. Never. George is a good sort, honorable. And I'm a good girl. We simply . . ."

"You simply like each other," Phoebe finished for her.

Connie nodded sadly. A tear splashed her pinafore. "Thank you, my lady. My family . . . they depend on what I can send home. Just not having to worry about feeding me eases their burdens."

"I understand. Your father—did he fight in the war?"

"He did, my lady, until they sent him home on account of the shell shock." The swinging door to the butler's pantry opened, and Douglas appeared with a covered tray. Connie reached for it and set it on the sideboard. "Well . . . I'd better help bring up the rest." She followed Douglas out of the room, but Phoebe stayed where she was, studying the closed door and remembering what Dora had told Eva. She had overheard Connie threatening to kill Henry if he ever touched her again.

People said things like that in anger. She herself had half-wanted to kill Henry Christmas night. Still . . .

She moved to the window. The clouds had thickened, creating an artificial dusk. Beyond the fountain a deer scampered across the main path. Closer, the ice coating the box hedge beneath the window tinkled like tiny chimes as the wind rattled the branches.

"Longing for spring, Lady Phoebe?"

She jumped and discovered Lord Owen by her side. She hadn't heard him come in. How did a man his size move so silently? She glanced to meet his gaze, then just as quickly dropped her own. Too late. Something in his expression traveled through her, sending a rush of fire to her cheeks.

Good heavens, she would die of mortification should he ever glimpse her fancies.

She gave a little sniff, hoping to emulate one of Julia's disdainful gestures. "I am longing, my lord, for answers, and for this dreadful episode to be behind us."

"Yes, of course. I'm sorry." His voice plummeted to a deep murmur. She heard only sincerity in his voice; nothing of mockery or teasing. That encouraged her to lower her guard.

"Why should you be sorry? You were only trying to make conversation. I'm the one who was rude."

"Not at all." He, too, faced out the window. Beyond the gardens and the forest, an upswell in the land revealed the closest pastures of the tenant farms, each lined with rock walls and dotted with the winter skeletons of oak and elm and laurel. Yesterday, bare earth showed in patches where the wind had swept the snow away; this morning those patches were blanketed in white. "I suppose you'll never quite look out over this park the same way again."

"An understatement." They stood in companionable silence for a moment, and Phoebe rejoiced inwardly that those infernal flames seemed to have stopped lapping at her cheeks. In fact, she felt quite normal. Adult. Able to speak with the man on an equal footing. "Did you know him well? Henry, I mean."

He hesitated for a fraction of a moment. "No, not well. We crossed paths numerous times during the war. And we had people in common. Your family, for instance."

"Business dealings, perhaps?"

Did she imagine the pause before he said, "No, his interests and mine never coincided."

A wash of relief followed his reply, and considering what Julia had told her last night, she fervently hoped he spoke the truth. She and Eva had talked this morning, and both agreed they needed some evidence of Henry's perfidy or the inspector would dismiss their claim out of hand.

"Did you like Henry?" she persisted, trying to learn of any connection, if one existed, between the two men. "Did you find him a decent sort?"

This time his hesitation stretched, and she felt the weight of his scrutiny. Her cheeks tingled, and she searched for something out the window—anything—to point to, comment upon, to change the subject. Finally, he said, "As decent a sort as many others in his position. Why do you ask?"

She frowned, filled with a sense that Lord Owen was purposely omitting something. "What an odd way to phrase it. Then you didn't like him."

"Does that make me a suspect?"

She pulled back with a start. "Of course not. I didn't say that. I—"

His teasing chuckle cut her off short. "I know you've been asking questions and poking about. Do you believe you can do a better job than your inspector?"

Though part of her felt she should be offended, she couldn't help matching his chuckle with one of her own. "Frankly, yes. But how do you know what I've been doing? Have you been watching me?"

Despite the challenge she managed to inject into her voice, goose bumps spread over her arms beneath her shirtwaist and the lamb's wool jumper she had donned over it. *Had* Lord Owen been watching her? Was he that aware of her? She had thought he barely knew she existed.

Footsteps behind them forestalled his reply. He turned at the sound. "Ah, Julia. Good morning." He left Phoebe's side and crossed the room to her sister, taking her hand and lightly kissing the backs of her knuckles. Together they went to the sideboard and filled their coffee cups.

Phoebe sighed. Forgotten yet again, just as on that day at the Sandown races with Oliver Prestwich four years ago. Goodness, Phoebe hadn't thought of him in ages. She had met him, the second son of the Earl of Trenton, at Sandown Park, where her family had been invited to view the races from his parents' box in the grandstand. As the week progressed he had taken to saving a seat for her right beside him, and she had been so certain of the genuineness of his attentions. She had never before experienced such a flurry inside her, like an entire flock of sparrows taking wing. Until Julia happened by, having grown tired of watching the races with friends of her own. Ten minutes with Julia and suddenly Oliver had few smiles to spare for Phoebe. He invited Julia to view the races with him the next day, and forgot to include Phoebe at all. . . .

Why couldn't Julia have stayed away?

Now, as then, Phoebe wondered about her sister's intentions. Had she meant to steal Oliver from her? Julia had never shown interest in a second son before—nor after, for that matter. Perhaps she found it an amusing game to simply collect people. It might have begun innocently enough, the natural result of being the pretty child of the family, only to later become a habit—a way of life. Could she comprehend at all how girls like Phoebe felt to be left standing alone, their words unspoken and their hearts in their hands?

A hollowness formed in the pit of her stomach and she went back to staring out the window. Sometimes she felt exactly the way the garden looked today. Gray and plain, with nothing vibrant to recommend it, while a bright sun shone nearby, yet a world away and out of her reach.

Well, she could blame Julia all she wished, not that it mattered. Lord Owen *had* been invited to provide Julia a second chance at marriage in the event things didn't work out with Henry. If that contented the two of them, Phoebe certainly wouldn't stand in their way.

She was about to paste on a neutral expression, select

her breakfast, and join them at the table when that plain gray garden once more seized her attention. The footprints. As she had noted from upstairs, the fresh snowfall had all but filled them in, but not quite, and now, with the morning light angled just so across them . . . A possibility startled her. Quickly she ate a piece of toast and went in search of Eva.

"Can I refill your cup for you, Nick?" Sitting at the table in the servants' hall, Eva lifted the coffeepot. They were alone, the other servants having left minutes ago to continue their morning chores. Eva had already attended to her ladies' morning needs, and these quiet moments following breakfast were a privilege of being a lady's maid Eva always enjoyed before she set to work polishing boots and jewelry, ironing shirtwaists, and making any desired alterations to her mistresses' wardrobes.

She had just filled Nick's cup and then her own, when Lady Phoebe appeared in the doorway. "Eva, I need to speak with you." She stopped short and glanced from Eva to Nick and back. "I'm sorry. I didn't realize you weren't alone."

Both Eva and Nick came to their feet. Eva said, "What can I do for you, my lady?"

"It's about . . ." She glanced over at Nick.

"I'll leave the two of you alone." He started for the door, and Phoebe moved aside to let him pass.

"Nick, wait one moment." Eva held out a hand, gesturing for him to remain, then spoke to Phoebe. "If it's about the matter we've been looking into, I believe Mr. Hensley might be of service to us. At least, he has as much reason as anyone to wish justice done in this matter."

"Lord Allerton was my employer, Lady Phoebe," he said with a deferential bob of his head. "I accompanied him into the trenches of France as well. Frankly, I don't know if your footman is guilty or not, but either way, I don't believe enough evidence has been gathered. I wish to help."

Phoebe's assessing glance roamed up and down Nick's length not once, but twice. She nodded, and glanced back out into the hallway, where Douglas and Connie were busily carrying empty platters and dirty dishes from the back stairs to the scullery. She said quickly, "A third pair of eyes might be useful. Will you two please dress warmly and meet me in the garden in a few minutes?"

"What do you think this is about?" Nick asked once Phoebe left them.

"It must be about the footprints Lord Allerton left the morning he disappeared. There is nothing else out there that could be connected to the case. Though with last night's snowfall, I can't imagine what could have been revealed that we haven't seen already."

She was soon to revise that opinion. She and Phoebe went out the library doors as usual, while Nick exited through the service courtyard and made his way along the perimeter of the garden past the fountain. Eva understood. For Phoebe to have invited a visiting valet out for a walk would be seen as exceedingly odd, not to mention inappropriate, by the family. But by the time he joined them beyond the footbridge, they were far enough away that anyone happening to look out would probably not even notice the trio out walking together, or if they did it would appear as nothing more than happenstance.

At the sound of the snow-laden branches creaking with the breeze, Eva shivered and tried to hunker deeper into her coat. "What is this about, my lady?"

"I'm sorry to bring you out into the cold," she replied. Her lips curled in a cunning smile. "Haven't you noticed? Mr. Hensley, you were too far away until now, but, Eva, haven't you looked down at all?"

Eva did look down, scanning the snow at their feet. "I only see a new accumulation of snow, my lady, which has all but filled in the footprints."

"All *but*," Phoebe repeated. "Come closer."

She crouched and gestured for them to do the same. Nick flashed Eva a curious look and then they did Phoebe's bidding, Eva beside her and Nick a respectful few feet away.

"Well? Do you see now?"

"I'm not sure what I'm looking for, my lady."

Before Eva had quite completed the statement, Nick spoke in a voice devoid of inflection. "They're not the same. One set leading away from the house is . . ."

"More labored, as if someone had difficulty walking out, but somehow lightened their burden for the trip back." Phoebe sat back on her heels, tucking her burgundy wool skirt around her legs. "It's a very subtle difference, and I only noticed it today because the new snow filled each set of prints in differently. See how the outgoing prints are farther apart and heavier, as if each step cost an effort? On the trip back, the steps are closer together, implying a faster gait. It's almost as if two men of slightly different builds made each set."

Eva considered this, her gaze following both trails to the edge of the wood. "You mean one man walked out and another walked in?"

"Or one man walked out carrying a bundle and returned lighter," Phoebe corrected her.

"But returned from where?" Nick stood and continued trekking toward the treeline. Eva helped Phoebe to her feet and they followed. Once they passed through the birch copse, Nick thrust aside evergreen branches, releasing a powdery shower of snow. "The trail goes cold here at the edge of the forest."

"I don't believe it does." Phoebe gave her skirts a shake

to dislodge the snow from her hems. "Just because a trail isn't obvious doesn't mean there isn't one."

"So what do you suggest, my lady? Hounds?"

"No, Mr. Hensley, I'm afraid we no longer have hounds on hand. The last of the ones that didn't go to war died over a year ago and my grandfather hasn't had the heart to bring any new dogs onto the estate. Hunting was something he and my father used to do together, you see." She paused, and a gust of wind rattled through the trees to echo the hollow sadness Eva felt on her mistress's behalf. As quickly as the wind dropped, however, Phoebe seemed to recover from the memory. "I do believe that on closer inspection, we might be able to detect minute signs of a trek through the woods. Crushed undergrowth, broken branches, and the like."

The possibility seemed doubtful to Eva, until she remembered something. "Nick, you were once a gamekeeper's assistant, right here at Foxwood. In fact, wasn't it your job to see to the hounds? Perhaps you remember a few tracking techniques."

"That was a long time ago." He looked uncomfortable and slightly embarrassed. "But I suppose it's worth a try."

"Wait a moment." Phoebe crossed the treeline into the frigid shadows and went still.

Eva hurried to her. "My lady? What is it?"

"Gamekeepers, hounds . . ." She whirled about to face Eva and Nick. "Constable Brannock and his men will never find him in the house, because he isn't there. We need to check the gamekeeper's cottage."

Eva's stomach sank at the thought of trekking through the woods for such a distance in this weather. "But didn't Constable Brannock say his men already searched there?"

"Yes, he did." Phoebe raised her chin in defiance. "But *if* he was telling the truth rather than merely attempting to placate me, they obviously must have missed something. It only makes sense. The gamekeeper's cottage is the only building on the estate no one ever uses. Where better to hide a body?"

Phoebe led the way at a brisk stride, or as brisk as icy, rutted ground, tangled brambles, and sharp rocks would allow. She heard Eva and Mr. Hensley thrashing through the dormant vegetation behind her, but she didn't slow down for them. Her lungs felt as if frosty daggers stabbed at them by the time she broke through into the well-manicured clearing of the stable yard. Here, beyond the shelter of the forest, snow once again blanketed the ground in fresh drifts. A hodgepodge of human and horse tracks littered the way between the stable doors and the closest paddock, where the remaining groom exercised Grams's carriage team and Amelia's sweet, aging Blossom daily.

Several buildings inhabited the clearing, slate-roofed and constructed of creamy Cotswolds stone. Phoebe entered the main stable and welcomed its relative warmth. A moment later, Eva and Mr. Hensley stepped into the building behind her.

Though far less pungent than in the old days when the stalls were fully inhabited, the odors of horse and hay still had the same steadying effect on her now as then. As if she entered another world where war and strife and sadness simply didn't exist. How she had loved spending hours here, feeding, brushing, even mucking—when Grams wasn't about. And then mounting Stormy and flying round the paddock and, again when Grams wasn't about, along the riding lanes that wove through the forest.

"My lady, surely you don't believe Lord Allerton is somewhere here?"

She started at the sound of Eva's voice. Quickly she wiped a coat sleeve across her eyes before the others could glimpse the moisture that had gathered there. "No, but it doesn't hurt to ask if Trevor saw or heard anything that night." She called out the groom's name. "Are you here?"

"I am, my lady." Once only a groom's assistant, Trevor Reeve, the new head groom, walked out from the office adjoined to the tack room. Like so many of the others remaining on the estate, Trevor was young, no more than eighteen, Phoebe guessed. Before the war he had been a shy, pale boy, rail thin, who always seemed much more at home with the animals than people. Though he had filled out to a man's proportions, that last hadn't changed, and he removed his cap and held it awkwardly in his hands. "Would you like the carriage?"

"No, nothing like that, Trevor." Phoebe walked down the center aisle to him, pausing to stroke Blossom's nose along the way. "I'm wondering if you noticed anything unusual yesterday morning."

"Something related to Lord Allerton's disappearance, my lady?"

Shy perhaps, but not unobservant. "Yes. Could someone have passed through here that morning or the night before? Do you lock up each night?"

"All doors are always locked at night, my lady. The one you entered through, the outside door to the office, and the big ones that open onto the main drive." He used his hat to point to the opposite end of the building. The horses were led out to be exercised through the doors through which Phoebe had entered. The other set of doors led out to the expansive, cobbled courtyard where, in the old days, motorcars and carriages would deliver the family and their guests for the great hunting parties held each autumn. Phoebe could almost hear the rumble of engines, the clopping of hooves, and the hurrying feet of the footmen as they served refreshments before everyone mounted up and the eager hounds were loosed. She wondered, would Foxwood see such happy activity again? Or had those old traditions died along with so many others during the war?

"My lady?" Eva touched her arm and Phoebe jumped.

"I was remembering . . ." She smiled weakly. "Never mind. So you say the doors are always kept locked at night, Trevor?"

"Indeed, my lady, I explained to the police—"

"So they've been here, then?"

"They were here with their search party," Trevor told her. "They turned the place upside down early this morning, but found nothing."

She thanked Trevor and led the way through the building and out the main doors. The courtyard showed signs of footprints and motorcar tracks beneath last night's fresh fall of snow. The search party, of course. If anyone else had come through here, all signs of the direction he might have taken had been obliterated. Phoebe started down the tree-lined lane that connected the stables and gamekeeper's cottage to the main house.

Eva and Mr. Hensley followed in her wake, and she could sense both their curiosity and their doubts. Where the lane forked, she followed partially obscured footprints and once again entered the woods. They walked for several minutes, picking their way over branches and rocks strewn across the once-wide and manicured path. It struck Phoebe how quickly nature had taken over this once frequently traveled route. Another couple of years and there might be no path left at all.

The cottage stood in a small clearing framed by a thick growth of trees. The branches were no longer tidily trimmed as they had been previously, and hung over the cottage in places and even scraped the roof. The place lay eerily silent except for the light screeching of wood against slate, reminding Phoebe of the ghost stories Grampapa used to tell her and Julia when they were young, before death had stolen their mother away. After that no one told ghost stories at Foxwood Hall.

She examined the clearing. Low mounds of snow tufted the ground and showed signs of a recent trampling. "Well, it does appear as if Mr. Brannock's search party has been here. Still, let's have a look inside," she said, and turned around to realize she had been talking to herself. Eva and Mr. Hensley hadn't caught up to her yet.

The cottage comprised small living quarters for the gamekeeper and an equipment room, each with their own entrance but connected from inside. It was to the latter she headed first. She strode to the oak door and tugged. The latch jiggled but held stubbornly in its locked position.

"Oh, hang it." She kicked lightly at the door. "I should have thought to ask Mr. Giles for the keys." She had never thought much about locked doors in the old days. The servants had always known the family's plans ahead of time and made all the necessary preparations.

How naïve—and oblivious—she and the family had been then.

She turned and this time saw Eva and Mr. Hensley negotiating the last bit of trail. She hadn't realized she had walked so fast and felt a little pang of guilt as the other two trod none too quietly through the brush and into the clearing. Eva panted from the exertion and Mr. Hensley appeared to be favoring his right leg.

"Are you all right, Mr. Hensley?"

"Yes, fine, my lady."

"Nick, I didn't realize you'd hurt yourself," Eva exclaimed. "Why didn't you say something?"

"I'm fine, Evie. What ails my leg happened a while back."

"Oh." Eva appeared to understand his meaning. "The war . . ."

"It rarely pains me anymore. But the cold combined with the walk . . ."

"I'm so sorry," Phoebe was quick to say.

He nodded and, apparently dismissing the subject, joined her at the shed door.

"It's locked," she told him, resisting the urge to deliver another, harder kick to the solid panels. She would only succeed in bruising a toe. "I'm sorry I dragged you both all the way out here for no good reason."

"Well, as long as we're here . . ." Mr. Hensley gave the door a tug as she had, though much more forcefully. Upon receiving the same result, he studied the lock, then looked about him. "You say no one ever uses the cottage anymore?"

"That's right," Phoebe replied.

Mr. Hensley nodded. "We need a sturdy rock."

Eva returned to the edge of the woods and toed the snowy ground with her boot. Then she stooped. "How is this?" With both hands she hefted a rough stone about the size of a wood used in lawn bowls.

Mr. Hensley smiled as he took the rock from her. He hit the latch once, again, and a third time. Clanging filled the air and made Phoebe cringe. She was glad they were far enough away from the house that no one would hear them.

On his fifth try, Mr. Hensley was rewarded with the crack of metal breaking; a piece of the latch thudded to the ground. Phoebe clapped her gloved hands. "You did it, Mr. Hensley."

"I can only hope I won't be apprehended for breaking and entering," he said wryly.

"You won't. Now . . ." Phoebe pushed and the door creaked open several inches. A waft of musty abandonment poured out from the murkiness within, making her nose tingle and her throat itch. "That's dreadful. They *can't* have been in here long."

"Who can't have?" Eva asked.

"The search party. If they had conducted a thorough search, the place would have aired out, at least somewhat." She thought of the inadequate search the inspector conducted of Henry's bedroom. "They must have been in and out in a matter of moments. And they could easily have missed something." She drew a breath. "Let's go in."

Eva stepped up beside her. "Would you like me to go first?"

"No, I should go first," Mr. Hensley offered.

"This was my idea, and I dragged you both out here." Phoebe stepped boldly across the threshold into the nearly black storeroom. "We'll need to open the curtains."

CHAPTER 11

Dust clouds billowed when Eva parted the heavy burlap curtains on the room's two windows. Light struggled to penetrate the panes, begrimed inside and out from years of neglect. She coughed and fanned at the air. "That doesn't light the room much, does it?"

"Enough to serve our purposes." Phoebe stood before a long glass-fronted case mounted to one wall. "The rifles have all been moved up to the house, along with anything of value that was out here. But as for the rest . . ." She sniffed the air. "It's horribly dank in here."

"Yes, but not putrid, my lady." Eva refrained from explaining further, but Phoebe's tightened features indicated she understood the reference to a decaying body.

"No, you're right about that," she said. "Still, we should look about. After all, the freezing temperatures would forestall the . . . the rotting of the . . ."

Corpse. Eva cringed. *Good heavens.*

One half of the room contained crates piled high and pushed up against the wall, stacked folding chairs, and a dusty mound of folded blankets. "There's nowhere on this side a body might be concealed," Eva said. "The crates are all too small."

"Not unless . . ." Phoebe's lips flattened. "Unless our culprit didn't stop at Lord Allerton's fingers, if you catch my meaning."

For all their euphemisms, there seemed no avoiding being distastefully blunt. But then, there was nothing gentile about what happened to Lord Allerton. With a hand pressed to her stomach, partly due to a vague queasiness and partly in a futile effort to shield herself, Eva approached the array of storage containers. She squinted to make out details and leaned down closer to examine surfaces. "No fingerprints in the dust," she announced with relief. "Nothing here looks as though it were disturbed in years, neither by the inspector's men nor by the killer."

They scanned the rest of the room. Several cages of various sizes occupied a corner. Eva knew these had been used by the gamekeeper, part of whose job it was to release the quarry in the desired area so the earl and guests might enjoy their day of riding, picnicking, and the triumphant climax of watching the hounds corner a poor, beleaguered fox against a tree or outcropping. Eva shuddered at the image that conjured.

"Are you all right? Cold?" Nick began unbuttoning his woolen overcoat.

Eva stopped him with a hand over his, imagining she could feel the warmth of his skin through their gloves. "No, it isn't that. This may seem silly coming from a farmer's daughter, especially when that farmer raises cattle for the local butchers, but anything to do with hunting always makes me sad . . . and a little angry, I'm afraid."

"I agree." Phoebe crouched beside a trunk on the less cluttered side of the room. "I loved the riding and being outdoors, but I always returned home before the others closed in for their pretend kill. At least they ultimately spared the creatures' lives. They only terrified them, the poor dears. Of course mallards and geese were another matter." She fingered the trunk's clasp. "This doesn't appear to be locked."

"Allow me to help you with that, my lady." Nick crossed the room to her but hesitated before lifting the lid. "Please go stand with Eva, my lady. Just in case."

She looked about to argue, but instead nodded and moved away. She reached for Eva's hand, and even as Eva sucked in a breath she felt Phoebe stiffen and do the same. The lid whined in protest.

"Nothing," Nick said with obvious relief. "Looks like . . ." He peered in closer, squinting as Eva had done in the pale light. "Extra tack. Even a few horseshoes."

"Supplies were kept here in case anyone threw a shoe or the like during the hunt." Phoebe next turned to a cupboard in the rear corner. Once again, Nick preceded her and reached for the latch. As before, he hesitated, then stood so his back would block the contents from Eva's and Phoebe's view.

Another disagreeable odor filled the air, dank and moldy. But Eva detected no hint of rotting flesh. Neither did Phoebe, apparently.

"I'm beginning to believe I was quite wrong about this," she said.

"Are you disappointed, my lady?"

"In a way, yes. Lord Allerton must be found, and given everything we've learned so far, this seemed the most likely place to hide a . . . body. I was just so convinced the authorities missed . . . I don't know . . . something . . ."

"Let's keep searching." Nick headed for the only other door. "Another cupboard, or does this lead into the living quarters?"

"Yes, that would be the kitchen." Phoebe went past him

and turned the door handle. The door stuck, and she gave it a shove that sent it swinging open to bang against the inside wall. Eva jumped at the sound, then peered into a smaller room fitted out with a fireplace, a coal stove, an old-fashioned sink with a water pump, and cupboards ranged above the work counter.

Nick followed her in and began opening cupboard doors. Remembering Phoebe's comment about the assailant perhaps having not stopped with merely severing Lord Allerton's fingers, Eva found herself holding her breath again with each creaking door that opened.

"Nothing but dust and mold," Phoebe griped minutes later. They had gone through the third room that had served as both parlor and bedroom for the gamekeeper.

"I suppose there's nothing left but to go." Eva started toward the door through which they had originally entered, but stopped when she realized Lady Phoebe hadn't moved to follow. Instead she stood staring up at the ceiling, an odd expression on her face. "My lady?"

"We need a ladder," she said, still gazing upward. Eva followed her line of sight and gasped.

"The attic!"

"Indeed." Lady Phoebe finally dragged her gaze away from the square trapdoor cut into the ceiling. "We'll need a ladder. . . ."

"Hang a ladder." Quickly Nick grabbed the nearest crate and set it on the floor directly beneath the trapdoor. As he reached for another, both Eva and Phoebe each bent to lift two more. Soon they had fashioned a makeshift ladder. "I'll go up."

"Do be careful, Mr. Hensley." Phoebe stood watching with hands clasped, her brow furrowed. "I know this is it. I *know* it is."

Eva moved to hold the crates steady as Nick climbed until he was able to press his palms against the trapdoor. It gave easily enough, and he slid it to one side of the attic floor before maneuvering himself higher, until his head and shoulders disappeared through the opening.

"What do you see?" Phoebe bounced on the balls of her feet.

With one hand fisted against her mouth, Eva watched with rather more apprehension, not at all certain she wished to know what sight might be confronting Nick at this very moment. The seconds seemed to drag on unendurably. . . .

"It's quite dark. . . ." His voice emerged from above, echoing hollowly against the rafters. "But . . ." He pulled himself higher, until only his legs dangled into the storage room. Finally, he said, "There is nothing up here, my lady. Nothing at all."

"But . . ." Phoebe seemed to lose inches from her stature. "I was so sure . . ."

Eva put an arm across her shoulders. "Come, my lady, let's start back. It was a good hunch, and if nothing else we did rule out the cottage altogether. Now we need never wonder if Inspector Perkins might have missed something."

Phoebe allowed Eva to guide her back outside. She kept her eyes on the ground and continually shook her head with a baffled expression. "It doesn't make sense. The footprints leaving the house *are* deeper than those returning, and I believe that to be significant to Lord Allerton's disappearance."

"It may yet prove significant, my lady." Nick gazed off through the trees as they returned to the trail. "Perhaps he's lying somewhere in the woods."

"If that's the case," Eva said, "it could take weeks or even months to find him."

"Unless the inspector were to expand his search party and—"

Eva stiffened at the sound that cut Phoebe's words

short. It was a snap unlike that of the trees bending to the weight of the snow or protesting the push of the wind. More like underbrush being stepped upon. An animal? She hoped so. Nick tensed, his face raised. His eyes glittered in concentration. Phoebe inched closer to Eva and slipped a hand into hers.

They listened another several moments, but the sound didn't come again.

"Did we imagine it?" Phoebe whispered.

"We must have. Or it was a deer, perhaps." But Eva's heart hadn't stopped its staccato rhythm.

Nick remained unmoving and cast wary glances into the shadows beneath the trees. "Let's get back."

"Yes, let's." Phoebe released Eva's hand. Her stride lengthened, taking her several paces ahead of Eva and Nick. Where a fallen branch blocked the path, Phoebe stepped nimbly over it. Nick offered his arm to assist Eva over.

He did not release her once they safely reached the other side. Instead he placed his hand over her own where it rested in the crook of his elbow. Eva found herself smiling. Even through their gloves, she liked the sensation of her hand nestled beneath Nick's larger, sturdier one.

Phoebe stood with her ear to her bedroom door, listening. Her room lay in darkness but for a thin band of moonlight falling through a gap in the curtains. The silence from the corridor persuaded her to turn the knob and soundlessly open the door. She stepped lightly onto the hall runner and paused, again pricking her ears. Only the steady tick of the grandfather clock echoing from the Great Hall disturbed the midnight hush. She set her feet in motion, finding her way by memory in the gloom.

Even through the rug and her slippers, the marble floors breathed their chill into her feet. She hugged her wrapper tighter about her as she reached the gallery, bathed in moonlight shining through the clerestory windows high above the front doors. Rather than comforting, the glare made her feel exposed and she hurried across, passing the open door of the darkened billiard room and seeking the guest wing of the house. Once there, she counted off the doors and slowed as she came to the bedroom Henry had inhabited.

She listened again for signs that anyone might be awake, and scanned beneath each nearby door for telltale signs of lamplight inside. By all appearances their guests were deep in slumber. Still, one never knew and she dared not take too long in her errand. Would she find the evidence Henry had claimed to hold over Julia? Or better still, would she discover proof of Henry's manipulation of war bonds? Victory Bonds, England had called them, yet these particular ones sounded as if they had brought victory to no one—not those who had invested their savings in "the cause," and certainly not Henry, wherever he lay.

She would have liked to conduct this search sooner, but with the inspector's men constantly underfoot she'd had no choice but to wait for her opportunity. Had Julia already been here?

She and Theo had acknowledged a need to destroy evidence. Yet it wasn't Julia's style to go snooping about. Instead, she tended to keep her nose in the air and ignore situations until they erupted in front of her, whereupon she relied on her considerable skills to talk her way out of any difficulty. She could envision Julia doing just that no matter what evidence ultimately surfaced. Beyond a doubt, whatever it was, she would have Grampapa believing the exact opposite of the truth before the day was out.

Phoebe steeled herself before wrapping both hands around the doorknob. With the utmost care not to make a sound, she turned the knob and paused again before pushing inward. Despite her bravado in the forest today, snooping came no more easily to her than to Julia, though perhaps for different reasons.

Holding her breath, she opened the door, then instantly pulled it closed again but for an inch. A gasp pushed its way to her lips, but she found the presence of mind to clamp them shut. Across Henry's room, in a small circle of light cast by a kerosene lantern, Lord Owen sat at the desk with his back to her. She recognized him by his height, the lines of his shoulders, his tapering torso clothed only in a shirt and waistcoat. Just beyond his elbow angled the lid of what appeared to be a travel desk, Henry's no doubt, open upon its hinges. The sound of fluttering pages sifted through the air. Even if she hadn't recognized Lord Owen by sight, she would have known him by how nimbly he rifled through whatever items inhabited the portable desk. Theo, with his debilitated hands, could not have pored through so quickly and quietly.

She started to back away, but the fluttering abruptly stopped. Lord Owen held something up to the light. Phoebe strained her eyes to see, but Owen's shoulder blocked whatever it was. His chin turned until the light gilded his strong profile. She tensed, inched backward, but then he turned his head back to his task. He slid whatever he held into his waistcoat. Her curiosity burgeoned, but with no options available other than to reveal herself, she started to back away. Suddenly something on the floor winked a glimmer of light into her eye.

Acting on instinct, she crouched, widened the door, and slipped her arm through the gap. Her fingers closed tight around a tiny object. Her heart thundering in her ears, she pulled her arm back through, scooted backward, and used the wainscoting beside her to pull to her feet.

Dare she close the door again? Her instincts told her no, at least not all the way. He might hear the click. Better to retreat at once and let Lord Owen believe what he will. As long as he didn't see her. But what was he doing there, and what had he found?

And what had *she* found?

Turning, she raced on tiptoe back down the corridor, only to nearly barrel straight into Julia, who appeared before her like a ghost in a fluttering cloud of pale nightgown and wrapper.

"Oh!"

"Gracious!"

"Shhhh!" Phoebe snatched her sister's hand and pulled her along as she darted across the gallery. Julia tugged, tried to dig in her heels, but Phoebe kept on, determined to drag Julia if she must. They reached Julia's room and with a firm grip still on her hand, Phoebe dodged inside and shut the door behind them.

Once released, Julia stood with her arms folded and her eyes a dark glitter against her translucent skin. "What in heaven's name was that about?"

"I could ask you the same. You were headed to Henry's room, weren't you?"

"Perhaps. Perhaps not. What were *you* doing in that part of the house?"

"Oh, Julia, what else could you have been intending?" Phoebe blew out a breath and stepped up onto the platform that held Julia's four-poster. She perched on the edge. A sigh drained a portion of the tension from her limbs. "*I* was about to slip into Henry's room. He has yet to be found, and we have yet to discover any reason why someone would wish to harm him. And no, I refuse to believe Vernon is guilty, or if he is," she quickly added when Julia's lips parted, "I don't believe the authorities have sufficient evidence to prove it. A man's life must not hinge on such flimsy reasoning. But as far as that goes, Inspector

Perkins has treated the entire matter with kid gloves. It's far easier to accuse a servant than find fault in a nobleman."

"That nobleman being Henry?"

"Among others. You yourself enlightened me to Henry's double-dealings." Phoebe raised an eyebrow in challenge. "It follows that whoever is responsible for his disappearance is somehow connected to those double-dealings."

Julia's chin rose to a haughty angle, as if she found the entire matter amusing. "And so did you discover anything useful?"

Phoebe opened her hand. She hadn't had time to identify the item plucked from Henry's floor. A dark glimmer winked from the center of her palm.

Julia gasped. "Is that blood?"

Phoebe shook her head. "No, it appears to be one of Henry's shirt studs." She met her sister's gaze. "The ones he was wearing Christmas night. Do you suppose he lost it in a struggle?"

Julia dismissed the notion with a wave. "Henry wasn't the tidiest of men. He probably merely dropped it while removing his shirt. What else did you find?"

"Nothing. I never actually went inside."

"Why ever not? Lose your nerve, did you? I never thought you had it in you to be cunning."

"As you are cunning, Julia?" Phoebe closed her fist around the garnet stud. Julia was probably correct, but even if Henry had lost it in a struggle, the stud brought her no closer to identifying the assailant. "Never mind, you needn't answer that. You're probably right, except in this case I didn't lose my nerve. I lost my opportunity. Someone beat me to it."

Julia's golden eyebrows pulled inward, and she stepped up to sit beside Phoebe on the bed. "Who?"

She hesitated. How much did she wish to confide in her

sister? The memory of how quickly Lord Owen had left Phoebe's side in the morning room to join Julia—to kiss her hand—sparked an ember of envy, but of caution as well. Just how chummy were they? Would Julia run to Lord Owen the moment Phoebe left her?

"Come now, Phoebe, you know what's at stake for me."

"Do I?" She studied Julia's even features, the perfect bow of her lips, the smooth slant of her nose. In the pale nightgown and matching robe, and with her hair hanging in a gleaming flaxen braid over one shoulder, she seemed much younger, even fragile, a mere wraith beneath the steely mask she showed the world. Only her eyes belied that image, with their depths of knowledge and guile and pride. "You've told me precious little," Phoebe said. "Perhaps if you were more forthcoming I'd know if I could trust you. You obviously don't trust me."

Julia sprang up from the bed. "I've had quite enough games for one night. You should go."

"Julia, sit down." Phoebe made a snap decision based on very little besides the realization that revealing the identity of the man who presently occupied Henry's room might produce an enlightening reaction.

Julia returned to sit beside her, though with obvious reluctance. "Well?"

"I discovered Lord Owen in Henry's room just now, going through his desk."

"Lord Owen?" Julia blinked, shook her head, and wrinkled her nose. Though an accomplished actress when she wished to be, she seemed nonetheless genuinely taken aback. "How odd. Very odd, indeed."

"Has he said anything about Henry to you?"

"No, nothing other than to express sympathy for Henry's likely fate." She stared into the dim outlines of the room's furnishings, hand-painted and painstakingly carved in Italy. "Lord Owen . . . hmm. This is puzzling. He's always been such a gentleman. Not like Henry at all. And with his war service, he certainly doesn't seem like a man who would . . ."

"Destroy a woman's reputation?" Julia looked alarmed, but Phoebe went on. "How much do we really know about him? He might be trying to help, looking for something to link Henry to whoever attacked him."

"What if he's looking for evidence that ties himself to Henry?"

"Such as Henry's scheme with the war bonds?" Yes, that had certainly occurred to Phoebe. What *had* he slid into his waistcoat?

Julia nodded slowly. "What if Lord Owen is responsible for what happened to Henry?"

CHAPTER 12

Eva rose earlier than usual Sunday morning and hurried below stairs to see how she could help with the morning chores. The family had decided against going to church in the village, and that left her with more time to offer her assistance to the other staff. Upon reaching the servants' corridor, however, she stepped into a maelstrom of anger.

"Where is that girl?" Mrs. Sanders gripped Connie's bucket of cleaning tools in one hand, while with the other she batted a feather duster at the air. Tiny particles flitted about her head like gnats on a humid summer's day.

Eva hurried down the remaining stairs. "Mrs. Sanders, is Connie missing?"

"Missing? Sleeping is more like it, the lazy hussy."

"Mrs. Sanders—"

"The table isn't set in the servants' hall, the linens are still stacked where the laundress left them, and the hot-water heaters haven't been turned on anywhere in the house. I just sent Dora up to drag the girl out of bed by her ankles. As if we can spare anyone down here for even a minute." Mrs. Sanders stalked to the stairs and plunked the pail on the bottom step. She thrust the duster in and gave the pail a kick with the toe of her lace-up boot for good measure.

"I'll lay the table." Eva made short work of the task, throwing on a cloth and not worrying overly much about how neatly she placed the napkins and silverware.

"Let me help you with that." Nick entered with a spring in his step and began straightening Eva's haphazard place settings. He whistled a few notes of "Keep the Home Fires Burning."

"You seem cheerful this morning."

"I am, Evie." He straightened and beamed at her. "Lord Owen called for me last night. He's offered me temporary employment as his valet. His own died in France, you know, of the influenza."

"No, I didn't know."

"Yes, well, if things work out, the position could become permanent. My troubles could be over."

"I'm so glad. But . . . there's a bit of a problem below stairs this morning. Would you mind finishing up in here— I hate to ask it of you—"

"Say no more, Evie." He circled the table and crouched to stoke the fire in the hearth.

Eva hurried down the corridor to the service entrance, to the row of pegs holding the servants' winter cloaks. One peg poked nakedly out from the wall, creating a gap in the draping wool garments. Someone had gone outside. A hunch had her reaching for the next convenient cloak, which she swung around her shoulders on her way out the door.

"Connie?" She spoke in a stage whisper, hoping her voice wouldn't carry into the house. She went to the delivery gates, but the lane to the main road appeared deserted as well. There was no telling for certain which way the girl might have gone, for too many comings and goings earlier had churned the snow to an icy, nondescript slush.

At the snippet of a giggle she whirled about and crossed

the courtyard to the garden gate. She peered down the dormant rows of the kitchen garden and caught a flash of movement over near the greenhouses. She set off at a brisk stride around the garden. More giggles, louder now, drew her along.

She reached the rear of the first glass-encased structure, fogged by the heaters blazing inside. She leaned as far as she dared around the corner, to see without being seen. There was Connie, near the greenhouse entrance, cradling a basket in her arms, and a bevy of children surrounding her, each holding out hands garbed in ragged mittens. Into each Connie placed a bundle, whereupon the child would either curtsy or bow and with a delighted giggle secret the bundle inside a coat Eva deemed far too thin. Connie repeated the little ritual with more than a half-dozen children that she could count, and she wondered how many had already wandered off back home.

Soon the basket was empty and the last of the children gone, having trotted off through the woods, presumably down to the main road. Connie stood watching a moment longer. Then, with a wistful smile, she swung the basket in one hand and started in Eva's direction.

Eva stepped out from her hiding place, and Connie jerked to stillness, her features frozen in alarm.

"I saw," Eva said simply.

Connie slowly closed the distance between them. She wore the missing cloak. A scarf covered her head and was tied beneath her chin. "And . . . you'll tell?"

"I don't see that we have much choice. Have you any idea of the time? Mrs. Sanders is on a rampage searching for you."

"I hadn't realized . . . I thought I had time to get back inside before anyone came down."

"Connie, have you forgotten everyone is rising earlier because we're shorthanded?"

"I . . . I guess I didn't think of that. Can't we say . . ." She trailed off, staring down into her empty basket. "I'll be sacked. Again."

"You were sacked from your last position?"

Connie nodded, loose hairs falling in her face.

"For the same infraction?"

Another nod.

"What was in those bundles? I'm assuming food, but from where?"

Her head came up, her eyes glazed with self-righteousness. "I didn't steal it! It was leftover and would have been tossed in the bins."

"Leftovers from above stairs?"

The maid retreated beneath those loose tendrils and tucked her chin into her scarf. She nodded again.

"Connie, why didn't you simply ask? I'm sure Mrs. Ellison and Mrs. Sanders would have been agreeable. You're feeding children, after all."

"But what if they weren't agreeable? They weren't at the last house I served in. They said it wasn't their business to feed every ragtag child who came begging. So I did it anyway. I took a chance." A sob entered her voice. "I had to, Miss Huntford. I know what it's like to be hungry."

Eva's eyes misted and she blinked to clear them. It was no use becoming emotional; she had to find a way to avoid Connie being sacked. Would Mrs. Sanders understand? If only they could get inside the greenhouse, they might fill Connie's basket with the herbs Mrs. Ellison needed and claim Connie had only been trying to help. Dora usually came out for that, but only when Mrs. Ellison sent her with the key. The doors would be locked now.

"Come on, Connie. We'll face Mrs. Sanders and Mrs. Ellison together."

Connie dropped her head again and started walking, a slow, dragging stride as if she were a condemned criminal being led to the gallows. "It's not my first brush with trouble, Miss Huntford. I'll be sacked for sure this time."

Eva's first thought was to ask Connie why, all things considered, she would take such a risk. But as Connie said, she knew what it was to be hungry, and Eva's heart went out to her. And then a thought came to her. It was due to Lady Phoebe that Connie had been spared dismissal when her romance with Vernon came to light. Could Phoebe work her magic again?

The three women occupying Mrs. Sanders's office jumped up from their seats as Phoebe entered. She wished to tell them to sit, but she knew Mrs. Sanders would have none of it until she herself was seated. Mrs. Sanders stood before her desk chair. Two chairs from the servants' hall appeared to have been brought in for Eva and Connie, while Mrs. Sanders's overstuffed chair seemed to have been reserved to Phoebe. She wasted no time in crossing the room to it.

Still, the others remained standing, Mrs. Sanders with her hands clasped at her waist and a pained expression drawing her aging features tight. Connie's shoulders shook with her visible effort to stem the tide of tears and muffle her sniffles. Eva alone faced Phoebe with a modicum of confidence that Phoebe hoped not to disappoint.

"My lady," Mrs. Sanders began in the gravest of tones, "I do hope you can forgive this interruption of your morning. As you know I abhor bothering the family with staff trivialities, but Miss Huntford insisted." Nostrils flared, she tossed a recriminating glance at Eva.

"She was quite right, Mrs. Sanders," Phoebe was quick to say. "I do appreciate being included. Now, then, from what I already understand, Connie has been taking leftovers and doling them out to some of our more unfortunate children here in Little Barlow."

"Indeed, she has, Lady Phoebe, quite without permission. I apologize for not having caught her in her pilfering sooner."

"Pilfering, Mrs. Sanders?" Phoebe crossed one leg over the other beneath her skirts, a habit Grams termed unladylike but which Phoebe seemed unable to break. Leaning forward in her chair, she said, "Please, all of you, sit down and let us discuss this."

Mrs. Sanders's frown deepened, especially as she regarded Connie lowering herself into the hard-backed dining chair. No doubt in the housekeeper's view, the accused should remain standing while the evidence was reviewed.

"Now, then, my question to you, Mrs. Sanders, is what is usually done with the leftovers from the family meals?"

The woman seemed taken aback by the question, as if Phoebe was accusing her in turn. "As my lady very well knows, the edible leftovers are sent each week to St. Margaret's Workhouse for Indigent Women."

"And the inedible leftovers?" Phoebe caught Eva's twitch of a smile.

"Why, they are thrown out, of course. What else would we do with them, my lady?"

"And in your opinion, Mrs. Sanders, what constitutes edible and inedible leftovers?" This Phoebe asked gently. Mrs. Sanders had served her family almost as long as Mr. Giles. She took great pride in her work and put all her energy into it. Phoebe had no desire to belittle her efforts.

"Anything left on the serving trays is edible, my lady." Mrs. Sanders sent a puzzled glance at each of them in turn, even Connie.

Phoebe turned to Connie. "What do *you* consider edible leftovers?"

"Oh, I . . ." She pulled herself up taller and fidgeted with a fold in her skirt. Her bottom lip disappeared for a moment between her teeth, and Phoebe saw the hint of new tears forming.

Thankfully, Eva leaned across the space between them and patted her hand. "Go ahead, dear. It's all right."

"Edible is anything not eaten, my lady," she said in a whisper so low that Phoebe, too, found herself leaning closer to hear her.

"But that's ridiculous!" Mrs. Sanders came to her feet. "I don't believe you were handing out half-eaten food. Who would deign to eat it?"

"It's better than starving, ma'am." Connie's voice picked up volume and, along with it, a note of defiance Phoebe couldn't help but applaud.

"You've been stealing from the larder, haven't you?"

"Mrs. Sanders," Phoebe said calmly, "please sit down. Now, Connie, are we to understand you've been scraping plates to feed these children?"

"M-mostly, my lady."

"Mostly," Mrs. Sanders repeated with emphasis. "Then what about the rest?"

"I save some of my own share of the meals for them."

Mrs. Sanders's scowl proclaimed her less than convinced, but Phoebe stood, prompting the others to surge to their feet again as well. "There, then. No harm done. What Connie has been doing doesn't hurt anyone, and in fact helps some of our local families. Mrs. Sanders, I shall clear it with my grandparents, but I'd like you to plan on setting food aside for the children, especially during these winter months when the fields lay dormant. Meanwhile, Connie stays on, but"—she broke off and moved to stand directly before the maid—"no more secrets. No more actions on the sly, no matter how well intended. Is that very clear?"

"Very, my lady. Th-thank you, my lady. I cannot say it enough."

"Once is sufficient." Phoebe smiled. "Now that that's settled, I'll let you all get back to work." But as the others filed to the door, she remembered something Eva had told her, something Connie had let slip out by the greenhouse. "Connie, one more moment, please. Mrs. Sanders, do you mind if Connie and I stay behind here?"

The woman's curiosity was glaringly apparent, but she merely said, "Of course not, my lady."

Phoebe closed the door behind them and turned to face the girl, her face red and swollen from crying. "Do sit down again, Connie."

Connie visibly tensed. She sat rod straight, hands clasped tightly.

Phoebe took the seat Eva had vacated, rather than return to Mrs. Sanders's overstuffed chair. "Connie, this isn't the first time you've faced this sort of thing, is it? Your last position . . . Were you sacked?"

"Did Miss Huntford . . . ?"

"Yes, Miss Huntford did. But you mustn't blame her. She's devoted to this house and wants the best for everyone in it. Including you, Connie. Now tell me, what happened at your last place of employment? You came to us with a letter of recommendation. Was that letter true?"

The girl dropped her chin and shook her head. "Not exactly, my lady. I was sacked for sneaking food out to hungry children, but then someone intervened on my behalf."

"Who? It's all right, you won't get yourself into trouble again."

"Lord Allerton, my lady."

Phoebe's hand flew to her mouth, but she recovered and just as quickly lowered it. "Lord Allerton? How was he involved?"

"He was a guest there, my lady."

"At Stonebridge Park, where you worked in Yorkshire?"

Connie shook her head. "No, my lady, I never worked there. I worked for Sir Michael and Lady Helen Smythe, in London. It was them who sent me packing. Lord Allerton was their guest for several days last summer. And he persuaded his friend, Lord Bellington of Stonebridge Park, to have the reference written for me."

Phoebe shook her head as she tried to make sense of the convoluted story. "Why on earth would Lord Allerton, a marquess and a colonel in His Majesty's service, go to so much trouble to see you gainfully employed after being dismissed?"

The girl shrank even further into herself, if that were possible. Her voice, when it emerged from her half-bitten lips, was shaky and filled with fear. "He wanted me where he could find me again, my lady, should he wish to."

For several moments Connie's words buzzed round and round Phoebe's head like a swarm of bees. Yet one by one, the implications fell into their logical order, and Phoebe understood. "Dear merciful heavens. Lord Allerton . . . he'd been . . . forcing himself on you all along . . ."

Connie only nodded, and Phoebe felt ill.

Eva wasn't at all surprised when Phoebe appeared in the service room some five minutes later. Without a word she came in, slid onto a stool at the table, and sat with her chin in her hand.

Eva set aside the blouse Julia had given her last night with the request that the mother-of-pearl buttons be replaced with ones sporting real pearls in solid gold settings. "You look troubled, my lady."

"I am." She reached for one of the plainer buttons, held it in her palm a moment, then fisted her fingers around it. "Lord Allerton deserved what happened to him, Eva."

"My lady, don't—"

"I'm sorry, Eva. I don't like saying such things. It's wicked, I know. But in this case . . ."

"Connie had more than that one run-in with him, I'm guessing?"

"At the place of her last employment, in London."

Eva pulled another stool to the table and perched on it. "But I thought she last worked in Yorkshire, at an estate called Stonebridge, I believe."

"No, she worked for a family called the Smythes, in London. When they caught her slipping food out the back door they dismissed her, but one of their guests at the time arranged to have false references written up for her. He engaged his friend, Lord Bellington, who owns Stonebridge."

"But why . . . ?" The dismay on Phoebe's young face supplied Eva with her answer, or at least enough of one. She didn't wish to know more. "I see."

"He sent her here, to us, for convenience sake. I suppose he thought after the war, he could have his dalliances without his mother catching on, which she might have if he'd have carried on at home."

"Oh, my lady . . ." Immeasurably sad, Eva trailed off. What could she say to her young mistress? That she didn't want Phoebe so much as thinking such thoughts? That it pained her dreadfully that sweet Phoebe should not only know about such things, but must suffer them to occur here, in her own home?

It was too late for any of that. Too late to draw a curtain of innocence across a window that had been thrown wide. She could only be what she was to Phoebe: her maid, her friend, and if needed, her protector. "My lady, shall I make you tea?"

"Thank you, Eva, but no. I don't need tea. I need answers." Rising, she went to the door and closed it. When she returned to the table, she pointed to Julia's blouse. "I'm sure my sister will be wanting that. You sew, and we'll talk."

Eva picked up her needle, already threaded with a length of the fine silk thread she had purchased at Henderson's haberdashery. She positioned one of the precious pearl buttons, not gotten from Henderson's but on Julia's trip to

London last summer. "In your mind, has Connie incrimi-
nated herself in regards to Lord Allerton? She certainly
had motive."

"I don't believe so," Phoebe replied, "at least I don't
wish to. Someone willing to risk her own employment not
once but twice in order to feed hungry children? That's not
a likely candidate for murder, is it?"

Eva experienced another painful twinge to hear the
word *murder* from Phoebe's lips, yet one more concept she
should never have to think about.

"But there's something else I wished to tell you, Eva. It
happened last night."

Eva looked up from her task, her needle poised in midair.
She narrowed her eyes, taking in what she hadn't previously
noticed in Mrs. Sanders's office: the dark smudges beneath
Phoebe's eyes. "You were up late, my lady."

"Yes, I waited until everyone was in bed, or so I thought,
before going to Lord Allerton's bedroom."

"My lady, you didn't. What if someone had seen you?"

"Someone almost did," she replied so calmly Eva was
possessed of an urge to tug her own hair. "When I opened
the door—luckily without a sound—I discovered . . ." She
glanced over her shoulder at the closed door, then continued lower, "I found Lord Owen Seabright inside, going
through Lord Allerton's travel desk. He removed something from among the documents."

Eva set her work aside. "You must go to your grandparents. They should know about this."

"I'm not so sure of that. Lord Owen might have been
doing the same as you and me—searching for the truth."

"But, my lady, you don't know that. A guest traipsing
about the house at night, searching through a man's possessions. This doesn't set Lord Owen in a positive light—
not a positive light at all."

"Again, it's nothing I hadn't intended doing myself. I

did find something just over the threshold, and managed to snatch it up before I retreated from the room. It was one of the shirt studs Lord Allerton wore on Christmas."

"Do you think that means something significant?"

"On its own, perhaps not. But it might prove there was a struggle in Henry's room. It's what I need to find out."

"Take it to the inspector, then. You're becoming too involved, my lady. You've done enough."

"The inspector will likely declare that Lord Allerton was untidy with his possessions."

"Which might be the truth."

Phoebe sighed. "Really, Eva, sometimes you seem to be taking Inspector Perkins's side in not wishing to ruffle feathers. Someone has to dig at the truth."

"It's not that I agree with the inspector, my lady. It's that I do not wish *you* to be the person doing all the digging. Will you at least consider speaking with Constable Brannock?"

"Possibly, except there are some extenuating circumstances that occurred last night. On my way out of the guest wing, I ran straight into Julia. Now, where do you suppose she was going?"

"Oh, my. You all might have had quite a gathering in Lord Allerton's room. Please don't do that again, my lady. It could be dangerous."

"Don't worry, Eva, for now I'll leave Lord Allerton's room alone. It's Lord Owen's room I'd like to explore next."

"My lady—" Eva heard her own voice becoming shrill. She drew a breath and whispered no less fiercely, "Don't you dare!" A ghost of a smile from Phoebe made her want to shake the girl. "I fail to see anything amusing in this."

The maddening smile persisted. "I'm sorry. I was just wondering if you ever speak to Julia this way. Or Amelia, for that matter."

Eva's chin came up defensively. "I do not, my lady. With Julia I would not dare. And with Amelia there is no need."

"Oh, I see." All trace of amusement vanished from Phoebe's features. "Then you find me wanting when compared with my sisters." She stared at Eva, her gaze full of contention and pride and stubbornness. A Renshaw through and through, Eva thought wryly.

Her own resolve softened, and she shook her head. "No, my lady. Not less. More. Much more. I love your sisters, but I know in my heart your achievements will be so very much greater than either Amelia or Julia could ever imagine."

Phoebe blinked, and the fight visibly drained from her. "Oh, Eva, I hope you're correct. Sometimes the future is like glimpsing a vista through a veil. I wish to step through, but there isn't a path in sight and I've no inkling where I might end up."

"Of course not, my lady. You're young and your future hasn't yet been shaped. Not yet imagined or invented, not for women. You'll do the inventing, my lady. I know you will, but you must also learn prudence, not to curb your spirit but to safeguard it."

The silence stretched. Had Eva overstepped her bounds? If she had, she didn't—couldn't—regret it. She would rather see herself sacked than allow harm to come to Phoebe. Then Phoebe's smile returned, no longer amused or mocking but something so much more, something deeper, that tugged at Eva's heartstrings. Phoebe hopped off her stool and came around the table, and suddenly they were hugging like sisters. Just for one long, precious moment before their arms dropped and Phoebe cleared her throat.

"Thank you, Eva. I believe I needed to hear that. It certainly trumps Fox telling me I should be content in the roles for which God designed women." She burst out laughing and Eva joined her, until a new thought silenced her.

"I have an idea concerning Lord Owen. He's engaged Mr. Hensley as his valet, on a trial basis—"

"I'm so glad!"

"Yes, and I was thinking he might be able to discover whether Lord Owen and Lord Allerton perhaps knew each other better than he admitted to you."

"Good thinking. Servants know everything."

"Well, I wouldn't say everything, my lady, but they do know who comes and goes, as well as to whom their employers send mail. I'll ask Ni—er—Mr. Hensley if he'd be so kind as to make some inquiries for us. Considering the circumstances, I'm sure he could come up with a feasible excuse for his questions."

"As long as he doesn't endanger his new position."

"If Lord Owen had anything to do with Lord Allerton's disappearance, my lady, I highly doubt Mr. Hensley would wish to continue in his employ."

"Yes, that's true, isn't it?"

"I'll just go and find him, then."

"No, you finish Julia's blouse or you'll never hear the end of it. I'll speak with Mr. Hensley."

CHAPTER 13

Luncheon promised to be a somber affair that afternoon. Lady Cecily joined them, along with Theo and Lord Owen. Lady Allerton had again opted to have a tray sent up to her room. Though she showed a braver face than Phoebe previously would have given her credit for, the strain of her son having not yet been found was taking its toll. It was taking its toll on all of them, to the point that even Fox kept his unwanted opinions to a minimum as the serving dishes were passed round. Grams and Grampapa made a valiant attempt to lead the conversation, even if the only neutral subject they could devise focused primarily on the weather and reports of an approaching storm.

Julia sighed at the news. "Then we'll be trapped here indefinitely."

"Planning to go somewhere, are you?" Grams's question dripped with irony.

"Nothing definite," Julia replied with her trademark half shrug, either not catching Grams's tone or choosing to ignore it. "But one does like to have options."

Amelia looked up from her steak and kidney pie. "And where would you go? Let's make a game of it. If we could be anywhere else in the world, where would we each choose? I'll go first. Oh, is it all right to play a game, under the circumstances?"

Amelia caught Phoebe's eye and Phoebe nodded encouragement. Anything to lift the pall that pressed harder on Foxwood Hall with each passing day. Grampapa also lent his approval in the form of a hearty "Yes, yes, indeed, my dear."

"Well, then, I would go to Rome, where it's warm, and we could tour the museums and churches."

"If you want warm," Julia said, "the south of France. That's where I would go. In a heartbeat," she added in an undertone that spoke of an impatient desire to escape.

Fox bounced in his seat. "I'd go to Germany."

"Germany," Julia shot back. "Are you mad?"

"No, I'd go to gloat that we won the war and they lost."

Phoebe was tempted to deliver a kick under the table. A range of disbelieving gawks and disapproving frowns—even from Lady Cecily—circulated round the table, but it was Theo who responded.

"War isn't a thing to gloat over, Fox. No side ever truly wins."

"How can you say that—ouch!"

Phoebe struck, guessing she caught her brother in the side of his shin with the pointed toe of her velvet-stamped pump. At the same time, fiery outrage on Theo's behalf crept from her neck to her hairline. Even Julia glared daggers at Fox. A dreadful silence gripped the table, until Theo held up his hands and spoke again.

"You see these burns, Fox. And here." He pointed to the side of his chin. "I got these, as you probably know, at the Battle of Somme."

"You were a hero," Fox interjected, his voice catching and breaking as it had begun to do in recent weeks, but mostly in times of duress.

Theo nodded slowly. "Perhaps. The gas rolled across no-man's-land and poured into the trenches. There weren't enough masks—I gave mine to an enlisted boy and tried to cover as well as I could with my clothing. But my hands were exposed, as well as the side of my face."

"You *were* a hero, Theo," Amelia said with a note of wonder, but it was the admiring shimmer in Gram's eyes that most caught Phoebe's attention.

Theo shook his head. "No, Amelia. There were greater heroes than me, on both sides of the war. And men who lost much more than I did. Lives, limbs, their sanity, and the ability to earn a livelihood. German, French, English—now the war is over it doesn't make much difference. We all lost a great deal."

"Indeed we did." Grampapa reached around Grams to clap a broad hand on Theo's shoulder. "Thank you for reminding us of that, dear boy." With a sweeping glance he encompassed Fox, Phoebe, and her sisters in manner uniquely his, a manner that never failed to make them all sit up straighter. "Patriotism is one thing, but war is never a matter to be glorified."

"But—" A sharp hiss from Grams forestalled whatever Fox might have said, and thank goodness. Phoebe needed a moment to take in the past few minutes. Never had she heard Theo Leighton speak so many words, nor so eloquently. At least not since before the war, when they were all young and unaware of how drastically life would change.

She never would have attributed to him such tolerance either, but the way he answered Fox—so intelligently and patiently—impressed her greatly. There was more to the Theo who returned from the war than she had suspected, or that he had let on. This was something she needed to ponder, and discuss with Eva. Despite Lord Owen's suspicious behavior, they hadn't ruled out Theo as the possible culprit in Henry's disappearance. Only now . . . She glanced again at the stretched and pitted skin beneath the corner of his mouth. Now she hoped it wasn't Theo.

"I suggest a return to Amelia's game," he said at length, bringing a second uncomfortable silence to an end. "I've seen enough of the world to last me several years, so I would simply choose to remain in England. I think I should like to spend next summer on the Cornish coast. Owen?"

With a slight smile Lord Owen shifted his sights to Phoebe, only to send a new wave of heat to her face—this time not due to anger, but to the familiar and disconcerting chagrin that seemed always to overtake her at his slightest attention. "Like Theo," he said, "I've seen enough of the world for a while, although if I had to choose, I believe it would be somewhere in the tropics. South America, perhaps, or Polynesia."

"How wildly exotic of you, Owen." Grams gave a little shiver. "Too rich for my blood, to be sure. I'm with Julia— the south of France sounds heavenly. And civilized," she added with emphasis. "Cecily, how about you, dear?"

"Must one choose? Couldn't I board a ship and go round the whole world?"

"Of course you may, if you like," Grams said, spearing a roasted asparagus tip with her fork. "But which way? East to west, or vice versa?"

Lady Cecily didn't answer, but with a puzzled frown twirled her finger one way and then the other, as if she couldn't quite grasp the concept of Grams's question.

"And I would gladly escort Amelia to Rome." Grampapa beamed fondly across the table at her. "Would you suffer your old Grampapa to escort you round the churches, my dear?"

"I would wish no other," Amelia declared, and raised her glass of lemonade in tribute. "May we, Grampapa?"

"Perhaps next year, my darling, when the world has recovered."

Amelia looked glum a moment, before brightening and turning to Phoebe. "What about you? You haven't said yet."

"I don't know. . . ." After Theo's earnest disclosure, even contemplating a holiday seemed trite. Where would she go? Like him, she couldn't envision much beyond England right now. Their country needed so much, needed every able-bodied citizen to contribute to rebuilding—what? Surely not the old ways, with their restrictions and silly notions of keeping people in their so-called rightful places. But building something new . . . yes, England needed that, and perhaps she could help. "I'd stay home—" she began, but Lord Owen interrupted before she could explain.

"Come now, Lady Phoebe, you must play." His coaxing sounded more like a command, and all eyes turned expectantly toward her. Yet it was *his* gaze alone that made her feel singled out in a most discomfiting way. She suddenly didn't like this game of Amelia's, wished it were over, wished her face didn't feel so hot. Did the others see it? Did *he*?

He held her gaze so steadily, Phoebe wished to crawl under the table. Was he doing this on purpose? And did she detect a mocking hint of one-upmanship in his manner? But why? She had wondered if he noticed her blushing; but what if it was worse than that? What if he knew she had peeked in on him in Henry's room last night? He had never turned around. . . . At least she didn't think he had. . . .

He smiled, all mockery gone, and said in a kindly voice, "Surely there is somewhere that captures your imagination, where all things seem possible."

As if by magic an answer came to her, so swiftly she barely knew where it originated, and hadn't time to ponder it before she said, "America. The United States. New York, I should think."

"Why ever would you wish to go there?" This came from Julia, with a look of distaste. "The Americans are so . . . common. I met numerous ones in London last summer, officers, mind you, yet even they exhibited a familiarity just this side of vulgar. Then again, you do seem to enjoy their penny-dreadful novels."

"Where were you meeting American officers?" Grams demanded from beneath the severe slash of her silver eyebrows. "You know I didn't approve of you going to London. Far too dangerous, even if those horrid Gotha bombers were no longer the threat they had been. Seems there were other threats equally as treacherous. American officers, indeed."

Luckily for Julia, the subject ended abruptly when Fox saw fit to interject one of his unasked-for judgments. "Phoebe would only get in trouble in America," he declared with a smirk.

Indignation had her pulling up straighter. "I'll have you both know—"

She had been about to point out that those novels to which Julia referred characterized the Americans as innovative, enlightened, and brave, when the door opened upon Mr. Giles. Giving away nothing by his expression, he came to the table and leaned low to whisper in Grams's ear, whereupon she paled and surged to her feet.

"Archibald, one of my father's priceless daggers has been stolen!"

Constable Brannock removed his pocket square and dragged it across his brow in a gesture so reminiscent of Inspector Perkins, Phoebe half expected him to reach next for his hip flask. At Grams's frantic summons he had hurried down from the attic, where the search for Henry was expected to reach its conclusion this evening, at least as far as the house was concerned. The outbuildings and greenhouses had all been searched as well, an icy endeavor for those involved. After this, the search must take to the forest and the surrounding environs. Henry could be anywhere, anywhere at all, and oftentimes Phoebe wondered if he would ever be found. When she thought about the contents of the Christmas boxes . . . well, she wondered how much of Henry even remained to be found.

Weariness dragged at Mr. Brannock's features and made him appear older than when he arrived only three days ago, suggesting he shared Phoebe's doubts. He stuffed the handkerchief back into his coat pocket and faced Grams squarely. "Why did no one think to inform either Inspector Perkins or myself about the existence of these knives, my lady?"

Grams scowled, no doubt finding his tone impertinent. The constable had wished to speak with Grams privately, but she had refused. The news from Mr. Giles had left her uncharacteristically ruffled, even shaky. The stolen dagger turned out to be a third-century Roman pugio with a leaf-shaped blade and a steel hilt emblazoned with solid gold. Priceless and in surprisingly good condition, the dagger had likely been a ceremonial piece owned by a general or statesman rather than a common soldier.

Did Grams fear the theft might make her a suspect? Or someone else in the family? Or was it merely being required to speak to the authorities that left her bristling? Either way, she had insisted she needed her family around her. Phoebe and Julia flanked her on the sofa in the Rosalind sitting room, while Grampapa looked on from an easy chair. Amelia had wished to be here as well, but Grams had wisely charged her with seeing to their guests' comfort, a task that satisfied Amelia with its importance. Equally wise, Grampapa had sent Fox back to his room for looking far too elated about this latest development.

He had gone off mumbling about never being allowed to have any fun.

"My young man, they are not *knives*," Grams testily corrected Constable Brannock. She tugged her silk shawl tighter around her shoulders. "They are daggers. Very old, very valuable daggers representing every significant era of European history. It took my father a lifetime to amass his collection."

The constable didn't look impressed. "That may be, my lady, but we should have been alerted to the presence of these weapons in this house. Can you hazard a guess as to when the dagger in question went missing?"

"*Pugio*, and how on earth should we know that?" Grams shrugged, her expression proclaiming this an absurd question. "No one here takes these weapons out to play, Mr. . . . er . . ."

"Constable Brannock, Grams," Phoebe leaned to whisper.

Grams waved a hand in dismissal. "The only reason we discovered the theft today is because Mr. Giles sent Douglas to retrieve them from their case in the billiard room for their monthly polishing. They must be oiled regularly or the old steel will rust."

"So sometime between last month and today, this pugio went missing." At Grams's pained look, Constable Brannock jotted a note in his writing tablet. "And they are kept in the billiard room, you say?"

"In a locked, glass-fronted case," Grampapa said. "In the old days I might have noticed the absence immediately, but since I rarely play billiards anymore, I don't tend to enter that room much."

No, Phoebe thought sadly, not since Papa went off to war.

The constable made another notation, murmuring, "Perhaps we've finally found what we were looking for."

"What are you saying?" Obviously startled, Grams appealed to Grampapa. "Archibald, what is he saying?"

It was Phoebe who answered. "He is saying, Grams, that he found it doubtful the harm done to Henry could be attributed to Mrs. Ellison's cleaver." She looked up at the man for consensus. "Isn't that what you told my maid? That the damage to Henry's hands could not have been achieved with such an unwieldy weapon."

"Are you saying Father's pugio is responsible for . . ." Grams's face filled with disbelief or, as Phoebe couldn't help noting, a refusal to believe.

Julia, on the other hand, blanched as horrified comprehension dawned in her eyes. Had her sister only now grasped the awful thing that had happened to Henry?

Grampapa, seeing Julia's distress, stood and held out his arms to her. She jumped up from the sofa hurriedly crossed the room to him.

"I thought you were searching for Lord Allerton," Grams said in shaky, though no less sharp, accusation.

"Indeed, we have been, Lady Wroxly, but as Lady Phoebe said, I have also been hoping to find a weapon more likely than the cleaver to have caused Lord Allerton's injuries. Such a weapon could exonerate your footman."

With Julia having taken up position at his side, Grampapa said, "But not without incriminating someone else."

"Not without," Constable Brannock agreed.

The reality of this pronouncement gripped all of them, and Phoebe regarded the others, as they did her and each other, with a sense of growing apprehension. Could one of them be responsible for Henry? Phoebe was helpless to prevent her gaze from returning to one individual in particular.

"Why do you keep gawking at me?" Julia's chin went up, and her dark eyes glared malice in return.

"I'm not," she replied, though she made a poor effort of her denial.

"Let's all take a breath and gain our bearings," Grampapa suggested, but Constable Brannock seemed to be assessing each member of the family with the shrewd eye of a bird of prey. Phoebe didn't doubt he took in every nuance, every twitch and furtive gaze.

"Lady Wroxly," he said finally, "who has access to this cabinet?"

"I do, of course. My husband, and Mr. Giles. Our butler has keys to all the important doors and cupboards in the house. But we trust him implicitly, don't we, Archibald?"

"We most certainly do."

Phoebe sucked her bottom lip between her teeth. Should she say something about the way Mr. Giles had been acting recently? His confusion? Perhaps he had mislaid his keys somewhere and someone picked them up. She only half listened while the constable asked Grams and Grampapa a few more questions and scribbled notes in his tablet. She should tell him, at least mention Mr. Giles's recent befuddlement, while stressing his many years of unwavering loyalty and service to the family. Yet she couldn't persuade her tongue to move or her lips to open.

"That will be all for now," the constable said. "Thank you, Lady Wroxly, and I hope you'll accept my apologies if this has upset you."

Grampapa moved to Grams and offered his arm to her. She leaned heavily on it and rose unsteadily to her feet. But like Julia, she raised her chin in a show of bravado and once again waved a dismissive hand at the policeman's words. "I realize you are only performing your job, young man."

They left the room and Julia moved to follow. Phoebe hesitated. She had decided to explain to the constable about Mr. Giles. It was a form of evidence and she would be wrong to hide it.

"Constable Brannock—"

"Lady Julia," he called at the same time. Phoebe bit back the words she'd been about to say as he continued, "Another word, if you please. You, too, Lady Phoebe."

Eva grabbed a tray piled with dirty luncheon dishes off the counter in the butler's pantry and headed down the back staircase. Dora followed her, while Douglas waited at the bottom for them to pass so he could go up for another tray.

Eva didn't much mind the extra work. She had done it all before, years ago when she first entered into service. True, she had the benefit of an education thanks to a local scholarship that enabled her to attend classes at nearby Haverleigh's School for Young Ladies, and yes, she had improved her diction and widened her reading tastes, but she wasn't so arrogant as to believe that made her better than any other servant. More than anything, it had been sheer chance that brought her to her present position, when the lady's maid engaged for Julia suddenly became engaged herself—to be married. Mrs. Sanders had been about to place a new advertisement in the local papers when she happened upon Eva in town shopping for her former mistress.

Eva brought the tray into the scullery, and when she turned to exit, a figure filling the doorway caused her to stop short with a yelp. "Nick! Good heavens." She pressed a hand to her chest and laughed. "I didn't realize you were there."

"Sorry, Evie. I've been looking for you. I have a small piece of news."

Eva's breath caught. She stepped across the threshold and out of Dora's hearing. "About Lord Owen?"

Nick cast a glance over his shoulder. Mrs. Sanders walked briskly out of her office, seemed about to say something to them, but continued down the corridor to one of the store-rooms. Nick took Eva's hand and whisked her into the valet's service room.

"I did as you asked. I made small talk with Lord Owen while I helped him prepare for luncheon, which was re-markably easy as he's rather an amiable chap, for a toff. Our both having served in the war opened up a common avenue of conversation. In fact, it was he who initiated it. From there I deftly steered him into civilian matters by commenting on how much I hoped his interests didn't suf-fer during the war, as so many did."

"And?" Eva's impatience grew as she waited for Nick to state his point.

"And it turns out he and my former employer did in fact share some financial interests. Lord Owen owns several woolen mills, and I remember Lord Allerton planning to invest in English textiles. Once Lord Owen revealed the lo-cations of his mills, I knew for certain these were among the very same Lord Allerton expressed an interest in."

"Are you sure?"

"Evie, I was the man's valet. He often discussed such matters with me, not for my opinions, of course, but sim-ply to voice his thoughts aloud. Not to mention I collected his post, both outgoing and incoming."

Eva eased around the table and pulled out a stool. Once seated, she leaned her chin on her hands and considered. "Could their business dealings have gone awry?"

"It's possible, although my money is still on Lord Theodore and I'll tell you why. A business dealing gone awry stands no chance of being remedied if one of the interested parties is dead."

"There could be circumstances we don't yet under-stand."

"Could be, but consider this. Lord Theodore had every-thing to gain by his brother's death. Title, status, fortune, and my word, Eva, the man returned from the war as cold as a stone. It isn't all that difficult to imagine, is it?"

A shiver went through her. "I don't suppose it is. But dear me, Nick, I feel no closer to knowing who harmed Lord Allerton than before."

"I'm sorry, Evie." Nick straightened his coat with a tug. "I tried my best."

Eva slid off her stool and went to him. "Of course you did. You've brought another clue to light and it could prove important. Thank you, Nick, from Lady Phoebe and me both."

His grin filled her view, and she saw little else as he leaned down closer. Suddenly his lips touched hers. Eva ran hot and cold and hot again as her lips sank into his. The sensation was startling, and lovely, and . . .

With a start she pulled back, shocked and aghast—at him, at herself, at the fact that she had allowed such a thing to happen. To happen for several long seconds before she ended it.

What did that mean? What did that make her? What kind of example could she be to Phoebe and her sisters?

"Evie, I'm sorry. Please look at me. I didn't mean to offend you."

She hesitated, staring at the floor, and then slowly glanced up, half-afraid at what she'd see lurking in his eyes. Did he hold her in slight regard? Or was he truly sorry?

Yes, perhaps he was, for his brows were knotted, his face pained. He looked every inch a man waiting to hear his sentence for a crime he couldn't deny having committed.

"Forgive me, Evie."

She nodded. "Yes, yes, of course. Let us speak no more of it, shall we." She moved past him, feeling his stare hot on her back as she hurried into the corridor. She practically ran up the backstairs to the second floor and into Amelia's bedroom. She had clothing to prepare for tonight's dinner and . . .

Blast. Why had Nick done such a thing?

"Yes?" Phoebe was more curious than anything else about why the constable had called her and Julia back. Julia, on the other hand, sat imperiously back down on the settee and appeared not the slightest bit interested.

He regarded them in silence for several moments, his focus shifting back and forth between them until uneasiness settled in Phoebe's stomach. Then he said, "Is there something I should know? Something concerning the two of you?"

"Whatever are you alluding to?" With a bored air Julia looked down at her meticulously manicured fingernails.

"I am alluding to what transpired between the two of you minutes ago, when we spoke of exonerating your footman. Would either of you care to tell me what that was all about?"

"I haven't the foggiest notion what you mean." Julia switched her attention to the view outside the window.

"Don't you, Lady Julia? What about you, Lady Phoebe? You've a look on your face I've seen before, and it tells me you're being reticent by design."

Phoebe said nothing as Julia wrinkled her nose. "What on earth is that supposed to mean?"

"It means your sister is hiding something," Constable Brannock retorted, all pretense of deference abandoned. "I've about had it with the lot of you. A man was murdered—"

"Or so we believe," Julia put in.

He rounded on her, moving startlingly close and leaning to bring his face level with hers. "I assure you, Lady Julia, all things considered, the marquess is quite dead. Inspector Perkins might be content to gloss over the details, but I am not. Nor am I inclined to continue treating all of you as though you're made of glass. Not when a man's life is at stake."

"Where *is* Inspector Perkins?" Julia continued to behave with her typical hubris, as if none of this concerned her at all. "Why has he left the investigation entirely in your hands?"

Constable Brannock straightened. "Inspector Perkins is at this moment preparing his case to present to the district magistrate, so that trial proceedings against your footman may begin."

Phoebe could endure no more. "Julia, say something!"

Her sister paled, and the constable pressed thumb and forefinger to the bridge of his nose as Grams often did when attempting to ward off an approaching headache. But when she expected him to entreat Julia once more, he instead switched his attention to her.

"Lady Phoebe, *you* say something or I'll bring both of you into the village for questioning in more official surroundings."

"You wouldn't dare!"

He turned back to Julia. "On the contrary, my lady. Indeed I would."

"My grandfather would see you on the streets—"

"Julia, stop it. Just *stop* it." Phoebe threw her hands up, then hugged them about her middle. "Constable, Julia and Henry were expected to become engaged, but—"

"Phoebe." With a threatening look, Julia came to her feet, but Phoebe pressed on.

"Julia broke it off Christmas night and they argued."

He considered this a long moment. "That's all? They argued? Did you think I'd suspect your sister because she argued with her beau?"

"Henry was not my beau," Julia said adamantly.

The constable acknowledged this with a backward wave of his hand. "If that were the case, Lady Phoebe, virtually every female in the whole of England would be sitting in a jail cell."

A knock at the door silenced them all, and in the next instant Eva entered the room. "Lady Wroxly sent me," she said in explanation.

Phoebe might have known Grams had heard the constable's request that she and Julia remain behind, and that she would send in reinforcements.

Eva narrowed her eyes in that assessing way of hers. "Have you been upsetting my ladies, sir?"

"I've been asking them some simple questions, Miss Huntford."

Her lips flattened and her nose flared. "And have you received your answers? Because if so . . ."

She didn't complete the sentence, but her meaning was clear, so clear the constable's eyes sparked with anger at this obvious affront to his authority. Dear Eva, so valiant and unafraid when it came to her duties. Phoebe couldn't help smiling, albeit weakly. Feeling suddenly drained, she sank into the chair Grampapa had vacated earlier. She wanted this over, wanted justice done so they could carry on with their lives, Julia and her reticence be damned.

"There's more to this story than a mere argument," she said bluntly. "There is the reason Henry and Julia argued in the first place."

"Very well." Julia blew out a breath and collapsed back onto the sofa. "Henry—Lord Allerton—was a swindler. He'd been playing with Victory Bonds and war news, convincing people to keep investing due to fake reports of the war continuing indefinitely."

"How did you discover this?" Constable Brannock put aside his derision and gave Julia the whole of his attention.

"I overheard things while in his company last summer, things he probably thought I neither understood nor deigned to concern myself with."

"Did you alert anyone?"

"You mean the authorities?" She raised her eyebrows in a show of naïveté that might have deceived the constable but didn't fool Phoebe one bit. "No, I feared what might happen to me if I did. He frightened me, you see."

Phoebe traded a glance with Eva and pursed her lips.

"Yes, I do see." Constable Brannock nodded. "Then what gave you the courage to break off your courtship with the man?"

"Being here, surrounded by my family, of course."

Phoebe wanted to wretch, and even Eva looked doubtful. There was so much more to this, yet she couldn't deny Julia's skills in making herself out a victim deserving of sympathy.

"It would have been better all around if you had been honest from the start, Lady Julia," the constable said in a mildly scolding tone. "These facts might be important to the case."

Julia opened her eyes wide. "How so?"

"For one thing, we might be able to learn which of Henry Leighton's acquaintances fell victim to his investment scheme."

"Hmm. Clever. Well, we should leave you to it, then. May we go now?" Julia came to her feet gracefully. She didn't wait for permission, but swept from the room, her head held high.

"Oh, Julia." Muttering, Phoebe pulled herself out of the chair. With a start she realized they had neglected yet another part of the story. How had she allowed Julia to so sidetrack her she forgot all about Henry's threats of revealing her own secret? Would Constable Brannock dismiss Julia's argument with Henry if he knew the entire truth?

CHAPTER 14

Eva closed the sitting-room door after Julia and Miles Brannock left, effectively preventing Lady Phoebe from following. She had news to tell her.

"You've learned something," Phoebe correctly guessed, her voice a low murmur. She sat back down, this time on the settee.

Eva took the liberty of sitting beside her on the hundred-year-old Regency piece, her serviceable black dress making a dreary contrast with the fine silk. "Mr. Hensley managed to speak with Lord Owen, and he's been able to piece together that Lord Allerton had invested in the Seabright woolen mills."

Phoebe's eyes went wide, then narrowed. "Oh, Eva, the nail is being driven farther and farther into Lord Owen's coffin." Her brow furrowed.

"And that grieves you, my lady?"

Lady Phoebe nodded, her cheeks turning pink, but then she quickly said, "But no more so than with any other occupant of this house. It certainly makes a decision for me."

Eva didn't like the sound of that, or the seriousness of Phoebe's tone. "What decision, my lady?"

"I need access to Lord Owen's room."

"Absolutely not." Eva had been saying that a lot lately, usually to no avail. "Look what almost happened when you tried to search Lord Allerton's room."

"Yes, I caught Lord Owen removing a document or something from Lord Allerton's travel desk. Now your Mr. Hensley has discovered a connection between the two men that Lord Owen lied about when I asked him how well he knew Lord Allerton."

"My lady—"

"Don't tell me to go to Constable Brannock, at least not until I find something definite. All I need is a good plan. . . ."

"My lady, I could ask Mr. Hensley to search Lord Owen's room. It would be much easier to explain his presence there than yours, since he is serving as his lordship's valet."

To Eva's frustration, the obstinate girl shook her head. "No, I won't have Mr. Hensley risk his future. Were he caught, and Lord Owen proved innocent, the consequences could be dire. As for me, at worst I would suffer from acute embarrassment and a scolding from my grandparents. Nothing I couldn't recover from."

"At least let me stand guard somewhere, so that if Lord Owen were to return to his room, I could warn you somehow."

Phoebe grinned. "Now that is a very good idea. But not you. You would run the same risk as your Mr. Hensley."

It didn't escape Eva's notice that Phoebe had termed Nick Hensley *hers* not once but twice. Could she somehow know what occurred in the service room this morning? No, that wasn't possible. The door had been closed. Phoebe would have to have been crouching on the ground outside and peering through the ice-glazed windows.

"He is not *my* Mr. Hensley, my lady. We knew each other a long time ago, and then not very well."

"Then why are you blushing?" Phoebe crossed her arms and waited for a response. But pointing out Eva's blush only sent another rush of prickling heat to her cheeks.

"My lady, I . . ."

"Eva, don't be silly." She laughed, a sound filled with delight. "It's perfectly all right with me if you've taken a fancy to Mr. Hensley, and he to you. I promise not to breathe a word of it in Mrs. Sanders's hearing."

"Please don't tease me, my lady." Eva had yet to decide how she felt about Nick's overture. If only she could be certain of his motives and his regard for her. But a man who steals kisses without warning must be viewed with some measure of suspicion, mustn't he? It could very well mean he didn't hold her in high esteem or believe her worth the time and effort of proper courting.

Was she reading too much into this? And wanting too much from him, more than she herself had suspected?

"Eva." Phoebe came to sit beside her and took her hand. "Mr. Hensley seems like a good man. Why, he might have gone straight to the inspector once he learned you and I were attempting a search of our own, but he didn't. Or he might have washed his hands of the whole affair, but again, he did not, but insisted on accompanying us, and then questioning Lord Owen."

Eva nodded, her spine rigid. "He has been most accommodating."

Phoebe released her hand. "All right, have it your way. Be mysterious. Just know I'm on your side, come what may."

Eva was about to thank her wholeheartedly, but the door abruptly opened. Lady Amelia regarded them both from the threshold and fisted her hands on her hips.

"Were you looking for me?" Phoebe asked her.

"Yes, I'm looking for you," Amelia said with no small amount of sarcasm. "I'm tired of being shoved in the background. I want to know what is going on."

Eva rose and headed for the door. "I'll leave you two alone."

"Stop right there, Eva." Amelia's command halted her in her tracks. "You're as involved as Phoebe is, no use denying it."

"Amelia, please." Phoebe stood and reached out to finger the lace trim on Amelia's collar, adjusting here, smoothing there. "Nothing is going on. The constable simply had some questions to ask Grams, and she wanted us with her for moral support."

"That much may be true, but you and Eva have been conspiring like a pair of thieves. I wish to know what's going on. I'm almost sixteen. I'm not a child anymore—"

"Yes, you are."

"You know I am not, Phoebe, and I wish to help. Don't you think I care about what happens to Vernon? Don't you think I want justice for Henry?"

The tiny catch in Amelia's voice tempted Eva to put her arms around her, or better yet tuck her into bed with a cup of warm milk and cinnamon. Yet she heard too much of Phoebe in this younger sister's demands. Had she thought Phoebe the only young Renshaw with spark? How wrong she had been.

Lady Phoebe saw it, too, for she stopped fussing over Amelia's collar and stepped back to regard her. "I'm sorry, Amelia. It's all too easy to go on seeing you as you were. I suppose the same way Grams and Grampapa see us all, as sweet little dolls who never change and never grow up. They want to keep us safe all the time, but if we allowed that we'd never see much of life, would we?"

"No," Amelia whispered. Louder, she said, "Then you'll tell me what you know and let me help?"

Phoebe turned to Eva. "What do you think?"

Eva raised both hands. "It is not my decision, my lady,

and it sounds to me as if you already made up your mind anyway."

"I have." She grasped Amelia's shoulders. "I have an idea how you can help me this very night. Eva, don't scowl. I promise my little sister will neither come to harm nor find herself in trouble. Now, here's what we're going to do."

At the sound of footsteps in the gallery, Phoebe and Amelia poked their heads outside Phoebe's bedroom door. "It's him," Amelia announced in an excited whisper, and Phoebe shushed her.

"I can see that," she said calmly, though inside she felt anything but. Strolling along the gallery, Lord Owen gave an adjusting tug on his tailcoat and pressed two fingers to his bowtie as if to test the integrity of the knot. "He's dressed for dinner. It isn't likely he'll return upstairs until sometime after the dessert course." She eased out of her bedroom and down the corridor, acutely aware of Amelia following so close behind her she could hear her breathing and even felt an occasional puff against her nape. At the edge of the gallery, they stopped and listened to Lord Owen's receding footsteps downstairs in the hall.

"He's gone to the drawing room," Phoebe said.

"About time. Let's go, then." Amelia took a step, which brought her thumping into Phoebe's back.

"Hold up a moment." Phoebe impatiently straightened her bodice where it had slid askew thanks to Amelia's bumping into her. "We know the others have gone down, all but Lady Allerton."

"She's probably eating in her room again. . . ."

"Probably." But Phoebe made no move to cross the gallery until she felt satisfied that if Lady Allerton had decided to dine with the others, she would have made an appearance by now. Minutes ago, Amelia had made her excuses to their grandparents by saying Phoebe needed help with some tangled strands of beads and didn't wish to bother Eva. That meant Phoebe had at most a quarter hour to make a quick search of Lord Owen's room while the others mingled in the drawing room before dinner was served. Should she linger past that, Grams would surely send someone looking for both her and Amelia.

"All right, let's go." Together they scurried across the gallery, their breaths held lest they be seen from below. Thankfully the hall remained empty. They made it across and into the guest wing without mishap. "Now, then, you remember what to say should Lord Owen take it into his head to return to his room before dinner?"

"He won't, will he?" The sudden worry in Amelia's eyes fractured Phoebe's confidence in having recruited her sister as her accomplice. Too late now. Phoebe didn't dare enter Lord Owen's room without a lookout. She had promised Eva. Actually, Eva had made her take a solemn oath.

"There is no reason why he would, Amellie." She used Amelia's nickname from when they were little, and it had the desired effect. The worry vanished from her gaze and she gave a determined nod.

"Well, then, *if* he were to return, I'll pretend I was just coming from Lady Allerton's room and claim I was checking to see if she intended coming down for dinner. I'll say she didn't respond to my knock and is probably sleeping. Then I'll ask Lord Owen to escort me to the drawing room."

"That's right. Being a gentleman, he cannot refuse. Just remember to speak in a loud voice so I'll be sure to hear you."

Amelia nodded her understanding, and Phoebe left her to continue down the hall to Lord Owen's bedroom. To her relief the doorknob turned in her hand. She opened the door only wide enough to slip inside and then closed it securely behind her. She went straight into the bathroom, not expecting to find anything there but wanting to rule it out quickly. As she supposed, nothing but extra towels, bars of soap, and Lord Owen's leather-encased shaving kit occupied the shelves. She returned to the bedroom.

The layout of the room was similar to Henry's, with a carved bedstead flanked by two end tables, a towering armoire, a seating arrangement around the fireplace, and a heavy mahogany desk. She went there first.

And found nothing of importance. As with the other guests rooms, a writing tablet, each page emblazoned at the top with the Wroxly coat of arms, sat on the leather desktop, accompanied by an assortment of pens and a pot of ink. A gilded porcelain bowl in the shape of an oak leaf held a few coins. She slid out the first drawer to her left and then the one beneath it. Both were empty. She made short work of the others and found only a few scraps of paper and a stub of a pencil most likely left there by a previous guest.

She took another quick survey of the room. If Owen Seabright had brought a travel desk as Henry had, he'd apparently hidden it. Quickly she crossed to one of the end tables, pulled out the drawer, and then flung open the cabinet beneath it. Both were empty but for a book: *Don Quixote,* an 1885 English translation by John Ormsby.

She paused and flipped to a page, then another, and stared down at the familiar words. She and Grampapa had spent weeks reading this book together. It was one of her favorites. She'd found it at once whimsical and sad, filled with hope and yet so tragic. She would not have thought a man like Owen Seabright—a commander, a leader of men— would read such a fanciful story. It showed another side to him, to be sure. A more tender side. The notion made her uncomfortable. Her snooping was meant to yield evidence that he was involved in the attack on Henry, or not. It wasn't meant to provide a window into the man's soul.

Carefully she replaced the book and closed the drawer.

If Lord Owen had something to hide, where would he put it? Under the mattress? She knelt and slid her arms beneath the down tick as far as they could reach, then ran around to do the same on the other side. She flipped over the corners of the Persian rug. Coming to her feet, she again scanned the room, struck by the impersonal nature of her surroundings. Did the man travel with nothing but the clothes on his back? She must remember to ask Mr. Hensley what he thought of Lord Owen's utter lack of possessions.

All right, then, that left the armoire.

Behind the left-hand door some dozen suits of clothing hung above a perfectly straight row of shoes and boots, while to the right a bank of drawers held shirts, collars, ties, accessories, and such parts of a man's wardrobe that aroused a sense of inappropriate intimacy. She was about to roll the last drawer back into place when a bit of paper peeked out from beneath a linen under chemise. Upon reaching for it she realized it was not merely paper, but something thicker. A photograph. With shaking fingers she turned it over and beheld an image—albeit a clouded, slightly blurry one as if taken at a distance through a window—of Julia standing on the threshold of what appeared to be the open door of a city building, perhaps an apartment building or a townhouse.

With a man.

The breath went out of her. Even given the fuzzy quality of the photograph, she recognized the straight black hair, wide mouth, and the slight bump in the bridge of his nose: Lord Bellington, one of Henry's friends and the individual who wrote Connie's false letter of recommendation. In the photograph, Julia had her face angled to receive Lord Bellington's kiss on her cheek.

Phoebe pressed a hand to her throat. Lord Bellington was married. *Married.*

She tunneled her hand through the folded piles of Lord Owen's underthings and found two more photographs of Julia with Lord Bellington. In one they occupied the front seat of a motorcar, Lord Bellington at the wheel. In the other, again apparently taken through a window, they sat together inside a café. It was dark, shadowy, but Phoebe made out the image all the same. Lord Bellington's hand lay over Julia's.

Julia, how could you? Phoebe's vision blurred and an ill sensation roiled up inside her. Perhaps nowadays Julia might have gotten away with seeing a man unchaperoned, but a married man? Her reputation—the entire *family's* reputation—would never endure it. And even Phoebe, with all her notions of women's independence and the easing of society's traditions, could not condone behavior such as this.

"Oh, Julia," she whispered. "Why?"

But why had Lord Owen taken these photographs? What did he plan to do with them? Julia had acted puzzled over his presence in Henry's room last night, but was that all it was—acting? Perhaps Henry and Owen both vied for Julia's affections. But Henry, Owen, *and* Lord Bellington?

And then an urgent thought struck her: the negatives. She burrowed her hand back into the drawer, in between, around, all the way down to the satin drawer liner. "They aren't here," she murmured. She was about to search through the other drawers again, but surely she would have seen something the first time—an envelope, perhaps.

"Good evening, Lord Owen."

Amelia's high-pitched, rapid greeting just barely penetrated the bedroom door. Phoebe gasped, shoved the photographs back into the folds of linen, and for an instant agonized over whether she could approximate the exact positions of the drawer's contents. Those concerns fled in the next moment.

"I was checking on Lady Allerton," Amelia said in the

same frenetic tone, "but it seems she is sleeping. Would you mind escorting me down to dinner?"

"I would be very happy to, my lady," Lord Owen replied. These words Phoebe only just made out, for he apparently didn't share Amelia's need to shout. "If you'll wait here but one moment, I need to stop in my room first."

Phoebe's eyes flew wide and her breath caught in her throat. Blood pounding in her temples, she glanced around wildly, but the turning of the doorknob left her with only one option. She stepped up into the left side of the armoire, knocking over a pair of boots in the process. She left them where they lay and pulled the doors closed behind her. She parted the suits, stepped behind them, and arranged them in front of her. With her back pressed against hard mahogany and the serge, tweeds, and superfine hanging right up against her face, it was all she could do to draw breath. Not that she dared.

His footfalls were muffled against the carpet and she tried to picture where in the room he was. A drawer opened, closed. More footsteps, a creak from the floor beneath the rug, and then a pause. What was he doing? What was he looking at? Had she closed the doors properly? A maddening itch seized her nose, but she daren't reach up to scratch. Another tickled between her shoulder blades. Her knees began to tremble.

The thudding steps sounded again, becoming subtly louder until she pictured him standing right in front of the armoire doors. She bit down on her bottom lip as an urge to cry out gripped her. *Please, please, don't look inside. . . . Go away. . . .*

She almost sagged with relief when the footsteps receded. She heard them louder against the wooden floor where the rug ended, and then the bedroom door closed again. Her heart hammered against her ribs so violently her entire body shook, and now she did sag, just slowly collapsed into a crouch against the back of the armoire. That brought her face close to the footwear lined up in front of her, the pungency of leather mingling with the scents of wool. She sneezed—she couldn't help it—but as she reached out to crack one of the doors a fraction of an inch, the utter stillness of the room assured her she was now safe. Amelia's muffled voice, and then Owen's, drifted from the corridor. She pushed the door wider, but froze.

The tip of a blade protruded from inside one of the boots she had knocked over. *Grams's pugio,* she thought with a start. She reached out, fingered the tip, then carefully caught it between her thumb and forefinger and slid it free.

The boot clunked against the floor of the armoire. Phoebe absently set it and its mate upright as she stared down at the weapon dangling from her hand. Not Grams's pugio. . . .

A bayonet, some twelve inches long, its edges as well as its point razor sharp.

CHAPTER 15

Eva knocked on Julia's bedroom door. At a reply from inside, she stepped inside, then took a startled stride backward. "Oh! My lady, I'm sorry, I thought you said to come in. I didn't realize . . ."

Julia stared up at her from the chaise longue set just beyond the dais that held her canopied bed. As eldest daughter, Julia had been allotted the largest and most elaborate room, second only to the one shared by Lord and Lady Wroxly. With rose-colored upholsteries and carved white furniture inlaid with mother-of-pearl accents, the room suited Julia—it complemented her beauty, satisfied her pride, and showcased her aristocratic tastes. Yes, when Eva pictured Julia Renshaw, it was usually here in this fairytale room, a princess holding court until just the right prince swept her off her feet.

She had never envisioned that such a prince might be embodied in the person of Theodore Leighton, yet here he was, standing near the hearth, the glow of the fire gilding the scars on his chin and neck.

Eva took quick assessment of the scene before her. They were still wearing their dinner clothes—all of them—and she had detected no sudden movements when she opened the door, such as Lord Theodore attempting to put distance between them in a show of innocence. Still . . .

"Forgive me, my lady," she said with a bobbed curtsey. "I'll come back later."

Julia laughed. "Nonsense, Eva. Lord Theodore was just leaving." She raised her chin to look up at him, the motion bringing a graceful curve to her elegant neck. "Weren't you, Theo?"

"Yes, it's late. I'll see you tomorrow, Julia." He crossed the room to her and leaned to peck her offered cheek. Eva found herself having to step out of his way as he strode to the door, or he might have barreled into her. She couldn't resist turning and watching him disappear into the corridor.

"Eva, do stop staring. The man doesn't bite."

"Doesn't he?" she said so quietly she doubted Lady Julia could have heard as she rose from the chaise in a rustle of silk and beading.

"No, he does not." Standing at her dressing table, Lady Julia sent Eva a pointed glare through the centermost panel of the triptych mirror. She kicked off her high-heeled silk shoes. "Come help me get this dress off, would you? All this beading weighs a ton."

"Certainly, my lady." Eva detoured into the dressing room for a nightgown, wrapper, and slippers. Upon returning she unbuttoned each tiny gold button down the back of Julia's dress, helped her off with stockings and brassier, and slipped the lacy nightgown over her head. Julia sat at the dressing table and Eva went to work on her hair, first removing the jeweled combs on either side. Then she searched for each pin and gently slid it free. "I know it's none of my business, my lady, but entertaining a gentleman in your room alone—"

"I understand your concern, Eva, but I was not *enter-*

taining Lord Theodore. He was merely inquiring as to my welfare, and I his."

"Excuse me, my lady, but is that not something that can be done downstairs, among the others?"

"No, it cannot. I don't expect you to understand, Eva."

"Nor is it my place to understand, my lady," she said calmly. "I only wish to make certain no harm comes to you, or either of your sisters. It doesn't do to put one's trust in the wrong sort."

"And have you decided Lord Theodore is the wrong sort? Why?"

The edge in Julia's tone was subtle, but unmistakable. "My lady, there have been such goings-on here lately. How can you know whom to trust?"

Julia went still. "What do you know about Theo Leighton, Eva? Have the servants been gossiping again?"

Dared she reveal what she had learned? Would it be a betrayal of Phoebe's trust? But no, this in particular she had learned from Vernon, who had served as Lord Theodore's valet. She steeled herself with a breath and slid another pin from Julia's hair. "There has been some talk, my lady. It's said Lord Theodore might not have slept in his bed Christmas night."

Julia took several long moments before answering, and when she did speak, her voice was cold and lacking inflection. "And does this incriminate him in your mind?"

"N-no, my lady. But it does raise a question or two."

Julia reached up and placed a hand over Eva's, stilling it in midair. "I shall put those questions to rest here and now. Lord Theodore was with me for hours Christmas night."

"My lady!"

"Not in *that* way. I'd just broken it off with his brother and was terribly upset. I met Theo in the gallery and he saw immediately something was wrong. We sat in the billiard room for hours talking. Even played a few rounds." She released Eva and folded her hands in her lap. "Theo and I share something of a bond now. We were the two people closest to Lord Allerton when he died—Theo as his brother, and me as the woman both our families believed would become his wife."

Eva's heartbeat, startled to a gallop by her misunderstanding of Julia's disclosure a moment ago, gradually resumed its normal pace. So this was the reason Theodore Leighton hadn't appeared to have slept in his bed that night, and why he wore the same clothes as the previous evening when Vernon saw him the next morning.

A turn of phrase Julia had used struck her as odd. "Your families believed. Did you not believe it, my lady?"

"No, not really." Julia shook her head and shrugged one slender shoulder. "For a short time I considered the notion. But only a very short time."

Eva found the last of the pins and now all of Julia's lustrous blond hair cascaded down her back. Eva reached for the silver-backed brush on the dressing table. She started at the side part in Julia's hair and stroked evenly down to the ends in a meticulous, steady rhythm.

"You've changed your mind many a time over suitors, my lady."

"That's an impertinent observation," Julia quipped, but a light hint of laughter let Eva know she hadn't taken offense. Julia confirmed this with her next words. "I've yet to find a man who satisfies all of my preconceived notions of what a husband should be."

"And what is that, my lady?"

"Full of questions tonight, aren't you? All right, I'll play along. But do keep brushing, please." Julia tilted her head back and with closed eyes shook her hair out until it fanned over her shoulders and danced nearly to her waist. "A man, in my opinion, should above all else be rich."

"Wasn't Lord Allerton rich, my lady?"

Julia sent her a playful look through the mirror. "I'm not finished yet. He should be rich, British through and through and preferably a Peer, splendidly tall, broad in the shoulders, and wear impeccably tailored clothing at all times. And I do mean all. Even his smoking jacket should fit him like a second skin."

"No foreigners, then, my lady? No Italians or Frenchmen or Spaniards?"

"No, I shan't have a foreigner. I want an Englishmen and a highly educated one at that. Eaton, and then Oxford or Cambridge. Nothing less will do.

"Well, Lord Allerton was certainly all that, my lady."

Julia suddenly pulled forward, out of reach of Eva's brushing. She propped her elbows on the tabletop and dropped her chin in her hands. With a sigh she regarded herself in the mirror. Her eyes clouded, became darker than the darkest sapphire. "The man I marry must be worthy of my respect."

When she explained no further, Eva asked, "And how may a man earn your respect, my lady?"

She remained silent a long moment before replying. "I don't know, Eva. That's the problem. I only know, at least I hope, I'll feel it when it happens. So far, it simply hasn't." She glanced over her shoulder at Eva. "Am I being foolish?"

Eva reached around Julia to set the brush down. "No, my lady. I think you're wise to wait for the right gentleman."

"Even if it takes years?"

"Better that than spending the rest of your life unhappily married."

"Grams wouldn't agree. She wants all of us girls married off as soon as possible. She sees it as the best way to keep Fox's inheritance intact."

"Perhaps, my lady, but it hasn't escaped my notice that your grandparents seem well-suited and happily married. I don't believe it's too much to want the same for yourself." With a hand on her shoulder, Eva gently turned Julia back to face the mirror, separated her hair into three sections, and began plaiting its length. Julia watched her through the mirror, a speculative light dancing in her eyes. "There now, my lady," Eva said as she secured the bottom of Julia's braid with a velvet ribbon that matched the blue of her nightgown. "Will there be anything else?"

"Thank you, Eva, you may go. And do find out what's got my sister's knickers in such a twist."

"I'm sorry?"

Julia rolled her eyes. "You'll see."

A few minutes later, Eva knocked at Phoebe's door. It sprang open as if the girl had been standing on the other side waiting for her. She seized Eva's wrist.

"Come in. Oh, Eva, such goings-on!"

Phoebe swung the door closed again. Eva took a moment to study her appearance, noting Phoebe's high color and the sore spot on her lower lip that suggested she had been biting it like she used to do during thunderstorms. "What is it, my lady? Your sister told me you . . ." She thought better of repeating Julia's exact words. "That you seemed agitated this evening."

"I'm assuming you mean Julia. Believe me, she doesn't know the half of it. Eva, I believe I know who our killer is."

Phoebe didn't mean to lose her composure, but hot, stinging tears filled her eyes.

"My lady, what is it?" Eva's arm went around her and she felt herself led to the little settee near the fireplace. Shudders racked her in an outpouring she had been holding in check all through dinner, dessert, and the eternal moments she'd had to spend with the others before she could politely excuse herself for bed. How draining it had all been. Now she could no longer contain the strain and fear that had held her in a chokehold in Lord Owen's bedroom—inside his armoire, with those damning pictures of Julia and Lord Bellington, and the weapon that very probably had . . .

She shut her eyes, exhaled, and tried not to think of Henry's final moments.

"I don't understand, Eva. He seems so steady and honorable and . . . he's a war hero."

"Who?" Eva grasped her shoulders and held her at arm's length. "Who are you talking about, my lady?"

"Lord Owen, of course. Lord Owen murdered Henry—Lord Allerton. I'm all but completely certain of it."

Eva's grip tightened on Phoebe's shoulders. "First, where is Amelia? Is she all right?"

Phoebe nodded. "She walked Grams up to her room. We haven't been able to speak of what happened yet, but I know she suffered a terrible fright." She sniffed and blinked away her last few tears.

Eva patted her cheek before reaching into a pocket in her skirt and taking out one of the handkerchiefs Phoebe and Amelia had embroidered for her for Christmas. "It's clean," she said. "I never use them, they're too precious. But I always carry one with me." She showed Phoebe one of her kindly smiles.

Phoebe reached to grasp the fabric, but a horrible notion prompted her to let it slip from her fingers and flutter to the floor.

Eva bent to retrieve it. "My lady?"

"It was in the box, Eva. In your Christmas box, with . . ."

"Yes, that's true." Eva frowned. "But you and Amelia wrapped them so well, they aren't tainted, my lady. I could never think of them as anything but the perfect gift they are. So here, dry your tears and tell me what happened."

As Phoebe's tale unfolded, she found she couldn't look Eva in the eye, for all her maid had helped devise the plan to search Lord Owen's bedroom. She had assured both Eva and Amelia of the foolproof nature of that plan, never expecting Lord Owen to deviate from the scenario she'd envisioned.

"This must end, my lady. It's too dangerous."

"Yes, I knew you would say that and perhaps you're right. We can debate it later. Right now, Eva, tell me what you think. Does that bayonet signify that Lord Owen is guilty?"

A knock forestalled Eva's answer. The door burst open upon Amelia, still in her evening clothes. She shut the door quickly and hurried across the room to them. "Phoebe, it was so awful. I tried to prevent him—"

"I know, Amelia." Standing, Phoebe embraced her sister. Though they'd traded numerous urgent looks across the dining table, they hadn't found a moment until now to speak of their near debacle. "I heard you try to persuade him to go downstairs. He wouldn't be deterred."

"Well, what happened when he came in?" Amelia demanded. "Where did you hide?"

Phoebe shuddered at the memory. "In the armoire. It's quite all right, Amellie, he didn't catch me. Do you know why he returned to his room? Was he holding anything when he came out?"

"Nothing I could see, but that doesn't mean he didn't put something in his pocket. He's still downstairs with Grampapa. Perhaps it had to do with whatever they're discussing. Oh!" She gasped. "Do you think it's all right for Grampapa to be alone with him? Perhaps I should return. . . ."

Phoebe shook her head. "No, Grampapa will be safe, I'm quite sure of it. Don't you agree, Eva?"

Eva didn't hesitate in nodding. "Lady Amelia, whoever

attacked Lord Allerton did so out of rage. It's unlikely such a beastly act will be repeated anytime soon."

"A crime of passion," Amelia said, "as they say in the penny dreadfuls. But how can you know that?"

"By the nature of the crime, my lady." Eva came to her feet and reached out to stroke Amelia's lovely golden hair. A few loose strands suggested she had been fidgety this evening—for good reason, Phoebe silently admitted. "Why don't I help you both take down your hair," Eva said, "and Phoebe can tell us if she discovered anything unusual in Lord Owen's room." Yet as soon as those words left her lips, she gazed in silent appeal at Phoebe.

Phoebe gave a slight nod. She had no intention of revealing to Amelia what she had found in Lord Owen's room. Her youngest sister might indeed be growing up, but Phoebe saw no reason to endanger her life. The less she knew, the better. They moved to the dressing table, and Phoebe scooted to one side of the tufted satin bench so Amelia could sit beside her.

"What I found," she said as Eva released her simple coiffeur, "was a decided lack of possessions. Lord Owen travels exceedingly light."

"What does that say about him?" Amelia's question had a statement-like quality, as if she already knew the answer. "A man who travels light can make the quickest getaway."

Phoebe couldn't contain a chirp of laughter, subdued in the next instant at Amelia's hurt expression. Amelia's chin came up in a show of defiance, and then she, too, chuckled. Simultaneously, they said, "Penny dreadfuls." Behind them, Eva joined in their laughter and released one of the ribbons that held Amelia's hair.

"Yes, I suppose you're right," Amelia conceded. "But I don't believe Henry is anywhere to be found in this house. There has been no blood found anywhere, and it's certain the poor man bled when that awful thing was done to him. In my opinion, he left the premises, by will or by force, and was put upon somewhere else. The question is where."

"Unfortunately, that's a question we might never be able to answer." Eva ran her fingertips down the length of Amelia's wavy hair. "My lady, why don't you wait for me in your room while I help your sister into bed."

"All right. I'll go say good night to Julia, too." Amelia kissed Phoebe on the cheek and ran out.

Eva immediately turned to Phoebe. "So you discovered a bayonet in Lord Owen's room. One could argue that any number of former soldiers have such an item in their possession. Did you find anything else that could establish a link between him and Lord Allerton?"

Phoebe covered her momentary hesitation with a cough and hoped Eva wouldn't see through the ploy. "No, only the bayonet."

"What about your great-grandfather's Roman dagger?" She helped Phoebe off with her dress and underthings and slipped her nightgown over her head.

"The bayonet could just as easily have been used against Henry." Phoebe used her forearm to sweep her hair out from the neckline of the flannel gown.

"Then why would someone steal the dagger?"

Phoebe tossed up her hands. "I don't know. A diversion?" She couldn't say why she hid the truth of those photographs from Eva. She trusted Eva, she truly did, but it still seemed a betrayal of her sister to tell anyone. She sat back down at the dressing table. She needed time to think, to decide what was best to do. How she wished those pictures didn't exist. . . .

She could have destroyed them. Perhaps she should have. But if Owen was responsible for Henry, the photographs might be the only substantial evidence to prove it, especially if the negatives where carefully hidden away somewhere. Not for the first time, she agonized over whether leaving the images behind had been the right decision. Would Lord Owen have noticed them missing? He most likely would, and from there he would recognize Amelia's attempt to distract him and conclude it could have been none other than Phoebe snooping through his room.

"I discovered something tonight, too, my lady."

Phoebe snapped out of her reverie. "You did? Go on, please."

"I found Lord Theodore in Julia's room when I went in to help her to bed."

"I *knew* there was something between them." Her heart sank. In the course of a mere six months Julia had gone from Henry to Lord Bellington and now Theo? Oh, yes, and possibly Lord Owen. The back of her neck prickled. Julia seemed to be at the center of this entire matter.

"She denied any romantic goings-on."

"And you believed her?"

"Well, when I entered her room she was sitting on the chaise and Lord Theodore was standing by the fireplace. The scene they presented seemed an entirely innocent one. Even so, I couldn't help overstepping my bounds by cautioning her against entertaining gentlemen in her room, or trusting the wrong people."

Phoebe stood up and went to sit on the bed. "To which she said what?"

"That she and Lord Theodore shared a kind of bond, being the two people closest to Lord Allerton right before he died."

" 'Close' she called it?" Phoebe threw back her head and let go a laugh. That was the very last word she'd have used to describe Julia's relationship with Henry right before he died. Toxic was more like it. And bitter. Not to mention angry.

Eva showed no sign of joining in Phoebe's wry mirth. "She also told me Lord Theodore was with her for several hours Christmas night—merely talking. She was upset after breaking it off with Lord Allerton, and Lord Theodore lent a sympathetic ear."

"He did, did he?" Phoebe started to chew her lip, then stopped when the raw spot she'd created earlier rebelled with a stab of pain. "This does change things, though. I was so certain Lord Owen must be guilty. . . ."

"I still don't understand why, my lady."

"Because . . ." She trailed off, realizing the photographs had persuaded her most of all. Could Lord Owen have taken them from Henry's room, not because they linked him to any crime, but because he wished to protect Julia? An uneasy sensation balled in the pit of her stomach at the notion of Lord Owen sweeping in to play the gallant for Julia.

Always Julia.

Growing up, she and everyone else had simply accepted that others would be drawn to her beautiful, vivacious older sister. Julia had been that sort of golden, engaging child, accomplished early on in singing and dancing and playing the piano, as well as being skilled in the art of conversation. Even in the schoolroom, she would talk circles around their governess to forestall any subject she didn't wish to study that day. Poor Miss Dawson often hadn't even realized she'd been duped. But Julia always earned high marks, both at home and at finishing school. She reaped praise Phoebe had sometimes deserved as well, but didn't always receive because Phoebe hadn't made a point of making sure everyone knew of her accomplishments. Still, she couldn't rightly blame Julia for that, could she?

Julia hadn't been unkind in those days. In fact, whenever she had gleaned some favor or privilege due to her charms, she had almost always shared her good fortune with Phoebe. She herself hadn't wanted the kind of attention Julia enjoyed. It simply wasn't in her nature to crave the notice of others. She much preferred her books and horses and tramping around the estate with Grampapa. Even later, when young men began tripping over one another for a chance to woo the Earl of Wroxly's stunning eldest granddaughter, Phoebe hadn't minded so much. Until, of course, that last glorious spring before the war began, when she met Oliver Prestwich at the Sandown Races. Phoebe had been fifteen, Julia eighteen and newly out in society. Even now Phoebe didn't know if Julia had intended what happened, or if it had merely been a matter of course.

Papa had assured Phoebe her turn would come, but instead the war came four months later. The men all shipped off to France, and Oliver with them. Phoebe meanwhile became caught up in the home efforts to support the soldiers fighting far away, and she had forgotten about her disappointment. There had been no time to worry about such trifles.

Then Papa died, along with Oliver and so many others, and everything changed. Julia had changed. Where once she had been charming, she became calculating, and the generosity she had shown Phoebe became scarcer and scarcer until Julia seemed to hold every advantage she had ever enjoyed as a kind of bulwark around herself. If Julia did include Phoebe, perhaps because Grams insisted, there had typically been an accompanying charitable sentiment. Phoebe hadn't wished to acknowledge it, had wished to continue believing in the genuineness of her sister's generosity, but now she wasn't so sure. Perhaps even when they were younger Julia's largess had merely been a way to ensure Phoebe's loyalty, to prevent Phoebe from running to Mama and Papa with tales of Julia's discreet misdeeds.

Perhaps. The difference between now and then was she

had learned, by necessity, to get on with her life without Julia's favors. Julia shut her out, shut out everyone, really, except where she believed she might benefit. As perhaps she sought to benefit now from Lord Owen—*use* him— and Phoebe guessed he would let her without ever realizing the truth, or perhaps he wouldn't mind because Julia was beautiful and for so many men that would be enough.

Phoebe minded, very much, but felt helpless to do anything about it.

"My lady? Won't you share your thoughts?"

"Sorry, Eva, I was just thinking . . ." She shook her memories and her envious thoughts away. "As I said, I caught Owen Seabright in Lord Allerton's room and tonight I discovered that bayonet. But now with this news of Julia and Theodore's budding friendship . . . it seems we've gone round in yet another circle."

A scream, muffled by the door, sent Phoebe to her feet. A shout followed, and by the time Phoebe reached the corridor, Grams, Fox, Julia, and Amelia were already hurrying to the gallery. Phoebe ran after them, with Eva close behind. The screams persisted, coming from the guest wing.

"It's mine! Give it back, you insolent thing!"

CHAPTER 16

In a flurry of nightgowns and wrappers, Phoebe and the others scurried into the guest wing. Lady Allerton's door opened and she, too, came running out to the corridor. The shouts continued, two female voices raised in a furious debate.

"Give it to me!"

"No, my lady, I shan't. Now move away from the door, I beg you!"

"Not till you do as I say!"

Phoebe recognized at least one of those voices—Lady Cecily, though she had never heard such a tone from the woman before.

"Sounds like they're about to come to blows," Fox announced gleefully. Theo's door opened and in shirtsleeves he peered out.

"What on earth?" Grams muttered and went to Lady Allerton's side. "Lucille, is that your aunt we're hearing?"

Lady Allerton gave a start. "Oh, Maude, I think it must be. And her maid. They woke me from a sound sleep."

"Has someone been hurt? Ladies? Fox? What is this all about?"

Phoebe turned to see Grampapa and Lord Owen striding toward them from the gallery. Owen stopped to speak with Theo. Grampapa placed a hand on Phoebe's shoulder as he went by. Though Theo remained on his threshold, Lord Owen continued until he reached the others and then hovered, as if unsure whether to remain on hand or go to his own room and mind his business. He glanced back once at Theo, who hadn't moved. Remaining on hand seemed to win out after another shout erupted, words Phoebe would not have repeated. Fox chuckled under his breath. Lady Allerton winced, clutched her wrapper tight beneath her chin, and ran in slippered feet to her aunt's door.

"Lucille, please allow me." Grampapa went to the door in question and rapped his knuckles loudly. "Cecily, dear?" He raised his baritone to be heard over the clamor within. "Are you quite all right, Cecily? I'm going to open the door now."

Inside the room, all fell immediately silent. And then a voice that was not Lady Cecily's called out, "Someone help, please!"

Grampapa opened the door, and the dropping of both his and Lady Allerton's jaws sent Phoebe and the others hurrying to see what the matter was all about. Inside, the same voice that had cried out for help now exclaimed, "Lady Cecily, no!"

"There now, Cecily, it's all right." With a hand extended, Grampapa stepped into the fray. From the doorway Phoebe saw Lady Cecily and her red-haired lady's maid facing each other only inches apart, their hands raised above their heads. Lady Cecily's hands were empty, but one could easily see that she was reaching for an object the maid held just beyond her reach.

Phoebe gasped and pointed. "Grams, your pugio!" What did this mean? Had Lady Cecily stolen the dagger from the case in the billiard room?

Lady Cecily jumped as she attempted to dislodge the

pugio from her maid's grip. Waving her hands in the air, Lady Allerton rushed in. "Aunt, what are you doing? Stop it at once. At once, I tell you!"

The maid stood on tiptoe and teetered when Lady Cecily jumped again. Thank goodness the dagger could do no harm buried inside its sheath. His face alight with excitement, Fox squeezed past Phoebe and into the room. He pressed himself against the wall, no doubt to make himself as inconspicuous as possible and avoid being sent away. Amelia, Julia, Eva, and Lord Owen lingered in the corridor, their riveted faces holding expressions of bafflement and shock in varying degrees. Phoebe's gaze rested a moment on Lord Owen. Of them all, he seemed the least surprised. She wondered why.

Grampapa motioned for silence. The maid took the opportunity to lower the pugio behind her back and step away from Lady Cecily.

"There, there now, Cecily," Grampapa said in a placating tone. "All is well."

Was it, Phoebe wondered? They had just found in a confused, elderly woman's possession the weapon possibly responsible for Henry's demise. Could Lady Cecily have . . . to her own great nephew?

"Aunt Cecily, whatever are you doing with a keepsake left to our dear Maude by her father?"

Now that the commotion had died down, Phoebe noticed in Lady Allerton's question a resignation that suggested such bizarre behavior was nothing new for Aunt Cecily.

The elderly woman dropped her arms to her sides and angled a sheepish glance at the audience she only now seemed to notice. As tame as a kitten, she batted her eyelashes. "It is mine. I found it," she said in a girlish whine.

"Oh, Aunt. You didn't find it at all." With a deep sigh Lady Allerton cupped Lady Cecily's shoulder and said, as though attempting to persuade a child to tell the truth, "You took it, didn't you?"

"I'd have given it back. . . ."

Lady Allerton turned to address the others. "She's developed this odd fascination with knives and swords. Last year it was screws."

At this Fox snickered. Grams silenced him with a look, and said, "Screws? As in furniture and gadgets?"

"Indeed, Maude. She stole a screwdriver from our man-of-all-work and went about the house unscrewing table legs, door hinges, and even lamps before we caught her at it. I cannot understand these obsessions of hers, but so far they've all been temporary and for the most part quite harmless."

Grampapa looked astonished, and not a little concerned. *"For the most part?"*

"She doesn't mean to cause difficulties, Archibald. She can't help herself." Lady Allerton's chins jiggled as she aimed a scowl at the maid, still holding the pugio, but out of sight in the folds of her dress. "You should have been watching her more closely, you lazy thing. You know how indisposed I've been. First my Henry, and now this. . . ." She raised a forearm to her brow. "A body can only endure so much!"

"Now, Lucille, don't faint! Not again." Grams took hold of Lady Allerton's wrist with one hand and with the other lightly tapped her cheeks.

Discreetly the maid slipped the dagger into Grampapa's waiting hand. "I found it under her pillow, my lord." Phoebe noted the woman offered no apologies or explanations addressing the charge of laziness Lady Allerton had leveled at her.

Grampapa seemed in no mind to berate her. "Good job. Thank you." He dropped the sheathed blade into the pocket of his cutaway coat. It weighed the garment down, causing it to hang crookedly on his frame. "I think it might be a good idea if you went below while we continue to calm your mistress. Please make her some tea, and you might have some yourself as well. I'll have someone send for you when it's safe to return." He scanned the faces hovering in the doorway. "Eva, please go with her."

The maid curtsied and turned into the corridor. Eva followed her.

"But, Aunt . . ." Lady Allerton seemed recovered from her near faint. "Why do you persist in taking things you know quite well don't belong to you? That is stealing, and stealing is wrong."

"No, no, I merely *borrowed* it, dear. I wished to see it up close." Lady Cecily smiled now, the last traces of her agitation gone. "I'd have returned it in the morning. Or sometime soon."

Grams spoke gently. "But, Cecily, how did you open a locked case?"

Lady Cecily shrugged and raised a hand to her curly coiffeur. "A hairpin, of course."

"But if you had simply asked me, I would have shown it to you myself."

"Would you have?" Lady Cecily sounded genuinely surprised. "You're such a dear, Maude. You always were."

While Grams took this in, Grampapa said to the others, "Everything is under control now and no harm done. You may all return to your rooms. Fox, that especially goes for you."

"Oh . . ."

"Get along, young sir." But then he called Phoebe to him and handed her the pugio. "My dear, take this with you. I'll come for it in a little while."

The dagger was cold and heavy against her palm. "I'll guard it with my life, Grampapa."

He kissed her forehead and she left the room. The others had already dispersed and Theo had apparently retreated into his bedroom. Perhaps he had come to view scenes such as this as a matter of course.

Phoebe could hear Julia's and Amelia's light chatter from the corridor on the far side of the gallery. She sped her steps to catch up to them, but as she entered the gallery a male voice called her name softly.

She couldn't see him, but she recognized Lord Owen's voice immediately. A shiver traveled up her back and tingled in her cheeks, and this time not due to her capricious fascination with him. What could he want, calling to her from the shadows? "Where are you? Show yourself, please."

"I'm sorry. I didn't mean to frighten you." He appeared in the billiard room doorway, outlined by the darkness behind him. Why hadn't he switched on a light?

"You didn't frighten me. I simply couldn't see you."

"As I couldn't see you earlier tonight, yet I knew you were there."

Her spine went rigid. She attempted to swallow and couldn't. She knew better than to stand there engaging in conversation with this man, yet something kept her rooted to the spot. "What do you want?"

"To speak with you."

"It's late, and we've had rather too much excitement for one night. I'd prefer to talk about whatever it is in the morning." She moved to go, but he stepped out and grasped her wrist. Not a tight hold. In fact, she barely felt his skin against her own, yet when she tried to pull away she found it impossible to either slip free or open the circle of his fingers. Her heart thrashed against her ribs as a frisson of fear rushed through her. "Lord Owen, if you please."

Without a word he drew her into the billiard room, again with that strange insistence that needed no force of strength. The only light came from the dimmed sconces in the gallery and the reflections off the snow outside. Yet his presence surrounded her, made it difficult to breathe. She felt trapped even after he released her wrist. "What were you doing in my room earlier?"

Instinct told her cry out or hurry away. Yet surely he wouldn't dare overpower her, here in her own home with Grandpapa but several rooms away. She held her ground. "How did you know?"

He smiled and inhaled deeply. "Your fragrance . . . violets, is it? Julia prefers rosewater and Amelia uses a citrusy scent, as many young girls do. And you didn't shut the armoire doors properly after you ducked inside." He crossed his arms before him. "What were you searching for, if I may be so bold as to ask?"

"What were *you* looking for in Henry's room the other night?" The moment the question left her lips she regretted it. She had just admitted to creeping about the house in the middle of the night. What else would Lord Owen surmise but that she, too, had intended to search Henry's room?

He smiled again. At least, she saw the glint of his teeth and hoped that signified a smile and not a snarl. Her fingertips trembled at her sides and she fisted her hands to still them. "You suspect me of . . . what, my lady? Killing Henry Leighton? I can't fathom any other reason for you to go skulking through a man's private possessions."

"Those photographs are not your private possessions," she blurted, then wanted to bite her tongue.

"So you found those. I thought so. See here." He gently grasped her beneath the elbow and drew her farther into the room; once again, she let him, or had no choice, or . . . She didn't know which, but she waited in silence while he paused, perhaps to listen for any approaching individuals. She realized then that he hadn't shut the door to the gallery, and in this she took a measure of comfort. Surely if he intended to harm her he would have sealed them inside.

He leaned down to bring his face closer to hers. "Let's

stop all pretense. You need to believe two things. One, those pictures were brought here by Henry to persuade your sister—"

"I know all about that. Why did you take them?"

"On the contrary, Lady Phoebe, you do not know all about that, nor do you need to know why I confiscated them, at least not at present. But you do need to believe my having them will in no way bring harm to Julia."

The way he carelessly tossed out Julia's name stirred a whisper of jealousy—again. Phoebe narrowed her eyes, not that that brought him into any sharper focus. Her vision had adjusted to the dark, but Lord Owen remained a vague series of outlines, like a wall before her. "Why should I believe you?"

"That brings me to my second point. You need to believe me when I say this is more dangerous than you apparently realize, though why you'd have trouble understanding the malicious nature of the individual with whom we are dealing is beyond me. Leave it alone, and tell your maid to leave it alone as well."

"Of course I realize this is dangerous. But I am not about to let an innocent man hang for a crime he didn't commit."

"You can't know that for certain, can you?" His voice had become a rough, impatient hiss. She heard him swallow; then he said more evenly, "Just as you cannot know for certain whether I or even Lady Cecily, for that matter, is innocent. She had a perfectly good murder weapon at her disposal, didn't she?"

"Lady Cecily, indeed. That confused old woman, a killer?"

"I give you that she isn't in her right mind, but that doesn't rule out the possibility that she snapped, or that someone else didn't put her up to stealing the dagger. The point is you cannot know what someone is capable of. When the dagger went missing, we all assumed it could have been the weapon used on Henry, if it wasn't the cleaver."

"All right, then, tell me this." She raised her chin to him and hoped he could make out the defiant gesture. "What is your involvement with Henry and Julia? Is she aware you have those photographs, and do you intend to give them to her?"

Suddenly his hands came down on her shoulders, and this time she felt the full brunt of the warning communicated by his steely fingertips. She started to shrink away, but he held her firm and gave her a little shake for good measure. "Too many questions. I said leave it alone. Say nothing to Julia for now and believe that if your footman is innocent, he shall go free. If not . . ."

He left the sentence hanging and strode away from her. Phoebe stood alone in the billiard room, more confused than ever, and believing only one thing Lord Owen had attempted to press upon her.

Except for her grandparents, Amelia, and Eva, she could trust no one.

"I tell you, Evie, his lordship was in the strangest mood this morning. If I didn't have the evidence of my own eyes, I'd have thought I was serving Lord Theodore, not Lord Owen." Nick dipped the scrub brush he was holding into the cleaning solution of water, baking soda, and bleach, and gently but thoroughly scoured it back and forth across the first of several dress shirt collars, a pre-scrub before the collars were sent to the laundress. "It's not at all like him to be sullen tempered. I hope it's nothing to do with my services. I keep hoping this position will become permanent."

"I'm sure it was nothing to do with you," Eva tried to assure him. She felt a moment's desperation on his behalf. Were he to lose his employment in the dead of winter, it might be months before he worked again, unless he were to accept the most menial position at the lowest wages. How would he survive?

She stood at the ironing board, waiting for the new electric iron to heat. Miss Shea had insisted on replacing the old flatirons, which Eva had been quite used to heating on the potbellied stove in the corner of the valet service room. Miss Shea had claimed the electric iron would cut ironing time in half, but sometimes Eva felt she spent more effort untangling herself from the electrical cord than she did alternating between two stove-heated flatirons.

"I wonder if Lord Owen's mood this morning has anything to do with what happened last night."

The brush went still and Nick glanced up from his task. "I heard Dora and Douglas whispering earlier. Something about Lady Cecily?"

"Such a scene." She stopped to listen for a moment and, hearing no one in the corridor, continued quietly, "Lady Cecily had taken an antique dagger from a locked case in Lord Wroxly's billiard room." Using her fingertips, she sprinkled starch over Amelia's new silk shirtwaist. "But then, having lived in the Leighton household, I wonder if this comes as such a surprise to you."

"Yes and no. Her ladyship has a penchant for mischief, I'm afraid. But as for daggers . . . that's something new. And to be discouraged as adamantly as possible."

Eva nodded absently. "To be sure. So, then . . . you don't think her ladyship had anything to do with . . ."

"With what happened to Lord Allerton?" He looked personally affronted, as Eva would have been if someone accused a member of the Renshaw family of a horrendous crime.

She shook her head. "Silly question. My apologies."

They worked in silence for several moments. Nick stood brushing away at Lord Owen's collars, scrubbing stains that didn't exist. He sucked his cheeks between his teeth. Eva set down her iron.

"Something is clearly on your mind, Nick. Why don't you have out with it?"

He smiled guiltily. "There is something. Lord Owen confided in me last night as I helped ready him for dinner. It's about . . . well . . . Lady Julia."

"What about Lady Julia?" In a sudden bout of defensiveness, she snapped the question at him.

"Just that Lord Owen is well aware of the family's motive in inviting him."

"And that motive would be?"

"A second choice for Lady Julia should an engagement with Lord Allerton not be forthcoming." He shrugged. "And it certainly doesn't appear forthcoming now, does it?"

Eva spoke through pinched lips. "And do you think Lady Julia is a commodity to be pawned off on the next available bachelor?"

"No, I do not. And neither does Lord Owen, apparently. I was about to tell you the family will be disappointed to learn that while he greatly esteems Lady Julia, he has no wish to marry her."

"He told you this?"

"He did."

"You've certainly earned his confidence in a short time, haven't you?" She carefully pressed a sleeve. "I'm glad. It suggests he has every intention of keeping you on."

"I think so, too. But do you think Lady Julia will be terribly—"

He broke off as Miss Shea and Mr. Phelps came into the room. The countess's lady's maid carried an armful of black wool with beaded taffeta trim and regarded Eva and Nick with a sneer of disapproval. "It sounds like there's a lot of talking going on in here. Eva, as long as you're ironing, do be agreeable and touch up Lady Wroxly's gabardine suit. She may wish to go into the village tomorrow." She laid the suit across the table, well away from Mr. Hensley's bleaching solution. "Be mindful of the pleats. You know how particular Lady Wroxly is about her pleats. Nor would her ladyship appreciate any burn marks. If you place a wet cloth over the fabric—"

"Yes, Miss Shea, I do know how to steam pleats, thank you." She bit back any further retort. Miss Shea was her superior and it wouldn't do her any good to anger the woman.

"I'll leave you to it, then." Miss Shea turned about with a haughty flounce of her skirts.

Mr. Phelps placed the leather case he held on the table. "For that matter, Hensley, I don't suppose you'll mind sharpening Lord Wroxly's straight razor." He flipped the latch and opened the case to reveal a shaving kit trimmed in silver inlaid with ivory. "I'm sure you've been eager to earn your keep here. You'll find a strop and paste on those shelves behind you."

"Yes, Mr. Phelps, I know where the sharpening equipment is."

Eva slammed the iron onto its trivet. "Mr. Phelps, I'll have you know Mr. Hensley has found a position with Lord Owen. He is no longer unemployed and is earning his keep quite nicely." She specifically left out the part about the position being tentative, for she had every confidence Lord Owen would keep Nick on.

"I'm happy to hear it," the man replied stiffly and with no small amount of indifference. "I've an important errand for Lord Wroxly in town." He gave a slight roll of the eyes. "He's having me tend to Vernon in his jail cell. I'll return later for the shaving kit."

Eva decided to ignore his sarcasm. "How kind of Lord Wroxly to send you. It must mean he doesn't believe Vernon is guilty."

"One supposes not, but with Vernon all but convicted it seems rather cruel to allow him to become accustomed to any sort of luxuries. He'll receive no such favors in penitentiary, nor on the scaffold."

"Mr. Phelps!"

Before Eva could say more, Nick spoke up. "See here, Mr. Phelps. That kind of talk before a lady is completely out of line."

The valet made a point of gazing first to his left, then to his right. "I see no ladies present."

Nick was around the table before Eva could blink and had his hands around Mr. Phelps's lapels by the time she hurried over. She seized Nick by the backs of his arms. "Gentlemen, please. The strain is clearly affecting everyone's judgment. Nick, strictly speaking I am not a lady, not in the sense that the female members of the family are ladies. Isn't that what you meant, Mr. Phelps?"

She was being overly generous, of course, for she recognized Mr. Phelps's observation for the slight it had been meant to be. Better to swallow her pride than have the two of them going at it like a pair of hardheaded rams.

"Indeed, Miss Huntford, I meant no offense." His aquiline nose flared, and although he held himself upright with all the dignity he could muster, lingering alarm flickered in his eyes.

Nick released him and stepped back. He drew a breath. "I'm sorry, Phelps. I believed you to be insulting our Miss Huntford, and as she and I are old friends, I couldn't endure it."

Mr. Phelps gave a sniff. "Perhaps Lord Owen should be made aware of his new valet's temper."

"Please, that isn't necessary—"

"No, it's all right, Eva," Nick interrupted her. "If Mr. Phelps feels the need to inform our respective employers of this incident, I shan't stop him. It is his prerogative."

Mr. Phelps hesitated, then eased toward the door. "I'll be back later for his lordship's shaving kit."

Nick smiled and inclined his head. "I'll have it ready."

Moments after they were left alone, Eva said, "What will Lord Owen think? I'll come to your defense, you can be sure of it."

"Never mind, Evie." Going back around the table, he tossed the collar he had scrubbed clean into the pile of the others ready for the laundress. "He won't say a word to Lord Owen."

"How can you be so sure?"

"Because I just reminded him that his own employer would inevitably become involved and would therefore discover what a boorish, pompous ass he employs as his valet."

Eva burst out laughing and then whisked a hand to her mouth to muffle the sound. But she quickly sobered. "I do wish Lord Wroxly hadn't sent Phelps to tend to Vernon. One can only imagine the disheartening comments he'll make in Vernon's hearing."

Nick nodded his agreement. "I'll tell you what. I'll finish up with this last collar, sharpen Lord Wroxly's razor, and ask Lord Owen's leave for an hour or so. I'll check in on Vernon myself and try to undo any harm caused by Phelps."

"That would be wonderful, Nick. Thank you."

A mischievous gleam entered his eye, and Eva looked quickly away. Not quickly enough, however, for Nick said softly, "Are you contemplating a more tangible means of thanking me, Evie? Say, a kiss? The first one we shared was awfully nice."

She wanted to deny it, but that would be a lie. "Yes, it was," she murmured so low Nick frowned as if not sure she had even spoken. Louder, she continued. "But it was wrong, Nick. My position . . . yours . . . We mustn't risk—"

"Living?"

"You know what I mean." She retrieved her forgotten iron. "Either of us could get the sack for lesser indiscretions than that."

"Since when is living an indiscretion? Besides, I know the rules. No courting other members of the staff. Well, I'm not a member of the staff here, Evie. Even by Old Ironheart's unreasonable standards we wouldn't be doing anything wrong."

"Don't call her that." Eva placed the iron on the trivet once more. "This has nothing to do with Mrs. Sanders, really. *I* felt it to be wrong, Nick. I suppose I'm not a modern woman. Not when it comes to matters like this. I need . . . time."

He moved closer and Eva tensed, wanting him to stop several safe paces away, yet at the same time yearning to catch the scent of his shaving soap as she had when he kissed her. He stopped a couple of feet away and smiled. "Take all the time you need, Evie."

CHAPTER 17

"Why on earth hasn't the fire been laid in this room?" Grams addressed her question to no one in particular. The family and guests came to an abrupt halt as they entered the library, where they had planned to spend the time between luncheon and tea. Grams had declared the drawing room was beginning to feel as large and vacuous as a sepulcher, and Grampapa had suggested the cozier surroundings of books and leather.

Surely the servants would have been notified that this room would be in use today. Puzzled, Phoebe stared at the empty grate while the other women wrapped their arms around themselves as if suddenly propelled headlong into arctic temperatures, despite the furnaces sending ample hot water up into the radiators. The men, on the other hand, gathered around the fireplace as if to find a ready solution to their dilemma. None would be found, of course, until one of the servants arrived.

The only person who seemed unperturbed was Lady Cecily, who made herself comfortable on the brocade settee and folded her hands on her lap as if waiting for some sort of entertainment to begin. Her lady's maid took up position behind the sofa; she had been charged with keeping a close eye on her mistress for the remainder of the woman's stay at Foxwood.

Julia pivoted on her heel. "I'm going upstairs to the sitting room. It's always warmer there, fire or no."

"I'm coming with you." The sleeves of her afternoon dress flowing out behind her, Lady Allerton followed Julia out. She didn't so much as glance at her aunt. Obviously Lady Allerton was only too happy to relinquish the job of supervising Lady Cecily to the maid.

Amelia stared after her. "Shall we all go, Phoebe?"

"If you like, but I'm going below to see what's happening. I do hope there hasn't been another crisis."

"Yes, do," Grams concurred with a flick of her hand. "I hope none of the servants is ill, or worse, gone missing. Who is it usually lays the fires?"

"Connie, I should think," Amelia replied. "And then Vernon or Douglas lights them right before we need the room."

Connie. A warning prickling at her nape, Phoebe hastened her steps. Lord Owen followed her out of the room and she thought he intended to accompany her downstairs—why, she couldn't fathom. But he only stared after her before she heard him return to the library.

In the service hallway, she discovered Eva striding from room to room, looking briefly into each one. Her face troubled, Eva stopped when she spotted Phoebe.

"I'm looking for Connie," they said at the same time, then paused, then started to speak again.

"You first, my lady," Eva said.

"The fire wasn't lit in the library, although my grandfather left instructions with Mr. Giles that we'd be using the room after luncheon."

Douglas turned into the hallway looking harried and none too pleased. In one hand he carried a coal bin and in the other a basket of twisted paper and kindling. "I'm on my way up right now, my lady. My apologies. I went to light the fire a little while ago, but the hearth was empty."

"That's Connie's job, isn't it?"

"It is, my lady," Eva murmured. They both stepped aside to let Douglas pass. "I've been searching for her everywhere."

"Thank you, Douglas," Phoebe called after the footman as he climbed the stairs. "Please tell the family Connie is . . . indisposed . . . and that's why the mix-up with the fire." Then she whispered to Eva, "How long has she been missing?"

"It's hard to say. I saw her this morning. She laid the servants' table and helped Dora ready tea for Mrs. Sanders and Mr. Giles. I thought she went upstairs next to distribute the linens and turn on the water heaters. She might have done, or not. I really can't say. I didn't think to keep an eye on her."

"No, of course not." Phoebe thought a moment. "The morning fires were all properly lit and no one complained of cold water. Which suggests she disappeared sometime around luncheon."

Mrs. Sanders appeared in her office doorway. "When I get my hands on that girl—" She broke off and rearranged her angry scowl into look of concern. "My lady. I didn't know you'd come down."

"I'm worried about Connie, Mrs. Sanders."

"As are we all, my lady. I only wish I could say it was unlike her to be scarce when there was work to be done. But we know what happened the other day. Eva, have you checked outside for her?"

"No, but I will."

"I'll come with you." Phoebe followed Eva to the courtyard door and selected a cloak at random from the pegs. The garment hit the floor with fabric to spare, and she raised the hem clear with both hands. "It doesn't make sense that she'd sneak out with food for the children again. Not after last time, and especially when she knows we've made arrangements for just that very thing."

"I don't understand it either, my lady."

Phoebe loathed saying her next words, but they needed to be voiced. "I can only plead her case so far. If she proves completely undependable, I cannot go on insisting Mrs. Sanders spare her the sack."

Eva hugged her cloak tighter about her. "I know," was all she said.

They went out through the courtyard gate and made their way past the kitchen garden to the hothouses. "There are no new footprints," Phoebe observed.

"Nor any sign of village children. Nor Connie, for that matter."

"Did someone check her room? Perhaps she's ill." Phoebe couldn't help hoping that was the case. But Eva shook her head.

"Dora went up. Connie wasn't there." Then Eva's eyebrows went up and a slight smile curved her lips. "Wait a moment. I think I might know where she is. With Nick Hensley. Come, my lady, let's return to the house."

"But why would she be with Mr. Hensley?" Phoebe pushed the question out with her frigid breath as they hurried back to the service courtyard. As they reached it, a motor came rumbling up the drive, parking just outside the courtyard wall. A moment later, Mr. Hensley himself came trudging through the open gates. He slipped on the snow, now an icy slush, and waved his arms about to catch his balance.

Eva ran to his side and reached to steady him. "Is Connie with you?"

"Hello to you, too, Evie." His gaze lighted on Phoebe, and he immediately straightened and retrieved his arm from Eva's hold. He bobbed his head. "My lady. Is there something wrong?"

"Yes, Connie seems to be missing, Mr. Hensley. Please say she went to town with you. I assumed you went to town in the groundkeeper's lorry."

The old lorry with its open bed and wooden railings was used by the servants to haul equipment around the estate, or to drive into town and back. Phoebe herself had driven it during the war to bring their Red Cross supplies to Bristol and Gloucester. Clearly Mr. Hensley had gotten Mr. Giles's permission to motor into town.

"I went to visit Vernon, my lady," he said. "But Connie wasn't with me."

Eva heaved a sigh. "She's nowhere else. I was almost certain she must have gone with you." She cast an imploring look at Phoebe. "Now what?"

Mr. Hensley frowned. "You don't think she's run off, do you?"

"I don't see why she would," Eva replied.

"Come, let's go back inside." Phoebe motioned to the door. "We're not helping Connie by catching our deaths out here."

As soon as she spoke, she wished she hadn't, or hadn't used the word *death*. What if Connie hadn't shirked her duties today? What if something infinitely more dreadful had happened to her?

Once Lady Phoebe left to return to the library, Eva and Nick went to continue their chores in the valet service room. She had finished with Lady Wroxly's suit and now turned her attention to pressing the wrinkles out of her ladies' fine silk chemises and petticoats. "So tell me, Nick, how was Vernon?"

"Grateful for the books you sent."

"That's not what I mean."

"I know. He's despondent, I'm afraid. Certain he'll be found guilty."

"It does seem more and more likely that he'll go to trial. There must be something we're missing. Some clue that would lead us to the real killer."

"Assuming it isn't Vernon," Nick said quietly.

"How can you say that?" she snapped.

"I'm sorry. I don't know Vernon at all well, and so I cannot go on faith alone. And neither can the police, I'm afraid. You're quite right. Without any other substantial clues, he'll go to trial."

Eva's stomach sank. "And be convicted."

"In all likelihood."

Voices in the corridor penetrated the gloom that settled around her, and upon recognizing the slight brogue of one of them, Eva crossed the room to look out. "What's he doing back? Maybe he knows something about Connie."

"Who's back, Evie?"

Without answering she strode into the hall. "Constable Brannock, what brings you to Foxwood?"

Standing with Mrs. Sanders, Miles Brannock tipped his helmet to her as he unwrapped the muffler from around his neck. "Certain questions, Miss Huntford. If that's all right with you." He grinned as he spoke, but that didn't soften his intended mockery. Eva angled her chin at him.

"I thought you might be bringing news about Connie, our housemaid. She hasn't been seen since before luncheon."

Mrs. Sanders spoke before the constable could reply. "He's not here about Connie. I'm afraid that girl's whereabouts are still a mystery."

A wave of disappointment swept through Eva, followed by a smidgeon of hope. "Have you learned something new, then? Something to help Vernon?"

Before replying, the constable said to Mrs. Sanders, "Please send for Mr. Phelps, ma'am." When the obviously puzzled housekeeper walked away to use the inter-house telephone in her office, Miles Brannock turned back to Eva. "I might have, Miss Huntford, but there's nothing conclusive yet."

"It involves Mr. Phelps?"

His gaze slid past her. "I can't say."

A quick glance over her shoulder confirmed that Nick stood watching from the service room. Eva turned back to Constable Brannock and crossed her arms defensively. "It must, if you're having him sent for."

"Now that I think about it, Miss Huntford, I might ask you the very same questions I have for Mr. Phelps. I haven't forgotten what was inside your Christmas box either."

"Me? I've already been questioned."

"So has Mr. Phelps. Come with me." He led the way to Mrs. Sanders's office and poked his head inside. "Ma'am, might I use your office for a few minutes?"

Mrs. Sanders rose from behind her desk. "I have to confer with the Countess about tonight's dinner anyway, so, yes, you may use my office. Mr. Phelps is on his way."

The constable didn't bother closing the door, but he drew Eva to the desk and spoke in a murmur. "What do you know about Lord Allerton's Victory Bond fraud?"

"What?" The question took her by surprise. "Very little. Only what Lady Julia told us yesterday when you were here."

"And have you ever heard anyone in this house, staff or family, talk about these bonds?"

"No, never."

"Had *you* purchased these Victory Bonds at Lord Allerton's instigation?"

"Of course not. As I said, I hadn't heard about them until yesterday."

"Well . . ." He lowered his voice another notch. "Mr. Phelps did. I did a little research between yesterday and today."

"That was awfully quick work."

"The miracles of our modern age along with some help-ful connections of mine in London, Miss Huntford. Any-way, he purchased the bonds during the summer, like many of the others. Any idea how he might have heard of them?"

"I don't know . . ." She thought a moment. "Lord Wroxly did go up to London briefly last summer. Lady Julia went with him, and I assume he would have brought Mr. Phelps. Perhaps he somehow overheard Lady Julia speak of them, and believed them to be legitimate."

"Perhaps. . . ." His hand went to his chin as he seemed to weigh the possibility.

"Are you thinking this could be a motive?" She lowered her voice yet more. "That Mr. Phelps might have—"

Footsteps drew their attention to the doorway. Mr. Phelps emerged from the corridor.

"You wished to see me, Constable?" He looked down the length of his curving nose. "I do hope you'll be quick about it, as Lord Wroxly might send for me at any time. We are quite shorthanded nowadays, as I'm sure you're aware."

"I won't take up much of your time." He turned back to Eva. "Miss Huntford, that will be all for now, thank you. I'll let you know if I have further questions."

Eva hesitated at the door. "Will you look into Connie's disappearance?"

"I'll alert our search parties to keep an eye out for her, Miss Huntford, but she hasn't been missing long enough for us to consider her disappearance a matter of urgency."

"How can you say that? Time could be of the essence. She might at this very moment need our help and if we wait—"

"Miss Huntford, did you not understand me when I said Lord Wroxly might send for me at any moment?" Mr. Phelps raised a disapproving eyebrow. "This is not the first time the chit has been derelict in her duties. Your questions are only serving to delay me and obstruct official police business."

"Of all the arrogant—"

Miles Brannock stepped between them. "Miss Huntford, I'll do my best where your missing housemaid is concerned."

"Thank you."

Eva turned about and left them, though she burned to stay and hear Mr. Phelps's answers to what he was sure to consider exceedingly impertinent questions. But the constable closed the office door. She was even tempted to press her ear to the wood. She couldn't help but wonder why the policeman had confided in her. Was he gauging her reaction and judging whether she knew more about the matter than she admitted? Could Mr. Phelps truly be a suspect? She supposed that depended upon how much he lost in his investment. The prospect should have brought her a renewed sense of optimism for Vernon, yet despite Mr. Phelps's condescending and often infuriating attitudes, he was still a member of this household and she didn't wish him to be guilty either. It was a situation where there could be no happy outcome.

And then there was Connie, still missing . . .

"What was all that about?" Nick asked when she returned to the valet's service room.

She very nearly blurted out the gist of her conversation with Constable Brannock. He hadn't sworn her to secrecy, yet her silence in the matter had seemed implied. Once taken into someone's confidence—anyone's confidence—Eva would not betray their trust. It was a simple code she had learned from her father.

"Nothing, really," she said. "He just wanted to verify a

couple of points. Nothing that seemed as if it would help Vernon."

Unless, of course, the Victory Bond investments proved motivation enough for murder.

"He's never going to be found. Heaven help me, it's time I accepted it." Lady Allerton dissolved into sobs and collapsed onto the Grecian bench on the half landing of the staircase.

Phoebe and her siblings stopped halfway down the lower steps and turned around to see Grams sink beside their guest and speak quietly in Lady Allerton's ear. Lady Allerton raised a hand as if to push Grams away but stopped just short of doing so. Grampapa had come to an uncertain halt a few steps above them, his usual calm features a jumble of confusion. He looked down at Phoebe and her sisters and raised his hands in defeat. He obviously had no idea what to do or say. What reassurances could he possibly offer?

From below them in the Grand Hall, Theo groaned and clutched the bannister. He re-climbed the steps and sat stiffly at his mother's other side. "You know, Mother, this isn't going to help Henry."

"But it's all so hopeless," she wailed. Beside Phoebe, Amelia flinched. Julia, however, continued down to the hall and murmured something to Lord Owen that Phoebe couldn't distinguish.

"Come now, Mother." Theo gripped Lady Allerton's hand none too gently and came to his feet. "We're going downstairs for dinner and we are not going to give up on Henry."

At his prompting, Lady Allerton slowly stood. "Theo, don't you believe he's most certainly . . . gone?"

"What I believe, Mother, is that whatever has befallen Henry, we can't change it by falling apart."

"He does have a point, dear," Lady Cecily called up from the Grand Hall. "And you know how Henry despises displays of maudlin sentimentality."

"He'd depend on you to set an example for others," Grams added.

"Good heavens, yes, yes, you're quite right." The marchioness gave herself a shake. "Nothing can be gained from losing our heads. One must always maintain one's dignity, my father always said. Maude, Archibald, do forgive me."

"Think nothing of it, Lucille. Already forgotten." Grampapa descended to the half landing and offered an arm both to Lady Allerton and to Grams, who came to her feet with a weary sigh. "A fine man, your father. Shall we?"

He sent a look down to the others, one that indicated the crisis was over and time to disperse. Lord Owen and Julia were already heading for the library, she on his arm and looking quite comfortable there, Phoebe noted with a pang she didn't care to examine too closely. Fox surprised her by offering her his own arm.

She regarded him with surprise. "Thank you, Fox."

He snickered, and said in an undertone, "So where have you been sneaking off to lately? And with the servants, I might add. Searching for Henry? Or do you already know where he is?"

She might have known he hadn't suddenly blossomed into a considerate young gentleman. She shrugged. "No, I don't know where Henry is, but I had a hunch I decided to investigate and yes, Eva came with me. Why wouldn't she? Unfortunately we found nothing."

"Where did you look?"

She saw no reason not to tell him. "The gamekeeper's cottage. But it was empty, except for some old equipment."

"Eva wasn't the only servant following along. I saw

Henry's valet, too. Don't deny it." They reached the library, but rather than release Eva, Fox gripped her wrist. "Why did you need Henry's valet along?"

"I didn't particularly, but I thought a third pair of eyes might come in handy. Besides, Mr. Hensley was able to open the door of the gamekeeper's cottage when I couldn't." She left out the part about breaking the lock. Fox didn't need to know that.

"You're up to something."

"I'm not, Fox. Don't be ridiculous. If I can do anything to help Vernon I will, but I am not 'up' to anything nefarious." She gave a vicious yank that freed her hand, only to turn and notice Theo hovering behind them in the doorway and watching them intently. Had he been eavesdropping? The others ranged themselves around the fireplace, this time lit with an enthusiastic blaze. Why had Theo lingered on the threshold?

Phoebe decided she didn't care; what did it matter if Theo heard or not? She'd done nothing wrong, and neither had Eva nor Mr. Hensley. And for their pains they had discovered nothing—surely nothing worthy of eavesdropping.

And yet as Fox sauntered away from her, Theo remained where he was, his brow furrowed. Phoebe followed his line of sight and saw only their reflections in the darkened windowpanes.

"Phoebe, why are you loitering alone in the middle of the room?" Grams motioned to her. "Do come and sit."

With a last glance at Theo, Phoebe took a seat on the wide ottoman Grampapa would normally have propped his feet on when settling in with a book. Though intent on ignoring Theo, she couldn't help glancing up at the doorway again. He was gone.

Gone without a word. What could spur a man—even

Theo—to behave in so ill-mannered a fashion? Especially knowing his mother's frame of mind. Had Phoebe and Fox's talk of Henry upset him? Or . . .

Had mention of the gamekeeper's cottage set off some kind of alarm only he could hear? The garden-facing windows had suddenly become an object of fascination for him, and what was out there but the footprints that led to the woods . . . and ultimately, perhaps, to the gamekeeper's cottage.

The more Phoebe considered, the more her heart raced and her ears rang, until she no longer heard the conversation around her.

"Phoebe? Phoebe!" Julia snapped her fingers. "I asked you about your plans to start up a new aid project for veterans and their families. Now the war is over, don't you think people will wish to focus their energies elsewhere?"

"I'm sorry, Phoebe," Amelia put in quickly, a worried look on her face, "was I not supposed to mention it?"

"Just please don't tell me you intend driving lorries again." Grams pursed her lips. "That was all very well during the war, but I should think you'd wish to return to more, well, normal pursuits now life has settled down. Archibald, don't you agree Phoebe should focus her attentions on more refined activities?"

"First things first," Fox mumbled into his cravat. "Let's get her married off."

Ordinarily Phoebe might have pinched him, but tonight the comment hardly registered, nor did Grams's observation: "Yes, as a married woman you may choose any charities you wish."

"Not to interfere, but . . ." Sitting in the Louis XV armchair across from Phoebe, Lord Owen casually crossed one leg over the other. "There is a great need among veterans and their families, so many of whom have been left with few or no means of earning a livelihood. On their behalf, I commend Lady Phoebe for her generosity and I do hope, Lord and Lady Wroxly, that you'll support the endeavor."

For the first time, Owen Seabright's attentions didn't send a blush creeping into Phoebe's cheeks. On one level she silently thanked him, yet at the same time she dismissed his encouragement while her own thoughts bandied about her brain. Then she was on her feet.

"Excuse me, everyone. I'll be back. I . . ." She never finished the sentence, didn't know how she *would* have finished the sentence, and in fact forgot she left a roomful of gaping individuals as soon as she crossed the threshold.

She found Eva below in the kitchen, wrapped in a starched white apron as she helped Mrs. Ellison and Dora fill the serving platters with the night's dinner. Phoebe's arrival brought a look of horror to Mrs. Ellison's face.

"Lady Phoebe! Are we late bringing dinner up?" The cook's reddening complexion made a startling contrast to her own white apron and cap.

"No, Mrs. Ellison, everything is fine upstairs. I realize you're very busy, but may I borrow Eva for a few moments?"

"Of course, my lady. I'm only sorry I have her ladling soup and spooning out potatoes. No fit work for a lady's maid, to be sure, but with Connie missing . . ."

Eva placed the ladle on a trivet beside the copper soup pot and placed the lid on the porcelain tureen. "I told you I don't mind helping out, Mrs. Ellison." She crossed the room to Phoebe. "What is this about, my lady? Not more ill news I hope."

"Come with me." Phoebe took her hand and brought her into the valet's service room, where she judged they'd have the most privacy. "Something most peculiar happened just now in the library," she said in a rush. "Fox began interrogating me as to where you and Mr. Hensley and I were going the other day, and I saw no reason not to tell him I'd decided to have a look about the gamekeeper's cottage."

"Well and good, my lady. There was nothing to hide about that, I suppose."

"No, you wouldn't think so. But then I noticed Lord Theodore listening in. He became very distracted, lost in thought, and then he disappeared without a word to anyone. Just turned around and left the library without a by-your-leave. What do you make of that?"

"Are you sure the gamekeeper's cottage was the cause of his distraction?"

"There couldn't have been anything else. He was fine before that. Even when his mother nearly broke down as we were all coming downstairs, he persuaded her that losing their heads wouldn't help her eldest son. He seemed rational and in control, only to behave most irrationally minutes later. The only thing that occurred between the two incidents was my conversation with Fox. I *knew* the cottage played a significant part in all this, and now it seems I was right."

Eva paused to take this in, then said, "What do you propose we do about it?"

"First thing in the morning we need to reexamine the cottage. We must have missed something vital."

"But, my lady, assuming you're correct, Lord Theodore might even now be on his way back to the cottage to dispose of any evidence he left behind."

"Goodness, Eva, you're right. But to stumble around the woods in the dark . . . We should telephone Constable Brannock. Except I very much doubt he'll take me seriously. Perhaps if you called . . ."

"He was here earlier. Too bad he left already."

"Excuse me, but did I just hear mention of the old gamekeeper's cottage?"

Phoebe whirled about to see Mr. Giles standing in the doorway, and she could have bitten her tongue for having spoken in so unguarded a fashion. But suddenly she realized her incaution could yield a benefit.

"Mr. Giles, you've been at Foxwood for ages, haven't you?"

"Indeed, my lady. I came as an under footman many years ago. In those days, many more servants were employed in the running of the house. Footmen and parlor maids aplenty, practically one for each room, and a host of underlings to assist. Ah, but times have changed, haven't they? That kind of extravagant living is no longer the way of things, more's the pity—"

"Mr. Giles," Phoebe interrupted, "can you tell me anything about the gamekeeper's cottage? For instance, are there any . . . well . . . secret storage nooks. Anything like that?"

"Well, when I first came to Foxwood, the gamekeeper lived in the older cottage to the west. A cramped, drafty old place it was. And then the additional storage cellars were built here in the main house, which meant he needn't live there any longer."

Oh dear, Phoebe thought. Was poor Mr. Giles becoming confused again? She traded a glance with Eva, who frowned slightly. "What do the storage cellars have to do with the gamekeeper's cottage?"

"We no longer needed to store the winter produce in the old root cellar."

Phoebe resisted the urge to press her palms to her temples in frustration. She asked as calmly as she could, "What root cellar, Mr. Giles?"

"Why, the one beneath the present gamekeeper's cottage. The whole place was once used, as I said, to—"

"To store the winter produce," Phoebe and Eva echoed

at the same time. They both gasped, and Phoebe's heart thundered. "Where is this root cellar, Mr. Giles?"

"Just to the left of the storage entrance doors. But it's well covered over. Your grandfather insisted there be no chance of accidents, nor of mischievous young boys taking it into their heads to play underground. Your father was an adventurous youth, to say the least, my lady, and he—"

"Thank you, Mr. Giles. That's all *very* interesting. But I . . . er . . . mustn't keep you any longer."

"No, indeed, my lady. I must see to the serving of dinner now."

Phoebe watched him traverse the corridor, and as soon as he stepped out of sight she rounded on Eva and gripped her hands. "That's it—that's where Henry is. I had no idea of the existence of such a cellar . . . but Lord Theodore might very well have learned of it as a boy. It's the kind of thing boys have an uncanny knack for knowing."

"Do you still want me to telephone Miles Brannock?"

Phoebe nodded emphatically. "Yes, do. I'll wait here and you can tell me what he says. Even if Lord Theodore is not involved, we might just have discovered where Lord Allerton lay."

Eva hurried out to use the telephone in Mrs. Sanders's office. While Phoebe waited she surveyed the room around her—the shoes waiting to be polished, her grandfather's overcoat that needed a brisk brushing, several shirts that wanted ironing, including one of Phoebe's own blouses, and then there were the items lining the shelves. Some were tools of a valet's or lady's maid's trade: brushes, polish, cleaning solutions. . . . Phoebe's gaze fell upon Grampapa's shaving kit, probably brought down for cleaning and sharpening. She walked over to it, placing her hand on the silver latch.

"Lady Phoebe, good evening." Surprise laced Mr. Hensley's greeting. He stopped short on the threshold, his expression quizzical.

"I'm sorry to intrude, Mr. Hensley. I'm just waiting for Eva to return from . . ." She trailed off, uncertain why his presence made her feel like a trespasser, or why she felt the need to make excuses for being there. His gaze fell to where her hand rested on the tooled leather case of the shaving kit, and for some odd reason she snatched her hand back as if the razor inside could somehow slice her fingers.

Her fingers . . .

"My lady, the con—" Eva rounded the corner into the room and came to a halt. "Nick, I didn't see you come down. Have you come to help with dinner?"

"I certainly will if you need me, but actually Mr. Phelps asked me to bring up Lord Wroxly's shaving kit. It seems our Lady Phoebe has already claimed it."

"No, I was only looking . . ." Awkwardness came over her again, sending excuses to stumble from her lips. She moistened them, then clamped them shut.

"Nick, you'll never guess," Eva said in a murmur. "We think we know where Lord Allerton is."

"Good heavens, Evie! Where?"

"Well, I expect we must have trod over the very place . . ."

Phoebe wanted to shush her—why, she didn't know. But it was too late, and as Eva went on to explain, her thoughts took a sharp turn. Valets had access to their masters' shaving kits—it was their job to keep the brushes clean, the blades flawlessly sharp. A nicked chin would never do, nor a scraped neck. . . .

She studied Mr. Hensley, looking distinguished in his severe black suit. But the man wasn't always a valet. He once worked at Foxwood. First as a gamekeeper's assistant, later as an under footman. He'd been a boy when he first entered into service here.

What had Phoebe herself said? *Boys have an uncanny knack for knowing . . .*

Mr. Hensley might have known . . . in all likelihood *had* known . . . about the old root cellar.

The silence jarred her from her thoughts. Eva was studying her with a curious expression. "Are you all right, my lady?"

"She's fine," Mr. Hensley answered, his mouth curving in a smile, his eyes sharp with cunning, and the tiniest of silver handguns pointed in her direction.

CHAPTER 18

At first Eva didn't understand the gleam of light flashing in Nick's hand. And why did Lady Phoebe look like that—shocked and frightened and deathly pale?

"Nick, whatever are you doing? Good heavens, put that thing away before you hurt someone. Where on earth did you get it?"

It was Phoebe who replied, in a voice devoid of inflection. "It's Lord Allerton's, isn't it, Mr. Hensley? You gave out six others of his belongings, and you kept his pistol along with whatever other satisfaction you had in murdering him."

"My lady, no, I'm sure you're quite wrong. Nick would never . . ." Eva regarded the weapon in Nick's hand. Surely he had a reasonable explanation. "They served together in the war. . . ."

"But he did kill Henry, Eva. It wasn't Lord Owen or Lord Theodore, or Julia or anyone else. It was Mr. Hensley."

Aghast, Eva turned back to him. "Nick, please say something. Please tell Lady Phoebe she's wrong."

"We're leaving." He gave a waggle of that insidious little weapon, as if it controlled invisible strings attached to

Eva and Phoebe. Neither of them budged. Phoebe's face mirrored the burgeoning horror flowing through Eva.

"You'll never get us out of here without being seen," Phoebe said. "The rest of the staff—"

"Are all busy carrying up dinner." Nick waved the gun again.

"Then they'll be calling for me to help." Eva latched on to hope. "Someone will be here any moment looking for me."

"No, they won't." Phoebe shook her head gravely. She released a breath. "They won't come, Eva, because I took you away from the kitchen. They'll make do shorthanded rather than risk offending me by insisting you return. Blast."

Eva dug in her heels. "Well, then, I've already ca—" She broke off as Phoebe shot her a fierce message with her eyes. Why *not* tell Nick that Miles Brannock had already been alerted? But then she realized Constable Brannock would go directly to the gamekeeper's cottage. She could only hope and pray that was where Nick intended to take them. But if Nick knew of Constable Brannock's involvement, he might do something drastic, such as take them to some other location and kill them both.

Lady Phoebe—*her* Phoebe—dying in some icy ditch. Eva's throat closed. The room began to spin, turned fuzzy and dark. She reached out to clutch her young lady to her but found only the hard edge of the worktable. Phoebe called her name, and something small and cold nudged the middle of her back.

Those two things were all she needed. Tightening her grip on the table, she straightened and shook her head to clear it. As the blood flowed more normally, she heard Nick speaking.

"We're leaving *now*. We'll go out through the servants' courtyard. I suggest you both take a cloak. It's deadly cold outside."

His voice and his steely eyes were deadly cold as well.

Outside, Eva and Phoebe, having taken the advice to wrap woolen cloaks around them, walked arm in arm with Nick following, and always that threatening weapon trained on their backs. When Eva and Phoebe turned toward the garden gate, he stopped them.

"This way. There isn't time for a stroll through the gardens, ladies, nor would it be a particularly good idea with the dining-room windows overlooking the path."

"My family will wonder where I am, you know. I imagine Amelia has already gone upstairs looking for me." Despite her brave words, Lady Phoebe trembled against Eva's side.

"Yes, one would assume." Nick gave a low chuckle. "That's why we'll take the lorry. Mr. Giles has grown quite careless about keys, hasn't he, my lady?" He prodded Eva to unlatch the service gates while he kept the gun leveled on Phoebe and then ordered them to walk through. A dozen different means of resisting ran through Eva's mind, but she dismissed them all as too great a risk to Phoebe's life.

"You didn't take the lorry the night Henry died," Phoebe said, and Eva wished she would stop engaging Nick in pointless conversation. What if she angered him?

"No, my lady. Didn't think of it, really. I had to do something quick, so I switched my shoes for his boots and began walking." They reached the truck parked in its bay hidden from view of the house. He opened the driver's side door. "You first, Evie."

Yes, she should have known he would keep Phoebe close beside him at all times. She climbed in and slid to the far end of the cold leather seat. Phoebe hesitated. "Why did you murder him?"

Eva's heart skipped a beat. Why did the girl persist in

challenging him? "Phoebe, please, just do as he says and get in."

"Yes, do get in, my lady. There will be time for talk later."

Would there? Was Nick going to spare them? It seemed illogical to Eva, but she held on to the hope. Soon they were rumbling down the estate road past the stables. The truck slid on icy patches, prompting Eva to stifle more than one cry. She held an arm across Phoebe's torso as if that could keep her safely in her seat if they crashed. Phoebe sat with her teeth clenched so tightly her jaw visibly pulsed, but otherwise she showed no fear. Several minutes after passing the stables Nick pulled the truck off the road and shut the engine. With the dousing of the headlights, the only illumination was that of the moon reflecting dimly on the snow.

"All right, I go first, then Lady Phoebe."

When they were all three standing on the frigid ground, Phoebe shivered and pulled her cloak tighter. "Now will you tell us why you killed Henry?"

He gave a cavalier shrug. "Start walking and I'll explain. You take the lead, Evie."

She wanted to claw his face each time he called her *Evie,* but with outward calm she began moving icy branches aside to find the path to the cottage.

"I think once you hear the truth you'll agree I did the right thing," Nick said almost amiably. "It started years ago, during the war. Lord Allerton had always been the devil's own whelp, but the war brought out the weasely coward in him as well. Men lost their lives because of him. Then about a year ago he proved himself no better than a St. Giles cutthroat. Our camp had been shelled all day, and anytime a soldier so much as poked a finger out of the trenches, he was peppered by machine gunfire. Lord Allerton and I were on the rear lines—where we were relatively safe—but even so, we could feel the men reaching their breaking point. Finally, an order to pull back came over the wire, but at the same time the shelling stopped."

Eva kept pushing through the brittle foliage, not sure if she had found the path or not. She wasn't even sure they were walking in the right direction, but since Nick didn't correct her she kept going, but slowly, stumbling on purpose and stalling for time.

Please hurry, Constable Brannock. . . .

Nick's voice came again, eerily muffled by the trees and the hissing snow that began falling in dry, sharp flakes. "The shelling stopped, and Lord Allerton decided the Germans must have given up. Perhaps their arsenal had run short, he said. So instead of sounding the retreat . . . Good God . . ."

His voice broke, and the raw emotion of it brought Eva to a halt. She turned, and rather than seeing the fiend who held them at gunpoint, she perceived a soldier caught in the throes of grief and terror. "What did he do, Nick?"

"He gave the order to attack. Thought he'd use the opportunity to make a name for himself, the selfish, stupid wretch. He'd already been awarded a Distinguished Service Order—not that he deserved it—and I suppose he was hoping for a Victoria Cross this time. He sent boys and young men charging out into no-man's-land . . . and that's when the shelling started again, like a firestorm." He groaned as if with physical pain. "Evie, your brother, Danny. Myron Henderson from the village, and the tailor's elder son. There were others—the uncle of your hall boy, Josh. And the village boy who intended asking Dora to marry him when he got home. You see, our battalion was made up of Cotswolds men. And that bastard, that miserable excuse for a man, sent them all either to their deaths or, like

Myron, to a future where they must live without the limbs God gave them. Still others haven't recovered from the shell shock and probably never will."

Eva barely heard anything past her brother's name. The battalion should have retreated. Danny might still be alive. Might even now be helping her father with the farm . . . A weight descended on her chest, crushing and painful, and for a second time that night she struggled to breathe.

"And you thought you could make it up to them by killing Henry and dispersing a few of his baubles?" Phoebe's anger rivaled the frigid air in bitterness. Eva started to caution her, but she kept relentlessly on with the blind bravado of youth. "No, Eva, I will not be silenced. Mr. Hensley, your actions were no better than those of a lawless vigilante. If Henry sacrificed the lives of others due to his reckless decision, you could have brought it to the attention of the authorities. Didn't his commanding officers notice he disobeyed orders?"

Nick shook his head, staring at the ground in obvious misery. "He lied. He said the lines were down, that the order didn't reach him until after he sent our soldiers out. Even the men in the trenches didn't know the truth. Only I knew. I knew because I was with him when the order came."

"But why now?" Phoebe persisted. "Why did you wait so long?"

A change came over Nick's expression, the sorrow vanishing and ruthlessness returning. "You ask too many questions, my lady." He flicked a gaze at Eva and back to Phoebe. "Walk."

They continued along the trail, until the cottage came into view in its little clearing, the snow on its roof glowing blue against the darkness. Eva saw no sign of Miles Brannock and knew their time was swiftly running out. "Nick, leave us here and take the lorry. You can be long gone from Little

Barlow before Phoebe and I make it even halfway back to the house. There is no need to—"

"Wait a minute," Phoebe said, the challenge rising in her voice once more. "Mr. Phelps also received one of your ghastly surprises in his Christmas box. He didn't fight in the war and to my knowledge he didn't lose anyone either. So why him? And again, why now?"

Her questions brought them to another halt at the edge of the clearing, beneath the overhanging branches of a towering Scots pine.

"You're awfully demanding for a young lady who's run out of options. So like your kind you are—arrogant and oblivious." Nick's eyes narrowed, and Eva almost fell to her knees in fear when his finger twitched on the trigger. "But there's no reason why you can't know. You won't be able to tell anyone. Our dear Lord Allerton had served up a Victory Bond scam—"

"Yes, we know all about that," Phoebe said.

Nick frowned in puzzlement before smiling vaguely. "I'll add *clever* to your list of attributes, my lady. When we were in London on leave last summer, I overheard him convincing an acquaintance to invest, and damn my own stupidity, I believed the opportunity to be real. I invested. Heavily. Only to find out when the war ended a month ago the bonds I purchased were worthless. As were the ones I encouraged Harlan Phelps to invest in. Luckily for me, the man's pride has stilled his tongue."

"That's why he refused to share his room with you," Eva said. "He's angry about his losses and blames you."

"Can't say as I blame him," Nick muttered.

"Money." Phoebe shook her head. "I knew it had to be a motive. It so often is."

Nick lurched toward her and Eva darted between them. The pistol struck her shoulder. The pain was sharp and radiated down her arm. She braced for the sting of a bullet, but in the next instant realized the pistol hadn't discharged. Nick stood toe-to-toe with her, his breath heaving and his nostrils flaring. He looked nothing short of a demon in the shadows of the forest. He shoved Eva backward. She stumbled into Phoebe and the two tumbled to the ground.

Nick stood above them. His teeth were bared, his chest rising and falling, the pistol extended down at them. "Don't try that again, Eva, or you'll both be dead."

"Let Phoebe go, Nick."

"No." Nick and Phoebe spoke at the same time. With her knees bent beneath her cloak, she looked like a vulnerable waif abandoned in the cold.

"I'm not leaving you, Eva," she said in a voice that brooked no debate. Eva's chest constricted.

"Get up," Nick ordered, almost a shout that made Phoebe flinch. But to Eva, his short outburst meant he didn't suspect anyone else might soon be arriving. Perhaps if she stalled him long enough . . .

Once she and Phoebe were back on their feet, Eva said, "Nick, I believe it was more than money that spurred you to do what you did. You aren't that shallow." Perhaps a show of sympathy would distract him from his purpose.

"By God, Evie, you've no idea how right you are. I went to him, still having no clue he was in on the scam. I told him how much I'd lost—I was essentially ruined, every bit of the money I'd saved gone. And do you know what he did?"

When his pause stretched on with seemingly no end, Eva asked, "No, please tell me. What did he do, Nick?"

His expression suddenly twisted with rage, and he once again lurched toward them. Eva wrapped her arms around Phoebe and pulled her back, but Nick stopped within a couple of feet of them, so close Eva swore she felt the heat of his anger. "He laughed! Laughed at me, Evie! Said a servant should know his place and not presume to eavesdrop on his betters. Said I got what I deserved."

It was all Eva could do to muster an appearance of commiseration. "Oh, Nick, how dreadful. I'm so sorry."

"But that's not all. After he said those things, he shrugged me off and sat down at his piano. His *beloved* piano. As I stood there gaping, he played some frivolous melody that made me want to murder him right then and there. But I didn't. I waited. I hoped he might take pity on me and help me find a way to recoup my losses."

"But he didn't, did he, Mr. Hensley?" This time Phoebe's voice held no challenge. Like Eva, she managed to project a convincing empathy.

"I asked him again Christmas night. I thought perhaps the spirit of the season had mellowed him. And I believed him to have become engaged that night . . ." His scowl returned. "To your blasted sister, my lady."

With nothing to say to that, Phoebe only compressed her lips.

"That night as I helped him out of his evening clothes, I raised the issue again. And this time . . . *this* time he said I was lucky to even have employment. He said I was no more deserving of recompense than the many shopkeepers to whom he owed money. If they could wait on payment, so could I. At that moment, I'd had enough." Nick barked out a laugh. "He cared as little as he did the day he sent all those soldiers to their deaths. Lord Allerton didn't deserve to breathe another day longer."

"You strangled him." Phoebe paused, obviously considering. "That would explain a lack of blood. What did you use, his cravat?"

Eva winced at her calculated guess. Nick smiled.

"Very good, Lady Phoebe. You are rather skilled at this. His cravat proved a most convenient weapon, being right there at my fingertips."

Phoebe's eyes widened and her mouth dropped open for an instant. Then she said, "The shirt stud. Henry must have torn it off as the two of you struggled. Of course! Eva, don't you see, it was the only clue he could leave us."

"Did he?" Nick raised one eyebrow as if he and Phoebe were engaged in an academic debate. "I hadn't realized. But how was that a clue? He was always careless with his wardrobe. One of the banes of my existence."

"Exactly, Mr. Hensley. Your job was to see to his clothing." Phoebe's chin took on a triumphant tilt. "Buttons and other such notions fall under a valet's domain. It was Henry's way of telling us who attacked him. Only I wasn't clever enough to realize it."

"Enough." Eva threw her hands in the air. "Nick, whatever you intend doing out here, please reconsider. Phoebe is only a child—"

"I'm not!"

Eva spoke over her. "You can make your escape without hurting either of us." She took a step toward him.

The gun swung toward her. "Stay there, Evie. I never intended hurting anyone else—not you or your precious Lady Phoebe, not Connie or even Theo Leighton, though he's another of the devil's brood."

"Connie and Theo!" Phoebe gasped and pressed a hand to her mouth.

"His lordship apparently reached the same conclusion you did, Lady Phoebe." Nick bared his teeth again. "Little meddling fool, you are. You were talking about this cottage and Theo realized I would know about it. He came running below stairs with . . ." He laughed and extended the gun farther. "Well, with this little weapon of his. Unfortunately I had the better of him and, to say the least, he won't be needing his pistol again."

"Oh, Theo . . . he's . . . dead?" Tears glistened on Phoebe's cheeks. "I suspected him . . . I never much liked him. . . ."

Eva tightened her arm around her. "Nick, you can't keep on like this. Two lives gone, and Vernon sitting in a jail cell for a crime you committed—" Eva's thoughts became lost in a tide of fresh horror. "And Connie. Is she alive or dead?"

Phoebe gasped again and stared at Nick. "Where is she? What have you done with her? And *why* Connie?"

"She saw me sharpening Lord Wroxly's razor. She didn't even have to say anything, I saw it in her eyes and knew what she was thinking. I was disposing of her while you believed I'd gone to town today, Evie."

The breath whooshed out of Eva and she feared she would faint. Still, she pushed the question out. "Disposed of her where?"

"You're about to find out. Move."

Panic caught Phoebe in a choke hold. From the corners of her eyes she took in her surroundings. She remembered the rock he had used to break the lock on the cottage door. Could she find another? The falling snow made it difficult to discern one thing from another. Besides, could she retrieve a rock and use it fast enough before he shot one or both of them?

Her foot slid on the slippery ground, and instinctively she reached out for balance. Eva quickly came to her rescue, securing a hold on her arm. But with her other hand Phoebe kept reaching, because her fingers had brushed pine needles and an idea sprang to life. She grabbed one of the lower boughs and tugged for all she was worth, and succeeded in breaking loose a shower of snow from not only the one branch, but several.

The weight of it knocked all three of them off balance. Phoebe seized the opportunity by lunging into Mr. Hensley's side. Eva wasted no time but barreled into him as well, and the two of them plunged to the ground.

"Phoebe, run!"

It was a suggestion she ignored, instead launching herself onto the heap Eva and Mr. Hensley had become. Wildly she threw punches, praying none of them landed on Eva. An explosion stung Phoebe's ears and a high-pitched ringing grew to a deafening pitch. The gun had gone off.

"Eva?"

"I'm all right!"

Mr. Hensley swore. His arm lay flat out on the ground, the pistol pointing into the forest, his hand covered in black powder. Phoebe flung herself at his wrist, using every bit of her determination and all of her weight to pin the weapon to the frozen ground. Mr. Hensley struggled beneath her and she despaired of restraining him for much longer. Eva was struggling to untangle her legs from his and finally managed to drag herself out from under him.

Suddenly, blood flew in droplets in the air and splattered Phoebe's coat. Mr. Hensley bellowed and went rigid, his arm once more hitting the ground beneath her weight. Phoebe looked up to see Eva kneeling over him. Blood dripped from her closed fist. Phoebe found the source: Mr. Hensley's nose—a nose that now tilted to one side.

On all fours Eva scrambled around him and prized the gun from Mr. Hensley's fingers. A violent shove from the valet sent Phoebe hurtling dizzily onto her side. At the same time, Eva gained her feet, drew back her foot, and kicked. The blow landed square in Mr. Hensley's ribs. He gave a wet roar, the blood now running into his mouth, and when Eva kicked out again, he caught her ankle and yanked. Eva's other foot came out from under her and she crashed onto her back with a sharp cry. His nose streaming, Mr. Hensley started to push to his feet. Phoebe charged bull-like on all fours, intending to hit him full-on—

A second shot stopped her cold. Blinking, Eva sat up and pointed the pistol at Nick. "Touch my lady Phoebe again, Nick Hensley, and the next shot goes straight into your miserable heart."

But who had fired the shot? Not Eva, Phoebe was sure of it. The next moments were a confusion of shouts, running feet, a twisted jumble of arms and legs as Mr. Hensley was dragged away from her, and then, finally, a soothing voice in her ear.

"Phoebe, it's all right, you're safe now. Are you hurt?"

CHAPTER 19

At first Phoebe could make little sense of the commotion around her, or of the voice speaking softly to her or the arms gently encircling her. An electric lantern clicked on, flooding the scene with a garish glare that temporarily blinded her. And then some of the fog of confusion cleared and she recognized the handsome features hovering above her. "Lord Owen?"

He smiled. "Owen will do. Can you stand?"

"Yes, I . . . I think so."

Two other men flanked Mr. Hensley, each gripping an arm and hauling him to his feet. He was snarling, swearing—and then fell silent. He stared, even as Phoebe stared in disbelief, at the man to his right.

"You're dead." Mr. Hensley spat blood with each word. "I killed you."

"I'm afraid not." Theo traded a mirthless grin with Miles Brannock, who stood at Mr. Hensley's other side.

"Surely you'll have one devil of a headache for the next several days, milord," the constable said.

Theo nodded ruefully. "Should have shot me, Nick."

"Would have done, if it weren't for the racket it would've

made," the valet muttered bitterly, and spat another mouthful of blood.

Phoebe rose with Owen's help. A raw gash at Theo's hairline filled her with remorse for ever suspecting him. "Oh, Theo, I'm so happy you're not dead." Her gaze took in both Theo and Lord Owen. "Eva had called Constable Brannock, but how do you two come to be here as well?"

"First Theo left the library, then you," Owen said with a half shrug. "I knew something was going on, so I followed. I'd assumed you both went upstairs, and I arrived in the gallery to see Theo slipping out of his room with his little pistol in hand." When Eva held the weapon up, Owen nodded. "That tweaked my suspicions—sorry, Theo—so I followed, but at a great enough distance that he wouldn't detect me. I trailed him down the back staircase, but by the time I came upon him, he was a heap on one of the landings." He glanced over at Theo. "There was a moment there I thought you were well and truly dead. Thank God you came around."

"And I realized it must be Nick Hensley who'd done Henry in when you and Fox talked about the game-keeper's cottage," Theo said. "I remembered about the root cellar, and I knew Hensley knew about it, too. We'd all been there as boys. The pieces all fell into place."

"We need to secure him and get that root cellar open." Miles Brannock's brogue was clipped with authority. He slipped his own gun—not a dainty silver pistol but something heavy and black and unforgiving—into a holster hidden beneath his overcoat. Then he helped Eva up off the ground.

The three men made short work of restraining Mr. Hensley. Miles Brannock linked a pair of handcuffs around a tree limb and secured Mr. Hensley's hands above his head. He wouldn't be going anywhere.

Phoebe couldn't resist approaching him. She looked him

up and down as a bitter taste rose in her mouth. "I'm on to you, Mr. Hensley."

He laughed bitterly. "Really? How is that?"

"Killing Lord Allerton was never about the war, was it? It wasn't about making up for the losses of others. It was all about what you lost. The money. You snapped and killed him, and afterwards panicked. I think you made up the rest to convince yourself he deserved it, to soothe your guilty conscience."

"I didn't make up what happened a year ago, you silly girl. Men died because of him."

"I understand it happened, and I believe it was most likely Lord Allerton's fault. But you . . ." She paused and looked back at Theo, who was silently watching and listening. "Lord Theodore wouldn't have you for his valet. There must be a good reason for that."

Theo came forward and set a hand on her shoulder. "My brother spoke of that day to me not long after. Said they might have pushed the Germans back if the men hadn't forgotten to bring their spines along with them when they charged. It made me sick to hear it, but you, Mr. Hensley, you nodded and laughed under your breath. Thought no one noticed, did you? No one notices the valet?" He moved closer to Mr. Hensley, and whispered, "*I* noticed, you . . ."

His voice plunged lower still, and Phoebe couldn't hear what he called Mr. Hensley.

Constable Brannock spoke from close behind her. "Milord?"

Theo stood another moment in front of Mr. Hensley before nodding and moving away. He approached the cottage, stopping a few yards to the right of the storage room door. He began kicking at the ground, his ear tilted. Phoebe detected no difference from one strike of his foot to another, but he reached a spot where he kicked multiple times. Bits of snow and earth flew up from the heel of his boot. "This is it."

"There are shovels and things inside, and the door isn't locked." Phoebe started to hurry over to Theo, but Owen stopped her.

"We'll handle it. But it would be a good idea for you and Miss Huntford to wait inside, out of the cold."

"It'll be just as cold inside as out." Phoebe went to stand with Eva. "We'll wait here."

Theo didn't go for the shovel. He merely crouched, brushed aside layers of snow, dead leaves, and twigs, and began clawing at the ground. Miles Brannock helped him. Chunks of earth scattered.

Phoebe knew frozen ground didn't break apart so easily. The spot had already been dug up once and recently, then carefully replaced to appear natural to the casual eye. She certainly hadn't noticed anything amiss when they'd been here last. Dear heavens, if she or Eva *had* noticed, what would Mr. Hensley have done? Would either of them be standing here now?

Theo soon uncovered the wooden planks and iron latch of a trap door. Phoebe slipped her arm through Eva's. "It won't be long now." She spoke through clenched teeth. In tense silence they ventured closer to the others.

Theo who reached for the latch. "Everyone ready?"

At their nods he pulled. The door let out a protesting grind, the sound jarring in the quiet wood. Theo let it fall completely open and it hit the ground with a thwack. "Nothing for it," he said, but Constable Brannock grasped his arm before he could descend the first stone step.

"I'll go first, milord." He took up the lantern, holding it out before him as he picked his way down the ancient steps.

"Do you see anything, Constable?" Phoebe called down after him.

His answer came immediately. "Are there any blankets in the cottage?"

"Yes, there are." Eva hurried inside and returned carrying a bundle.

"Toss them down. Better yet, Lord Owen, would you please bring them down."

Phoebe frowned, then pressed a hand to her mouth. "Is Henry *alive*?"

"No, milady, but Connie Robson is and I'll need help carrying her out."

That next day Eva's heart squeezed as Lord Wroxly's sapphire blue Rolls Royce came around the drive and stopped in front of Foxwood Hall's main entrance. Despite the cold, the staff and even the family had assembled outside in a formal receiving line typically reserved for illustrious visitors. After the chauffeur opened the door and assisted Lord Wroxly out of the vehicle, the earl in turn offered his own assistance to George Vernon. Lord Wroxly had insisted on collecting Vernon himself this morning, had brought him a fresh suit of clothes as well as Mr. Phelps to help him prepare for his homecoming.

Applause broke out, turning Vernon's fair complexion several shades ruddier. He smiled shyly and looked askance, but the sound of his name repeatedly called out coaxed his lips into a wide grin and brought assurance to his step as he came forward to greet the others. Mr. Giles hurried forward and in an uncharacteristic show of affection, caught Vernon in a bear hug.

"Thank you, everyone." Vernon's voice was gruff, an attempt, Eva guessed, to hide the emotion he was feeling. "It's good to be home. And I can't thank you enough, Lord Wroxly."

The earl slapped his back. "Never doubted you, my boy."

"No, indeed, Vernon," the countess chimed in. "We're delighted to have you home again, where you belong."

"Welcome home," Phoebe said simply, and offered her hand to Vernon.

"I know I have you to thank for my being here, my lady. And Miss Huntford, too." He smiled over at Eva where she stood among the other servants. His nod expressed all the thanks Eva needed, and she returned the gesture.

"Come, everyone, back inside. Before we all catch our deaths."

Lord Wroxly's hearty declaration was met with a moment's stunned silence. They had had enough talk of death to last a lifetime. But chatter swiftly filled the air as the servants closed around Vernon and the gathering funneled through the front door. Connie, who should have been in bed but could not be restrained there today, walked at Vernon's side, her arm through his. Eva spied Mrs. Sanders's disapproving look, but their budding romance would be a matter to be dealt with another day.

For today, there would be no work for the servants. Lord Wroxly had declared this a holiday for all of them; there would be food and drink, and Lady Wroxly had her gramophone carried down to the servants' hall for the occasion.

When Eva lagged behind the others, Phoebe sought her out in the Great Hall. "Aren't you going down, Eva?"

"I'm afraid I don't much feel like celebrating, my lady. I'm thrilled for Vernon, and for Connie, too, but . . ." She turned and faced her young mistress full-on. "I trusted him, my lady. I feel so foolish, and I endangered you and everyone with my blindness."

Phoebe took her hand and squeezed gently. "No, Eva. You couldn't have known."

"But you knew before I did. So did Connie, and Lord

Theodore. I was the only one taken in by him to the very last."

"Excuse me, Miss Huntford?"

She and Phoebe turned to see Miles Brannock handing his coat to Mr. Giles. He removed his domed helmet and came toward them. What on earth could he want?

"Miss Huntford, I wondered if I might have a word," he said.

Phoebe spoke before Eva could gather her thoughts. "What is this about, Constable? I thought everything had been resolved."

"It is, my lady, to be sure." He paused, his eyes on Eva. A small smile played on his lips. With each passing second Eva's confusion mounted. "I just thought . . . since you've got your coat on . . . would you care to take a walk?"

"A walk?" Eva frowned. What on earth could he mean by that?

"Yes, a walk. With your leave, of course, Lady Phoebe."

"No . . . I don't think . . ." Eva started to say.

"Of course, she may. Why, today has been declared a servants' holiday, so Eva has leave to walk all she wishes." Phoebe gave her a nudge, and silently Eva vowed to accidentally stick her with a brooch pin at the next opportunity. "Go on, and have a nice walk." The girl had the audacity to wink.

With little choice short of being rude, Eva buttoned up her coat. She pretended not to notice the arm Miles Brannock offered her and instead walked back outside with a respectable distance between them. She had been fooled once; the bitterness of it stung and would for a long time to come. She would not be vulnerable again. Besides, what did she really know about this man who had survived the war with nary a scratch?

*   *   *

Phoebe felt oddly at loose ends after Eva left with Constable Brannock. She briefly wondered what might come of it, hoped the constable might help Eva forget the past week, then dismissed the matter from her mind. She climbed the stairs, planning to spend a quiet afternoon reading in her room, and if she didn't experience a bit of excitement for these next several months, so much the better.

At the top of the stairs, a voice beckoned.

"Phoebe."

She looked about, saw no one, then realized where the voice had come from. She stepped into the billiard room and into Owen Seabright's embrace. "I thought you were packing to leave," she whispered, her skin heating where his arms encircled her.

"I was. But I wasn't about to depart before seeing you. Alone." He leaned back a bit to study her. "How are you? Any lasting effects from last night?"

"Only a new resolve not to interfere in police business."

He laughed softly. "Resolves are meant to be broken and something tells me it's only a matter of time before that one snaps like a twig." He raised her chin with the tips of his fingers. "I'd been investigating Henry since the summer. Once he began swindling friends of mine there was no chance I'd let him get away with his little game. Others have already been apprehended, but Henry had covered his tracks fairly well. With Julia's help, and Lord Bellington's, we were amassing enough evidence against him to have him declared a traitor to the realm and stripped of his title."

"Lord Bellington! Then those pictures of Julia with him—"

"Yes, I know how they looked. Henry thought they were having an affair and we let him, but she was supplying us with information. I stole those pictures last week because I didn't know then if we could trust Theo or not. I couldn't take the chance that he might find them first and use them against us somehow."

"Apparently Julia trusted him," she said. "I overheard the two of them talking about those pictures, although at the time I didn't understand the reference."

"Hmm, yes. Unfortunately your sister never told me she had already confided in Theo. Not that her faith in him would have exonerated him in my mind, not without further proof. Still, she might have mentioned it."

"That's Julia. She tends to err on the side of reticence." Phoebe angled her chin. "But you certainly could have mentioned *your* involvement to me, instead of trying to frighten me off like you did."

"No, Phoebe, I couldn't have. Not until I knew who posed a danger to you and who didn't. Until then I thought it best you knew as little as possible. I didn't want you involved."

"Did Julia know of your efforts to investigate Henry?" He nodded, and the notion of Julia being in this man's confidence was like a stab to her side. Remembering the reason he'd been invited to spend Christmas at Foxwood, she stepped out of his arms. "Well, then, you and she work quite well together, don't you? What a splendid couple the two of you will make."

"Couple?" He looked utterly mystified for all of three seconds, then laughed. "Ah, that little scheme Fox and your grandmother cooked up in the event things didn't work out with Henry. Rest assured, my lady, Julia is not the Renshaw sister who interests me, nor am I the man who interests her."

With that he leaned in and caught Phoebe's lips in a warm little kiss that ended all too soon, before she could decipher its meaning—to him, to herself—and before she could quite decide if she wished it to end or go on and on. He smiled again, bowed slightly, and left the room.

Blindly, Phoebe left the billiard room, too, with hardly a notion of where she was going or what she passed along the way. No wonder she bumped into Julia in the corridor.

"What on earth is wrong with you, Phoebe? Watch where you're going."

"Julia . . . sorry. I—"

"Goodness, Phoebe, you what? Did you take a blow to the head in the midst of your derring-do last night?" Julia narrowed her eyes and leaned closer to study her. "Or perhaps you caught a head cold from being out in the snow."

"Neither. I'm fine, it's just that . . . Oh, Julia." Suddenly overcome with an admiration she hadn't felt for her sister in a very long time, she threw her arms around Julia.

"What on earth is this?"

Phoebe pulled back. "What you did—your part in bringing Henry to justice—to think you let me believe you'd behaved dishonorably when all along your actions were nothing short of heroic."

Julia's beautiful features pulled taut in a scowl. "Don't you go shoving me onto any pedestals, little sister, or the whole lot will come tumbling down around your naïve little ears. What I did was as much motivated by self-interest as any other reason. I detested Henry, and the idea of seeing him brought low filled me with glee. I didn't wish death on him, mind you, but ostracized, penalized—oh yes, I wanted him to have what he deserved. Now, if you'll excuse me."

With that, Julia brushed by her and continued to the gallery. Phoebe stood where she was for several long moments, dazed by her encounters with both her sister and Owen. As to the latter . . . hmm . . . she didn't know. Simply didn't know. It was all so unexpected and so . . . so not the sort of thing that happened to girls like her.

As for Julia . . . a smile dawned on Phoebe's lips. For all her protests, Julia *had* been heroic and that meant she had *cared* enough about something—anything—to rouse herself to action. And that meant Julia was finally coming alive again. Phoebe's smile persisted as she continued on to her room, her mind abuzz with all manner of new possibilities and hopes for the future.